NORWEGIAN WOOD

Haruki Murakami was born in Kyoto in 1949 and lives near Tokyo. His work has been translated into thirty-four languages, and the most recent of his many honours is the Yomiuri Literary Prize, whose previous recipients include Yukio Mishima, Kenzaburo Ōe and Kobo Abe.

Jay Rubin is a professor of Japanese Literature at Harvard University. He is the author of *Haruki Murakami and the Music of Words* and he has also translated Murakami's *The Wind-up Bird Chronicle* and *After the Quake*.

ALSO BY HARUKI MURAKAMI

Fiction

Dance Dance Dance

The Elephant Vanishes

Hard-boiled Wonderland and the End of the World

A Wild Sheep Chase

The Wind-Up Bird Chronicle

South of the Border, West of the Sun

Sputnik Sweetheart

After the Quake

Kafka on the Shore

Blind Willow, Sleeping Woman

Non-Fiction

*Underground: The Tokyo Gas Attack and
the Japanese Psyche*

Edited

Birthday Stories

HARUKI MURAKAMI

Norwegian Wood

TRANSLATED FROM THE JAPANESE BY
Jay Rubin

VINTAGE BOOKS
London

Published by Vintage 2006

2 4 6 8 10 9 7 5 3 1

First published in 1987 with the title *Noruwei no mori* by
Kodansha Ltd, Tokyo

First published in Great Britain in 2000 by The Harvill Press

First published by Vintage in 2003

Vintage
Random House, 20 Vauxhall Bridge Road, London SW1V 2SA

Random House Australia (Pty) Limited
20 Alfred Street, Milsons Point, Sydney
New South Wales 2061, Australia

Random House New Zealand Limited
18 Poland Road, Glenfield, Auckland 10, New Zealand

Random House (Pty) Limited
Isle of Houghton, Corner of Boundary Road & Carse O'Gowrie,
Houghton, 2198, South Africa

Random House Publishers India Private Limited
301 World Trade Tower, Hotel Intercontinental Grand Complex,
Barakhamba Lane, New Delhi 110 001, India

The Random House Group Limited Reg. No. 954009
www.randomhouse.co.uk/vintage

A CIP catalogue record for this book
is available from the British Library

ISBN 9780099490784 (from Jan 2007)
ISBN 0099490781

Papers used by Random House are natural, recyclable
products made from wood grown in sustainable forests. The
manufacturing processes conform to the environmental
regulations of the country of origin

Printed and bound in Great Britain by
Cox & Wyman Limited, Reading, Berkshire

For Many Fêtes

第 1 章

I was 37 then, strapped in my seat as the huge 747 plunged through dense cloud cover on approach to Hamburg airport. Cold November rains drenched the earth, lending everything the gloomy air of a Flemish landscape: the ground crew in waterproofs, a flag atop a squat airport building, a BMW billboard. So – Germany again.

Once the plane was on the ground, soft music began to flow from the ceiling speakers: a sweet orchestral cover version of the Beatles' "Norwegian Wood". The melody never failed to send a shudder through me, but this time it hit me harder than ever.

I bent forward, my face in my hands to keep my skull from splitting open. Before long one of the German stewardesses approached and asked in English if I were sick.

"No," I said, "just dizzy."

"Are you sure?"

"Yes, I'm sure. Thanks."

She smiled and left, and the music changed to a Billy Joel tune. I straightened up and looked out of the window at the dark clouds hanging over the North Sea, thinking of all I had lost in the course of my life: times gone for ever, friends who had died or disappeared, feelings I would never know again.

The plane reached the gate. People began unfastening their

1

seatbelts and pulling luggage from the overhead lockers, and all the while I was in the meadow. I could smell the grass, feel the wind on my face, hear the cries of the birds. Autumn 1969, and soon I would be 20.

The stewardess came to check on me again. This time she sat next to me and asked if I was all right.

"I'm fine, thanks," I said with a smile. "Just feeling kind of blue."

"I know what you mean," she said. "It happens to me, too, every once in a while."

She stood and gave me a lovely smile. "Well, then, have a nice trip. *Auf Wiedersehen.*"

"*Auf Wiedersehen.*"

Eighteen years have gone by, and still I can bring back every detail of that day in the meadow. Washed clean of summer's dust by days of gentle rain, the mountains wore a deep, brilliant green. The October breeze set white fronds of head-high grasses swaying. One long streak of cloud hung pasted across a dome of frozen blue. It almost hurt to look at that far-off sky. A puff of wind swept across the meadow and through her hair before it slipped into the woods to rustle branches and send back snatches of distant barking – a hazy sound that seemed to reach us from the doorway to another world. We heard no other sounds. We met no other people. We saw only two bright red birds leap startled from the centre of the meadow and dart into the woods. As we ambled along, Naoko spoke to me of wells.

Memory is a funny thing. When I was in the scene I hardly paid it any attention. I never stopped to think of it as something that would make a lasting impression, certainly never

2

imagined that 18 years later I would recall it in such detail. I didn't give a damn about the scenery that day. I was thinking about myself. I was thinking about the beautiful girl walking next to me. I was thinking about the two of us together, and then about myself again. I was at that age, that time of life when every sight, every feeling, every thought came back, like a boomerang, to me. And worse, I was in love. Love with complications. Scenery was the last thing on my mind.

Now, though, that meadow scene is the first thing that comes back to me. The smell of the grass, the faint chill of the wind, the line of the hills, the barking of a dog: these are the first things, and they come with absolute clarity. I feel as if I can reach out and trace them with a fingertip. And yet, as clear as the scene may be, no one is in it. No one. Naoko is not there, and neither am I. Where could we have disappeared to? How could such a thing have happened? Everything that seemed so important back then – Naoko, and the self I was then, and the world I had then: where could they have all gone? It's true, I can't even bring back her face – not straight away, at least. All I'm left holding is a background, pure scenery, with no people at the front.

True, given time enough, I can remember her face. I start joining images – her tiny, cold hand; her straight, black hair so smooth and cool to the touch; a soft, rounded earlobe and the microscopic mole just beneath it; the camel-hair coat she wore in the winter; her habit of looking straight into my eyes when asking a question; the slight trembling that would come to her voice now and then (as though she were speaking on a windy hilltop) – and suddenly her face is there, always in profile at first, because Naoko and I were always out walking together, side by side. Then she turns to me and smiles, and tilts her head just a little, and begins to speak, and she looks into my eyes as if trying to catch the image of a minnow that has darted across the pool of a limpid spring.

It takes time, though, for Naoko's face to appear. And as the years have passed, the time has grown longer. The sad truth is that what I could recall in 5 seconds all too soon needed 10, then 30, then a full minute – like shadows lengthening at dusk. Someday, I suppose, the shadows will be swallowed up in darkness. There is no way around it: my memory is growing ever more distant from the spot where Naoko used to stand – where my old self used to stand. And nothing but scenery, that view of the meadow in October, returns again and again to me like a symbolic scene in a film. Each time it appears, it delivers a kick to some part of my mind. *Wake up*, it says. *I'm still here. Wake up and think about it. Think about why I'm still here*. The kicking never hurts me. There's no pain at all. Just a hollow sound that echoes with each kick. And even that is bound to fade one day. At Hamburg airport, though, the kicks were longer and harder than usual. Which is why I am writing this book. To think. To understand. It just happens to be the way I'm made. I have to write things down to feel I fully comprehend them.

Let's see, now, what was Naoko talking about that day?

Of course: the "field well". I have no idea whether there was such a well. It might have been an image or a sign that existed only inside Naoko, like all the other things she used to spin into existence inside her mind in those dark days. Once she had described it to me, though, I was never able to think of that meadow scene without the well. From that day forward, the image of a thing I had never laid eyes on became inseparably fused to the actual scene of the field that lay before me. I can describe the well in minute detail. It lay

4

precisely on the border where the meadow ended and the woods began – a dark opening in the earth a yard across, hidden by grass. Nothing marked its perimeter – no fence, no stone curb (at least not one that rose above ground level). It was nothing but a hole, a wide-open mouth. The stones of its collar had been weathered and turned a strange muddy-white. They were cracked and chunks were missing, and a little green lizard slithered into an open seam. You could lean over the edge and peer down to see nothing. All I knew about the well was its frightening depth. It was deep beyond measuring, and crammed full of darkness, as if all the world's darknesses had been boiled down to their ultimate density.

"It's really, *really* deep," said Naoko, choosing her words with care. She would speak that way sometimes, slowing down to find the exact word she was looking for. "But no one knows where it is," she continued. "The one thing I know for sure is that it's around here somewhere."

Hands thrust into the pockets of her tweed jacket, she smiled at me as if to say "It's true!"

"Then it must be incredibly dangerous," I said. "A deep well, but nobody knows where it is. You could fall in and that'd be the end of you."

"The end. Aaaaaaaah! Splat! Finished."

"Things like that must happen."

"They do, every once in a while. Maybe once in two or three years. Somebody disappears all of a sudden, and they just can't find him. So then the people around here say, 'Oh, he fell in the field well'."

"Not a nice way to die," I said.

"No, it's a terrible way to die," said Naoko, brushing a cluster of grass seed from her jacket. "The best thing would be to break your neck, but you'd probably just break your leg

5

and then you couldn't do a thing. You'd yell at the top of your lungs, but nobody would hear you, and you couldn't expect anyone to find you, and you'd have centipedes and spiders crawling all over you, and the bones of the ones who died before are scattered all around you, and it's dark and soggy, and high overhead there's this tiny, tiny circle of light like a winter moon. You die there in this place, little by little, all by yourself."

"Yuck, just thinking about it makes my flesh creep," I said. "Somebody should find the thing and build a wall around it."

"But nobody *can* find it. So make sure you don't go off the path."

"Don't worry, I won't."

Naoko took her left hand from her pocket and squeezed my hand. "Don't *you* worry," she said. "You'll be OK. *You* could go running all around here in the middle of the night and you'd *never* fall into the well. And as long as I stick with you, I won't fall in, either."

"Never?"

"Never!"

"How can you be so sure?"

"I just know," she said, increasing her grip on my hand and walking along in silence. "I know these things. I'm always right. It's got nothing to do with logic: I just feel it. For example, when I'm really close to you like this, I'm not the least bit scared. Nothing dark or evil could ever tempt me."

"Well, that's the answer," I said. "All you have to do is stay with me like this all the time."

"Do you mean that?"

"Of course."

Naoko stopped short. So did I. She put her hands on my shoulders and peered into my eyes. Deep within her own pupils a heavy, black liquid swirled in a strange whirlpool pattern. Those beautiful eyes of hers were looking inside me for a long, long time. Then she stretched to her full height and touched her cheek to mine. It was a marvellous, warm gesture that stopped my heart for a moment.

"Thank you."

"My pleasure," I answered.

"I'm so happy you said that. Really happy," she said with a sad smile. "But it's impossible."

"Impossible? Why?"

"It would be wrong. It would be terrible. It – "

Naoko clamped her mouth shut and started walking again. I could tell that all kinds of thoughts were whirling around in her head, so rather than intrude on them I kept silent and walked by her side.

"It would be wrong – wrong for you, wrong for me," she said after a long pause.

"Wrong how?" I murmured.

"Don't you see? It's just not possible for one person to watch over another person forever and ever. I mean, suppose we got married. You'd have to work during the day. Who's going to watch over me while you're away? Or if you go on a business trip, who's going to watch over me then? Can I be glued to you every minute of our lives? What kind of equality would there be in that? What kind of relationship would that be? Sooner or later you'd get sick of me. You'd wonder what you were doing with your life, why you were spending all your time babysitting this woman. I couldn't stand that. It wouldn't solve any of my problems."

"But your problems are not going to continue for the rest of your life," I said, touching her back. "They'll end eventually. And when they do, we'll stop and think about how to go on

7

from there. Maybe *you* will have to help *me*. We're not running our lives according to some account book. If you need me, use me. Don't you see? Why do you have to be so rigid? Relax, let down your guard. You're all tensed up so you always expect the worst. Relax your body, and the rest of you will lighten up."

"How can you say that?" she asked in a voice drained of feeling.

Naoko's voice alerted me to the possibility that I had said something I shouldn't have.

"Tell me how you could say such a thing," she said, staring at the ground beneath her feet. "You're not telling me anything I don't know already. 'Relax your body, and the rest of you will lighten up.' What's the point of saying that to me? If I relaxed my body now, I'd fall apart. I've always lived like this, and it's the only way I know how to go on living. If I relaxed for a second, I'd never find my way back. I'd go to pieces, and the pieces would be blown away. Why can't you see that? How can you talk about watching over me if you can't see that?"

I said nothing.

"I'm confused. Really confused. And it's a lot deeper than you think. Deeper . . . darker . . . colder. But tell me something. How could you have slept with me that time? How could you have done such a thing? Why didn't you just leave me alone?"

Now we were walking through the frightful silence of a pine forest. The desiccated corpses of cicadas that had died at the end of summer littered the surface of the path, crunching beneath our shoes. As if searching for something we'd lost, Naoko and I continued slowly along the path.

"I'm sorry," she said, taking my arm and shaking her head.

"I didn't mean to hurt you. Try not to let what I said bother you. Really, I'm sorry. I was just angry at myself."

"I suppose I don't really understand you yet," I said. "I'm not all that smart. It takes me a while to understand things. But if I *do* have the time, I *will* come to understand you – better than anyone else in the world."

We came to a stop and stood in the silent forest, listening. I tumbled pinecones and cicada shells with my toecap, then looked up at the patches of sky showing through the pine branches. Hands in pockets, Naoko stood there thinking, her eyes focused on nothing in particular.

"Tell me something, Toru," she said. "Do you love me?"

"You know I do."

"Will you do me two favours?"

"You can have up to three wishes, Madame."

Naoko smiled and shook her head. "No, two will do. One is for you to realize how grateful I am that you came to see me here. I hope you'll understand how happy you've made me. I know it's going to save me if anything will. I may not show it, but it's true."

"I'll come to see you again," I said. "And what is the other wish?"

"I want you always to remember me. Will you remember that I existed, and that I stood next to you here like this?"

"Always," I said. "I'll always remember."

She walked on without speaking. The autumn light filtering through the branches danced over the shoulders of her jacket. A dog barked again, closer than before. Naoko climbed a small mound, walked out of the forest and hurried down a gentle slope. I followed two or three steps behind.

"Come over here," I called towards her back. "The well might be around here somewhere." Naoko stopped and smiled and took my arm. We walked the rest of the way side by side.

"Do you really promise never to forget me?" she asked in a near whisper.

"I'll never forget you," I said. "I *could* never forget you."

Even so, my memory has grown increasingly dim, and I have already forgotten any number of things. Writing from memory like this, I often feel a pang of dread. What if I've forgotten the most important thing? What if somewhere inside me there is a dark limbo where all the truly important memories are heaped and slowly turning into mud?

Be that as it may, it's all I have to work with. Clutching these faded, fading, imperfect memories to my breast, I go on writing this book with all the desperate intensity of a starving man sucking on bones. This is the only way I know to keep my promise to Naoko.

Once, long ago, when I was still young, when the memories were far more vivid than they are now, I often tried to write about her. But I couldn't produce a line. I knew that if that first line would come, the rest would pour itself onto the page, but I could never make it happen. Everything was too sharp and clear, so that I could never tell where to start – the way a map that shows too much can sometimes be useless. Now, though, I realize that all I can place in the imperfect vessel of writing are imperfect memories and imperfect thoughts. The more the memories of Naoko inside me fade, the more deeply I am able to understand her. I know, too, why she asked me not to forget her. Naoko herself knew, of course. She knew that my memories of her would fade. Which is precisely why she begged me never to forget her, to remember that she had existed.

The thought fills me with an almost unbearable sorrow. Because Naoko never loved me.

第 2 章

Once upon a time, many years ago – just 20 years ago, in fact – I was living in a dormitory. I was 18 and a first-year student. I was new to Tokyo and new to living alone, and so my anxious parents found a private dorm for me to live in rather than the kind of single room that most students took. The dormitory provided meals and other facilities and would probably help their unworldly 18-year-old survive. Expenses were also a consideration. A dorm cost far less than a private room. As long as I had bedding and a lamp, there was no need to buy a lot of furnishings. For my part, I would have preferred to rent a flat and live in comfortable solitude, but knowing what my parents had to spend on enrolment fees and tuition at the private university I was attending, I was in no position to insist. And besides, I really didn't care where I lived.

Located on a hill in the middle of the city with open views, the dormitory compound sat on a large quadrangle surrounded by a concrete wall. A huge, towering zelkova tree stood just inside the front gate. People said it was at least 150 years old. Standing at its base, you could look up and see nothing of the sky through its dense cover of green leaves.

The paved path leading from the gate circumvented the tree and continued on long and straight across a broad quadrangle, two three-storey concrete dorm buildings facing each other on either side of the path. They were large with lots of windows and gave the impression of being either flats that had been converted into jails or jails that had been converted into flats. However there was nothing dirty about them, nor did they feel dark. You could hear radios playing through open windows, all of which had the same cream-coloured curtains that the sun could not fade.

Beyond the two dormitories, the path led up to the entrance of a two-storey common building, the first floor of which contained a dining hall and bathrooms, the second consisting of an auditorium, meeting rooms, and even guest rooms, whose use I could never fathom. Next to the common building stood a third dormitory, also three storeys high. Broad green lawns filled the quadrangle, and circulating sprinklers caught the sunlight as they turned. Behind the common building there was a field used for baseball and football, and six tennis courts. The complex had everything you could want.

There was just one problem with the place: its political smell. It was run by some kind of fishy foundation that centred on this extreme right-wing guy, and there was something strangely twisted – as far as I was concerned – about the way they ran the place. You could see it in the pamphlet they gave to new students and in the dorm rules. The proclaimed "founding spirit" of the dormitory was "to strive to nurture human resources of service to the nation through the ultimate in educational fundamentals", and many financial leaders who endorsed this "spirit" had contributed their private funds to the construction of the place. This was the public face of the project, though what lay behind it was extremely vague. Some said it was a tax dodge, others saw it as a publicity stunt for the contributors, and still others claimed that the construction of the dormitory was a cover for swindling the public out of a prime piece of real estate. One thing was certain, though: in the dorm complex there existed a privileged club composed of elite students from various universities. They formed "study groups" that met several times a month and included some of the founders. Any member of the club could be assured of a good job after graduation. I had no idea which – if any – of these theories was correct, but they all shared the assumption that there was "something fishy" about the place.

In any case, I spent two years – from the spring of 1968 to the spring of 1970 – living in this "fishy" dormitory. Why I put up with it so long, I can't really say. In terms of everyday life, it made no practical difference to me whether the place was right wing or left wing or anything else.

Each day began with the solemn raising of the flag. They played the national anthem, too, of course. You can't have one without the other. The flagpole stood in the very centre of the compound, where it was visible from every window of all three dormitories.

The Head of the east dormitory (my building) was in charge of the flag. He was a tall, eagle-eyed man in his late fifties or early sixties. His bristly hair was flecked with grey, and his sunburned neck bore a long scar. People whispered that he was a graduate of the wartime Nakano spy school, but no one knew for sure. Next to him stood a student who acted as his assistant. No one really knew this guy, either. He had the world's shortest crewcut and always wore a navy-blue student uniform. I didn't know his name or which room he lived in, never saw him in the dining hall or the bath. I'm not even sure he was a student, though would think he must have been, given the uniform – which quickly became his nickname. In contrast to Sir Nakano, "Uniform" was short, pudgy and pasty-faced. This creepy couple would raise the banner of the Rising Sun every morning at six.

When I first entered the dormitory, the sheer novelty of the event would often prompt me to get up early to observe this patriotic ritual. The two would appear in the quadrangle at almost the exact moment the radio beeped the six o'clock signal. Uniform was wearing his uniform, of course, with black leather shoes, and Nakano wore a short jacket and white trainers. Uniform held a ceremonial box of untreated paulownia wood, while Nakano carried a Sony tape recorder at his side. He placed this at the base of the flagpole, while Uniform opened the box to reveal a neatly folded banner. This he reverentially proffered to Nakano, who would clip it to the rope on the flagpole, revealing the bright red circle of the Rising Sun on a field of pure white. Then Uniform pressed the switch for the playing of the anthem.

"May Our Lord's Reign . . ."

And up the flag would climb.

"Until pebbles turn to boulders . . ."

It would reach halfway up the pole.

"And be covered with moss."

Now it was at the top. The two stood to attention, rigid, looking up at the flag, which was quite a sight on clear days when the wind was blowing.

The lowering of the flag at dusk was carried out with the same ceremonial reverence, but in reverse. Down the banner would come and find its place in the box. The national flag did not fly at night.

I didn't know why the flag had to be taken down at night. The nation continued to exist while it was dark, and plenty of people worked all night – railway construction crews and taxi drivers and bar hostesses and firemen and night watchmen: it seemed unfair to me that such people were denied the protection of the flag. Or maybe it didn't matter all that much and nobody really cared – aside from me. Not that I really cared, either. It was just something that happened to cross my mind.

The rules for room assignments put first- and second-year students in doubles while third- and final-year students had single rooms. Double rooms were a little longer and narrower than nine-by-twelve, with an aluminium-framed window in the wall opposite the door and two desks by the window arranged so the inhabitants of the room could study back-to-back. To the left of the door stood a steel bunk bed. The furniture supplied was sturdy and simple and included a pair of lockers, a small coffee table, and some built-in shelves. Even the most well-disposed observer would have had trouble calling this setting poetic. The shelves of most rooms carried such items as transistor radios, hairdryers, electric carafes and cookers, instant coffee, tea bags, sugar cubes, and simple pots and bowls for preparing instant ramen. The walls bore pin-ups from girlie magazines or stolen porno movie posters. One guy had a photo of pigs mating, but this was a far-out exception to the usual naked women, girl pop singers or actresses. Bookshelves on the desks held textbooks, dictionaries and novels.

The filth of these all-male rooms was horrifying. Mouldy mandarin skins clung to the bottoms of waste-paper baskets. Empty cans used for ashtrays held mounds of cigarette butts, and when these started to smoulder they'd be doused with coffee or beer and left to give off a sour stink. Blackish grime and bits of indefinable matter clung to all the bowls and dishes on the shelves, and the floors were littered with instant ramen wrappers and empty beer cans and discarded lids from one thing or another. It never occurred to anyone to sweep up and throw these things in the bin. Any wind that blew through would raise clouds of dust. Each room had its own horrendous smell, but the components of that smell were always the same: sweat, body odour and rubbish. Dirty clothes would pile up under the beds, and without anyone bothering to air the mattresses on a regular basis, these sweat-impregnated pads would give off odours beyond redemption. In retrospect, it seems amazing that these shitpiles gave rise to no killer epidemics.

My room, on the other hand, was as sanitary as a morgue. The floor and window were spotless, the mattresses were aired each week, all pencils stood in the pencil holders, and even the curtains were washed once a month. My room-mate was a cleanliness freak. None of the others in the dorm believed me when I told them about the curtains. They didn't know that curtains *could* be washed. They believed, rather, that curtains were semi-permanent parts of the window. "There's something wrong with that guy," they'd say, labelling him a Nazi or a storm trooper.

We didn't even have pin-ups. No, we had a photo of a canal in Amsterdam. I had put up a nude shot, but my room-mate had pulled it down. "Hey, Watanabe," he said, "I-I'm not too crazy about this kind of thing," and up went the canal photo instead. I wasn't especially attached to the nude, so I didn't protest.

"What the hell's *that*?" was the universal reaction to the Amsterdam photo whenever any of the other guys came to my room.

"Oh, Storm Trooper likes to wank looking at this," I said.

I meant it as a joke, but they all took me seriously – *so* seriously that I began to believe it myself.

Everybody sympathized with me for having Storm Trooper as a room-mate, but I really wasn't that upset about it. He left me alone as long as I kept my area clean, and in fact having him as my room-mate made things easier for me in many ways. He did all the cleaning, he took care of sunning the mattresses, he threw out the rubbish. He'd give a sniff and suggest a bath for me if I'd been too busy to wash for a few days. He'd even point out when it was time for me to go to the barber's or trim my nasal hair. The one thing that bothered me was the way he would spray clouds of insecticide if he noticed a single fly in the room, because then I had to take refuge in a neighbouring shitpile.

Storm Trooper was studying geography at a national university.

As he told me the first time we met, "I'm studying m-m-maps."

"You like maps?" I asked.

"Yup. When I graduate, I'm going to work for the Geographical Survey Institute and make m-m-maps."

I was impressed by the variety of dreams and goals that life could offer. This was one of the very first new impressions I received when I came to Tokyo for the first time. The thought struck me that society *needed* a few people – just a few – who were interested in and even passionate about map-making. Odd, though, that someone who wanted to work for the government's Geographical Survey Institute should stutter every time he said the word "map". Storm Trooper often didn't stutter at all, except when he pronounced the word "map", for which it was a 100 per cent certainty.

"W-what are *you* studying?" he asked me.

"Drama," I said.

"Gonna put on plays?"

"Nah, just read scripts and do research. Racine, Ionesco, Shakespeare, stuff like that."

He said he had heard of Shakespeare but not the others. I hardly knew anything about the others myself, I'd just seen their names in lecture handouts.

"You like plays?" he asked.

"Not especially."

This confused him, and when he was confused, his stuttering got worse. I felt sorry I had done that to him.

"I could have picked anything," I said. "Ethnology, Asian history. I just happened to pick drama, that's all," which was not the most convincing explanation I could have come up with.

"I don't get it," he said, looking as if he really didn't get it. "I like m-m-maps, so I decided to come to Tokyo and get my parents to s-send me money so I could study m-m-maps. But not you, huh?"

His approach made more sense than mine. I gave up trying to explain myself. Then we drew lots (matchsticks) to choose bunks. He got the upper bunk.

Tall, with a crewcut and high cheekbones, he always wore the same outfit: white shirt, black trousers, black shoes, navy-blue jumper. To these he would add a uniform jacket and black briefcase when he went to his university: a typical right-wing student. Which is why everybody called him Storm Trooper. But in fact he was totally indifferent to politics. He wore a uniform because he didn't want to be bothered choosing clothes. What interested him were things like changes in the coastline or the completion of a new railway tunnel. Nothing else. He'd go on for hours once he got started on a subject like that, until you either ran away or fell asleep.

He was up at six each morning with the strains of "May Our Lord's Reign". Which is to say that that ostentatious flag-raising ritual was not entirely useless. He'd get dressed, go to the bathroom and wash his face – for ever. I sometimes got the feeling he must be taking out each tooth and washing it, one at a time. Back in the room, he would snap the wrinkles out of his towel and lay it on the radiator to dry, then return his toothbrush and soap to the shelf. Finally he'd do radio callisthenics with the rest of the nation.

I was used to reading late at night and sleeping until eight o'clock, so even when he started shuffling around the room and exercising, I remained unconscious – until the part where he started jumping. He took his jumping seriously and made the bed bounce every time he hit the floor. I stood it for three days because they had told us that communal life called for a certain degree of resignation, but by the morning of the fourth day, I couldn't take it any more.

"Hey, can you do that on the roof or somewhere?" I said. "I can't sleep."

"But it's already 6.30!" he said, open-mouthed.

"Yeah, I *know* it's 6.30. I'm still supposed to be asleep. I don't know how to explain it exactly, but that's how it works for me."

"Anyway, I can't do it on the roof. Somebody on the third floor would complain. Here, we're over a storeroom."

"So go out on the quad. On the lawn."

"That's no good, either. I don't have a transistor radio. I need to plug it in. And you can't do radio callisthenics without music."

True, his radio was an old piece of junk without batteries. Mine was a transistor portable, but it was strictly FM, for music.

"OK, let's compromise," I said. "Do your exercises but cut out the jumping part. It's so damned noisy. What do you say?"

"J-jumping? What's that?"

"Jumping is jumping. Bouncing up and down."

"But there isn't any jumping."

My head was starting to hurt. I was ready to give up, but I wanted to make my point. I got out of bed and started bouncing up and down and singing the opening melody of NHK's radio callisthenics. "I'm talking about *this*," I said.

"Oh, *that*. I guess you're right. I never noticed."

"See what I mean?" I said, sitting on the edge of the bed. "Just cut out that part. I can put up with the rest. Stop jumping and let me sleep."

"But that's impossible," he said matter-of-factly. "I can't leave anything out. I've been doing the same thing every day for ten years, and once I start I do the whole routine unconsciously. If I left something out, I wouldn't be able to do any of it."

There was nothing more for me to say. What *could* I have said? The quickest way to put a stop to this was to wait for him to leave the room and throw his goddamn radio out the goddamn window, but I knew if I did that all hell would break loose. Storm Trooper treasured everything he owned. He smiled when he saw me sitting on the bed at a loss for words, and tried to comfort me.

"Hey, Watanabe, why don't you just get up and exercise with me?" And he went off to breakfast.

Naoko chuckled when I told her the story of Storm Trooper and his radio callisthenics. I hadn't been trying to amuse her, but I ended up laughing myself. Though her smile vanished in an instant, I enjoyed seeing it for the first time in a long while.

We had left the train at Yotsuya and were walking along the embankment by the station. It was a Sunday afternoon in the middle of May. The brief on-and-off showers of the morning had cleared up before noon, and a south wind had swept away the low-hanging clouds. The brilliant green leaves of the cherry trees stirred in the air, splashing sunlight in all directions. This was an early summer day. The people we passed carried their jumpers or jackets over their shoulders or in their arms. Everyone looked happy in the warm Sunday afternoon sun. The young men playing tennis in the courts beyond the embankment had stripped down to their shorts. Only where two nuns in winter habits sat talking on a bench did the summer light seem not to reach, though both wore looks of satisfaction as they enjoyed chatting in the sun.

Fifteen minutes of walking and I was sweaty enough to take off my thick cotton shirt and go with a T-shirt. Naoko had rolled the sleeves of her light grey sweatshirt up to her elbows. It was nicely faded, obviously having been washed many times. I felt as if I had seen her in that shirt long before. This was just a feeling I had, not a clear memory. I didn't have that much to remember about Naoko at the time.

"How do you like communal living?" she asked. "Is it fun to live with a lot of other people?"

"I don't know, I've only been doing it a month or so. It's not that bad, I can stand it."

She stopped at a fountain and took a sip, wiping her mouth with a white handkerchief she took from her trouser pocket. Then she bent over and carefully retied her laces.

"Do you think I could do it?"

"What? Living in a dorm?"

"Uh-huh."

"I suppose it's all a matter of attitude. You could let a lot of things bother you if you wanted to – the rules, the idiots who think they're hot shit, the room-mates doing radio

21

callisthenics at 6.30 in the morning. But it's pretty much the same anywhere you go, you can manage."

"I guess so," she said with a nod. She seemed to be turning something over in her mind. Then she looked straight into my eyes as if peering at some unusual object. Now I saw that her eyes were so deep and clear they made my heart thump. I realized that I had never had occasion to look into her eyes like this. It was the first time the two of us had ever gone walking together or talked at such length.

"Are you thinking about living in a dorm or something?" I asked.

"Uh-uh," she said. "I was just wondering what communal life would be like. And . . ." She seemed to be trying – and failing – to find exactly the right word or expression. Then she sighed and looked down. "Oh, I don't know. Never mind."

That was the end of the conversation. She continued walking east, and I followed just behind.

Almost a year had gone by since I had last seen Naoko, and in that time she had lost so much weight as to look like a different person. The plump cheeks that had been a special feature of hers were all but gone, and her neck had become delicate and slender. Not that she was bony now or unhealthy-looking: there was something natural and serene about the way she had slimmed down, as if she had been hiding in some long, narrow space until she herself had become long and narrow. And a lot prettier than I remembered. I wanted to tell her that, but couldn't find a good way to put it.

We had not planned to meet but had run into each other on the Chuo commuter line. She had decided to see a film by herself, and I was headed for the bookshops in Kanda – nothing urgent in either case. She had suggested that we leave the train, which we happened to do in Yotsuya, where the green embankment makes for a nice place to walk by the old castle moat. Alone together, we had nothing in particular to talk about, and I wasn't quite sure why Naoko had suggested we get off the train. We had never really had much to say to each other.

Naoko started walking the minute we hit the street, and I hurried after her, keeping a few paces behind. I could have closed the distance between us, but something held me back. I walked with my eyes on her shoulders and her straight black hair. She wore a big, brown hairslide, and when she turned her head I caught a glimpse of a small, white ear. Now and then she would look back and say something. Sometimes it would be a remark I might have responded to, and sometimes it would be something to which I had no idea how to reply. Other times, I simply couldn't hear what she was saying. She didn't seem to care one way or another. Once she had finished saying whatever she wanted to say, she'd face front again and keep on walking. Oh, well, I told myself, it was a nice day for a stroll.

This was no mere stroll for Naoko, though, judging from that walk. She turned right at Iidabashi, came out at the moat, crossed the intersection at Jinbocho, climbed the hill at Ochanomizu and came out at Hongo. From there she followed the tram tracks to Komagome. It was a challenging route. By the time we reached Komagome, the sun was sinking and the day had become a soft spring evening.

"Where are we?" asked Naoko, as if noticing our surroundings for the first time.

"Komagome," I said. "Didn't you know? We made this big arc."

"Why did we come here?"

"*You* brought us here. I was just following you."

We went to a shop by the station for a bowl of noodles. Thirsty, I had a whole beer to myself. Neither of us said a word from the time we gave our order to the time we finished eating. I was exhausted from all that walking, and she just sat there with her hands on the table, mulling something over again. All the leisure spots were crowded on this warm Sunday, they were saying on the TV news. And we just walked from Yotsuya to Komagome, I said to myself.

"Well, *you're* in good shape," I said when I had finished my noodles.

"Surprised?"

"Yeah."

"I was a long distance runner at school, I'll have you know. I used to do the 10,000 metres. And my father took me mountain climbing on Sundays ever since I can remember. You know our house – right there, next to the mountain. I've always had strong legs."

"It doesn't show," I said.

"I know," she answered. "Everybody thinks I'm this delicate little girl. But you can't judge a book by its cover." To which she added a momentary smile.

"And that goes for me, too," I said. "I'm worn out."

"Oh, I'm sorry, I've been dragging you around all day."

"Still, I'm glad we had a chance to talk. We've never done that before, just the two of us," I said, trying without success to recall what we had talked *about*.

She was playing with the ashtray on the table.

"I wonder . . ." she began, ". . . if you wouldn't mind . . . I mean, if it really wouldn't be any bother to you . . . Do you think we could see each other again? I know I don't have any right to be asking you this."

"Any *right*? What do you mean by that?"

She blushed. My reaction to her request might have been a little too strong.

"I don't know . . . I can't really explain it," she said, tugging the sleeves of her sweatshirt up over the elbows and down again. The soft hair on her arms shone a lovely golden colour in the lights of the shop. "I didn't mean to say 'right' exactly. I was looking for another way to put it."

Elbows on the table, she stared at the calendar on the wall, almost as though she were hoping to find the proper expression there. Failing, she sighed and closed her eyes and played with her hairslide.

"Never mind," I said. "I think I know what you're getting at. I'm not sure how to put it, either."

"I can never say what I want to say," continued Naoko. "It's been like this for a while now. I try to say something, but all I get are the wrong words – the wrong words or the exact *opposite* words from what I mean. I try to correct myself, and that only makes it worse. I lose track of what I was trying to say to begin with. It's like I'm split in two and playing tag with myself. One half is chasing the other half around this big, fat post. The *other* me has the right words, but this me can't catch her." She raised her face and looked into my eyes. "Does this make any sense to you?"

"Everybody feels like that to some extent," I said. "They're trying to express themselves and it bothers them when they can't get it right."

Naoko looked disappointed with my answer. "No, that's not it either," she said without further explanation.

"Anyway, I'd be glad to see you again," I said. "I'm always free on Sundays, and walking would be good for me."

We boarded the Yamanote Line, and Naoko transferred to the Chuo Line at Shinjuku. She was living in a tiny flat way out in the western suburb of Kokubunji.

"Tell me," she said as we parted. "Has anything changed about the way I talk?"

"I think so," I said, "but I'm not sure what. Tell you the truth, I know I saw you a lot back then, but I don't remember talking to you much."

"That's true," she said. "Anyway, can I call you on Saturday?"

"Sure. I'll be expecting to hear from you."

I first met Naoko when I was in the sixth-form at school. She was also in the sixth-form at a posh girls' school run by one of the Christian missions. The school was *so* refined you were considered *un*refined if you studied too much. Naoko was the girlfriend of my best (and only) friend, Kizuki. The two of them had been close almost from birth, their houses not 200 yards apart.

As with most couples who have been together since childhood, there was a casual openness about the relationship of Kizuki and Naoko and little sense that they wanted to be alone together. They were always visiting each other's homes and eating or playing mah-jong with each other's families. I double-dated with them any number of times. Naoko would bring a school friend for me and the four of us would go to the zoo or the pool or the cinema. The girls she brought were always pretty, but a little too refined for my taste. I got along better with the somewhat cruder girls from my own State school who were easier to talk to. I could never tell what was going on inside the pretty heads of the girls that Naoko brought along, and they probably couldn't understand me, either.

After a while, Kizuki gave up trying to arrange dates for

me, and instead the three of us would do things together. Kizuki and Naoko and I: odd, but that was the most comfortable combination. Introducing a fourth person into the mix would always make things a little awkward. We were like a TV talk show, with me the guest, Kizuki the talented host, and Naoko his assistant. He was good at occupying that central position. True, he had a sarcastic side that often struck people as arrogant, but in fact he was a considerate and fair-minded person. He would distribute his remarks and jokes fairly to Naoko and to me, taking care to see that neither of us felt left out. If one or the other stayed quiet too long, he would steer his conversation in that direction and get the person to talk. It probably looked harder than it was: he knew how to monitor and adjust the air around him on a second-by-second basis. In addition, he had a rare talent for finding the interesting parts of someone's generally uninteresting comments so that, while speaking to him, you felt you were an exceptionally interesting person with an exceptionally interesting life.

And yet he was not the least bit sociable. I was his only real friend at school. I could never understand why such a smart and capable talker did not turn his talents to the broader world around him but remained satisfied to concentrate on our little trio. Nor could I understand why he picked me to be his friend. I was just an ordinary kid who liked to read books and listen to music and didn't stand out in any way that would prompt someone like Kizuki to pay attention to me. We hit it off straight away, though. His father was a dentist, known for his professional skill and his high fees.

"Want to double-date Sunday?" he asked me just after we met. "My girlfriend goes to a girls' school, and she'll bring along a cute one for you."

"Sure," I said, and that was how I met Naoko.

27

The three of us spent a lot of time together, but whenever Kizuki left the room, Naoko and I had trouble talking to each other. We never knew what to talk *about*. And in fact there was no topic of conversation that we had in common. Instead of talking, we'd drink water or toy with something on the table and wait for Kizuki to come back and start up the conversation again. Naoko was not particularly talkative, and I was more of a listener than a talker, so I felt uncomfortable when I was left alone with her. Not that we were incompatible: we just had nothing to talk about.

Naoko and I saw each other only once after Kizuki's funeral. Two weeks after the event, we met at a café to take care of some minor matter, and when that was finished we had nothing more to say. I tried raising several different topics, but none of them led anywhere. And when Naoko did talk, there was an edge to her voice. She seemed angry with me, but I had no idea why. We never saw each other again until that day a year later we happened to meet on the Chuo Line in Tokyo.

Naoko might have been angry with me because I, not she, had been the last one to see Kizuki. That may not be the best way to put it, but I more or less understood how she felt. I would have swapped places with her if I could have, but finally, what had happened had happened, and there was nothing I could do about it.

It had been a nice afternoon in May. After lunch, Kizuki suggested we skip classes and go play pool or something. I had no special interest in my afternoon classes, so together we left school, ambled down the hill to a pool hall on the harbour, and played four games. When I won the first, easy-going game, he became serious and won the next three. This meant I paid, according to our custom. Kizuki didn't make a single joke as we played, which was most unusual. We smoked afterwards.

"Why so serious?" I asked.

"I didn't want to lose today," said Kizuki with a satisfied smile.

He died that night in his garage. He led a rubber hose from the exhaust pipe of his N-360 to a window, taped over the gap in the window, and revved the engine. I have no idea how long it took him to die. His parents had been out visiting a sick relative, and when they opened the garage to put their car away, he was already dead. His radio was going, and a petrol station receipt was tucked under the windscreen wiper.

Kizuki had left no suicide note, and had no motive that anyone could think of. Because I had been the last one to see him, I was called in for questioning by the police. I told the investigating officer that Kizuki had given no indication of what he was about to do, that he had been exactly the same as always. The policeman had obviously formed a poor impression of both Kizuki and me, as if it was perfectly natural for the kind of person who would skip classes and play pool to commit suicide. A small article in the paper brought the affair to a close. Kizuki's parents got rid of his red N-360. For a time, a white flower marked his school desk.

In the ten months between Kizuki's death and my exams, I was unable to find a place for myself in the world around me. I started sleeping with one of the girls at school, but that didn't last six months. Nothing about her really got to me. I applied to a private university in Tokyo, the kind of place with an entrance exam for which I wouldn't have to study much, and I passed without exhilaration. The girl asked me not to go to Tokyo – "It's 500 miles from here!" she pleaded – but I had to get away from Kobe at any cost. I wanted to begin a new life where I didn't know a soul.

"You don't give a damn about me any more, now that you've slept with me," she said, crying.

"That's not true," I insisted. "I just need to get away from this town." But she was not prepared to understand me. And so we parted. Thinking about all the things that made her so much nicer than the other girls at home, I sat on the bullet train to Tokyo feeling terrible about what I'd done, but there was no way to undo it. I would try to forget her.

There was only one thing for me to do when I started my new life in the dorm: stop taking everything so seriously; establish a proper distance between myself and everything else. Forget about green baize pool tables and red N-360s and white flowers on school desks; about smoke rising from tall crematorium chimneys, and chunky paperweights in police interrogation rooms. It seemed to work at first. I tried hard to forget, but there remained inside me a vague knot of air. And as time went by, the knot began to take on a clear and simple form, a form that I am able to put into words, like this:

Death exists, not as the opposite but as a part of life.

It's a cliché translated into words, but at the time I felt it not as words but as that knot of air inside me. Death exists – in a paperweight, in four red and white balls on a pool table – and we go on living and breathing it into our lungs like fine dust.

Until that time, I had understood death as something entirely separate from and independent of life. The hand of death is bound to take us, I had felt, but until the day it reaches out for us, it leaves us alone. This had seemed to me the simple, logical truth. Life is here, death is over there. I am here, not over there.

The night Kizuki died, however, I lost the ability to see death (and life) in such simple terms. Death was not the opposite of life. It was already here, within my being, it had always been here, and no struggle would permit me to forget that. When it took the 17-year-old Kizuki that night in May, death took me as well.

I lived through the following spring, at 18, with that knot of air in my chest, but I struggled all the while against becoming serious. Becoming serious was not the same thing as approaching the truth, I sensed, however vaguely. But death was a fact, a serious fact, no matter how you looked at it. Stuck inside this suffocating contradiction, I went on endlessly spinning in circles. Those were strange days, now that I look back at them. In the midst of life, everything revolved around death.

第 3 章

Naoko called me the following Saturday, and that Sunday we had a date. I suppose I can call it a date. I can't think of a better word for it.

As before, we walked the streets. We stopped somewhere for coffee, walked some more, had dinner in the evening, and said goodbye. Again, she talked only in snatches, but this didn't seem to bother her, and I made no special effort to keep the conversation going. We talked about whatever came to mind – our daily routines, our colleges; each a little fragment that led nowhere. We said nothing at all about the past. And mainly, we walked – and walked, and walked. Fortunately, Tokyo is such a big city we could never have covered it all.

We kept on walking like this almost every weekend. She would lead, and I would follow close behind. Naoko had a variety of hairslides and always wore them with her right ear exposed. I remember her most clearly this way, from the back. She would toy with her hairslide whenever she felt embarrassed by something. And she was always dabbing at her mouth with a handkerchief. She did this whenever she had something to say. The more I observed these habits of hers, the more I came to like her.

Naoko went to a girls' college on the rural western edge of Tokyo, a nice little place famous for its teaching of English.

Nearby was a narrow irrigation canal with clean, clear water, and Naoko and I would often walk along its banks. Sometimes she would invite me up to her flat and cook for me. It never seemed to concern her that the two of us were in such close quarters together. The room was small and neat and so lacking in frills that only the stockings drying in the corner by the window gave any hint that a girl lived there. She led a spare, simple life with hardly any friends. No one who had known her at school could have imagined her like this. Back then, she had dressed with real flair and surrounded herself with a million friends. When I saw her room, I realized that, like me, she had wanted to go away to college and begin a new life far from anyone she knew.

"Know why I chose this place?" she said with a smile. "Because nobody from home was coming here. We were all supposed to go somewhere more chic. You know what I mean?"

My relationship with Naoko was not without its progress, though. Little by little, she grew more accustomed to me, and I to her. When the summer holidays ended and a new term started, Naoko began walking next to me as if it were the most natural thing in the world to do. She saw me as a friend now, I concluded, and walking side by side with such a beautiful girl was by no means painful for me. We kept walking all over Tokyo in the same meandering way, climbing hills, crossing rivers and railway lines, just walking and walking with no destination in mind. We forged straight ahead, as if our walking were a religious ritual meant to heal our wounded spirits. If it rained, we used umbrellas, but in any case we walked.

Then came autumn, and the dormitory grounds were buried in zelkova leaves. The fragrance of a new season arrived when

I put on my first pullover. Having worn out one pair of shoes, I bought some new suede ones.

I can't seem to recall what we talked about then. Nothing special, I expect. We continued to avoid any mention of the past and rarely spoke about Kizuki. We could face each other over coffee cups in total silence.

Naoko liked to hear me tell stories about Storm Trooper. Once he had a date with a fellow student (a girl in geography, of course) but came back in the early evening looking glum. "Tell me, W-W-Watanabe, what do you talk about with g-g-girls?" I don't remember how I answered him, but he had picked the wrong person to ask. In July, somebody in the dorm had taken down Storm Trooper's Amsterdam canal scene and put up a photo of the Golden Gate Bridge instead. He told me he wanted to know if Storm Trooper could masturbate to the Golden Gate Bridge. "He loved it," I reported later, which prompted someone else to put up a picture of an iceberg. Each time the photo changed in his absence, Storm Trooper became upset.

"Who-who-who the hell is doing this?" he asked.

"I wonder," I said. "But what's the difference? They're all nice pictures. You should be grateful."

"Yeah, I s'pose so, but it's weird."

My stories of Storm Trooper always made Naoko laugh. Not many things succeeded in doing that, so I talked about him often, though I was not exactly proud of myself for using him this way. He just happened to be the youngest son in a not-too-wealthy family who had grown up a little too serious for his own good. Making maps was the one small dream of his one small life. Who had the right to make fun of him for that?

By then, however, Storm-Trooper jokes had become an

34

indispensable source of dormitory talk, and there was no way for me to undo what I had done. Besides, the sight of Naoko's smiling face had become my own special source of pleasure. I went on supplying everyone with new stories.

Naoko asked me one time – just once – if I had a girl I liked. I told her about the one I had left behind in Kobe. "She was nice," I said, "I enjoyed sleeping with her, and I miss her every now and then, but finally, she didn't move me. I don't know, sometimes I think I've got this hard kernel in my heart, and nothing much can get inside it. I doubt if I can really love anybody."

"Have you ever *been* in love?" Naoko asked.

"Never," I said.

She didn't ask me more than that.

When autumn ended and cold winds began tearing through the city, Naoko would often walk pressed against my arm. I could sense her breathing through the thick cloth of her duffel coat. She would entwine her arm with mine, or cram her hand in my pocket, or, when it was really cold, cling tightly to my arm, shivering. None of this had any special meaning. I just kept walking with my hands shoved in my pockets. Our rubber-soled shoes made hardly any sound on the pavement, except for the dry crackling when we trod on the broad, withered sycamore leaves. I felt sorry for Naoko whenever I heard that sound. My arm was not the one she needed, but the arm of someone else. My warmth was not what she needed, but the warmth of someone else. I felt almost guilty being me.

As the winter deepened, the transparent clarity of Naoko's eyes seemed to increase. It was a clarity that had nowhere to go. Sometimes Naoko would lock her eyes on to mine for no apparent reason. She seemed to be searching for something, and this would give me a strange, lonely, helpless sort of feeling.

I wondered if she was trying to convey something to me, something she could not put into words – something prior to words that she could not grasp within herself and which therefore had no hope of ever turning into words. Instead, she would fiddle with her hairslide, dab at the corners of her mouth with a handkerchief, or look into my eyes in that meaningless way. I wanted to hold her tight when she did these things, but I would hesitate and hold back. I was afraid I might hurt her. And so the two of us kept walking the streets of Tokyo, Naoko searching for words in space.

The guys in the dorm would always tease me when I got a call from Naoko or went out on a Sunday morning. They assumed, naturally enough, that I had found a girlfriend. There was no way to explain the truth to them, and no need to explain it, so I let them think what they wanted to. I had to face a barrage of stupid questions in the evening – what position had we used? What was she like down there? What colour underwear had she been wearing that day? I gave them the answers they wanted.

And so I went from 18 to 19. Each day the sun would rise and set, the flag would be raised and lowered. Every Sunday I would have a date with my dead friend's girl. I had no idea what I was doing or what I was going to do. For my courses I would read Claudel and Racine and Eisenstein, but they meant almost nothing to me. I made no friends at the lectures, and hardly knew anyone in the dorm. The others in the dorm thought I wanted to be a writer because I was always alone with a book, but I had no such ambition. There was nothing I wanted to be.

I tried to talk about this feeling with Naoko. She, at least, would be able to understand what I was feeling with some degree of precision, I thought. But I could never find the words to express myself. Strange, I seemed to have caught her word-searching sickness.

On Saturday nights I would sit by the phone in the lobby, waiting for Naoko to call. Most of the others were out, so the lobby was usually deserted. I would stare at the grains of light suspended in that silent space, struggling to see into my own heart. What did I want? And what did others want from me? But I could never find the answers. Sometimes I would reach out and try to grasp the grains of light, but my fingers touched nothing.

I read a lot, but not a lot of different books: I like to read my favourites again and again. Back then it was Truman Capote, John Updike, F. Scott Fitzgerald, Raymond Chandler, but I didn't see anyone else in my lectures or the dorm reading writers like that. They liked Kazumi Takahashi, Kenzaburo Oe, Yukio Mishima, or contemporary French novelists, which was another reason I didn't have much to say to anybody but kept to myself and my books. With my eyes closed, I would touch a familiar book and draw its fragrance deep inside me. This was enough to make me happy.

At 18 my favourite book was John Updike's *The Centaur*, but after I had read it a number of times, it began to lose some of its initial lustre and yielded first place to *The Great Gatsby*. *Gatsby* stayed in first place for a long time after that. I would pull it off the shelf when the mood hit me and read a section at random. It never once disappointed me. There wasn't a boring page in the whole book. I wanted to tell people what a wonderful novel it was, but no one around me had read *The*

Great Gatsby or was likely to. Urging others to read F. Scott Fitzgerald, although not a reactionary act, was not something one could do in 1968.

When I did finally meet the one person in my world who had read *Gatsby*, he and I became friends because of it. His name was Nagasawa. He was two years older than me, and because he was doing legal studies at the prestigious Tokyo University, he was on the fast track to national leadership. We lived in the same dorm and knew each other only by sight, until one day when I was reading *Gatsby* in a sunny spot in the dining hall. He sat down next to me and asked what I was reading. When I told him, he asked if I was enjoying it. "This is my third time," I said, "and every time I find something new that I like even more than the last."

"This man says he has read *The Great Gatsby* three times," he said as if to himself. "Well, any friend of *Gatsby* is a friend of mine."

And so we became friends. This happened in October.

The better I got to know Nagasawa, the stranger he seemed. I had met a lot of weird people in my day, but none as strange as Nagasawa. He was a far more voracious reader than me, but he made it a rule never to touch a book by any author who had not been dead at least 30 years. "That's the only kind of book I can trust," he said.

"It's not that I don't believe in contemporary literature," he added, "but I don't want to waste valuable time reading any book that has not had the baptism of time. Life is too short."

"What kind of authors *do* you like?" I asked, speaking in respectful tones to this man two years my senior.

"Balzac, Dante, Joseph Conrad, Dickens," he answered without hesitation.

"Not exactly fashionable."

"That's why I read them. If you only read the books that everyone else is reading, you can only think what everyone else is thinking. That's the world of hicks and slobs. Real people would be ashamed of themselves doing that. Haven't you noticed, Watanabe? You and I are the only real ones in this dorm. The other guys are crap."

This took me off guard. "How can you say that?"

"'Cause it's true. I know. I can see it. It's like we have marks on our foreheads. And besides, we've both read *The Great Gatsby*."

I did some quick calculating. "But Fitzgerald's only been dead 28 years," I said.

"So what? Two years? Fitzgerald's advanced."

No one else in the dorm knew that Nagasawa was a secret reader of classic novels, nor would it have mattered if they had. Nagasawa was known for being smart. He breezed into Tokyo University, he got good marks, he would take the Civil Service Exam, join the Foreign Ministry, and become a diplomat. He came from a wealthy family. His father owned a big hospital in Nagoya, and his brother had also graduated from Tokyo, gone on to medical school, and would one day inherit the hospital. Nagasawa always had plenty of money in his pocket, and he carried himself with real dignity. People treated him with respect, even the dorm Head. When he asked someone to do something, the person would do it without protest. There was no choice in the matter.

Nagasawa had a certain inborn quality that drew people to him and made them follow him. He knew how to stand at the head of the pack, to assess the situation, to give precise and tactful instructions that others would obey. Above his head hung an aura that revealed his powers like an angel's halo, the mere sight of which would inspire awe in people

39

for this superior being. Which is why it shocked everyone that Nagasawa chose me, a person with no distinctive qualities, to be his special friend. People I hardly knew treated me with a certain respect because of it, but what they did not seem to realize was that the reason for my having been chosen was a simple one, namely that I treated Nagasawa with none of the adulation he received from other people. I had a definite interest in the strange, complex aspects of his nature, but none of those other things – his good marks, his aura, his looks – impressed me. This must have been something new for him.

There were sides to Nagasawa's personality that conflicted in the extreme. Even I would be moved by his kindness at times, but he could just as well be malicious and cruel. He was both a spirit of amazing loftiness and an irredeemable man of the gutter. He could charge forward, the optimistic leader, even as his heart writhed in a swamp of loneliness. I saw these paradoxical qualities of his from the start, and I could never understand why they weren't just as obvious to everyone else. He lived in his own special hell.

Still, I think I always managed to view him in the most favourable light. His greatest virtue was his honesty. Not only would he never lie, he would always acknowledge his shortcomings. He never tried to hide things that might embarrass him. And where I was concerned, he was unfailingly kind and supportive. Had he not been, my life in the dorm would have been far more unpleasant than it was. Still, I never once opened my heart to him, and in that sense my relationship with Nagasawa stood in stark contrast to me and Kizuki. The first time I saw Nagasawa drunk and tormenting a girl, I promised myself never, under any circumstances, to open myself up to him.

There were several "Nagasawa Legends" that circulated throughout the dorm. According to one, he supposedly once ate three slugs. Another gave him a huge penis and had him sleeping with more than 100 girls.

The slug story was true. He told me so himself. "Three big mothers," he said. "Swallowed 'em whole."

"What the hell for?"

"Well, it happened the first year I came to live here," he said. "There was some shit between the first-years and the third-years. Started in April and finally came to a head in September. As first-year representative I went to work things out with the third-years. Real right-wing arseholes. They had these wooden kendo swords, and 'working things out' was probably the last thing they wanted to do. So I said, 'All right, let's put an end to this. Do what you want to me, but leave the other guys alone.' So they said, 'OK, let's see you swallow a couple of slugs.' 'Fine,' I said, 'Let's have 'em.' The bastards went out and got three huge slugs. And I swallowed 'em."

"What was it like?"

"'What was it like?' You have to swallow one yourself. The way it slides down your throat and into your stomach . . . it's cold, and it leaves this disgusting aftertaste . . . yuck, I get chills just thinking about it. I wanted to puke but I fought it. I mean, if I had puked 'em up, I would have had to swallow 'em all over again. So I kept 'em down. All three of 'em."

"Then what happened?"

"I went back to my room and drank a bucket of salt water. What else could I do?"

"Yeah, I guess so."

"But after that, nobody could say a thing to me. Not even the third-years. I'm the only guy in this place who can swallow three slugs."

"I bet you are."

Finding out about his penis size was easy enough. I just went to the dorm's communal shower with him. He had a big one, all right. But 100 girls was probably an exaggeration. "Maybe 75," he said. "I can't remember them all, but I'm sure it's at least 70." When I told him I had slept with only one, he said, "Oh, we can fix that, easy. Come with me next time. I'll get you one easy as that."

I didn't believe him, but he turned out to be right. It was easy. Almost too easy, with all the excitement of flat beer. We went to some kind of bar in Shibuya or Shinjuku (he had his favourites), found a pair of girls (the world was full of pairs of girls), talked to them, drank, went to a hotel, and had sex with them. He was a great talker. Not that he had anything great to say, but girls would get carried away listening to him, they'd drink too much and end up sleeping with him. I guess they enjoyed being with somebody so nice and handsome and clever. And the most amazing thing was that, just because I was with him, I seemed to become equally fascinating to them. Nagasawa would urge me to talk, and girls would respond to me with the same smiles of admiration they offered him. He worked his magic, a real talent he had that impressed me every time. Compared with Nagasawa, Kizuki's conversational gifts were child's play. This was a completely different level of accomplishment. As much as I found myself caught up in Nagasawa's power, though, I still missed Kizuki. I felt a new admiration for his sincerity. Whatever talents he had he would share with Naoko and me alone, while Nagasawa was bent on disseminating his considerable gifts to all around him. Not that he was dying to sleep with the girls he found: it was just a game to him.

I was not too crazy about sleeping with girls I didn't know. It was an easy way to take care of my sex drive of course, and I did enjoy all the holding and touching, but I hated the morning after. I'd wake up and find this strange girl sleeping next to me, and the room would reek of alcohol, and the bed and the lighting and the curtains had that special "love hotel" garishness, and my head would be in a hungover fog. Then the girl would wake up and start groping around for her knickers and while she was putting on her stockings she'd say something like, "I hope you used one last night. It's the worst day of the month for me." Then she'd sit in front of a mirror and start grumbling about her aching head or her uncooperative make-up while she redid her lipstick or attached her false eyelashes. I would have preferred not to spend the whole night with them, but you can't worry about a midnight curfew while you're seducing women (which runs counter to the laws of physics anyway), so I'd go out with an overnight pass. This meant I had to stay put until morning and go back to the dorm filled with self-loathing and disillusionment, sunlight stabbing my eyes, mouth coated with sand, head belonging to someone else.

When I had slept with three or four girls this way, I asked Nagasawa, "After you've done this 70 times, doesn't it begin to seem kind of pointless?"

"That proves you're a decent human being," he said. "Congratulations. There is absolutely nothing to be gained from sleeping with one strange woman after another. It just tires you out and makes you disgusted with yourself. It's the same for me."

"So why the hell do you keep it up?"

"Hard to say. Hey, you know that thing Dostoevsky wrote on gambling? It's like that. When you're surrounded by endless possibilities, one of the hardest things you can do is pass them up. See what I mean?"

"Sort of."

"Look. The sun goes down. The girls come out and drink. They wander around, looking for something. I can give them that something. It's the easiest thing in the world, like drinking water from a tap. Before you know it, I've got 'em down. It's what they expect. That's what I mean by possibility. It's all around you. How can you ignore it? You have a certain ability and the opportunity to use it: can you keep your mouth shut and let it pass?"

"I don't know, I've never been in a situation like that," I said with a smile. "I can't imagine what it's like."

"Count your blessings," Nagasawa said.

His womanizing was the reason Nagasawa lived in a dorm despite his affluent background. Worried that Nagasawa would do nothing else if allowed to live alone in Tokyo, his father had compelled him to live all four years at university in the dormitory. Not that it mattered much to Nagasawa. He was not going to let a few rules bother him. Whenever he felt like it, he would get an overnight permission and go girl-hunting or spend the night at his girlfriend's flat. These permissions were not easy to get, but for him they were like free passes – and for me, too, as long as he did the asking.

Nagasawa did have a steady girlfriend, one he'd been going out with since his first year. Her name was Hatsumi, and she was the same age as Nagasawa. I had met her a few times and found her to be very nice. She didn't have the kind of looks that immediately attracted attention, and in fact she was so ordinary that when I first met her I had to wonder why Nagasawa couldn't do better, but anyone who talked to her took an immediate liking to her. Quiet, intelligent, funny, caring, she always dressed with immaculate good taste. I liked her a lot and knew that if I could have a girlfriend like Hatsumi, I wouldn't be sleeping around with a bunch of easy marks. She liked me, too, and tried hard to fix me up with a first-year in her club so we could double-date, but I would make up excuses to keep from repeating past mistakes. Hatsumi went to the absolute top girls' college in the country, and there was no way I was going to be able to talk to one of those super-rich princesses.

Hatsumi had a pretty good idea that Nagasawa was sleeping around, but she never complained to him. She was seriously in love, but she never made demands.

"I don't deserve a girl like Hatsumi," Nagasawa once said to me. I had to agree with him.

That winter I found a part-time job in a little record shop in Shinjuku. It didn't pay much, but the work was easy – just watching the place three nights a week – and they let me buy records cheap. For Christmas I bought Naoko a Henry Mancini album with a track of her favourite "Dear Heart". I wrapped it myself and added a bright red ribbon. She gave me a pair of woollen gloves she had knitted. The thumbs were a little short, but they did keep my hands warm.

"Oh, I'm sorry," she said, blushing, "What a bad job!"

"Don't worry, they fit fine," I said, holding my gloved hands out to her.

"Well, at least you won't have to shove your hands in your pockets, I guess."

Naoko didn't go home to Kobe for the winter break. I stayed in Tokyo, too, working in the record shop right up to the end of the year. I didn't have anything especially fun to do in Kobe or anyone I wanted to see. The dorm's dining hall was closed for the holiday, so I went to Naoko's flat for meals. On New Year's Eve we had rice cakes and soup like everybody else.

A lot happened in late January and February that year, 1969.

At the end of January, Storm Trooper went to bed with a raging fever. Which meant I had to stand up Naoko that day. I had gone to a lot of trouble to get my hands on some free tickets for a concert. She had been especially eager to go because the orchestra was performing one of her favourites: Brahms' Fourth Symphony. But with Storm Trooper tossing around in bed on the verge of what looked like an agonizing death, I couldn't just leave him, and I couldn't find anyone stupid enough to nurse him in my place. I bought some ice and used several layers of plastic bags to hold it on his forehead, wiped his sweating brow with cold towels, took his temperature every hour, and even changed his vest for him. The fever stayed high for a day, but the following morning he jumped out of bed and started exercising as though nothing had happened. His temperature was completely normal. It was hard to believe he was a human being.

"Weird," said Storm Trooper. "I've never run a fever in my life." It was almost as if he were blaming me.

This made me mad. "But you *did* have a fever," I insisted, showing him the two wasted tickets.

"Good thing they were free," he said. I wanted to grab his radio and throw it out of the window, but instead I went back to bed with a headache.

It snowed several times in February.

Near the end of the month I got into a stupid fight with one of the third-years on my floor and punched him. He hit his head against the concrete wall, but he wasn't badly injured, and Nagasawa straightened things out for me. Still, I was called into the dorm Head's office and given a warning, after which I grew increasingly uncomfortable living in the dormitory.

The academic year ended in March, but I came up a few credits short. My exam results were mediocre – mostly "C"s and "D"s with a few "B"s. Naoko had all the grades she needed to begin the spring term of her second year. We had completed one full cycle of the seasons.

Halfway through April Naoko turned 20. She was seven months older than I was, my own birthday being in November. There was something strange about her becoming 20. I felt as if the only thing that made sense, whether for Naoko or for me, was to keep going back and forth between 18 and 19. After 18 would come 19, and after 19, 18, of course. But she turned 20. And in the autumn, I would do the same. Only the dead stay 17 for ever.

It rained on her birthday. After lectures I bought a cake nearby and took the tram to her flat. "We ought to have a celebration," I said. I probably would have wanted the same thing if our positions had been reversed. It must be hard to pass your twentieth birthday alone. The tram had been packed and had pitched so wildly that by the time I arrived at Naoko's room the cake was looking more like the Roman Colosseum than anything else. Still, once I had managed to stand up the 20 candles I had brought along, light them, close the curtains and turn out the lights, we had the makings of a birthday party. Naoko opened a bottle of wine. We drank, had some cake, and enjoyed a simple dinner.

"I don't know, it's stupid being 20," she said. "I'm just not ready. It feels weird. Like somebody's pushing me from behind."

"I've got seven months to get ready," I said with a laugh.

"You're so lucky! Still 19!" said Naoko with a hint of envy.

While we ate I told her about Storm Trooper's new jumper. Until then he had had only one, a navy-blue pullover, so two was a big move for him. The jumper itself was a nice one, red and black with a knitted deer motif, but on him it made everybody laugh. He couldn't work out what was going on.

"W-what's so funny, Watanabe?" he asked, sitting next to me in the dining hall. "Is something stuck to my forehead?"

"Nothing," I said, trying to keep a straight face. "There's nothing funny. Nice jumper."

"Thanks," he said, beaming.

Naoko loved the story. "I *have* to meet him," she said. "Just once."

"No way," I said. "You'd laugh in his face."

"You think so?"

"I'd bet on it. I see him every day, and still I can't help laughing sometimes."

We cleared the table and sat on the floor, listening to music and drinking the rest of the wine. She drank two glasses in the time it took me to finish one.

Naoko was unusually talkative that night. She told me about her childhood, her school, her family. Each episode was a long one, executed with the painstaking detail of a miniature. I was amazed at the power of her memory, but as I sat listening it began to dawn on me that there was something wrong with the way she was telling these stories: something strange, warped even. Each tale had its own internal logic, but the link from one to the next was odd. Before you knew it, story A had turned into story B, which had been contained in A, and then came C from something in B, with no end in sight. I found things to say in response at first, but after a while I stopped trying. I put on a record, and when it ended

I lifted the needle and put on another. After the last record I went back to the first. She only had six. The cycle started with *Sgt. Pepper's Lonely Hearts Club Band* and ended with Bill Evans' *Waltz for Debbie*. Rain fell past the window. Time moved slowly. Naoko went on talking by herself.

It eventually dawned on me what was wrong: Naoko was taking great care as she spoke not to touch on certain things. One of those things was Kizuki, of course, but there was more than Kizuki. And though she had certain subjects she was determined to avoid, she went on endlessly and in incredible detail about the most trivial, inane things. I had never heard her speak with such intensity before, and so I did not interrupt her.

Once the clock struck eleven, though, I began to feel nervous. She had been talking non-stop for more than four hours. I had to worry about the last train, and my midnight curfew. I saw my chance and cut in.

"Time for the troops to go home," I said, looking at my watch. "Last train's coming."

My words did not seem to reach her. Or, if they did, she was unable to grasp their meaning. She clamped her mouth shut for a split second, then went on with her story. I gave up and, shifting to a more comfortable position, drank what was left of the second bottle of wine. I thought I had better let her talk herself out. The curfew and the last train would have to take care of themselves.

She did not go on for long, though. Before I knew it, she had stopped talking. The ragged end of the last word she spoke seemed to float in the air, where it had been torn off. She had not actually finished what she was saying. Her words simply evaporated. She had been trying to go on, but had come up against nothing. Something was gone now, and I was probably the one who had destroyed it. My words might have finally reached her, taken their time to be understood, and obliterated whatever energy it was that had kept her talking so long. Lips slightly parted, she turned her half-focused eyes on mine. She looked like some kind of machine that had been humming along until someone pulled the plug. Her eyes appeared clouded, as if covered by some thin, translucent membrane.

"Sorry to interrupt," I said, "but it's getting late, and . . ."

One big tear spilled from her eye, ran down her cheek and splattered onto a record jacket. Once that first tear broke free, the rest followed in an unbroken stream. Naoko bent forwards on all fours on the floor and, pressing her palms to the mat, began to cry with the force of a person vomiting. Never in my life had I seen anyone cry with such intensity. I reached out and placed a hand on her trembling shoulder. Then, all but instinctively, I took her in my arms. Pressed against me, her whole body trembling, she continued to cry without a sound. My shirt became damp – then soaked – with her tears and hot breath. Soon her fingers began to move across my back as if in search of something, some important thing that had always been there. Supporting her weight with my left arm, I used my right hand to caress her soft, straight hair. And I waited. In that position, I waited for Naoko to stop crying. And I went on waiting. But Naoko's crying never stopped.

I slept with Naoko that night. Was it the right thing to do? I can't tell. Even now, almost 20 years later, I can't be sure. I suppose I'll never know. But at the time, it was all I could do. She was in a heightened state of tension and confusion, and she made it clear she wanted me to give her release. I turned the lights down and began, one piece at a time, with the gentlest touch I could manage, to remove her clothes. Then I undressed. It was warm enough, that rainy April night, for us to cling to each other's nakedness without a sense of chill. We explored each other's bodies in the darkness without words. I kissed her and held her soft breasts in my hands. She clutched at my erection. Her opening was warm and wet and asking for me.

And yet, when I went inside her, Naoko tensed with pain. Was this her first time? I asked, and she nodded. Now it was my turn to be confused. I had assumed that Naoko had been sleeping with Kizuki all that time. I went in as far as I could and stayed that way for a long time, holding Naoko, without moving. And then, as she began to seem calmer, I allowed myself to move inside her, taking a long time to come to climax, with slow, gentle movements. Her arms tightened around me at the end, when at last she broke her silence. Her cry was the saddest sound of orgasm I had ever heard.

When everything had ended, I asked Naoko why she had never slept with Kizuki. This was a mistake. No sooner had I asked the question than she took her arms from me and started crying soundlessly again. I pulled her bedding from the closet, spread it on the mat floor, and put her in beneath the covers. Smoking, I watched the endless April rain beyond the window.

The rain had stopped when morning came. Naoko was sleeping with her back to me. Or maybe she hadn't slept at all. Whether she was awake or asleep, all words had left her lips, and her body now seemed stiff, almost frozen. I tried several times to talk to her, but she would not answer or move. I stared for a long time at her naked shoulder, but in the end I lost all hope of eliciting a response and decided to get up.

The floor was still littered with record jackets, glasses, wine bottles and the ashtray I had been using. Half the caved-in birthday cake remained on the table. It was as if time had come to a halt. I picked up the things off the floor and drank two glasses of water at the sink. On Naoko's desk lay a dictionary and a French verb chart. On the wall above the desk hung a calendar, one without an illustration or photo of any kind, just the numbers of the days of the month. There were no memos or marks written next to any of the dates.

I picked up my clothes and dressed. The chest of my shirt was still damp and chilly. It had Naoko's smell. On the notepad lying on the desk I wrote: *I'd like to have a good long talk with you once you've calmed down. Please call me soon. Happy Birthday*. I took one last look at Naoko's shoulder, stepped outside and quietly shut the door.

No call came even after a week had passed. Naoko's house had no system for calling people to the phone, and so on Sunday morning I took the train out to Kokubunji. She wasn't there, and her name had been removed from the door. The windows and storm shutters were closed tight. The manager told me that Naoko had moved out three days earlier. He had no idea where she had moved to.

I went back to the dorm and wrote Naoko a long letter addressed to her home in Kobe. Wherever she was, they would forward it to her at least.

I gave her an honest account of my feelings. There was a lot I still didn't understand, I said, and though I was trying hard to understand, it would take time. Where I would be once that time had gone by, it was impossible for me to say now, which is why it was impossible for me to make promises or demands, or to set down pretty words. For one thing, we knew too little of each other. If, however, she would grant me the time, I would give it my best effort, and the two of us would come to know each other better. In any case, I wanted to see her again and have a good long talk. When I lost Kizuki, I lost the one person to whom I could speak honestly of my feelings, and I imagined it had been the same for Naoko. She and I had needed each other more than either of us knew. Which was no doubt why our relationship had taken such a major detour and become, in a sense, warped. *I probably should not have done what I did, and yet I believe that it was all I could do. The warmth and closeness I felt for you at that moment was something I have never experienced before. I need you to answer this letter. Whatever that answer may be, I need to have it.*

No answer came.

Something inside me had dropped away, and nothing came in to fill the empty cavern. There was an abnormal lightness to my body, and sounds had a hollow echo to them. I went to lectures more faithfully than ever. They were boring, and I never talked to my fellow students, but I had nothing else to do. I would sit by myself in the very front row of the lecture hall, speak to no one and eat alone. I stopped smoking.

The student strike started at the end of May. "Dismantle the University!" they all screamed. Go ahead, do it, I thought. Dismantle it. Tear it apart. Crush it to bits. I don't give a damn. It would be a breath of fresh air. I'm ready for anything. I'll help if necessary. Just go ahead and do it.

With the campus blockaded and lectures suspended, I started to work at a delivery company. Sitting with the driver, loading and unloading lorries, that kind of stuff. It was tougher than I thought. At first I could hardly get out of bed in the morning with the pain. The pay was good, though, and as long as I kept my body moving I could forget about the

53

emptiness inside. I worked on the lorries five days a week, and three nights a week I continued my job at the record shop. Nights without work I spent with whisky and books. Storm Trooper wouldn't touch whisky and couldn't stand the smell, so when I was sprawled on my bed drinking it straight, he'd complain that the fumes made it impossible for him to study and ask me to take my bottle outside.

"*You* get the hell out," I growled.

"But you know drinking in the dorm is a-a-against the rules."

"I don't give a shit. *You* get out."

He stopped complaining, but now I was annoyed. I went to the roof and drank alone.

In June I wrote Naoko another long letter, addressing it again to her house in Kobe. It said pretty much the same thing as the first one, but at the end I added: *Waiting for your answer is one of the most painful things I have ever been through. At least let me know whether or not I hurt you.* When I posted it, I felt as if the cavern inside me had grown again.

That June I went out with Nagasawa twice again to sleep with girls. It was easy both times. The first girl put up a terrific struggle when I tried to get her undressed and into the hotel bed, but when I began reading alone because it just wasn't worth it, she came over and started nuzzling me. And after I had done it with the second one, she started asking me all kinds of personal questions – how many girls had I slept with? Where was I from? Which university did I go to? What kind of music did I like? Had I ever read any novels by Osamu Dazai? Where would I like to go if I could travel abroad? Did I think her nipples were too big? I made up some answers and went to sleep, but next morning she said she wanted to have breakfast with me, and she kept up the stream of questions over the tasteless eggs and toast and coffee. What kind of work did my father do? Did I get good marks at school? What month was I born? Had I ever eaten frogs? She was giving me a headache, so as soon as we had finished eating I said I had to go to work.

"Will I ever see you again?" she asked with a sad look.

"Oh, I'm sure we'll meet again somewhere before long," I said, and left. What the hell am I doing? I started wondering as soon as I was alone, feeling disgusted with myself. And yet it was all I *could* do. My body was hungering for women. All the time I was sleeping with those girls I thought about Naoko: the white shape of her naked body in the darkness, her sighs, the sound of the rain. The more I thought about these things, the hungrier my body grew. I went up to the roof with my whisky and asked myself where I thought I was heading.

Finally, at the beginning of July, a letter came from Naoko. A short letter.

Please forgive me for not answering sooner. But try to understand. It took me a very long time before I was in any condition to write, and I have started this letter at least ten times. Writing is a painful process for me.

Let me begin with my conclusion. I have decided to take a year off from college. Officially, it's a leave of absence, but I suspect that I will never be going back. This will no doubt come as a surprise to you, but in fact I had been thinking about doing this for a very long time. I tried a few times to mention it to you, but I was never able to make myself begin. I was afraid even to pronounce the words.

Try not to get so worked up about things. Whatever happened – or didn't happen – the end result would have been the same. This may not be the best way to put it, and I'm sorry if it hurts you. What I am trying to tell you is, I don't want you to blame yourself for what happened with me. It is something I have to take on all by myself. I had been putting it off for more than a year, and so I ended up making things very difficult for you. There is probably no way to put it off any longer.

After I moved out of my flat, I came back to my family's house in Kobe and was seeing a doctor for a while. He tells me there is a place in the hills outside Kyoto that would be perfect for me, and I'm thinking of spending a little time there. It's not exactly a hospital, more a sanatorium kind of thing with a far freer style of treatment. I'll leave the details for another letter. What I need now is to rest my nerves in a quiet place cut off from the world.

I feel grateful in my own way for the year of companionship you gave me. Please believe that much even if you believe nothing else. You are not the one who hurt me. I myself am the one who did that. This is truly how I feel.

For now, however, I am not prepared to see you. It's not that I don't *want* to see you: I'm simply not prepared for it. The moment I feel ready, I will write to you. Perhaps then we can get to know each other better. As you say, this is probably what we should do: get to know each other better.

Goodbye.

I read Naoko's letter again and again, and each time I would be filled with that same unbearable sadness I used to feel whenever Naoko herself stared into my eyes. I had no way to deal with it, no place I could take it to or hide it away. Like the wind passing over my body, it had neither shape nor weight nor could I wrap myself in it. Objects in the scene would drift past me, but the words they spoke never reached my ears.

I continued to spend my Saturday nights sitting in the hall. There was no hope of a phone call, but I didn't know what else to do with the time. I would switch on a baseball game and pretend to watch it as I cut the empty space between me and the television set in two, then cut each half in two again, over and over, until I had fashioned a space small enough to hold in my hand.

I would switch the set off at ten, go back to my room, and go to sleep.

At the end of the month, Storm Trooper gave me a firefly. It was in an instant coffee jar with air holes in the lid and containing some blades of grass and a little water. In the bright room the firefly looked like some kind of ordinary black insect you'd find by a pond somewhere, but Storm Trooper insisted it was the real thing. "I know a firefly when I see one," he said, and I had no reason or basis to disbelieve him.

"Fine," I said. "It's a firefly." It had a sleepy look on its face, but it kept trying to climb up the slippery glass walls of the jar and falling back.

"I found it in the quad," he said.

"Here? By the dorm?"

"Yeah. You know the hotel down the street? They release fireflies in their garden for summer guests. This one made it over here."

Storm Trooper was busy stuffing clothes and notebooks into his black Boston bag as he spoke.

We were several weeks into the summer holidays, and he and I were almost the only ones left in the dorm. I had carried on with my jobs rather than go back to Kobe, and he had stayed on for a practical training session. Now that the training had ended, he was going back to the mountains of Yamanashi.

"You could give this to your girlfriend," he said. "I'm sure she'd love it."

"Thanks," I said.

After dark the dorm was hushed, like a ruin. The flag had been lowered and the lights glowed in the windows of the dining hall. With so few students left, they turned on only half the lights in the place, keeping the right half dark and the left lighted. Still, the smell of dinner drifted up to me – some kind of cream stew.

I took my bottled firefly to the roof. No one else was up there. A white vest hung on a clothesline that someone had forgotten to take in, waving in the evening breeze like the discarded shell of some huge insect. I climbed a steel ladder in the corner of the roof to the top of the dormitory's water tank. The tank was still warm with the heat of the sunlight it had absorbed during the day. I sat in the narrow space above the tank, leaning against the handrail and coming face-to-face with an almost full white moon. The lights of Shinjuku glowed to the right, Ikebukuro to the left. Car headlights flowed in brilliant streams from one pool of light to the other. A dull roar of jumbled sounds hung over the city like a cloud.

The firefly made a faint glow in the bottom of the jar, its light all too weak, its colour all too pale. I hadn't seen a firefly in years, but the ones in my memory sent a far more intense light into the summer darkness, and that brilliant, burning image was the one that had stayed with me all that time.

Maybe this firefly was on the verge of death. I gave the jar a few shakes. The firefly bumped against the glass walls and tried to fly, but its light remained dim.

I tried to remember when I had last seen fireflies, and where it might have been. I could see the scene in my mind, but was unable to recall the time or place. I could hear the sound of water in the darkness and see an old-fashioned brick sluice gate. It had a handle you could turn to open and close the gate. The stream it controlled was small enough to be hidden by the grass on its banks. The night was dark, so dark I couldn't see my feet when I turned out my torch. Hundreds of fireflies drifted over the pool of water held back by the sluice gate, their hot glow reflected in the water like a shower of sparks.

I closed my eyes and steeped myself in that long-ago darkness. I heard the wind with unusual clarity. A light breeze swept past me, leaving strangely brilliant trails in the dark. I opened my eyes to find the darkness of the summer night a few degrees deeper than it had been.

I twisted open the lid of the jar and took out the firefly, setting it on the two-inch lip of the water tank. It seemed not to grasp its new surroundings. It hobbled around the head of a steel bolt, catching its legs on curling scabs of paint. It moved to the right until it found its way blocked, then circled back to the left. Finally, with some effort, it mounted the head of the bolt and crouched there for a while, unmoving, as if it had taken its last breath.

Still leaning against the handrail, I studied the firefly. Neither I nor it made a move for a very long time. The wind continued sweeping past the two of us while the numberless leaves of the zelkova tree rustled in the darkness.

I waited for ever.

*

Only much later did the firefly take to the air. As if some thought had suddenly occurred to it, the firefly spread its wings, and in a moment it had flown past the handrail to float in the pale darkness. It traced a swift arc by the side of the water tank as though trying to bring back a lost interval in time. And then, after hovering there for a few seconds as if to watch its curved line of light blend into the wind, it finally flew off to the east.

Long after the firefly had disappeared, the trail of its light remained inside me, its pale, faint glow hovering on and on in the thick darkness behind my eyelids like a lost soul.

More than once I tried stretching my hand out in the dark. My fingers touched nothing. The faint glow remained, just beyond my grasp.

第 4 章

During the summer holidays the university called in the riot police. They broke down the barricades and arrested the students inside. This was nothing new. It's what all the students were doing at the time. The universities were not so easily "dismantled". Massive amounts of capital had been invested in them, and they were not about to dissolve just because a few students had gone wild. And in fact those students who had sealed off the campus had not wanted to dismantle the university either. All they had really wanted to do was shift the balance of power within the university structure, about which I couldn't have cared less. And so, when the strike was finally crushed, I felt nothing.

I went to the campus in September expecting to find rubble. The place was untouched. The library's books had not been carted off, the tutors' offices had not been destroyed, the student affairs office had not been burned to the ground. I was thunderstruck. What the hell had they been doing behind the barricades?

When the strike was defused and lectures started up again under police occupation, the first ones to take their seats in the classrooms were those arseholes who had led the strike. As if nothing had ever happened, they sat there taking notes and answering "present" when the register was taken. I found this incredible. After all, the strike was still in effect. There had been no declaration bringing it to an end. All that had happened was that the university had called in the riot police and torn down the barricades, but the strike itself was supposed to be continuing. The arseholes had screamed their heads off at the time of the strike, denouncing students who opposed it (or just expressed doubts about it), at times even trying them in their own kangaroo courts. I made a point of visiting those former leaders and asking why they were attending lectures instead of continuing to strike, but they couldn't give me a straight answer. What could they have said? That they were afraid of losing marks through lack of attendance? To think that these idiots had been the ones screaming for the dismantling of the university! What a joke. The wind changes direction a little, and their cries become whispers.

Hey, Kizuki, I thought, you're not missing a damn thing. This world is a piece of shit. The arseholes are getting good marks and helping to create a society in their own disgusting image.

For a while I attended lectures but refused to answer when they took the register. I knew it was a pointless gesture, but I felt so bad I had no choice. All I managed to do was isolate myself more than ever from the other students. By remaining silent when my name was called, I made everyone uncomfortable for a few seconds. None of the other students spoke to me, and I spoke to none of them.

By the second week in September I reached the conclusion that a university education was meaningless. I decided to think of it as a period of training in techniques for dealing with boredom. I had nothing I especially wanted to accomplish in society that would require me to abandon my studies straight away, and so I went to my lectures each day, took notes, and spent my free time in the library reading or looking things up.

And though that second week in September had rolled around, there was no sign of Storm Trooper. More than unusual, this was an earth-shattering development. University had started up again, and it was inconceivable that Storm Trooper would miss lectures. A thin layer of dust covered his desk and radio. His plastic cup and toothbrush, tea tin, insecticide spray and so on stood in a neat row on his shelf.

I kept the room clean in his absence. I had picked up the habit of neatness over the past year and a half, and without him there to take care of the room, I had no choice but to do it. I swept the floor each day, wiped the window every third day, and aired my mattress once a week, waiting for him to come back and tell me what a great job I had done.

But he never came back. I returned from lectures one day to find all his stuff gone and his name tag removed from the door. I went to the dorm Head's room and asked what had happened.

"He's withdrawn from the dormitory," he said. "You'll be alone in the room for the time being."

I couldn't get him to tell me why Storm Trooper had disappeared. This was a man whose greatest joy in life was to control everything and keep others in the dark.

Storm Trooper's iceberg poster stayed on the wall for a time, but I eventually took it down and replaced it with Jim Morrison and Miles Davis. This made the room seem a little more like my own. I used some of the money I had saved from work to buy a small stereo. At night I would drink alone and listen to music. I thought about Storm Trooper every now and then, but I enjoyed living alone.

At 11.30 a.m. one Monday, after a lecture on Euripides in History of Drama, I took a ten-minute walk to a little restaurant and had an omelette and salad for lunch. The place was on a quiet backstreet and was slightly more expensive than the student dining hall, but you could relax there, and they knew how to make a good omelette. "They" were a married couple who rarely spoke to each other, plus one part-time waitress. As I sat there eating by the window, a group of four students came in, two men and two women, all rather neatly dressed. They took the table near the door, spent some time looking over the menu and discussing their options, until one of them reported their choices to the waitress.

Before long I noticed that one of the girls kept glancing in my direction. She had extremely short hair and wore dark sunglasses and a white cotton mini-dress. I had no idea who she was, so I went on with my lunch, but she soon slipped out of her seat and came over to where I was sitting. With one hand on the edge of my table, she said, "You're Watanabe, aren't you?"

I raised my head and looked at her more closely. Still I could not recall ever having seen her. She was the kind of girl you notice, so if I had met her before I should have been able to recognize her immediately, and there weren't that many people in my university who knew me by name.

"Mind if I sit down?" she asked. "Or are you expecting somebody?"

Still uncertain, I shook my head. "No, nobody's coming. Please."

With a wooden clunk, she dragged a chair out and sat down

opposite, staring straight at me through her sunglasses, then glancing at my plate.

"Looks good," she said.

"It is good. Mushroom omelette and green pea salad."

"Damn," she said. "Oh, well, I'll get it next time. I've already ordered something else."

"What are you having?"

"Macaroni and cheese."

"Their macaroni and cheese isn't bad, either," I said. "By the way, do I know you? I don't recall . . ."

"Euripides," she said. "*Electra*. 'No god hearkens to the voice of lost Electra.' You know – the class just ended."

I stared hard at her. She took off her sunglasses. At last I remembered her – a first-year I had seen in History of Drama. A striking change in hairstyle had prevented me recognizing her.

"Oh," I said, touching a point a few inches below my shoulder, "your hair was down to here before the summer holidays."

"You're right," she said. "I had a perm this summer, and it was *just awful*. I was ready to kill myself. I looked like a corpse on the beach with seaweed stuck to my head. So I decided as long as I was ready to die, I might as well cut it all off. At least it's cool in the summer." She ran her hand through her pixie cut and gave me a smile.

"It looks good, though," I said, still munching my omelette. "Let me see your profile."

She turned away and held the pose a few seconds.

"Yeah, I thought so. It really looks good on you. Nicely shaped head. Pretty ears, too, uncovered like that."

"So I'm *not* mad after all! I thought I looked good myself once I cut it all off. Not one guy likes it, though. They all tell me I look like a concentration camp survivor. What's this thing that guys have for girls with long hair? Fascists, the whole bunch of them! Why do guys all think girls with long hair are the classiest, the sweetest, the most feminine? I mean, I myself know at least 250 *un*classy girls with long hair. Really."

"I think you look better now than you did before," I said. And I meant it. As far as I could recall, with long hair she had been just another cute student. A fresh and physical life force surged from the girl who sat before me now. She was like a small animal that has popped into the world with the coming of spring. Her eyes moved like an independent organism with joy, laughter, anger, amazement and despair. I hadn't seen a face so vivid and expressive in ages, and I enjoyed watching it live and move.

"Do you mean it?" she asked.

I nodded, still munching on my salad.

She put on her sunglasses and looked at me from behind them.

"You're not lying, are you?"

"I like to think of myself as an honest man," I said.

"Far out."

"So tell me: why do you wear such dark glasses?"

"I felt defenceless when my hair got short all of a sudden. As if somebody had thrown me into a crowd all naked."

"Makes sense," I said, eating the last of my omelette. She watched me with intense interest.

"You don't have to go back to them?" I asked, indicating her three companions.

"Nah. I'll go back when they serve the food. Am I interrupting your meal?"

"There's nothing left to interrupt," I said, ordering coffee when she showed no sign of leaving. The wife took my dishes and brought milk and sugar.

"Now *you* tell *me*," she said. "Why didn't you answer today when they called the register? You *are* Watanabe, aren't you? Toru Watanabe?"

"That's me."

"So why didn't you answer?"

"I just didn't feel like it today."

She took off her sunglasses again, set them on the table, and looked at me as if she were staring into the cage of some rare animal at a zoo. "'I just didn't feel like it today.' You talk like Humphrey Bogart. Cool. Tough."

"Don't be silly. I'm just an ordinary guy like everybody else."

The wife brought my coffee and set it on the table. I took a sip without adding sugar or milk.

"Look at that. You drink it black."

"It's got nothing to do with Humphrey Bogart," I explained patiently. "I just don't happen to have a sweet tooth. I think you've got me all wrong."

"Why are you so tanned?"

"I've been hiking around the last couple of weeks. Rucksack. Sleeping bag."

"Where'd you go?"

"Kanazawa. Noto Peninsula. Up to Niigata."

"Alone?"

"Alone," I said. "Found some company here and there."

"Some romantic company? New women in far-off places."

"Romantic? Now I *know* you've got me wrong. How's a guy with a sleeping bag on his back and his face all stubbly supposed to have romance?"

"Do you always travel alone like that?"

"Uh-huh."

"You enjoy solitude?" she asked, resting her cheek on her

hand. "Travelling alone, eating alone, sitting by yourself in lecture halls . . ."

"Nobody likes being alone that much. I don't go out of my way to make friends, that's all. It just leads to disappointment."

The tip of one earpiece in her mouth, sunglasses dangling down, she mumbled, "'Nobody likes being alone. I just hate to be disappointed.' You can use that line if you ever write your autobiography."

"Thanks," I said.

"Do you like green?"

"Why do you ask?"

"You're wearing a green polo shirt."

"Not especially. I'll wear anything."

"'Not especially. I'll wear anything.' I love the way you talk. Like spreading plaster, nice and smooth. Has anybody ever told you that?"

"Nobody," I said.

"My name's Midori," she said. "'Green'. But green looks terrible on me. Weird, huh? It's like I'm cursed, don't you think? My sister's name is Momoko: 'Peach girl'."

"Does she look good in pink?"

"She looks *great* in pink! She was *born* to wear pink. It's totally unfair."

The food arrived at Midori's table, and a guy in a madras jacket called out to her, "Hey, Midori, come 'n' get it!" She waved at him as if to say "I know".

"Tell me," she said. "Do you take lecture notes? In drama?"

"I do."

"I hate to ask, but could I borrow your notes? I've missed twice, and I don't know anybody in the class."

"No problem," I said, pulling the notebook from my bag.

After checking to make sure I hadn't written anything personal in it, I handed it to Midori.

"Thanks," she said. "Are you coming to lectures the day after tomorrow?"

"Yeah."

"Meet me here at noon. I'll give you back your notebook and buy you lunch. I mean . . . it's not as if you get an upset stomach or anything if you don't eat alone, right?"

"No," I said. "But you don't have to buy me lunch just because I'm lending you my notebook."

"Don't worry," she said. "I like buying people lunch. Anyway, shouldn't you write it down somewhere? You won't forget?"

"I won't forget. Day after tomorrow. Twelve o'clock. Midori. Green."

From the other table, somebody called out, "Hurry up, Midori, your food's getting cold!"

She ignored the call and asked me, "Have you always talked like that?"

"I think so," I said. "Never noticed before." And in fact no one had ever told me there was anything unusual about the way I spoke.

She seemed to be mulling something over for a few seconds. Then she stood up with a smile and went back to her table. She waved to me as I walked past their table, but the three others barely glanced in my direction.

At noon on Wednesday there was no sign of Midori in the restaurant. I thought I might wait for her over a beer, but the place started to fill up as soon as the drink arrived, so I ordered lunch and ate alone. I finished at 12.35, but still no Midori. Paying my bill, I went outside and crossed the street to a little shrine, where I waited on the stone steps for my head to clear and Midori to come. I gave up at one o'clock and went to read in the library. At two I went to my German lecture.

When it was over I went to the student affairs office and looked for Midori's name in the class list for History of Drama. The only Midori in the class was Midori Kobayashi. Next I flipped through the cards of the student files and found the address and phone number of a Midori Kobayashi who had entered the university in 1969. She lived in a north-west suburb, Toshima, with her family. I slipped into a phone box and dialled the number.

A man answered: "Kobayashi Bookshop." Kobayashi Bookshop?

"Sorry to bother you," I said, "but I wonder if Midori might be in?"

"No, she's not," he said.

"Do you think she might be on campus?"

"Hmm, no, she's probably at the hospital. Who's calling, please?"

Instead of answering, I thanked him and hung up. The hospital? Could she have been injured or fallen ill? But the man had spoken without the least sense of emergency. "She's probably at the hospital," he had said, as easily as he might have said "She's at the fish shop". I thought about a few other possibilities until thinking itself became too problematic, then I went back to the dorm and stretched out on my bed reading *Lord Jim*, which I'd borrowed from Nagasawa. When I had finished it, I went to his room to give it back.

Nagasawa was on his way to the dining hall, so I went with him for dinner.

"How'd the exams go?" I asked. The second round of upper-level exams for the Foreign Ministry had been held in August.

"Same as always," said Nagasawa as if it had been nothing.

"You take 'em, you pass. Group discussions, interviews . . . like screwin' a chick."

"In other words, easy," I said. "When do they let you know?"

"First week of October. If I pass, I'll buy you a big dinner."

"So tell me, what kind of guys make it to round two? All superstars like you?"

"Don't be stupid. They're a bunch of idiots. Idiots or weirdos. I'd say 95 per cent of the guys who want to be bureaucrats aren't worth shit. I'm not kidding. They can barely read."

"So why are you trying to join the Foreign Ministry?"

"All kinds of reasons," said Nagasawa. "I like the idea of working overseas, for one. But mainly I want to test my abilities. If I'm going to test myself, I want to do it in the biggest field there is – the nation. I want to see how high I can climb, how much power I can exercise in this insanely huge bureaucratic system. Know what I mean?"

"Sounds like a game."

"It *is* a game. I don't give a damn about power and money per se. Really, I don't. I may be a selfish bastard, but I'm incredibly cool about shit like that. I could be a Zen saint. The one thing I do have, though, is curiosity. I want to see what I can do out there in the big, tough world."

"And you have no use for 'ideals', I suppose?"

"None. Life doesn't require ideals. It requires standards of action."

"But there are lots of other ways to live, aren't there?" I asked.

"You like the way I live, don't you?"

"That's beside the point," I said. "I could never get into Tokyo University; I can't sleep with any girl I want whenever

71

I want to; I'm no great talker; people don't look up to me; I haven't got a girlfriend; and the future's not going to open up to me when I get a literature BA from a second-rate private university. What does it matter if I like the way you live?"

"Are you saying you *envy* the way I live?"

"No, I don't," I said. "I'm too used to being who I am. And I don't really give a damn about Tokyo University or the Foreign Ministry. The one thing I envy you for is having a terrific girlfriend like Hatsumi."

Nagasawa shut up and ate. When dinner was over he said, "You know, Watanabe, I have this feeling like, maybe 10 years or 20 years after we get out of this place, we're going to meet again somewhere. And one way or another, I think we're going to have some connection."

"Sounds like Dickens," I said with a smile.

"I guess it does," he said, smiling back. "But my hunches are usually right."

The two of us left the dining hall and went out to a bar. We stayed there drinking until after nine.

"Tell me, Nagasawa," I asked, "what is the 'standard of action' in *your* life?"

"You'll laugh if I tell you," he said.

"No I won't."

"All right," he said. "To be a gentleman."

I didn't laugh, but I nearly fell off my chair. "To be a gentleman? A *gentleman*?"

"You heard me."

"What does it mean to be a gentleman? How do you define it?"

"A gentleman is someone who does not what he *wants* to do but what he *should* do."

"You're the weirdest guy I've ever met," I said.

72

"You're the straightest guy I've ever met," he said. And he paid for us both.

I went to the following week's drama lecture, but still saw no sign of Midori Kobayashi. After a quick survey of the room convinced me she wasn't there, I took my usual seat in the front row and wrote a letter to Naoko while I waited for the lecturer to arrive. I wrote about my summer travels – the roads I had walked, the towns I had passed through, the people I had met. *And every night I thought of you. Now that I can no longer see you, I realize how much I need you. University is incredibly boring, but as a matter of self-discipline I am going to all my lectures and doing all the assignments. Everything seems pointless since you left. I'd like to have a nice, long talk with you. If possible, I'd like to visit your sanatorium and see you for several hours. And, if possible, I'd like to go out walking with you side by side the way we used to. Please try to answer this letter – even a short note. I won't mind.*

I filled four sheets, folded them, slipped them into an envelope, and addressed it to Naoko care of her family.

By then the lecturer had arrived, wiping the sweat from his brow as he took the register. He was a small, mournful-looking man who walked with a metal cane. While not exactly fun, the lectures in his course were always well prepared and worthwhile. After remarking that the weather was as hot as ever, he began to talk about the use of the *deus ex machina* in Euripides and explained how the concept of "god" was different in Euripides than in Aeschylus or Sophocles. He had been talking for some 15 minutes when the lecture-hall door opened and in walked Midori. She was wearing a dark blue sports shirt, cream-coloured cotton trousers and her usual sunglasses. After flashing a "sorry I'm late" kind of smile at the professor, she sat down next to me. Then she took a notebook – my notebook – from her shoulder bag, and handed it to me. Inside, I found a note: *Sorry about Wednesday. Are you angry?*

The lecture was about half over and the professor was drawing a sketch of a Greek stage on the blackboard when the door opened again and two students in helmets walked in. They looked like some kind of comedy team, one tall, thin and pale, the other short, round and dark with a long beard that didn't suit him. The tall one carried an armful of political agitation handbills. The short one walked up to the professor and said, with a degree of politeness, that they would like to use the second half of his lecture for political debate and hoped that he would cooperate, adding, "The world is full of problems far more urgent and relevant than Greek tragedy." This was more an announcement than a request. The professor replied, "I rather doubt that the world has problems far more urgent and relevant than Greek tragedy, but you're not going to listen to anything I have to say, so do what you like." Grasping the edge of the table, he set his feet on the floor, picked up his cane and limped out of the classroom.

While the tall student passed out his handbills, the round one went to the podium and started lecturing. The handbills were full of the usual simplistic sloganeering: "SMASH FRAUDULENT ELECTIONS FOR UNIVERSITY PRESIDENT!", "MARSHAL ALL FORCES FOR NEW ALL-CAMPUS STRIKE!", "CRUSH THE IMPERIAL-EDUCATIONAL-INDUSTRIAL COMPLEX!" I had no problem with what they were saying, but the writing was lame. It had nothing to inspire confidence or arouse the passions. And the round man's speech was just as bad – the same old tune with different words. The true enemy of this bunch was not State Power but Lack of Imagination.

"Let's get out of here," said Midori.

I nodded and stood, and the two of us made for the door. The round man said something to me at that point, but I couldn't catch it. Midori waved to him and said, "See ya later."

"Hey, are we counter-revolutionaries?" Midori asked me when we were outside. "Are we going to be strung upon telephone poles if the revolution succeeds?"

"Let's have lunch first, just in case."

"Good. There's a place I want to take you to. It's a bit far, though. Can you spare the time?"

"Yeah, I'm free until my two o'clock class."

Midori took me by bus to Yotsuya and showed me to a fancy boxed-lunch speciality shop in a sheltered spot just behind the station. The minute we sat down they served us soup and the lunch of the day in square, red-lacquered boxes. This was a place worth a bus ride to eat at.

"Great food," I said.

"And cheap, too. I've been coming here since school. My old school's just down the street. They were so strict, we had to sneak out to eat here. They'd suspend you if they caught you eating out."

Without the sunglasses, Midori's eyes looked somewhat sleepier than they had the last time. When she was not playing with the narrow silver bracelet on her left wrist, she would be rubbing at the corners of her eyes with the tip of her little finger.

"Tired?" I asked.

"Kind of. I'm not getting enough sleep. But I'm OK, don't worry," she said. "Sorry about the other day. Something important came up and I just couldn't get out of it. All of a sudden, in the morning. I thought about calling you at the restaurant, but I couldn't remember the name, and I didn't know your home number. Did you wait long?"

"No big deal. I've got a lot of time on my hands."

"A lot?"

"Way more than I need. I wish I could give you some to help you sleep."

Midori rested her cheek on her hand and smiled at me. "What a nice guy you are."

"Not nice. I just have time to kill," I said. "By the way, I called your house that day and somebody told me you were at the hospital. Something wrong?"

"You called my house?" she asked with a slight wrinkle forming between her eyebrows. "How did you get my number?"

"Looked it up in the student affairs office. Anyone can do that."

She nodded once or twice and started playing with the bracelet again. "I never would have thought of that. I suppose I could have looked up your number. Anyway, about the hospital, I'll tell you next time. I don't feel like it now. Sorry."

"That's OK. I didn't mean to pry."

"No, you're not prying. I'm just kind of tired. Like a monkey in the rain."

"Shouldn't you go home and get some sleep?"

"Not now. Let's get out of here."

She took me to her old school, a short walk from Yotsuya.

Passing the station, I thought about Naoko and our endless walking. It had all started from there. I realized that if I hadn't run into Naoko on the train that Sunday in May, my life would have been very different from what it was now. But then I changed my mind: no, even if we hadn't met that day, my life might not have been any different. We were

76

supposed to meet. If not then, some other time. I didn't have any basis for thinking this: it was just a feeling.

Midori Kobayashi and I sat on a park bench together, looking at her old school. Ivy clung to the walls, and pigeons huddled under the gables, resting their wings. It was a nice, old building with character. A great oak tree stood in the playground, and a column of white smoke rose straight up beside it. The fading summer light gave the smoke a soft and cloudy look.

"Do you know what that smoke is?" Midori asked me all of a sudden.

"No idea," I said.

"They're burning sanitary towels."

"Really?" I couldn't think of anything else to say.

"Sanitary towels, tampons, stuff like that," she said with a smile. "It *is* a girls' school. The old caretaker collects them from all the receptacles and burns them in the incinerator. *That's* the smoke."

"Whoa."

"Yeah, that's what I used to say to myself whenever I was in class and saw the smoke outside the window. 'Whoa'. Think about it: the school had almost a thousand girls. So, say 900 of them have started their periods, and maybe a fifth of them are menstruating at any one time: 180 girls. That's 180 girls' worth of towels in the receptacles every day."

"I bet you're right – though I'm not sure about the maths."

"Anyway, it's a lot. 180 girls. What do you think it feels like to collect and burn that much stuff?"

"Can't imagine," I said. How could I have imagined what the old man was going through? Midori and I went on watching the smoke.

"I really didn't want to go to this school," Midori said. She gave her head a little shake. "I wanted to go to an absolutely ordinary State school with ordinary people where I could relax and have fun like an ordinary teenager. But my parents thought it would look good for me to go to this fancy place. They're the ones who stuck me in here. You know: that's what happens when you do well in primary school. The teacher tells your parents 'With marks like hers, she ought to go *there*.' So that's where I ended up. I went for six years and I never liked it. All I could think about was getting out. And you know, I've got certificates of merit for never having been late or missed a day of school. That's how much I hated the place. Get it?"

"No, I don't get it."

"It's because I hated the place so much. I wasn't going to let it beat me. If I'd let it get to me once I'd be finished. I was scared I'd just keep slipping down and down. I'd crawl to school with a temperature of 103. The teacher would ask me if I was sick, but I'd say no. When I left they gave me certificates for perfect attendance and punctuality, plus a French dictionary. That's why I'm taking German now. I didn't want to owe this school *anything*. I'm not kidding."

"Why did you hate it so much?

"Did *you* like *your* school?"

"Well, no, but I didn't especially hate it, either. I went to an ordinary State school but I never thought about it one way or another."

"Well, *this* school," Midori said, scratching the corner of her eye with her little finger, "had nothing but upper-class girls – almost a thousand girls with good backgrounds and good exam results. *Rich* girls. They had to be rich to survive. High tuition, endless contributions, expensive school trips. For instance, if we went to Kyoto, they'd put us up in a first-class inn and serve us tea ceremony food on lacquer tables, and they'd take us once a year to the most expensive hotel in Tokyo to study table manners. I mean, this was no ordinary school. Out of 160 girls in my class, I was the only one from a middle-class neighbourhood like Toshima. I looked at the school register once to see where the others lived, and every single one of them was from a rich area. Well, no, there was one girl from way out in Chiba with the farmers, so I got kind of friendly with her. And she was really nice. She invited me to her house, though she apologized for how far I'd have to travel to get there. I went and it was *incredible*, this giant piece of land you'd have to walk 15 minutes to get around. It had this amazing garden and two dogs like compact cars they fed *steaks* to. But still, this girl felt embarrassed about living out in Chiba. This is a girl who would be driven to school in a Mercedes Benz if she was late! By a chauffeur! Like right out of the *Green Hornet*: the hat, the white gloves, the whole deal. And still she had this inferiority complex. Can you believe it?"

I shook my head.

"I was the only one in the whole school who lived in a place like Kita-Otsuka Toshima. And under 'parent's profession' it said 'bookshop owner'. Everybody in my class thought that was so neat: 'Oh, you're so lucky, you can read any book you like' and stuff. Of course, they were thinking of some monster bookshop like Kinokuniya. They could never have imagined the poor, little Kobayashi Bookshop. The door creaks open and you see nothing but magazines. The steady sellers are the women's glossies with illustrated pull-out sections on the latest sexual techniques. The local housewives buy them and sit at the kitchen table reading them from cover to cover, and give 'em a try when their husbands get home. And they've got the most incredible positions! Is this what housewives have on their minds all day? The comics are the other big-seller: *Magazine*, *Sunday*, *Jump*. And of course the weeklies. So this 'bookshop' is almost all magazines. Oh, there are a few books, paperbacks, mysteries and swashbucklers and romances. That's all that sells. And How-To books: how to win at *Go*, how to raise bonsai, how to give wedding speeches, how to have sex, how to stop smoking, you name it. We even sell writing supplies – stacks of ballpoint pens and pencils and notebooks next to the till. But that's it. No *War and Peace*, no Kenzaburo Oe, no *Catcher in the Rye*. That's the Kobayashi Bookshop. That's how 'lucky' I am. Do you think I'm lucky?"

"I can just see the place."

"You know what I mean. Everybody in the neighbourhood comes there, some of them for years, and we deliver. It's a good business, more than enough to support a family of four; no debts, two daughters in college, but that's it. Nothing to spare for extras. They should never have sent me to a school like that. It was a recipe for heartache. I had to listen to them grumble to me every time the school asked for a contribution, and I was always scared to death I'd run out of money if I went out with my school friends and they wanted to eat somewhere expensive. It's a miserable way to live. Is your family rich?"

"My family? No, my parents are absolutely ordinary working people, not rich, not poor. I know it's not easy for them to send me to a private university in Tokyo, but there's just me, so it's not that big a deal. They don't give me much to live on, so I work part-time. We live in a typical house with a little garden and our car is a Toyota Corolla."

"What's your job like?"

"I work in a Shinjuku record shop three nights a week. It's easy. I just sit there and mind the shop."

"You're joking?" said Midori. "I don't know, just looking

at you I sort of assumed you'd never been hard up."

"It's true. I *have* never been hard up. Not that I have tons of money, either. I'm like most people."

"Well, 'most people' in my school were *rich*," said Midori, palms resting on her lap. "That was the problem."

"So now you'll have plenty of chances to see a world without that problem. More than you want to, maybe."

"Hey, tell me, what do you think the best thing is about being rich?"

"I don't know."

"Being able to say you don't have any money. Like, if I suggested to a school friend we do something, she could say, 'Sorry, I don't have any money'. Which is something I could *never* say if the situation was reversed. If *I* said 'I don't have any money', it would *really mean* 'I don't have any money'. It's sad. Like, if a pretty girl says 'I look terrible today, I don't want to go out,' that's OK, but if an ugly girl says the same thing people laugh at her. That's what the world was like for me. For six years, until last year."

"You'll get over it."

"I hope so. University is such a relief! It's full of ordinary people."

She smiled with the slightest curl of her lip and smoothed her short hair with the palm of her hand.

"Do you have a job?" I asked.

"Yeah, I write map notes. You know those little pamphlets that come with maps? With descriptions of the different neighbourhoods and population figures and points of interest. Here there's so-and-so hiking trail or such-and-such a legend, or some special flower or bird. I write the texts for those things. It's *so* easy! Takes no time at all. I can write a whole booklet with a day of looking things up in the library. All you have to do is master a couple of secrets and all kinds of work comes your way."

"What kind of secrets?"

"Like you put in some little something that nobody else has written and the people at the map company think you're a literary genius and send you more work. It doesn't have to be anything at all, just some tiny thing. Like, say, when they built a dam in this particular valley, the water covered over a village, but still every spring the birds come up from the south and you can see them flying over the lake. Put in one little episode like that and people love it, it's so graphic and sentimental. The usual part-timer doesn't bother with stuff like that, but I can make decent money with what I write."

"Yeah, but you have to find those 'episodes'."

"True," said Midori with a tilt of her head. "But if you're looking for them, you usually find them. And if you don't, you can always make up something harmless."

"Aha!"

"Peace," said Midori.

She said she wanted to hear about my dormitory, so I told her the usual stories about the raising of the flag and Storm Trooper's radio callisthenics. Storm Trooper especially made Midori laugh, as he seemed to do with everyone. She said she thought it would be fun to have a look at the dorm. There was nothing fun about the place, I told her: "Just a few hundred guys in grubby rooms, drinking and wanking."

"Does that include you?"

"It includes every man on the face of the earth," I explained. "Girls have periods and boys wank. Everybody."

"Even ones with girlfriends? I mean, sex partners."

"It's got nothing to do with that. The Keio student living next door to me has a wank before every date. He says it relaxes him."

82

"I don't know much about that stuff. I was in a girls' school so long."

"I guess the glossy women's magazines don't go into that."

"Not at all!" she said, laughing. "Anyway, Watanabe, would you have some time this Sunday? Are you free?"

"I'm free every Sunday. Until six, at least. That's when I go to work."

"Why don't you visit me? At the Kobayashi Bookshop. The shop itself will be closed, but I have to hang around there alone all day. I might be getting an important phone call. How about lunch? I'll cook for you."

"I'd like that," I said.

Midori tore a page from a notebook and drew a detailed map of the way to her place. She used a red pen to make a large X where the house stood.

"You can't miss it. There's a big sign: 'Kobayashi Bookshop'. Come at noon. I'll have lunch ready."

I thanked her and put the map in my pocket. "I'd better get back to campus now," I said. "My German lecture starts at two." Midori said she had somewhere to go and took the train from Yotsuya.

Sunday morning I got up at nine, shaved, did my laundry and hung out the clothes on the roof. It was a beautiful day. The first smell of autumn was in the air. Red dragonflies flitted around the quadrangle, chased by neighbourhood kids swinging nets. With no wind, the Rising Sun flag hung limp on its pole. I put on a freshly ironed shirt and walked from the dorm to the tram stop. A student neighbourhood on a Sunday morning: the streets were dead, virtually empty, most shops closed. What few sounds there were echoed with special clarity. A girl wearing sabots clip-clopped across the asphalt roadway, and next to the tram shelter four or five kids were throwing rocks at a row of empty cans. A florist's was open, so I went in and bought some daffodils. Daffodils in autumn: that was strange. But I had always liked that particular flower.

Three old women were the only passengers on the Sunday morning tram. They all looked at me and my flowers. One of them gave me a smile. I smiled back. I sat in the last seat and watched the ancient houses passing close to the window. The tram almost touched the overhanging eaves. The laundry deck of one house had ten potted tomato plants, next to which a big black cat lay stretched out in the sun. In the garden of another house, a little girl was blowing soap bubbles. I heard an Ayumi Ishida song coming from somewhere, and could even catch the smell of curry cooking. The tram snaked its way through this private back-alley world. A few more passengers got on at stops along the way, but the three old women went on talking intently about something, huddled together face-to-face.

I got off near Otsuka Station and followed Midori's map down a broad street without much to look at. None of the shops along the way seemed to be doing very well, housed as they were in old buildings with gloomy-looking interiors and faded writing on some of the signs. Judging from the age and style of the buildings, this area had been spared the wartime air raids, leaving whole blocks intact. A few of the places had been entirely rebuilt, but just about all had been enlarged or repaired in places, and it was these additions that tended to look shabbier than the old buildings themselves.

The whole atmosphere of the place suggested that most of the original residents had become fed up with the cars, the filthy air, the noise and high rents and moved to the suburbs, leaving only cheap flats and company apartments and hard-to-sell shops and a few stubborn people who clung to old family properties. Everything looked blurred and grimy as though wrapped in a haze of exhaust fumes.

Ten minutes' walk down this street brought me to a corner petrol station, where I turned right into a small block of shops, in the middle of which hung the sign for the Kobayashi Bookshop. True, it was not a big shop, but neither was it as small as Midori's description had led me to believe. It was just a typical neighbourhood bookshop, the same kind I used to run to on the very day the boys' comics came out. A nostalgic mood overtook me as I stood in front of the place.

The whole front of the shop was sealed off by a big, roll-down metal shutter inscribed with a magazine advertisement: "WEEKLY BUNSHUN SOLD HERE THURSDAYS". I still had 15 minutes before noon, but I didn't want to kill time wandering through the block with a handful of daffodils, so I pressed the doorbell beside the shutter and stepped a few paces back to wait. Fifteen seconds went by without an answer, and I was debating with myself whether to ring again when I heard a window clatter open above me. I looked up to see Midori leaning out and waving.

"Come in," she yelled. "Lift the shutter."

"Is it OK? I'm kind of early," I shouted back.

"No problem. Come upstairs. I'm busy in the kitchen." She pulled the window closed.

The shutter made a terrific grinding noise as I raised it three feet from the ground, ducked under, and lowered it again. The shop was pitch black inside. I managed to feel my way to the back stairway, tripping over bound piles of magazines. I unlaced my shoes and climbed the stairs to the living area. The interior of the house was dark and gloomy. The stairs led to a simple parlour with a sofa and easy chairs. It was a small room with dim light coming in the window, reminiscent of old Polish films. There was a kind of storage area on the left and what looked like the door to a bathroom. I had to climb the steep stairway with care to reach the second floor, but once I got there, it was so much brighter than the first that I felt greatly relieved.

"Over here," called Midori's voice. To the right at the top of the stairs was what looked like a dining room, and beyond that a kitchen. The house itself was old, but the kitchen seemed to have been refitted recently with new cabinets and a bright, shiny sink and taps. Midori was preparing food. A pot was bubbling, and the air was filled with the smell of grilled fish.

"There's beer in the fridge," she said with a glance in my direction. "Have a seat while I finish this." I took a can and sat at the kitchen table. The beer was so cold it might have been in the fridge for the best part of a year. On the table lay a small, white ashtray, a newspaper, and a soy sauce dispenser. There was also a notepad and pen, with a phone number and some figures on the pad that seemed to be calculations connected with shopping.

"I should have this done in ten minutes," she said. "Can you stand the wait?"

"Of course I can," I said.

"Get good and hungry, then. I'm making a lot."

I sipped my beer and focused on Midori as she went on cooking, her back to me. She worked with quick, nimble movements, handling no fewer than four cooking procedures at once. Over here she tasted a boiled dish, and the next second she was at the cutting board, rat-tat-tatting, then she took something out of the fridge and piled it in a bowl, and before I knew it she had washed a pot she had finished using. From the back she looked like an Indian percussionist – ringing a bell, tapping a block, striking a water-buffalo bone, each movement precise and economical, with perfect balance. I watched in awe.

"Let me know if there's something I can do," I said, just in case.

"That's OK," said Midori with a smile in my direction. "I'm used to doing everything alone." She wore slim blue jeans and a navy T-shirt. An Apple Records logo nearly covered the back of the shirt. She had extremely narrow hips, as if she had somehow skipped puberty when the hips grow fuller, and this gave her a far more androgynous look than most girls have in slim jeans. The light pouring in from the kitchen window gave her figure a kind of vague outline.

"You really didn't have to put together such a feast," I said.

"It's no feast," answered Midori without turning my way. "I was too busy to do any real shopping yesterday. I'm just throwing together a few things I had in the fridge. Really, don't worry. Besides, it's Kobayashi family tradition to treat guests well. I don't know what it is, but we like to entertain. It's inborn; a kind of sickness. Not that we're especially nice or people love us or anything, but if somebody shows up we have to treat them well no matter what. We've all got the same personality flaw, for better or worse. Take my father, for example. He hardly drinks, but the house is full of alcohol. What for? To serve guests! So don't hold back: drink all the beer you want."

"Thanks," I said.

It suddenly dawned on me that I had left the daffodils downstairs. I had set them aside while unlacing my shoes. I slipped back downstairs and found the ten bright blossoms lying in the gloom. Midori took a tall, slim glass from the cupboard and arranged the flowers in it.

"I love daffodils," said Midori. "I once sang 'Seven Daffodils' in the school talent contest. Do you know it?"

"Of course."

"We had a folk group. I played guitar."

She sang 'Seven Daffodils' as she arranged the food on plates.

Midori's cooking was far better than I had expected: an amazing assortment of fried, pickled, boiled and roasted dishes using eggs, mackerel, fresh greens, aubergine, mushrooms, radishes, and sesame seeds, all cooked in the delicate Kyoto style.

"This is *great*," I said with my mouth full.

"OK, tell me the truth now," Midori said. "You weren't expecting my cooking to be very good, were you – judging from the way I look?"

"Not really," I said honestly.

"You're from the Kansai region, so you like this kind of delicate flavouring, right?"

"Don't tell me you changed style especially for me?"

"Don't be ridiculous! I wouldn't go to that much trouble. No, we always eat like this."

"So your mother – or your father – is from Kansai?"

"Nope. My father was born in Tokyo and my mother's from Fukushima. There's not a single Kansai person among my relatives. We're all from Tokyo or northern Kanto."

"I don't get it," I said. "How can you make this 100 per cent authentic Kansai-style food? Did somebody teach you?"

"Well, it's kind of a long story," she said, eating a slice of fried egg. "My mother hated housework of any kind, and she almost never cooked anything. And we had the business to think about, so it was always 'Today we're so busy, let's get a take-away' or 'Let's just buy some croquettes at the butcher's' and so on. I hated that even when I was little, I mean like cooking a big pot of curry and eating the same thing three days in a row. So then one day – I was in the fifth year of school – I decided I was going to cook for the family and do it right. I went to the big Kinokuniya in Shinjuku and bought the biggest, handsomest cookbook I could find, and I mastered it from cover to cover: how to choose a cutting board, how to sharpen knives, how to bone a fish, how to shave fresh bonito flakes, everything. It turned out the author of the book was from the Kansai, so all my cooking is Kansai style."

"You mean you learned how to make all this stuff from a book?!"

"I saved my money and went to eat the real thing. That's how I learned flavourings. I've got pretty good intuition. I'm hopeless as a logical thinker, though."

"It's amazing you could teach yourself to cook so well without having anyone to show you."

"It wasn't easy," said Midori with a sigh, "growing up in a house where nobody gave a damn about food. I'd tell them I wanted to buy decent knives and pots and they wouldn't give me the money. 'What we have now is good enough,' they'd say, but I'd tell them that was crazy, you couldn't bone a fish with the kind of flimsy knives we had at home, so they'd say, 'What the hell do you have to bone a fish for?' It was hopeless trying to communicate with them. I saved up my allowance and bought real professional knives and pots and strainers and stuff. Can you believe it? Here's a 15-year-old girl pinching pennies to buy strainers and whetstones and tempura pots when all the other girls at school are getting huge allowances and buying beautiful dresses and shoes. Don't you feel sorry for me?"

I nodded, swallowing a mouthful of clear soup with fresh junsai greens.

"When I was in the sixth-form, I *had* to have an egg fryer – a long, narrow pan for making this dashimaki-style fried egg we're eating. I bought it with money I was supposed to use for a new bra. For *three months* I had to live with *one bra*. Can you believe it? I'd wash my bra at night, go crazy trying to dry it, and wear it the next day. And if it didn't dry right, I had a tragedy to deal with. The saddest thing in the world is wearing a damp bra. I'd walk around with tears pouring from my eyes. To think I was suffering this for an egg fryer!"

"I see what you mean," I said with a laugh.

"I know I shouldn't say this, but actually it was kind of a relief to me when my mother died. I could run the family budget *my* way. I could buy what *I* liked. So now I've got a relatively complete set of cooking utensils. My father doesn't know a thing about the budget."

"When did your mother die?"

"Two years ago. Cancer. Brain tumour. She was in the hospital a year and a half. It was terrible. She suffered from beginning to end. Finally lost her mind; had to be doped up all the time, and still she couldn't die, though when she did it was practically a mercy killing. It's the worst kind of death – the person's in agony, the family goes through hell. It took every yen we had. I mean, they'd give her these shots – bang, bang, ¥20,000 a pop, and she had to have round-the-clock care. I was so busy with her, I couldn't study, had to delay university for a year. And as if that weren't bad enough – " She stopped in mid-sentence, put her chopsticks down and sighed. "How did this conversation turn so dark all of a sudden?"

"It started with the business about the bras," I said.

"So anyway, eat your eggs and think about what I just told you," Midori said with a solemn expression.

Eating my portion filled me up, but Midori ate far less. "Cooking ruins my appetite," she said. She cleared the table, wiped up the crumbs, brought out a box of Marlboro, put one in her mouth and lit up with a match. Taking hold of the glass with the daffodils, she studied the blooms for a while.

"I don't think I'll put them in a vase," she said. "If I leave them like this, it's like I just happened to pick them by a pond somewhere and threw them into the first thing that came to hand."

"I did pick them by the pond at Otsuka Station," I said.

She chuckled. "You *are* a weird one. Making jokes with a perfectly straight face."

Chin in hand, she smoked half her cigarette, then crushed it out in the ashtray. She rubbed her eyes as if smoke had got into them.

"Girls are supposed to be a little more elegant when they put out their cigarettes. You did that like a lumberjack. You shouldn't just cram it down in the ashtray but press it lightly around the edges of the ash. Then it doesn't get all bent up. And girls are *never* supposed to blow smoke through their noses. And most girls wouldn't talk about how they wore the same bra for three months when they're eating alone with a man."

"I *am* a lumberjack," Midori said, scratching next to her nose. "I can never manage to be chic. I try it as a joke sometimes, but it never sticks. Any more critiques for me?"

"Girls don't smoke Marlboro," I said.

"What's the difference? One tastes as bad as another." She turned the red Marlboro packet over and over in her hand. "I started smoking last month. It's not as if I was dying

91

for tobacco or anything. I just sort of felt like it."

"Why's that?" I asked.

She pressed her hands together on the table and thought about it for a while. "What's the difference? You don't smoke?"

"Stopped in June," I said.

"How come?"

"It was a pain. I hated running out of smokes in the middle of the night. I don't like having something control me that way."

"You're very clear about what you like and what you don't like," she said.

"Maybe so," I said. "Maybe that's why people don't like me. Never have."

"It's because you show it," she said. "You make it obvious you don't care whether people like you or not. That makes some people angry." She spoke in a near mumble, chin in hand. "But I like talking to you. The way you talk is so unusual. 'I don't like having something control me that way'."

I helped her wash the dishes. Standing next to her, I wiped as she washed, and stacked everything on the worktop.

"So," I said, "your family's out today?"

"My mother's in her grave. She died two years ago."

"Yeah, I heard that part."

"My sister's on a date with her fiancé. Probably on a drive. Her boyfriend works for some car company. He loves cars. I *don't* love cars."

Midori stopped talking and washed. I stopped talking and wiped.

"And then there's my father," she said after some time had gone by.

"Right," I said.

92

"He went off to Uruguay in June last year and he's been there ever since."

"Uruguay?! Why Uruguay?"

"He was thinking of settling there, believe it or not. An old army buddy of his has a farm there. All of a sudden, my father announces he's going, too, that there's no limit to what he can do in Uruguay, and he gets on a plane and that's that. We tried hard to stop him, like, 'Why do you want to go to a place like that? You can't speak the language, you've hardly ever left Tokyo.' But he wouldn't listen. Losing my mother was a real shock to him. I mean, it made him a little cuckoo. That's how much he loved her. Really."

There was not much I could say in reply. I stared at Midori with my mouth open.

"What do you think he said to my sister and me when our mother died? 'I would much rather have lost the two of you than her.' It knocked the wind out of me. I couldn't say a word. You know what I mean? You just can't *say* something like that. OK, he lost the woman he loved, his partner for life. I understand the pain, the sadness, the heartbreak. I pity him. But you don't tell the daughters you fathered 'You should have died in her place'. I mean, that's just too terrible. Don't you agree?"

"Yeah, I see your point."

"That's one wound that will never go away," she said, shaking her head. "But anyway, everyone in my family's a little different. We've all got something just a little bit strange."

"So it seems," I said.

"Still, it *is* wonderful for two people to love each other, don't you think? I mean, for a man to love his wife so much he can tell his daughters they should have died in her place . . . !"

"Maybe so, now that you put it that way."

"And then he dumps the two of us and runs off to Uruguay."

I wiped another dish without replying. After the last one, Midori put everything back in the cabinets.

"So, have you heard from your father?" I asked.

"One postcard. In March. But what does he write? 'It's hot here' or 'The fruit's not as good as I expected'. Stuff like that. I mean, give me a break! One stupid picture of a donkey! He's lost his marbles! He didn't even say whether he'd met that guy – that friend of his or whatever. He did add near the end that once he's settled he'll send for me and my sister, but not a word since then. And he never answers our letters."

"What would you do if your father said 'Come to Uruguay'?"

"I'd go and have a look around at least. It might be fun. My sister says she'd absolutely refuse. She can't stand dirty things and dirty places."

"Is Uruguay dirty?"

"Who knows? *She* thinks it is. Like the roads are full of donkey shit and it's swarming with flies, and the toilets don't work, and lizards and scorpions crawl all over the place. She maybe saw a film like that. She can't stand flies, either. All she wants to do is drive through scenic places in fancy cars."

"No way."

"I mean, what's wrong with Uruguay? I'd go."

"So who's running the shop?"

"My sister, but she hates it. We have an uncle in the neighbourhood who helps out and makes deliveries. And I help when I have time. A bookshop's not exactly hard labour, so we can manage. If it gets to be too much, we'll sell the place."

"Do you like your father?"

Midori shook her head. "Not especially."

"So how can you follow him to Uruguay?"

"I believe in him."

"Believe in him?"

"Yeah, I'm not that fond of him, but I believe in my father. How can I *not* believe in a man who gives up his house, his kids, his work, and runs off to Uruguay from the shock of losing his wife? Do you see what I mean?"

I sighed. "Sort of, but not really."

Midori laughed and patted me on the back. "Never mind," she said. "It really doesn't matter."

One weird thing after another came up that Sunday afternoon. A fire broke out near Midori's house and, when we went up to the third-floor laundry deck to watch, we sort of kissed. It sounds stupid when I put it like that, but that was how things worked out.

We were drinking coffee after the meal and talking about the university when we heard sirens. They got louder and louder and seemed to be increasing in number. Lots of people ran past the shop, some of them shouting. Midori went to a room facing the street, opened the window and looked down. "Wait here a minute," she said and disappeared; after which I heard feet pounding up stairs.

I sat there drinking coffee alone and trying to remember where Uruguay was. Let's see, Brazil was over here, and Venezuela there, and Colombia somewhere over here, but I couldn't recall the location of Uruguay. A few minutes later Midori came down and urged me to hurry somewhere with her. I followed her to the end of the hall and climbed a steep, narrow stairway to a wooden deck with bamboo laundry poles. The deck was higher than most of the surrounding rooftops and gave a good view of the neighbourhood. Huge clouds of black smoke shot up from a place three or four houses away and flowed with the breeze out towards the high street. A burning smell filled the air.

"It's Sakamoto's place," said Midori, leaning over the railing. "They used to make traditional door fittings and stuff. They went out of business some time ago, though."

I leaned over the railing with her and strained to see what was going on. A three-storey building blocked our view of the fire, but there seemed to be three or four fire engines over there working on the blaze. No more than two of them could squeeze into the narrow lane where the house was burning, the rest standing by on the high street. The usual crowd of gawkers filled the area.

"Hey, maybe you should gather your valuables together and get ready to evacuate this place," I said to Midori. "The wind's blowing the other way now, but it could change any time, and you've got a petrol station right there. I'll help you pack."

"What valuables?" said Midori.

"Well, you must have something you'd want to save – bank-books, seals, legal papers, stuff like that. Emergency cash."

"Forget it. I'm not running away."

"Even if this place burns?"

"You heard me. I don't mind dying."

I looked her in the eye, and she looked straight at me. I couldn't tell if she was serious or joking. We stayed like that for a while, and soon I stopped worrying.

"OK," I said. "I get it. I'll stay with you."

"You'll die with me?" Midori asked with shining eyes.

"No way," I said. "I'll run if it gets dangerous. If you want to die, you can do it alone."

"Cold-hearted bastard!"

"I'm not going to die with you just because you made lunch for me. Of course, if it had been dinner . . ."

"Oh, well . . . Anyway, let's stay here and watch for a while. We can sing songs. And if something bad happens, we can think about it then."

"Sing songs?"

Midori brought two floor pillows, four cans of beer and a guitar from downstairs. We drank and watched the black smoke rising. She strummed and sang. I asked her if she didn't think this might anger the neighbours. Drinking beer and singing while you watched a local fire from the laundry deck didn't seem like the most admirable behaviour I could think of.

"Forget it," she said. "We never worry about what the neighbours might think."

She sang some of the folk songs she had played with her group. I would have been hard pressed to say she was good, but she did seem to enjoy her own music. She went through all the old standards – "Lemon Tree", "Puff (The Magic Dragon)", "Five Hundred Miles", "Where Have All the Flowers Gone?", "Michael, Row the Boat Ashore". At first she tried to get me to sing bass harmony, but I was so bad she gave up and sang alone to her heart's content. I worked on my beer and listened to her sing and kept an eye on the fire. It flared up and died down several times. People were yelling and giving orders. A newspaper helicopter clattered overhead, took photographs and flew away. I worried that we might be in the picture. A policeman screamed through a loudspeaker for bystanders to get back. A little kid was crying for his mother. Glass shattered somewhere. Before long the wind began shifting unpredictably, and white ash flakes fell out of the air around us, but Midori went on sipping and singing. After she had gone through most of the songs she knew, she sang an odd one that she said she had written herself:

> *I'd love to cook a stew for you,*
> > *But I have no pot.*
> *I'd love to knit a scarf for you,*
> > *But I have no wool.*
> *I'd love to write a poem for you,*
> > *But I have no pen.*

"It's called 'I Have Nothing'," Midori announced. It was a truly terrible song, both words and music.

I listened to this musical mess thinking that the house would blow apart in the explosion if the petrol station caught fire. Tired of singing, Midori put down her guitar and slumped against my shoulder like a cat in the sun.

"How did you like my song?" she asked.

I answered cautiously, "It was unique and original and very expressive of your personality."

"Thanks," she said. "The theme is that I have nothing."

"Yeah, I kind of thought so."

"You know," she said, "when my mother died . . ."

"Yeah?"

"I didn't feel the least bit sad."

"Oh."

"And I didn't feel sad when my father left, either."

"Really?"

"It's true. Don't you think I'm terrible? Cold-hearted?"

"I'm sure you have your reasons."

"My reasons. Hmm. Things were pretty complicated in this house. But I always thought, I mean, they're my mother and father, of course I'd be sad if they died or I never saw them again. But it didn't happen that way. I didn't feel anything. Not sad, not lonely. I hardly even think of them. Sometimes I'll have dreams, though. Sometimes my mother will be glaring at me out of the darkness and she'll accuse me of being happy she died. But I'm *not* happy she died. I'm just not very sad. And to tell the truth, I never shed a single tear. I cried all night when my cat died, though, when I was little."

Why so much smoke? I wondered. I couldn't see flames, and the burning area didn't seem to be spreading. There was just this column of smoke winding up into the sky. What could have kept burning so long?

"But I'm not the only one to blame," Midori continued. "It's true I have a cold streak. I recognize that. But if they – my father and mother – had loved me a little more, I would have been able to feel more – to feel real sadness, for example."

"Do you think you weren't loved enough?"

She tilted her head and looked at me. Then she gave a sharp, little nod. "Somewhere between 'not enough' and 'not at all'. I was always hungry for love. Just once, I wanted to know what it was like to get my fill of it – to be fed so much love I couldn't take any more. Just once. But they never gave that to me. Never, not once. If I tried to cuddle up and beg for something, they'd just shove me away and yell at me. 'No! That costs too much!' It's all I ever heard. So I made up my mind I was going to find someone who would love me unconditionally 365 days a year. I was still in primary school at the time, but I made up my mind once and for all."

"Wow," I said. "And did your search pay off?"

"That's the hard part," said Midori. She watched the rising smoke for a while, thinking. "I guess I've been waiting so long I'm looking for perfection. That makes it tough."

"Waiting for the perfect love?"

"No, even I know better than that. I'm looking for selfishness. Perfect selfishness. Like, say I tell you I want to eat strawberry shortbread. And you stop everything you're doing

99

and run out and buy it for me. And you come back out of breath and get down on your knees and hold this strawberry shortbread out to me. And I say I don't want it any more and throw it out of the window. That's what I'm looking for."

"I'm not sure that has anything to do with love," I said with some amazement.

"It does," she said. "You just don't know it. There are times in a girl's life when things like that are incredibly important."

"Things like throwing strawberry shortbread out of the window?"

"Exactly. And when I do it, I want the man to apologize to me. 'Now I see, Midori. What a fool I've been! I should have known that you would lose your desire for strawberry short-bread. I have all the intelligence and sensitivity of a piece of donkey shit. To make it up to you, I'll go out and buy you something else. What would you like? Chocolate mousse? Cheesecake?'"

"So then what?"

"So then I'd give him all the love he deserves for what he's done."

"Sounds crazy to me."

"Well, to *me*, that's what love is. Not that anyone can understand me, though." Midori gave her head a little shake against my shoulder. "For a certain kind of person, love begins from something tiny or silly. From something like that or it doesn't begin at all."

"I've never met a girl who thinks like you."

"A lot of people tell me that," she said, digging at a cuticle. "But it's the only way I know how to think. Seriously. I'm just telling you what I believe. It's never crossed my mind that my way of thinking is different from other people's. I'm not *trying* to be different. But when I speak out honestly, everybody thinks I'm kidding or play-acting. When that happens, I feel like everything's such a pain!"

"And you want to let yourself die in a fire?"

"Hey, no, that's different. It's just a matter of curiosity."

"What? Dying in a fire?"

"No, I just wanted to see how you'd react," Midori said. "But, I'm not afraid of dying. Really. Like here, I'd just be overcome with smoke and lose consciousness and die before I knew it. That doesn't frighten me at all, compared to the way I saw my mother and a few relatives die. *All* my relatives die after suffering from some terrible illness. It's in the blood, I guess. It's always a *long, long* process, and at the end you almost can't tell whether the person is alive or dead. All that's left is pain and suffering."

Midori put a Marlboro between her lips and lit it.

"That's the kind of death that frightens me. The shadow of death slowly, slowly eats away at the region of life, and before you know it everything's dark and you can't see, and the people around you think of you as more dead than alive. I hate that. I couldn't stand it."

Another half hour and the fire was out. They had apparently kept it from spreading and prevented any injuries. All but one of the fire engines returned to base, and the crowd dispersed, buzzing with conversation. One police car remained to direct the traffic, its blue light spinning. Two crows had settled on nearby lamp-posts to observe the activity below.

Midori seemed drained of energy. Limp, she stared at the sky and barely spoke.

"Tired?" I asked.

"Not really," she said. "I just sort of let myself go limp and spaced out. First time in a long time."

She looked into my eyes, and I into hers. I put my arm around her and kissed her. The slightest twinge went through her shoulders, and then she relaxed and closed her eyes for several seconds. The early autumn sun cast the shadow of her lashes on her cheek, and I could see it trembling in outline.

It was a soft and gentle kiss, one not meant to lead beyond itself. I would probably not have kissed Midori that day if we hadn't spent the afternoon on the laundry deck in the sun, drinking beer and watching a fire, and she no doubt felt the same. After a long time of watching the glittering rooftops and the smoke and the red dragonflies and other things, we had felt something warm and close, and we both probably wanted, half-consciously, to preserve that mood in some form. It was that kind of kiss. But as with all kisses, it was not without a certain element of danger.

The first to speak was Midori. She held my hand and told me, with what seemed like some difficulty, that she was seeing someone. I said that I had sensed as much.

"Do you have a girl you like?" she asked.

"I do," I said.

"But you're always free on Sundays, right?"

"It's very complicated," I said.

And then I realized that the brief spell of the early autumn afternoon had vanished.

At five I said I had to go to work and suggested that Midori come with me for a snack. She said she had to stay home in case the phone rang.

"I hate waiting at home all day for a call. When I spend the day alone, I feel as if my flesh is rotting little by little – rotting and melting until there's nothing left but a green puddle that gets sucked down into the earth. And all that stays behind are my clothes. That's how it feels to me, waiting indoors all day."

"I'll keep you company next time you have to wait for a call," I said. "As long as lunch is included."

"Great," she said. "I'll arrange another fire for dessert."

Midori didn't come to the next day's History of Drama lecture. I went to the cafeteria afterwards and ate a cold, tasteless lunch alone. Then I sat in the sun and observed the campus scene. Two women students next to me were carrying on a long conversation, standing the whole time. One cradled a tennis racquet to her breast with all the loving care she might give a baby, while the other held some books and a Leonard Bernstein LP. Both were pretty and obviously enjoying their discussion. From the direction of the student club building came the sound of a bass voice practising scales. Here and there stood groups of four or five students expressing whatever opinions they happened to hold, laughing and shouting to one another. There were skateboarders in the car park. A professor with a leather briefcase in his arms crossed the car park, avoiding them. In the quadrangle a helmeted girl student knelt on the ground, painting huge characters on a sign with something about American imperialism invading Asia. It was the usual midday university scene, but as I sat watching it with renewed attention, I became aware of something. In his or her own way, everyone I saw before me looked happy. Whether they were really happy or just looked it, I couldn't tell. But they did look happy on this pleasant early afternoon in late September, and because of that I felt a kind of loneliness new to me, as if I were the only one here who was not truly part of the scene.

Come to think of it, what scene *had* I been a part of in recent years? The last one I could remember was a pool hall near the harbour, where Kizuki and I played pool together in a spirit of total friendship. Kizuki died that night, and ever since a cold, stiffening wind had come between me and the world. This boy Kizuki: what had his existence meant to me? To this question I could find no answer. All I knew – with absolute certainty – was that Kizuki's death had robbed me for ever of some part of my adolescence. But what that meant, and what would come of it, were far beyond my understanding.

I sat there for a long time, watching the campus and the people passing through it, and hoping, too, that I might see Midori. But she never appeared, and when the noon break ended, I went to the library to prepare for my German class.

Nagasawa came to my room that Saturday afternoon and suggested we have one of our nights on the town. He would arrange an overnight pass for me. I said I would go. I had been feeling especially muddle-headed for the past week and was ready to sleep with anybody, it didn't matter who.

Late in the afternoon I showered and shaved and put on fresh clothes – a polo shirt and cotton jacket – then had dinner with Nagasawa in the dining hall and the two of us caught a bus to Shinjuku. We walked around a lively area for a while, then went to one of our usual bars and sat there waiting for a likely pair of girls. The girls tended to come in pairs to this bar – except on this particular evening. We stayed there almost two hours, sipping whisky and sodas at a rate that kept us sober. Finally, two friendly-looking girls took seats at the bar, ordering a gimlet and a margarita. Nagasawa approached them straight away, but they said they were waiting for their boyfriends. Still, the four of us enjoyed a pleasant chat until their dates showed up.

Nagasawa took me to another bar to try our luck, a small

place in a kind of cul-de-sac, where most of the customers were already drunk and noisy. A group of three girls occupied a table at the back. We joined them and enjoyed a little conversation, the five of us getting into a nice mood, but when Nagasawa suggested we go somewhere else for a drink, the girls said it was almost curfew time and they had to go back to their dorms. So much for our "luck". We tried one more place with the same result. For some reason, the girls were just not coming our way.

At 11.30 Nagasawa was ready to give up. "Sorry I dragged you around for nothing," he said.

"No problem," I said. "It was worth it to me just to see you have your off days sometimes, too."

"Maybe once a year," he admitted.

In fact, I didn't care about getting laid any more. Wandering around Shinjuku on a noisy Saturday night, observing the mysterious energy created by a mixture of sex and alcohol, I began to feel that my own desire was a puny thing.

"What are you going to do now, Watanabe?"

"Maybe go to an all-nighter," I said. "I haven't seen a film in ages."

"I'll be going to Hatsumi's then," said Nagasawa. "Do you mind?"

"No way," I said. "Why should I mind?"

"If you'd like, I could introduce you to a girl who'd let you spend the night."

"Nah, I really am in the mood for a film."

"Sorry," said Nagasawa. "I'll make it up to you some time." And he disappeared into the crowd. I went into a fast food place for a cheeseburger and some coffee to kill the buzz, then went to see *The Graduate* in an old rep house. I didn't think it was all that good, but I didn't have anything better to do, so

105

I stayed and watched it again. Emerging from the cinema at four in the morning, I wandered along the chilly streets of Shinjuku, thinking.

When I tired of walking, I went to an all-night café and waited with a book and a cup of coffee for the morning trains to start. Before long, the place became crowded with people who, like me, were waiting for those first trains. A waiter came to ask me apologetically if I would mind sharing my table. I said it would be all right. It didn't matter to me who sat across from me: I was just reading a book.

My companions at the table turned out to be two girls. They looked about my age. Neither of them was a knockout, but they weren't bad. Both were reserved in the way they dressed and made up: they were definitely not the type to be wandering around Shinjuku at five in the morning. I guessed they had just happened to miss the last train. They seemed relieved to sit with me: I was neatly dressed, had shaved in the evening, and to cap it all I was absorbed in Thomas Mann's *The Magic Mountain*.

One of the girls was on the large side. She wore a grey parka and white jeans, carried a large vinyl pocketbook, and had large, shell-shaped earrings. Her friend was a small girl with glasses. She wore a blue cardigan over a checked shirt and had a turquoise ring. The smaller one had a habit of taking off her glasses and pressing her eyes with her fingertips.

Both girls ordered *café au lait* and cake, which it took them some time to consume as they carried on what seemed like a serious discussion in hushed tones. The large girl tilted her head several times, while the small one shook hers just as often. I couldn't make out what they were saying because of the loud stereo playing Marvin Gaye or the Bee Gees or something, but it seemed the small girl was angry or upset and the large girl was trying to comfort her. I alternated passages of my book with glances in their direction.

Clutching her shoulder bag to her breast, the smaller girl went to the ladies', at which point her companion spoke to me.

"I'm sorry to bother you, but I wonder if you might know of any bars in the neighbourhood that would still be serving drinks?"

Taken off guard, I set my book aside and asked, "After five o'clock in the morning?"

"Yes . . ."

"If you ask me, at 5.20 in the morning, most people are on their way home to get sober and go to bed."

"Yes, I realize that," she said, a bit embarrassed, "but my friend says she has to have a drink. It's kind of important."

"There's probably nothing much you can do but go home and have a drink."

"But I have to catch a 7.30 train to Nagano."

"So find a vending machine and a nice place to sit. It's about all you can do."

"I know this is asking a lot, but could you come with us? Two girls alone really can't do something like that."

I had had a number of unusual experiences in Shinjuku, but I had never before been invited to have a drink with two strange girls at 5.20 in the morning. Refusing would have been more trouble than it was worth, and time was no problem, so I bought an armload of sake and snacks from a nearby machine, and the three of us went to an empty car park by the west exit of the station to hold an impromptu drinking party.

The girls told me they had become friends working at a travel agency. Both of them had graduated from college this year and started their first jobs. The small one had a boyfriend she had been seeing for a year, but had recently discovered he was sleeping with another girl and she had taken it hard. The larger one was supposed to have left for the mountains of Nagano last night for her brother's wedding, but she had decided to spend the night with her depressed friend and take the first express on Sunday morning.

"It's too bad what you're going through," I said to the small one, "but how did you find out your boyfriend was sleeping with someone else?"

Taking little sips of sake, the girl tore at some weeds underfoot. "I didn't have to work anything out," she said. "I opened his door, and there he was, doing it."

"When was that?"

"The night before last."

"No way. The door was unlocked?"

"Right."

"I wonder why he didn't lock it?"

"How the hell should I know?"

"Yeah, how's she supposed to feel?" said the larger one, who seemed truly concerned for her friend. "What a shock it must have been for her. Don't you think it's terrible?"

"I really can't say," I answered. "You ought to have a good talk with your boyfriend. Then it's a question of whether you forgive him or not."

"Nobody knows how I feel," spat out the little one, still tearing grass.

A flock of crows appeared from the west and sailed over a big department store. It was daylight now. The time for the train to Nagano was approaching, so we gave what was left of the sake to a homeless guy downstairs at the west exit, bought platform tickets and went in to see the big girl off. After the train pulled out of sight, the small girl and I somehow ended up going to a nearby hotel. Neither of us was particularly dying to sleep with the other, but it seemed necessary to bring things to a close.

I undressed first and sat in the bath drinking beer with a vengeance. She got in with me and did the same, the two of us stretched out and guzzling beer in silence. We couldn't seem to get drunk, though, and neither of us was sleepy. Her skin was very fair and smooth, and she had beautiful legs. I complimented her on her legs, but her "Thanks" was little more than a grunt.

Once we were in bed, though, she was like a different person. She responded to the slightest touch of my hands, writhing and moaning. When I went inside her, she dug her nails into my back, and as her orgasm approached she called out another man's name exactly 16 times. I concentrated on counting them as a way to delay my own orgasm. Then the two of us fell asleep.

She was gone when I woke at 12.30. I found no note of any kind. One side of my head felt strangely heavy from having drunk at an odd hour. I took a shower to wake myself, shaved and sat in a chair, naked, drinking a bottle of juice from the fridge and reviewing in order the events of the night before. Each scene felt unreal and strangely distant, as though I were viewing it through two or three layers of glass, but the events had undoubtedly happened to me. The beer glasses were still sitting on the table, and a used toothbrush lay by the sink.

I ate a light lunch in Shinjuku and went to a telephone box to call Midori Kobayashi on the off chance that she might be home alone waiting for a call again today. I let it ring 15 times but no one answered. I tried again 20 minutes later with the same results. Then I took a bus back to the dorm. A special delivery letter was waiting for me in the letterbox by the entry. It was from Naoko.

第 5 章

Thanks for your letter, wrote Naoko. Her family had forwarded it *here*, she said. Far from upsetting her, its arrival had made her very happy, and in fact she had been on the point of writing to me herself.

Having read that much, I opened the window, took off my jacket and sat on the bed. I could hear pigeons cooing in a nearby roost. The breeze stirred the curtains. Holding the seven pages of writing paper from Naoko, I gave myself up to an endless stream of feelings. It seemed as if the colours of the real world around me had begun to drain away from my having done nothing more than read a few lines she had written. I closed my eyes and spent a long time collecting my thoughts. Finally, after one deep breath, I continued reading.

It's almost four months since I came here, she went on.

I've thought a lot about you in that time. The more I've thought, the more I've come to feel that I was unfair to you. I probably should have been a better, fairer person when it came to the way I treated you.

This may not be the most normal way to look at things, though. Girls my age *never* use the word "fair". Ordinary girls as young as I am are basically indifferent to whether things are fair or not. The central

110

question for them is not whether something is fair but whether or not it's beautiful or will make them happy. "Fair" is a man's word, finally, but I can't help feeling that it is also exactly the right word for me now. And because questions of beauty and happiness have become such difficult and convoluted propositions for me now, I suspect, I find myself clinging instead to other standards – like, whether or not something is fair or honest or universally true.

In any case, though, I believe that I have not been fair to you and that, as a result, I must have led you around in circles and hurt you deeply. In doing so, however, I have led myself around in circles and hurt myself just as deeply. I say this not as an excuse or a means of self-justification but because it is true. If I have left a wound inside you, it is not just your wound but mine as well. So please try not to hate me. I am a flawed human being – a far more flawed human being than you realize. Which is precisely why I do not want you to hate me. Because if you were to do that, I would really go to pieces. I can't do what you can do: I can't slip inside my shell and wait for things to pass. I don't know for a fact that you are really like that, but sometimes you give me that impression. I often envy that in you, which may be why I led you around in circles so much.

This may be an over-analytical way of looking at things. Don't you agree? The therapy they perform here is certainly not over-analytical, but when you are under treatment for several months the way I am here, like it or not, you become more or less analytical. "This was caused by that, and that means this, because of which such-and-such." Like that. I can't tell whether this kind of analysis is trying to simplify the world or complicate it.

In any case, I myself feel that I am far closer to recovery than I once was, and people here tell me this is true. This is the first time in a long while I have been able to sit down and calmly write a letter. The one I wrote you in July was something I had to squeeze out of me (though, to tell the truth, I don't remember what I wrote – was it terrible?), but this time I am very, very calm. Clean air, a quiet world cut off from the outside, a daily schedule for living, regular exercise: those are what I needed, it seems. How wonderful it is to be able to write someone a letter! To feel like conveying your thoughts to a person, to sit at your desk and pick up a pen, to put your thoughts into words like this is truly marvellous. Of course, once I *do* put them into words, I find I can only express a fraction of what I want to say, but that's all right. I'm happy just to be able to feel I want to write to someone. And so I am writing to you. It's 7.30 in the evening, I've had my dinner and I've just finished my bath. The place is silent, and it's pitch black outside. I can't see a single light through the window. I usually have a clear view of the stars from here, but not today, with the clouds. Everyone here knows a lot about the stars, and they tell me "That's Virgo" or "That's Sagittarius". They probably learn whether they want to or not because there's nothing to do here once the sun goes down. Which is also why they know so much about birds and flowers and insects. Speaking to them, I realize how ignorant

I was about such things, which is kind of nice.

There are about 70 people living here. In addition, the staff (doctors, nurses, office staff, etc.) come to just over 20. It's such a wide-open place, these are not big numbers at all. Far from it: it might be more accurate to say the place is on the empty side. It's big and filled with nature and everybody lives quietly – *so* quietly you sometimes feel that this is the normal, real world, which of course it's not. We can have it this way because we live here under certain pre-conditions.

I play tennis and basketball. Basketball teams are made up of both staff and (I hate the word, but there's no way around it) patients. When I'm absorbed in a game, though, I lose track of who are the patients and who are staff. This is kind of strange. I know this will *sound* strange, but when I look at the people around me during a game, they all look equally deformed.

I said this one day to the doctor in charge of my case, and he told me that, in a sense, what I was feeling was right, that we are in here not to correct the deformation but to accustom ourselves to it: that one of our problems was our inability to recognize and accept our own deformities. Just as each person has certain idiosyncrasies in the way he or she walks, people have idiosyncrasies in the way they think and feel and see things, and though you might want to correct them, it doesn't happen overnight, and if you try to force the issue in one case, something else might go funny. He gave me a very simplified explanation, of course, and it's just one small part of the problems we have, but I think I understand what he was trying to say. It may well be that we can never fully adapt to our own deformities. Unable to find a place inside ourselves for the very real pain and suffering that these deformities cause, we come here to get away from such things. As long as we are here, we can get by without hurting others or being hurt by them because we know that we are "deformed". That's what distinguishes us from the outside world: most people go about their lives unconscious of their deformities, while in this little world of ours the deformities themselves are a precondition. Just as Indians wear feathers on their heads to show what tribe they belong to, we wear our deformities in the open. And we live quietly so as not to hurt one another.

In addition to playing sports, we all participate in growing vegetables: tomatoes, aubergines, cucumbers, watermelons, strawberries, spring onions, cabbage, daikon radishes, and so on and on. We grow just about everything. We use greenhouses, too. The people here know a lot about vegetable farming, and they put a lot of energy into it. They read books on the subject and call in experts and talk from morning to night about which fertilizer to use and the condition of the soil and stuff like that. I have come to love growing vegetables. It's great to watch different fruits and vegetables getting bigger and bigger each day. Have you ever grown watermelons? They swell up, just like some kind of little animals.

We eat freshly picked fruits and vegetables every day. They also serve meat and fish of course, but when you're living here you feel less and less like eating those because the vegetables are so fresh and delicious. Sometimes we go out and gather wild plants and mushrooms. We have experts on that kind of thing (come to think of it, this place is crawling with experts) who tell us which plants to pick and which to avoid. As a result of all this, I've gained over six pounds since I got here. My weight is just about perfect, thanks to the exercise and the good eating on a regular schedule.

When we're not farming, we read or listen to music or knit. We don't have TV or radio, but we do have a very decent library with books and records. The record collection has everything from Mahler symphonies to the Beatles, and I'm always borrowing records to listen to in my room.

The one real problem with this place is that once you're here you don't want to leave – or you're afraid to leave. As long as we're here, we feel calm and peaceful. Our deformities seem natural. We think we've recovered. But we can never be sure that the outside world will accept us in the same way.

My doctor says it's time I began having contact with "outside people" – meaning normal people in the normal world. When he says that, the only face I see is yours. To tell the truth, I don't want to see my parents. They're too upset over me, and seeing them puts me in a bad mood. Plus, there are things I have to explain to you. I'm not sure I *can* explain them very well, but they're important things I can't go on avoiding any longer.

Still, you shouldn't feel that I'm a burden to you. The one thing I don't want to be is a burden to anyone. I can sense the good feelings you have for me. They make me very happy. All I am doing in this letter is trying to convey that happiness to you. Those good feelings of yours are probably just what I need at this point in my life. Please forgive me if anything I've written here upsets you. As I said before, I am a far more flawed human being than you realize.

I sometimes wonder: IF you and I had met under absolutely ordinary circumstances, and IF we had liked each other, what would have happened? IF I had been normal and you had been normal (which, of course, you are) and there had been no Kizuki, what would have happened? Of course, this "IF" is way too big. I'm trying hard at least to be fair and honest. It's all I can do at this point. I hope to convey some small part of my feelings to you this way.

Unlike an ordinary hospital, this place has free visiting hours. As long as you call the day before, you can come any time. You can even eat with me, and there's a place for you to stay. Please come and see me sometime when it's convenient for you. I look forward to seeing you. I'm enclosing a map. Sorry this turned into such a long letter.

I read Naoko's letter all the way through, and then I read it again. After that I went downstairs, bought a Coke from the vending machine, and drank it while reading the letter one more time. I put the seven pages of writing paper back into the envelope and laid it on my desk. My name and address had been written on the pink envelope in perfect, tiny characters that were just a bit too precisely formed for those of a girl. I sat at my desk, studying the envelope. The return address on the back said *Ami Hostel*. An odd name. I thought about it for a few minutes, concluding that the "ami" must be from the French word for "friend".

After putting the letter away in my desk drawer, I changed clothes and went out. I was afraid that if I stayed near the letter I would end up reading it 10, 20, who knew how many times? I walked the streets of Tokyo on Sunday without a destination in mind, as I had always done with Naoko. I wandered from one street to the next, recalling her letter line by line and mulling each sentence over as best I could. When the sun went down, I returned to the dorm and made a long-distance call to the Ami Hostel. A woman receptionist answered and asked my business. I asked if it might be possible for me to visit Naoko the following afternoon. I left my name and she said I should call back in half an hour.

The same woman answered when I called back after dinner. It would indeed be possible for me to see Naoko, she said. I thanked her, hung up, and put a change of clothes and a few toiletries in my rucksack. Then I picked up *The Magic Mountain* again, reading and sipping brandy and waiting to get sleepy. Even so, I didn't fall asleep until after one o'clock in the morning.

第 6 章

As soon as I woke at seven o'clock on Monday morning, I washed my face, shaved, and went straight to the dorm Head's room without eating breakfast to say that I was going to be gone for two days hiking in the hills. He was used to my taking short trips when I had free time, and reacted without surprise. I took a crowded commuter train to Tokyo Station and bought a bullet-train ticket to Kyoto, literally jumping onto the first *Hikari* express to pull out. I made do with coffee and a sandwich for breakfast and dozed for an hour.

I arrived in Kyoto a few minutes before eleven. Following Naoko's instructions, I took a city bus to a small terminal serving the northern suburbs. The next bus to my destination would not be leaving until 11.35, I was told, and the trip would take a little over an hour. I bought a ticket and went to a bookshop across the street for a map. Back in the waiting room, I studied the map to see if I could find exactly where the Ami Hostel was located. It turned out to be much farther into the mountains than I had imagined. The bus would have to cross several hills in its trek north, then turn around where the canyon road dead-ended and return to the city. My stop would be just before the end of the line. There was a footpath near the bus stop, according to Naoko, and if I followed it for 20 minutes I would reach Ami Hostel. No wonder it was such a quiet place, if it was that deep in the mountains!

The bus pulled out with about 20 passengers aboard, following the Kamo River through the north end of Kyoto. The tightly packed city streets gave way to more sparse housing, then fields and vacant land. Black tile roofs and vinyl-sided greenhouses caught the early autumn sun and sent it back with a glare. When the bus entered the canyon, the driver began hauling the steering wheel this way and that to follow the twists and curves of the road, and I began to feel queasy. I could still taste my morning coffee. By the time the number of curves began to decrease to the point where I felt some relief, the bus plunged into a chilling cedar forest. The trees might have been old growth the way they towered over the road, blocking out the sun and covering everything in gloomy shadows. The breeze flowing into the bus's open windows turned suddenly cold, its dampness sharp against the skin. The valley road hugged the river bank, continuing so long through the trees it began to seem as if the whole world had been buried for ever in cedar forest – at which point the forest ended, and we came to an open basin surrounded by mountain peaks. Broad, green farmland spread out in all directions, and the river by the road looked bright and clear. A single thread of white smoke rose in the distance. Some houses had laundry drying in the sun, and dogs were howling. Each farmhouse had firewood out front piled up to the eaves, usually with a cat resting somewhere on the pile. The road was lined with such houses for a time, but I saw not a single person.

The scenery repeated this pattern any number of times. The bus would enter cedar forest, come out to a village, then go back into forest. It would stop at a village to let people off, but no one ever got on. Forty minutes after leaving the city, the bus reached a mountain pass with a wide-open view. The driver stopped the bus and announced that we would be waiting there for five or six minutes: people could step down from the bus if they wished. There were only four passengers left now, including me. We all got out and stretched or smoked and looked down at the panorama of Kyoto far below. The driver went off to one side for a pee. A suntanned man in his early fifties who had boarded the bus with a big, rope-tied cardboard carton asked me if I was going out to hike in the mountains. I said yes to keep things simple.

Eventually another bus came climbing up from the other side of the pass and stopped next to ours. The driver got out, had a short talk with our driver, and the two men climbed back into their buses. The four of us returned to our seats, and the buses pulled out in opposite directions. It was not immediately clear to me why our bus had had to wait for the other one, but a short way down the other side of the mountain the road narrowed suddenly. Two big buses could never have passed each other on the road, and in fact passing ordinary cars coming in the other direction required a good deal of manœuvring, with one or the other vehicle having to back up and squeeze into the overhang of a curve.

The villages along the road were far smaller now, and the level areas under cultivation even narrower. The mountain was steeper, its walls pressed closer to the bus windows. They seemed to have just as many dogs as the other places, though, and the arrival of the bus would set off a howling competition.

At the stop where I got off, there was nothing – no houses, no fields, just the bus stop sign, a little stream, and the trail opening. I slung my rucksack over my shoulder and started up the track. The stream ran along the left side of the trail, and a forest of deciduous trees lined the right. I had been climbing the gentle slope for some 15 minutes when I came to a road leading into the woods on the right, the opening barely wide enough to accommodate a car. AMI HOSTEL. PRIVATE. NO TRESPASSING read the sign by the road.

Sharply etched tyre tracks ran up the road through the trees. The occasional flapping of wings echoed in the woods. The sound came through with strange clarity, as if amplified above the other voices of the forest. Once, from far away, I heard what might have been a rifle shot, but it was a small and muffled sound, as though it had passed through several filters.

Beyond the woods I came to a white stone wall. It was no higher than my own height and, lacking additional barriers on top, would have been easy for me to scale. The black iron gate looked sturdy enough, but it was wide open, and there was no one manning the guardhouse. Another sign like the last one stood by the gate: AMI HOSTEL. PRIVATE. NO TRESPASSING. A few clues suggested the guard had been there until some moments before: the ashtray held three butt-ends, a tea cup stood there half empty, a transistor radio sat on a shelf, and the clock on the wall ticked off the time with a dry sound. I waited a while for the person to come back, but when that showed no sign of happening, I gave a few pushes to something that looked as if it might be a bell. The area just inside the gate was a car park. In it stood a mini-bus, a four-wheel drive Land Cruiser, and a dark blue Volvo. The car park could have held 30 cars, but only those three were parked there now.

Two or three minutes went by, and then a gatekeeper in a navy-blue uniform came down the forest road on a yellow bicycle. He was a tall man in his early sixties with receding hair. He leaned the yellow bike against the guardhouse and said, "I'm very sorry to have kept you waiting," though

121

he didn't sound sorry at all. The number 32 was painted in white on the bike's mudguard. When I gave him my name, he picked up the phone and repeated it twice to someone on the other end, replied "Yes, uh-huh, I see" to the other person, then hung up.

"Go to the main building, please, and ask for Doctor Ishida," he said to me. "You take this road through the trees to a roundabout. Then take your second left – got that? Your *second* left – from the roundabout. You'll see an old house. Turn right and go through another bunch of trees to a concrete building. That's the main building. It's easy, just watch for the signs."

I took the second left from the roundabout as instructed, and where that path ended I came to an interesting old building that obviously had been someone's country house once. It had a manicured garden with well-shaped rocks and a stone lantern. It must have been a country estate. Turning right through the trees, I saw a three-storey concrete building. It stood in a hollowed-out area, and so there was nothing overwhelming about its three storeys. It was simple in design and gave a strong impression of cleanliness.

The entrance was on the second floor. I climbed the stairs and went in through a big glass door to find a young woman in a red dress at the reception desk. I gave her my name and said I had been instructed to ask for Doctor Ishida. She smiled and gestured towards a brown sofa, suggesting in low tones that I wait there for the doctor to come. Then she dialled a number. I lowered my rucksack from my back, sank down into the deep cushions of the sofa, and surveyed the place. It was a clean, pleasant lobby, with ornamental potted plants, tasteful abstract paintings, and a polished floor. As I waited, I kept my eyes on the floor's reflection of my shoes.

At one point the receptionist assured me, "The doctor will

be here soon." I nodded. What an incredibly quiet place! There were no sounds of any kind. It was as though everyone were taking a siesta. People, animals, insects, plants must all be sound asleep, I thought, it was such a quiet afternoon.

Before long, though, I heard the soft padding of rubber soles, and a mature, bristly-haired woman appeared. She swept across the lobby, sat down next to me, crossed her legs and took my hand. Instead of just shaking it, she turned my hand over, examining it front and back.

"You haven't played a musical instrument, at least not for some years now, have you?" were the first words out of her mouth.

"No," I said, taken aback. "You're right."

"I can tell from your hands," she said with a smile.

There was something almost mysterious about this woman. Her face had lots of wrinkles. These were the first thing to catch your eye, but they didn't make her look old. Instead, they emphasized a certain youthfulness in her that transcended age. The wrinkles *belonged* where they were, as if they had been part of her face since birth. When she smiled, the wrinkles smiled with her; when she frowned, the wrinkles frowned, too. And when she was neither smiling nor frowning, the wrinkles lay scattered over her face in a strangely warm, ironic way. Here was a woman in her late thirties who seemed not merely a nice person but whose niceness drew you to her. I liked her from the moment I saw her.

Wildly chopped, her hair stuck out in patches and the fringe lay crooked against her forehead, but the style suited her perfectly. She wore a blue work shirt over a white T-shirt, baggy, cream-coloured cotton trousers, and tennis shoes. Long and slim, she had almost no breasts. Her lips moved constantly to one side in a kind of ironic curl, and the wrinkles at the corners of her eyes moved in tiny twitches. She looked like a kindly, skilled, but somewhat world-weary female carpenter.

Chin drawn in and lips curled, she took some time to look me over from head to toe. I imagined that any minute now she was going to whip out her tape measure and start measuring me everywhere.

"*Can* you play an instrument?" she asked.

"Sorry, no," I said.

"Too bad," she said. "It would have been fun."

"I suppose so," I said. Why all this talk about musical instruments?

She took a pack of Seven Stars from her breast pocket, put one between her lips, lit it with a lighter and began puffing away with obvious pleasure.

"It crossed my mind that I should tell you about this place, Mr – Watanabe, wasn't it? – before you see Naoko. So I arranged for the two of us to have this little talk. Ami Hostel is kind of unusual – you might find it a little confusing without any background knowledge. I'm right, aren't I, in supposing that you don't know anything about this place?"

"Almost nothing."

"Well, then, first of all – " she began, then snapped her fingers. "Come to think of it, have you had lunch? I'll bet you're hungry."

"You're right, I am."

"Come with me, then. We can talk over food in the dining hall. Lunchtime is over, but if we go now they can still make us something."

She took the lead, hurrying down a corridor and a flight of stairs to the first-floor dining hall. It was a large room, with enough space for perhaps 200 people, but only half was in use, the other half partitioned off, like a resort hotel out of season. The day's menu listed a potato stew with noodles, salad, orange juice and bread. The vegetables turned out to be as delicious as Naoko had said in her letter, and I finished everything on my plate.

"You obviously enjoy your food!" said my female companion.

"It's wonderful," I said. "Plus, I've hardly eaten anything all day."

"You're welcome to mine if you like. I'm full. Here, go ahead."

"I will, if you really don't want it."

"I've got a small stomach. It doesn't hold much. I make up for what I'm missing with cigarettes." She lit another Seven Star. "Oh, by the way, you can call me Reiko. Everybody does."

Reiko seemed to derive great pleasure from watching me while I ate the potato stew she had hardly touched and munched on her bread.

"Are you Naoko's doctor?" I asked.

"Me?! Naoko's doctor?!" She screwed up her face. "What makes you think I'm a doctor?"

"They told me to ask for Doctor Ishida."

"Oh, I get it. No no no, I teach music here. It's a kind of therapy for some patients, so for fun they call me 'The Music Doctor' and sometimes 'Doctor Ishida'. But I'm just another patient. I've been here seven years. I work as a music teacher and help out in the office, so it's hard to tell any more whether I'm a patient or staff. Didn't Naoko tell you about me?"

I shook my head.

"That's strange," said Reiko. "I'm Naoko's room-mate. I like living with her. We talk about all kinds of things. Including you."

"What about me?"

"Well, first I have to tell you about this place," said Reiko, ignoring my question. "The first thing you ought to know is that this is no ordinary 'hospital'. It's not so much for treatment as for convalescence. We do have a few doctors, of course, and they give hourly sessions, but they're just checking people's conditions, taking their temperature and things like that, not administering 'treatments' as in an ordinary hospital. There are no bars on the windows here, and the gate is always wide open. People enter and leave voluntarily. You have to be suited to that kind of convalescence to be admitted here in the first place. In some cases, people who need specialized therapy end up going to a specialized hospital. OK so far?"

"I think so," I said. "But what does this 'convalescence' consist of? Can you give me a concrete example?"

Reiko exhaled a cloud of smoke and drank what was left of her orange juice. "Just living here is the convalescence," she said. "A regular routine, exercise, isolation from the outside world, clean air, quiet. Our farmland makes us practically self-sufficient; there's no TV or radio. We're like one of those commune places you hear so much about. Of course, one thing different from a commune is that it costs a bundle to get in here."

"A bundle?"

"Well, it's not ridiculously expensive, but it's not cheap. Just look at these facilities. We've got a lot of land here, a few patients, a big staff, and in my case I've been here a long time. True, I'm almost staff myself so I get concessions, but still . . . Now, how about a cup of coffee?"

I said I'd like some. She stubbed out her cigarette and went over to the counter, where she poured two cups of coffee from a warm pot and brought them back to where we were sitting. She put sugar in hers, stirred it, frowned, and took a sip.

"You know," she said, "this sanatorium is not a profit-making enterprise, so it can keep going without charging as much as it might have to otherwise. The land was a donation. They created a corporation for the purpose. The whole place used to be the donor's summer home about 20 years ago. You saw the old house, I'm sure?"

I said I had.

"That used to be the only building on the property. It's where they did group therapy. That's how it all got started. The donor's son had a tendency towards mental illness and a specialist recommended group therapy for him. The doctor's theory was that if you could have a group of patients living out in the country, helping each other with physical labour and have a doctor for advice and check-ups, you could cure certain kinds of sickness. They tried it, and the operation grew and was incorporated, and they put more land under cultivation, and put up the main building five years ago."

"Meaning, the therapy worked."

"Well, not for everything. Lots of people don't get better. But also a lot of people who couldn't be helped anywhere else managed a complete recovery here. The best thing about this place is the way everybody helps everybody else. Everybody knows they're flawed in some way, and so they try to help each other. Other places don't work that way, unfortunately. Doctors are doctors and patients are patients: the patient looks for help to the doctor and the doctor gives his help to the patient. Here, though, we all help each other. We're all each other's mirrors, and the doctors are part of us. They watch us from the sidelines and they slip in to help us if they see we need something, but it sometimes happens that we help them. Sometimes we're better at something than they are. For example, I'm teaching one doctor to play the piano, and another patient is teaching a nurse French. That kind of thing. Patients with problems like ours are often blessed with special abilities. So everyone here is equal – patients, staff – and you. You're one of us while you're in here, so I help you and you help me." Reiko smiled, gently flexing every wrinkle on her face. "You help Naoko and Naoko helps you."

"What should I do, then? Give me an example."

"First you decide that you want to help and that you need to be helped by the other person. Then you are totally honest. You will not lie, you will not gloss over anything, you will not cover up anything that might prove embarrassing to you. That's all there is to it."

"I'll try," I said. "But tell me, Reiko, why have you been in here for seven years? Talking with you like this, I can't believe there's anything wrong with you."

"Not while the sun's up," she said with a sombre look. "But when night comes, I start drooling and rolling on the floor."

"Really?"

"Don't be ridiculous, I'm kidding," she said, shaking her head with a look of disgust. "I'm completely well – for now, at least. I stay here because I enjoy helping other people get well, teaching music, growing vegetables. I like it here. We're all more or less friends. Compared to that, what have I got in the outside world? I'm 38, going on 40. I'm not like Naoko. There's nobody waiting for me to get out, no family to take me back. I don't have any work to speak of, and almost no friends. And after seven years, I don't know what's going on out there. Oh, I'll read a paper in the library every once in a while, but I haven't set foot outside this property all that time. I wouldn't know what to do if I left."

"But maybe a new world would open up for you," I said. "It's worth a try, don't you think?"

"Hmm, you may be right," she said, turning her cigarette lighter over and over in her hand. "But I've got my own set of problems. I can tell you all about them sometime if you like."

I nodded in response. "And Naoko," I said, "is she any better?"

"Hmm, we think so. She was pretty confused at first and we had our doubts for a while, but she's calmed down now and improved to the point where she's able to express herself verbally. She's definitely heading in the right direction. But she should have received treatment a lot earlier. Her symptoms were already apparent from the time that boyfriend of hers, Kizuki, killed himself. Her family should have seen it, and she herself should have realized that something was wrong. Of course, things weren't right at home, either . . ."

"They weren't?" I shot back.

"You didn't know?" Reiko seemed more surprised than I was.

I shook my head.

"I'd better let Naoko tell you about that herself. She's ready for some honest talk with you." Reiko gave her coffee another stir and took a sip. "There's one more thing you need to know," she said. "According to the rules here, you and Naoko will not be allowed to be alone together. Visitors can't be alone with patients. An observer always has to be present – which in this case means me. I'm sorry, but you'll just have to put up with me. OK?"

"OK," I said with a smile.

"But still," she said, "the two of you can talk about anything you'd like. Forget I'm there. I know pretty much everything there is to know about you and Naoko."

"Everything?"

"Pretty much. We have these group sessions, you know. So we learn a lot about each other. Plus Naoko and I talk about everything. We don't have many secrets here."

I looked at Reiko as I drank my coffee. "To tell you the truth," I said, "I'm confused. I still don't know whether what I did to Naoko in Tokyo was the right thing to do or not. I've been thinking about it this whole time, but I still don't know."

"And neither do I," said Reiko. "And neither does Naoko. That's something the two of you will have to decide for yourselves. See what I mean? Whatever happened, the two of you can turn it in the right direction – *if* you can reach some kind of mutual understanding. Maybe, once you've got *that* taken care of, you can go back and think about whether what happened was the right thing or not. What do you say?"

I nodded.

"I think the three of us can help each other – you and Naoko and I – if we really want to, and if we're really honest. It can be incredibly effective when three people work at it like that. How long can you stay?"

"Well, I'd like to get back to Tokyo by early evening the day after tomorrow. I have to work, and I've got a German exam on Thursday."

"Good," she said. "So you can stay with us. That way it won't cost you anything and you can talk without having to worry about the time."

"With '*us*'?" I asked.

"Naoko and me, of course," said Reiko. "We have a separate bedroom, and there's a sofa bed in the living room, so you'll be able to sleep fine. Don't worry."

130

"Do they allow that?" I asked. "Can a male visitor stay in a woman's room?"

"I don't suppose you're going to come in and rape us in the middle of the night?"

"Don't be silly."

"So there's no problem, then. Stay in our place and we can have some nice, long talks. That would be the best thing. Then we can really understand each other. And I can play my guitar for you. I'm pretty good, you know."

"Are you sure I'm not going to be in the way?"

Reiko put her third Seven Star between her lips and lit it after screwing up the corner of her mouth.

"Naoko and I have already discussed this. The two of us together are giving you a personal invitation to stay with us. Don't you think you should just politely accept?"

"Of course, I'll be glad to."

Reiko deepened the wrinkles at the corners of her eyes and looked at me for a time. "You've got this funny way of talking," she said. "Don't tell me you're trying to imitate that boy in *Catcher in the Rye*?"

"No way!" I said with a smile.

Reiko smiled too, cigarette in mouth. "You *are* a good person, though. I can tell that much from looking at you. I can tell these things after seven years of watching people come and go here: there are people who can open their hearts and people who can't. You're one of the ones who can. Or, more precisely, you can if you want to."

"What happens when people open their hearts?"

Reiko clasped her hands together on the table, cigarette dangling from her lips. She was enjoying this. "They get better," she said. Ash dropped onto the table, but she seemed not to notice.

Reiko and I left the main building, crossed a hill, and passed by a pool, some tennis courts, and a basketball court. Two men – one thin and middle-aged, the other young and fat – were on a tennis court. Both used their racquets well, but to me the game they were playing could not have been tennis. It seemed as if the two of them had a special interest in the bounce of tennis balls and were doing research in that area. They slammed the ball back and forth with a kind of strange concentration. Both were drenched in sweat. The young man, in the end of the court closer to us, noticed Reiko and came over. They exchanged a few words, smiling. Near the court, a man with no expression on his face was using a large mower to cut the grass.

Moving on, we came to a patch of woods where some 15 or 20 neat little cottages stood at some distance from each other. The same kind of yellow bike the gatekeeper had been riding was parked at the entrance to almost every house. "Staff members and their families live here," said Reiko.

"We have just about everything we need without going to the city," she said as we walked along. "Where food is concerned, as I said before, we're practically self-sufficient. We get eggs from our own chicken coop. We have books and records and exercise facilities, our own convenience store, and every week barbers and beauticians come to visit. We even have films at weekends. Anything special we need we can ask a staff member to buy for us in town. Clothing we order from catalogues. Living here is no problem."

"But you can't go into town?"

"No, that we can't do. Of course if there's something special, like we have to go to the dentist or something, that's another matter, but as a rule we can't go into town. Each person is completely free to leave this place, but once you've left you can't come back. You burn your bridges. You can't go off for a couple of days in town and expect to come back. It only stands to reason, though. Everybody would be coming and going."

Beyond the trees we came to a gentle slope along which, at irregular intervals, was a row of two-storey wooden houses that had something odd about them. What made them look strange it's hard to say, but that was the first thing I felt when I saw them. My reaction was a lot like what we feel when we see unreality painted in a pleasant way. It occurred to me that this was what you might get if Walt Disney did an animated version of a Munch painting. All the houses were exactly the same shape and colour, nearly cubical, in perfect left-to-right symmetry, with big front doors and lots of windows. The road twisted its way among them like the artificial practice course of a driving school. There was a well-manicured flowering shrubbery in front of every house. The place was deserted, and curtains covered all the windows.

"This is called Area C. The women live here. Us! There are ten houses, each containing four units, two people per unit. That's 80 people all together, but at the moment there are only 32 of us."

"Quiet, isn't it?"

"Well, there's nobody here now," Reiko said. "I've been given special permission to move around freely like this, but everyone else is off pursuing their individual schedules. Some are exercising, some are gardening, some are in group therapy, some are out gathering wild plants. Each person makes up his or her own schedule. Let's see, what's Naoko doing now? I think she was supposed to be working on new paint and wallpaper. I forget. There are a few jobs like that that don't finish till five."

Reiko walked into the building marked "C-7", climbed the stairs at the far end of the hallway, and opened the door on the right, which was unlocked. She showed me around the flat, a pleasant, if plain, four-room unit: living room, bedroom, kitchen, and bath. It had no extra furniture or unnecessary decoration, but neither was the place severe. There was nothing special about it, but being there was kind of like being with Reiko: you could relax and let the tension leave your body. The living room had a sofa, a table, and a rocking chair. Another table stood in the kitchen. Both tables had large ashtrays on them. The bedroom had two beds, two desks and a closet. A small night table stood between the beds with a reading lamp on top and a paperback turned face down. The kitchen had a small electric cooker that matched the fridge and was equipped for simple cooking.

"No bath, just a shower, but it's pretty impressive, wouldn't you say? Bath and laundry facilities are communal."

"It's almost too impressive. My dorm room has a ceiling and a window."

"Ah, but you haven't seen the winters here," said Reiko, touching my back to guide me to the sofa and sitting down next to me. "They're long and harsh. Nothing but snow and snow and more snow everywhere you look. It gets damp and chills you to the bone. We spend the winter shovelling snow. Mostly you stay inside where it's warm and listen to music or talk or knit. If you didn't have this much space, you'd suffocate. You'll see if you come here in the winter."

Reiko gave a deep sigh as if picturing wintertime, then folded her hands on her knees.

"This will be your bed," she said, patting the sofa. "We'll

134

sleep in the bedroom, and you'll sleep here. You should be all right, don't you think?"

"I'm sure I'll be fine."

"So, that settles it," said Reiko. "We'll be back around five. Naoko and I both have things to do until then. Do you mind staying here alone?"

"Not at all. I'll study my German."

When Reiko left, I stretched out on the sofa and closed my eyes. I lay there steeping myself in the silence when, out of nowhere, I thought of the time Kizuki and I went on a motorbike ride. That had been autumn, too, I realized. Autumn how many years ago? Yes, four. I recalled the smell of Kizuki's leather jacket and the racket made by that red Yamaha 125cc bike. We went to a spot far down the coast, and came back the same evening, exhausted. Nothing special happened on the way, but I remembered it well. The sharp autumn wind moaned in my ears, and looking up at the sky, my hands clutching Kizuki's jacket, I felt as if I might be swept into outer space.

I lay there for a long time, letting my mind wander from one memory to another. For some strange reason, lying in this room seemed to bring back old memories that I had rarely if ever recalled before. Some of them were pleasant, but others carried a trace of sadness.

How long did this go on? I was so immersed in that torrent of memory (and it was a torrent, like a spring gushing out of the rocks) that I failed to notice Naoko quietly open the door and come in. I opened my eyes, and there she was. I raised my head and looked into her eyes for a time. She was sitting on the arm of the sofa, looking at me. At first I thought she might be an image spun into existence by my own memories. But it was the real Naoko.

"Sleeping?" she whispered.

"No," I said, "just thinking." I sat up and asked, "How are you?"

"I'm good," she said with a little smile like a pale, distant scene. "I don't have much time, though. I'm not supposed to be here now. I just got away for a minute, and I have to go back right away. Don't you hate my hair?"

"Not at all," I said. "It's cute." Her hair was in a simple schoolgirl style, with one side held in place with a hairslide the way she used to have it in the old days. It suited her very well, as if she had always worn it that way. She looked like one of the beautiful little girls you see in woodblock prints from the Middle Ages.

"It's such a pain, I have Reiko cut it for me. Do you really think it's cute?"

"Really."

"My mother hates it." She opened the hairslide, let the hair hang down, smoothed it with her fingers, and closed the hairslide again. It was shaped like a butterfly.

"I wanted to see you alone before the three of us get together. Not that I had anything special to say. I just wanted to see your face and get used to having you here. Otherwise, I'd have trouble getting to know you again. I'm so bad with people."

"Well?" I asked. "Is it working?"

"A little," she said, touching her hairslide again. "But time's up. I've got to go."

I nodded.

"Toru," she began, "I really want to thank you for coming to see me. It makes me very happy. But if being here is any kind of burden to you, you shouldn't hesitate to tell me so. This is a special place, and it has a special system, and some

136

people can't get into it. So if you feel like that, please be honest and let me know. I won't be crushed. We're honest with each other here. We tell each other all kinds of things with complete honesty."

"I'll tell you," I said. "I'll be honest."

Naoko sat down and leaned against me on the sofa. When I put my arm around her, she rested her head on my shoulder and pressed her face to my neck. She stayed like that for a time, almost as if she were taking my temperature. Holding her, I felt warm in the chest. After a short while, she stood up without saying a word and went out through the door as quietly as she had come in.

With Naoko gone, I went to sleep on the sofa. I hadn't intended to do so, but I fell into the kind of deep sleep I had not had for a long time, filled with a sense of Naoko's presence. In the kitchen were the dishes Naoko used, in the bathroom was the toothbrush Naoko used, and in the bedroom was the bed in which Naoko slept. Sleeping soundly in this flat of hers, I wrung the fatigue from every cell of my body, drop by drop. I dreamed of a butterfly dancing in the half-light.

When I awoke again, the hands of my watch were pointing to 4.35. The light had changed, the wind had died, the shapes of the clouds were different. I had sweated in my sleep, so I dried my face with a small towel from my rucksack and put on a fresh vest. Going to the kitchen, I drank some water and stood there looking through the window over the sink. I was facing a window in the building opposite, on the inside of which hung several paper cut-outs – a bird, a cloud, a cow, a cat, all in skilful silhouette and joined together. As before, there was no sign of anyone about, and there were no sounds of any kind. I felt as if I were living alone in an extremely well-cared-for ruin.

People started coming back to Area C a little after five. Looking out of the kitchen window, I saw three women passing below. All wore hats that prevented me from telling their ages, but judging from their voices, they were not very young. Shortly after they had disappeared around a corner, four more women appeared from the same direction and, like the first group, disappeared around the same corner. An evening mood hung over everything. From the living room window I could see trees and a line of hills. Above the ridge floated a border of pale sunlight.

Naoko and Reiko came back together at 5.30. Naoko and I exchanged proper greetings as if meeting for the first time. She seemed truly embarrassed. Reiko noticed the book I had been reading and asked what it was. Thomas Mann's *The Magic Mountain*, I told her.

"How could you bring a book like that to a place like this?" she demanded. She was right, of course.

Reiko then made coffee for the three of us. I told Naoko about Storm Trooper's sudden disappearance and about the last day I saw him, when he gave me the firefly.

"I'm so sorry he's gone," she said. "I wanted to hear more stories about him." Reiko asked who Storm Trooper was, so I told her about his antics and got a big laugh from her. The world was at peace and filled with laughter as long as Storm Trooper stories were being told.

At six we went to the dining hall in the main building for supper. Naoko and I had fried fish with green salad, boiled vegetables, rice and miso soup. Reiko limited herself to pasta salad and coffee, followed by another cigarette.

"You don't need to eat so much as you get older," she said by way of explanation.

Some 20 other people were there in the dining hall. A few newcomers arrived as we ate, meanwhile some others left. Aside from the variety in people's ages, the scene looked pretty much like that of the dining hall in my dormitory. Where it differed was the uniform volume at which people conversed. There were no loud voices and no whispers, no one laughing out loud or crying out in shock, no one yelling with exaggerated gestures, nothing but quiet conversations, all carrying on at the same level. People were eating in groups of three to five, each with a single speaker, to whom the others would listen with nods and grunts of interest, and when that person had finished speaking, the next would take up the conversation. I could not tell what they were saying, but the way they said it reminded me of the strange tennis game I had seen at noon. I wondered if Naoko spoke like this when she was with them and, strangely enough, I felt a twinge of loneliness mixed with jealousy.

At the table behind me, a balding man in white with the authentic air of a doctor was holding forth to a nervous-looking young man in glasses and a squirrel-faced woman of middle age on the effects of weightlessness on the secretion of gastric juices. The two listened with an occasional "My goodness" or "Really?" but the longer I listened to the balding man's style of speaking, the less certain I became that, even in his white coat, he was really a doctor.

No one in the dining hall paid me any special attention. No one stared or even seemed to notice I was there. My presence must have been an entirely natural event.

Just once, though, the man in white spun around and asked me, "How long will you be staying?"

"Two nights," I said. "I'll be leaving on Wednesday."

"It's nice here this time of year, isn't it? But come again

139

in winter. It's *really* nice when everything's white."

"Naoko may be out of here by the time it snows," said Reiko to the man.

"True, but still, the winter's really nice," he repeated with a sombre expression. I felt increasingly unsure as to whether or not he was a doctor.

"What do you people talk about?" I asked Reiko, who seemed to not quite follow me.

"What do we talk about? Just ordinary things. What happened that day, or books we've read, or tomorrow's weather, you know. Don't tell me you're wondering if people jump to their feet and shout stuff like: 'It'll rain tomorrow if a polar bear eats the stars tonight!'"

"No, no, of course not," I said. "I was just wondering what all these quiet conversations were about."

"It's a quiet place, so people talk quietly," said Naoko. She made a neat pile of fish bones at the edge of her plate and dabbed at her mouth with a handkerchief. "There's no need to raise your voice here. You don't have to convince anybody of anything, and you don't have to attract anyone's attention."

"I guess not," I said, but as I ate my meal in those quiet surroundings, I was surprised to find myself missing the hum of people. I wanted to hear laughter and people shouting for no reason and saying overblown things. That was just the kind of noise I had become weary of in recent months, but sitting here eating fish in this unnaturally quiet room, I couldn't relax. The dining hall had all the atmosphere of a specialized-machine-tool trade fair. People with a strong interest in a specialist field came together in a specific place and exchanged information understood only by themselves.

*

Back in the room after supper, Naoko and Reiko announced that they would be going to the Area C communal bath and that if I didn't mind having just a shower, I could use the one in their bathroom. I would do that, I said, and after they were gone I undressed, showered, and washed my hair. I found a Bill Evans album in the bookcase and was listening to it while drying my hair when I realized that it was the record I had played in Naoko's room on the night of her birthday, the night she cried and I took her in my arms. That had been only six months ago, but it felt like something from a much remoter past. Maybe it felt that way because I had thought about it so often – too often, to the point where it had distorted my sense of time.

The moon was so bright, I turned the lights off and stretched out on the sofa to listen to Bill Evans' piano. Streaming in through the window, the moonlight cast long shadows and splashed the walls with a touch of diluted Indian ink. I took a thin metal flask from my rucksack, let my mouth fill with the brandy it contained, allowed the warmth to move slowly down my throat to my stomach, and from there felt it spreading to every extremity. After a final sip, I closed the flask and returned it to my rucksack. Now the moonlight seemed to be swaying with the music.

Twenty minutes later, Naoko and Reiko came back from the bath.

"Oh! It was so dark here, we thought you had packed your bags and gone back to Tokyo!" exclaimed Reiko.

"No way," I said. "I hadn't seen such a bright moon for years. I wanted to look at it with the lights off."

"It's lovely, though," said Naoko. "Reiko, do we still have those candles from the last power cut?"

"Probably, in a kitchen drawer."

Naoko brought a large, white candle from the kitchen. I lit it, dripped a little wax into a plate, and stood it up. Reiko used the flame to light a cigarette. As the three of us sat facing the candle amid these hushed surroundings, it began to seem as if we were the only ones left on some far edge of the world. The still shadows of the moonlight and the swaying shadows of the candlelight met and melded on the white walls of the flat. Naoko and I sat next to each other on the sofa, and Reiko settled into the rocking chair facing us.

"How about some wine?" Reiko asked me.

"You're allowed to drink?" I asked with some surprise.

"Well, not really," said Reiko, scratching an earlobe with a hint of embarrassment. "But they pretty much let it go. If it's just wine or beer and you don't drink too much. I've got a friend on the staff who buys me a little now and then."

"We have our drinking parties," said Naoko with a mischievous air. "Just the two of us."

"That's nice," I said.

Reiko took a bottle of white wine from the fridge, opened it with a corkscrew and brought three glasses. The wine had a clear, delicious flavour that seemed almost homemade. When the record ended, Reiko brought out a guitar from under her bed, and after tuning it with a look of fondness for the instrument, she began to play a slow Bach fugue. She missed her fingering every now and then, but it was real Bach, with real feeling – warm, intimate, and filled with the joy of performance.

"I started playing the guitar here," said Reiko. "There are no pianos in the rooms, of course. I'm self-taught, and I don't have guitar hands, so I'll never get very good, but I really love the instrument. It's small and simple and easy, kind of like a warm, little room."

She played one more short Bach piece, something from a suite. Eyes on the candle flame, sipping wine, listening to Reiko's Bach, I felt the tension inside me slipping away. When Reiko ended the Bach, Naoko asked her to play a Beatles song.

"Request time," said Reiko, winking at me. "She makes me play Beatles every day, like I'm her music slave."

Despite her protest, Reiko played a fine "Michelle".

"That's a good one," she said. "I really like that song." She took a sip of wine and puffed her cigarette. "It makes me feel like I'm in a big meadow in a soft rain."

Then she played "Nowhere Man" and "Julia". Now and then as she played, she would close her eyes and shake her head. Afterwards she would return to the wine and the cigarette.

"Play 'Norwegian Wood'," said Naoko.

Reiko brought a porcelain beckoning cat from the kitchen. It was a coin bank, and Naoko dropped a ¥100 piece from her purse into its slot.

"What's this all about?" I asked.

"It's a rule," said Naoko. "When I request 'Norwegian Wood,' I have to put ¥100 into the bank. It's my favourite, so I make a point of paying for it. I make a request when I really want to hear it."

"And that way I get my cigarette money!" said Reiko.

Reiko gave her fingers a good flexing and then played "Norwegian Wood". Again she played with real feeling, but never allowed it to become sentimental. I took a ¥100 coin from my pocket and dropped it into the bank.

"Thank you," said Reiko with a sweet smile.

"That song can make me feel *so* sad," said Naoko. "I don't know, I guess I imagine myself wandering in a deep wood. I'm all alone and it's cold and dark, and nobody comes to save me. That's why Reiko never plays it unless I request it."

"Sounds like *Casablanca*!" Reiko said with a laugh.

She followed "Norwegian Wood" with a few bossa novas while I kept my eyes on Naoko. As she had said in her letter, she looked healthier than before, suntanned, her body firm from exercise and outdoor work. Her eyes were the same deep clear pools they had always been, and her small lips still trembled shyly, but overall her beauty had begun to change to that of a mature woman. Almost gone now was the sharp edge – the chilling sharpness of a thin blade – that could be glimpsed in the shadows of her beauty, in place of which there now hovered a uniquely soothing, quiet calm. I felt moved by this new, gentle beauty of hers, and amazed to think that a woman could change so much in the course of half a year. I felt as drawn to her as ever, perhaps more than before, but the thought of what she had lost in the meantime also gave me cause for regret. Never again would she have that self-centred beauty that seems to take its own, independent course in adolescent girls and no one else.

Naoko said she wanted to hear about how I was spending my days. I talked about the student strike and Nagasawa. This was the first time I had ever said anything about him to her. I found it challenging to give her an accurate account of his odd humanity, his unique philosophy, and his uncentred morality, but Naoko seemed finally to grasp what I was trying to tell her. I hid the fact that I went out hunting girls with him, revealing only that the one person in the dorm I spent any real time with was this unusual guy. All the while, Reiko went through another practice of the Bach fugue she had played before, taking occasional breaks for wine and cigarettes.

"He sounds like a strange person," said Naoko.

"He *is* strange," I said.

"But you like him?"

"I'm not sure," I said. "I guess I can't say I *like* him. Nagasawa is beyond liking or not liking. He doesn't try to be liked. In that sense, he's a very honest guy, stoic even. He doesn't try to fool anybody."

"'Stoic' sleeping with all those girls? Now *that* is weird," said Naoko, laughing. "How many girls has he slept with?"

"It's probably up to 80 now," I said. "But in his case, the higher the numbers go, the less each individual act seems to mean. Which is what I think he's trying to accomplish."

"And you call that 'stoic'?"

"For him it is."

Naoko thought about my words for a minute. "I think he's a lot sicker in the head than I am," she said.

"So do I," I said. "But he can put all of his warped qualities into a logical system. He's brilliant. If you brought him here, he'd be out in two days. 'Oh, sure, I know all that,' he'd say. 'I understand everything you're doing here.' He's that kind of guy. The kind people respect."

"I guess I'm the opposite of brilliant," said Naoko. "I don't understand anything they're doing here – any better than I understand myself."

"It's not because you're not smart," I said. "You're normal. I've got tons of things I don't understand about myself. We're both normal: ordinary."

Naoko raised her feet to the edge of the sofa and rested her chin on her knees. "I want to know more about you," she said.

"I'm just an ordinary guy – ordinary family, ordinary education, ordinary face, ordinary exam results, ordinary thoughts in my head."

"You're such a big Scott Fitzgerald fan . . . wasn't he the one who said you shouldn't trust anybody who calls himself an ordinary man? You lent me the book!" said Naoko with a mischievous smile.

"True," I said. "But this is no affectation. I really, truly believe deep down that I'm an ordinary person. Can you find something in me that's *not* ordinary?"

"Of course I can!" said Naoko with a hint of impatience. "Don't you get it? Why do you think I slept with you? Because I was so drunk I would have slept with anyone?"

"No, of course I don't think that," I said.

Naoko remained silent for a long time, staring at her toes. At a loss for words, I took another sip of wine.

"How many girls have *you* slept with, Toru?" Naoko asked in a tiny voice as if the thought had just crossed her mind.

"Eight or nine," I answered truthfully.

Reiko plopped the guitar into her lap. "You're not even 20 years old!" she said. "What kind of life are you leading?"

Naoko kept silent and watched me with those clear eyes of hers. I told Reiko about the first girl I'd slept with and how we had broken up. I had found it impossible to love her, I explained. I went on to tell her about my sleeping with one girl after another under Nagasawa's tutelage.

"I'm not trying to make excuses, but I was in pain," I said to Naoko. "Here I was, seeing you almost every week, and talking with you, and knowing that the only one in your heart was Kizuki. It hurt. It really hurt. And I think that's why I slept with girls I didn't know."

Naoko shook her head for a few moments, and then she raised her face to look at me. "You asked me that time why I had never slept with Kizuki, didn't you? Do you still want to know?"

"I suppose it's something I really ought to know," I said.

"I think so, too," said Naoko. "The dead will always be dead, but we have to go on living."

I nodded. Reiko played the same difficult passage over and over, trying to get it right.

"I was ready to sleep with him," said Naoko, unclasping her hairslide and letting her hair down. She toyed with the butterfly shape in her hands. "And of course he wanted to sleep with me. So we tried. We tried a lot. But it never worked. We couldn't do it. I didn't know why then, and I still don't know why. I loved him, and I wasn't worried about losing my virginity. I would have been glad to do anything he wanted. But it never worked."

Naoko lifted the hair she had let down and fastened it with the slide.

"I couldn't get wet," she said in a tiny voice. "I never opened to him. So it always hurt. I was just too dry, it hurt too much. We tried everything we could think of – creams and things – but still it hurt me. So I used my fingers, or my lips. I would always do it for him that way. You know what I mean."

I nodded in silence.

Naoko cast her gaze through the window at the moon, which looked bigger and brighter now than it had before. "I never wanted to talk about any of this," she said. "I wanted to shut it up in my heart. I wish I still could. But I have to talk about it. I don't know the answer. I mean, I was plenty wet the time I slept with you, wasn't I?"

"Uh-huh," I said.

"I was wet from the minute you walked into my flat the night of my twentieth birthday. I wanted you to hold me. I wanted you to take off my clothes, to touch me all over and enter me. I had never felt like that before. Why is that? Why do things happen like that? I mean, I really loved him."

"And not me," I said. "You want to know why you felt that way about me, even though you didn't love me?"

"I'm sorry," said Naoko. "I don't mean to hurt you, but this much you have to understand: Kizuki and I had a truly special relationship. We had been together from the time we were three. It's how we grew up: always together, always talking, understanding each other perfectly. The first time we kissed – it was in the first year of junior school – was just wonderful. The first time I had my period, I ran to him and cried like a baby. We were that close. So after he died, I didn't know how to relate to other people. I didn't know what it meant to love another person."

She reached for her wineglass on the table but only managed to knock it over, spilling wine on the carpet. I crouched down and retrieved the glass, setting it on the table. Did she want to drink some more? I asked. Naoko remained silent for a while, then suddenly burst into tears, trembling all over. Slumping forward, she buried her face in her hands and sobbed with the same suffocating violence as she had that night with me. Reiko laid down her guitar and sat by Naoko, caressing her back. When she put an arm across Naoko's shoulders, she pressed her face against Reiko's chest like a baby.

"You know," Reiko said to me, "it might be a good idea for you to go out for a little walk. Maybe 20 minutes. Sorry, but I think that would help."

I nodded and stood, pulling a jumper on over my shirt. "Thanks for stepping in," I said to Reiko.

"Don't mention it," she said with a wink. "This is not your fault. Don't worry, by the time you come back she'll be OK."

My feet carried me down the road, which was illuminated by the oddly unreal light of the moon, and into the woods.

Beneath that moonlight, all sounds bore a strange reverberation. The hollow sound of my own footsteps seemed to come
from another direction as though I were hearing someone
walking on the bottom of the sea. Behind me, every now and
then, I would hear a crack or a rustle. A heavy pall hung over
the forest, as if the animals of the night were holding their
breath, waiting for me to pass.

Where the road sloped upwards beyond the trees, I sat and
looked towards the building where Naoko lived. It was easy to
tell her room. All I had to do was find the one window towards
the back where a faint light trembled. I focused on that point
of light for a long, long time. It made me think of something
like the final pulse of a soul's dying embers. I wanted to cup
my hands over what was left and keep it alive. I went on
watching it the way Jay Gatsby watched that tiny light on the
opposite shore night after night.

When I walked back to the front entrance of the building half
an hour later, I could hear Reiko practising the guitar. I padded
up the stairs and tapped on the door to the flat. Inside there
was no sign of Naoko. Reiko sat alone on the carpet, playing
her guitar. She pointed towards the bedroom door to let me
know Naoko was in there. Then she set down the guitar on the
floor and took a seat on the sofa, inviting me to sit next to her
and dividing what wine was left between our two glasses.

"Naoko is fine," she said, touching my knee. "Don't worry,
all she has to do is rest for a while. She'll calm down. She was
just a little worked up. How about taking a walk with me in
the meantime?"

"Good," I said.

Reiko and I ambled down a road illuminated by street
lamps. When we reached the area by the tennis and basketball

courts, we sat on a bench. She picked up a basketball from under the bench and turned it in her hands. Then she asked me if I played tennis. I knew how to play, I said, but I was bad at it.

"How about basketball?"

"Not my strongest sport," I said.

"What *is* your strongest sport?" Reiko asked, wrinkling the corners of her eyes with a smile. "Aside from sleeping with girls."

"I'm not so good at that, either," I said, stung by her words.

"Just kidding," she said. "Don't get angry. But really, though, what *are* you good at?"

"Nothing special. I have things I *like* to do."

"For instance?"

"Hiking. Swimming. Reading."

"You like to do things alone, then?"

"I guess so. I could never get excited about games you play with other people. I can't get into them. I lose interest."

"Then you *have* to come here in the winter. We do cross-country skiing. I'm sure you'd like that, tramping around in the snow all day, working up a good sweat." Under the street lamp, Reiko stared at her right hand as though she were inspecting an antique musical instrument.

"Does Naoko often get like that?" I asked.

"Every now and then," said Reiko, now looking at her left hand. "Every once in a while she'll get worked up and cry like that. But that's OK. She's letting out her feelings. The scary thing is *not* being able to do that. When your feelings build up and harden and die inside, then you're in big trouble."

"Did I say something I shouldn't have?"

"Not a thing. Don't worry. Just speak your mind honestly. That's the best thing. It may hurt a little sometimes, and someone may get upset the way Naoko did, but in the long run it's for the best. That's what you should do if you're serious about making Naoko well again. Like I told you in the beginning, you should think not so much about wanting to help her as wanting to recover yourself by helping her to recover. That's the way it's done here. So you have to be honest and say everything that comes to mind, while you're here at least. Nobody does that in the outside world, right?"

"I guess not," I said.

"I've seen all kinds of people come and go in my time here," she said, "maybe *too* many people. So I can usually tell by looking at a person whether they're going to get better or not, almost by instinct. But in Naoko's case, I'm not sure. I have absolutely no idea what's going to happen to her. For all I know, she could be 100 per cent recovered next month, or she could go on like this for years. So I really can't tell you what to do aside from the most generalized kind of advice: to be honest and help each other."

"What makes Naoko such a hard case for you?"

"Probably because I like her so much. I think my emotions get in the way and I can't see her clearly. I mean, I really like her. But aside from that, she has a bundle of different problems that are all tangled up with each other so that it's hard to unravel a single one. It may take a very long time to undo them all, or something could trigger them to come unravelled all at once. It's kind of like that. Which is why I can't be sure about her."

She picked up the basketball again, twirled it in her hands and bounced it on the ground.

"The most important thing is not to let yourself get impatient," Reiko said. "This is one more piece of advice I have for you: don't get impatient. Even if things are so tangled up you can't do anything, don't get desperate or blow a fuse and start yanking on one particular thread before it's ready to come undone. You have to realize it's going to be a long process and that you'll work on things slowly, one at a time. Do you think you can do that?"

"I can try," I said.

"It may take a very long time, you know, and even then she may not recover completely. Have you thought about that?"

I nodded.

"Waiting is hard," she said, bouncing the ball. "Especially for someone your age. You just sit and wait for her to get better. Without deadlines or guarantees. Do you think you can do that? Do you love Naoko that much?"

"I'm not sure," I said honestly. "Like Naoko, I'm not really sure what it means to love another person. Though she meant it a little differently. I do want to try my best, though. I have to, or else I won't know where to go. Like you said before, Naoko and I have to save each other. It's the only way for either of us to be saved."

"And are you going to go on sleeping with girls you pick up?"

"I don't know what to do about that either," I said. "What do you think? Should I just keep waiting and masturbating? I'm not in complete control there, either."

Reiko set the ball on the ground and patted my knee. "Look," she said, "I'm not telling you to stop sleeping with girls. If you're OK with that, then it's OK. It's *your* life after all, it's something *you* have to decide. All I'm saying is you shouldn't use yourself up in some unnatural form. Do you see what I'm getting at? It would be such a waste. The years 19 and 20 are a crucial stage in the maturation of character, and if you allow yourself to become warped when you're that age, it will cause you pain when you're older. It's true. So think about it carefully. If you want to take care of Naoko, take care of yourself, too."

I said I would think about it.

"I was 20 myself. Once upon a time. Would you believe it?"

"I believe it. Of course."

"Deep down?"

"Deep down," I said with a smile.

"And I was cute, too. Not as cute as Naoko, but pretty damn cute. I didn't have all these wrinkles."

I said I liked her wrinkles a lot. She thanked me.

"But don't ever tell another woman that you find her wrinkles attractive," she added. "I like to hear it, but I'm the exception."

"I'll be careful," I said.

She slipped a wallet from her trouser pocket and handed me a photo from the card-holder. It was a colour snapshot of a cute girl around ten years old wearing skis and a brightly coloured ski-suit, standing on the snow smiling sweetly for the camera.

"Isn't she pretty? My daughter," said Reiko. "She sent me this in January. She's – what? – nine years old now."

"She has your smile," I said, returning the photo. Reiko pocketed the wallet and, with a sniff, put a cigarette between her lips and lit up.

"I was going to be a concert pianist," she said. "I had talent, and people recognized it and made a fuss over me while I was growing up. I won competitions and had top marks in the conservatoire, and I was all set to study in Germany after graduation. Not a cloud on the horizon. Everything worked out perfectly, and when it didn't there was always somebody to fix it. But then one day something happened, and it all blew apart. I was in my final year at the conservatoire and there was a fairly important competition coming up. I practised for it constantly, but all of a sudden the little finger of my left hand stopped moving. I don't know why, but it just did. I tried massaging it, soaking it in hot water, taking a few days off from practice: nothing worked. So then I got scared and went to the doctor's. They tried all kinds of tests but they couldn't come up with anything. There was nothing wrong with the finger itself, and the nerves were OK, they said: there was no reason it should stop moving. The problem must be psychological. So I went to a psychiatrist, but he didn't really know what was going on, either. Probably pre-competition stress, he said, and advised me to get away from the piano for a while."

Reiko inhaled deeply and let the smoke out. Then she bent her neck to the side a few times.

"So I went to recuperate at my grandmother's place on the coast in Izu. I thought I'd forget about that particular competition and really relax, spend a couple of weeks away from the piano doing anything I wanted. But it was hopeless. Piano was all I could think about. Maybe my finger would never move again. How would I live if that happened? The same thoughts kept going round and round in my brain. And no wonder: piano had been my whole life up to that point. I had started playing when I was four and grew up thinking about the piano and nothing else. I never did housework so as not to injure my fingers. People paid attention to me for that one thing: my talent at the piano. Take the piano away from a girl who's grown up like that, and what's left? So then, *snap*! My mind became a complete jumble. Total darkness."

She dropped her cigarette to the ground and stamped it out, then bent her neck a few times again.

"That was the end of my dream of becoming a concert pianist. I spent two months in the hospital. My finger started to move shortly after I arrived, so I *was* able to return to the conservatoire and graduate, but something inside me had vanished. Some jewel of energy or something had disappeared – evaporated – from inside my body. The doctor said I lacked the mental strength to become a professional pianist and advised me to abandon the idea. So after graduating I took pupils and taught them at home. But the pain I felt was excruciating. It was as if my life had ended. Here I was in my early twenties and the best part of my life was over. Do you see how terrible that would be? I had such potential, then woke up one day and it had gone. No more applause, no one would make a big fuss over me, no one would tell me how wonderful I was. I spent day after day in the house teaching neighbourhood children Beyer exercises and sonatinas. I felt so miserable, I cried all the time. To think what I had missed! I would hear about people who were far less talented than me winning second place in a competition or holding a recital in such-and-such a hall, and the tears would pour out of me.

"My parents walked around on tiptoe, afraid of hurting me. But I knew how disappointed they were. All of a sudden the daughter they had been so proud of was an ex-mental-patient. They couldn't even marry me off. When you're living with people, you sense what they're feeling, and I hated it. I was afraid to go out, afraid the neighbours were talking about me. So then, *snap!* It happened again – the jumble, the darkness. It happened when I was 24, and this time I spent seven months in a sanatorium. Not this place: a regular insane asylum with high walls and locked gates. A filthy place without pianos. I didn't know what to do with myself. All I knew was I wanted to get out of there as soon as I could, so

I struggled desperately to get better. Seven months: a *long* seven months. That's when my wrinkles started."

Reiko smiled, her lips stretching from side to side.

"I hadn't been out of the hospital for long when I met a man and got married. He was a year younger than me, an engineer who worked in an aeroplane manufacturing company, and one of my pupils. A nice man. He didn't say a lot, but he was warm and sincere. He had been taking lessons from me for six months when all of a sudden he asked me to marry him. Just like that – one day when we were having tea after his lesson. Can you believe it? We had never dated or held hands. He took me totally off guard. I told him I couldn't get married. I said I liked him and thought he was a nice person but that, for certain reasons, I couldn't marry him. He wanted to know what those reasons were, so I explained everything to him with complete honesty – that I had been hospitalized twice for mental breakdowns. I told him *everything* – what the cause had been, my condition, and the possibility that it could happen again. He said he needed time to think, and I encouraged him to take all the time he needed. But when he came for his lesson a week later, he said he still wanted to marry me. I asked him to wait three months. We would see each other for three months, I said, and if he still wanted to marry me at that point, we would talk about it again.

"We dated once a week for three months. We went everywhere, and talked about everything, and I got to like him a lot. When I was with him, I felt as if my life had finally come back to me. It gave me a wonderful sense of relief to be alone with him: I could forget all those terrible things that had happened. So what if I hadn't been able to become a concert pianist? So what if I had spent time in mental hospitals? My life hadn't ended. Life was still full of wonderful things I hadn't experienced. If only for having made me feel that way, I felt tremendously grateful to him. After three months went by, he asked me again to marry him. And this is what I said to him: 'If you want to sleep with me, I don't mind. I've never slept with anybody, and I'm very fond of you, so if you want to make love to me, I don't mind at all. But marrying me is a whole different matter. If you marry me, you take on all my troubles, and they're a lot worse than you can imagine.

"He said he didn't care, that he didn't just want to sleep with me, he wanted to marry me, to share everything I had inside me. And he meant it. He was the kind of person who would only say what he really meant, and do anything he said. So I agreed to marry him. It was all I could do. We got married, let's see, four months later I think it was. He fought with his parents over me, and they disowned him. He was from an old family that lived in a rural part of Shikoku. They had my background investigated and found out that I had been hospitalized twice. No wonder they opposed the marriage. So, anyway, we didn't have a wedding ceremony. We just went to the registry office and registered our marriage and took a trip to Hakone for two nights. That was plenty for us: we were happy. And finally, I remained a virgin until the day I married. I was 25 years old! Can you believe it?"

Reiko sighed and picked up the basketball again.

"I thought that as long as I was with him, I would be all right," she went on. "As long as I was with him, my troubles would stay away. That's the most important thing for a sickness like ours: a sense of trust. If I put myself in this person's hands, I'll be OK. If my condition starts to worsen even the slightest bit – if a screw comes loose – he'll notice straight away, and with tremendous care and patience he'll fix it, he'll

157

tighten the screw again, put all the jumbled threads back in place. If we have that sense of trust, our sickness stays away. No more *snap*! I was so happy! Life was great! I felt as if someone had pulled me out of a cold, raging sea and wrapped me in a blanket and laid me in a warm bed. I had a baby two years after we were married, and then my hands were really full! I practically forgot about my sickness. I'd get up in the morning and do the housework and take care of the baby and feed my husband when he came home from work. It was the same thing day after day, but I was happy. It was probably the happiest time of my life. How many years did it last, I wonder? At least until I was 31. And then, all of a sudden, *snap*! It happened again. I fell apart."

Reiko lit a cigarette. The wind had died down. The smoke rose straight up and disappeared into the darkness of night. Just then I realized that the sky was filled with stars.

"Something happened?" I asked.

"Yes," she said, "something very strange, as if a trap had been laid for me. Even now, it gives me a chill just to think about it." Reiko rubbed a temple with her free hand. "I'm sorry, though, making you listen to all this talk about me. You came here to see Naoko, not listen to my story."

"I'd really like to hear it, though," I said. "If you don't mind, I'd like to hear the rest."

"Well," Reiko began, "when our daughter entered kindergarten, I started playing again, little by little. Not for anyone else, but for myself. I started with short pieces by Bach, Mozart, Scarlatti. After such a long blank period, of course, my feel for the music didn't come back straight away. And my fingers wouldn't move the way they used to. But I was thrilled to be playing the piano again. With my hands on the keys, I realized how much I had loved music – and how much

158

I hungered for it. To be able to perform music for yourself is a wonderful thing.

"As I said before, I had been playing from the time I was four years old, but it occurred to me that I had never once played for myself. I had always been trying to pass a test or practise an assignment or impress somebody. Those are all important things, of course, if you are going to master an instrument. But after a certain age you have to start performing for yourself. That's what music *is*. I had to drop out of the elite course and pass my thirty-first birthday before I was finally able to see that. I would send my child off to kindergarten and hurry through the housework, then spend an hour or two playing music I liked. So far so good, right?"

I nodded.

"Then one day I had a visit from one of the ladies of the neighbourhood, someone I at least knew well enough to say hello to on the street, asking me to give her daughter piano lessons. I didn't know the daughter – although we lived in the same general neighbourhood our houses were still pretty far apart – but according to the woman, her daughter used to pass my house and loved to hear me play. She had seen me at some point, too, and now she was pestering her mother to let me teach her. She was in her fourth year of school and had taken lessons from a number of people but things had not gone well for one reason or another and now she had no teacher.

"I turned her down. I had had that blank of several years, and while it might have made sense for me to take on an absolute beginner, it would have been impossible for me to pick up with someone who had had lessons for a number of years. Besides, I was too busy taking care of my own child and, though I didn't say this to the woman, nobody can deal with the kind of child who changes teachers constantly. So then the woman asked me to at least do her daughter the favour of meeting her once. She was a fairly pushy lady and I could see she was not going to let me off the hook that easily, so I agreed to meet the girl – but *just meet* her. Three days later the girl came to the house by herself. She was an absolute angel, with a kind of pure, sweet, transparent beauty. I had never – and have never – seen such a beautiful little girl. She had long, shiny hair as black as freshly ground Indian ink, slim, graceful arms and legs, bright eyes, and a soft little mouth that looked as if someone had just made it. I couldn't speak when I first saw her, she was so beautiful. Sitting on my sofa, she turned my living room into a gorgeous parlour. It hurt to look directly at her: I had to squint. So, anyway, that's what she was like. I can still picture her clearly."

Reiko narrowed her eyes as if she were actually picturing the girl.

"Over coffee we talked for a whole hour – talked about all kinds of things: music, her school, just everything. I could see straight away she was a smart one. She knew how to hold a conversation: she had clear, shrewd opinions and a natural gift for drawing out the other person. It was almost frightening. Exactly what it was that made her frightening, I couldn't tell at the time. It just struck me how frighteningly intelligent she was. But in her presence I lost any normal powers of judgement I might have had. She was so young and beautiful, I felt overwhelmed to the point where I saw myself as an inferior specimen, a clumsy excuse for a human being who could only have negative thoughts about her because of my own warped and filthy mind."

Reiko shook her head several times.

"If I were as pretty and smart as she was, I'd have been

160

a normal human being. What more could you want if you were that smart and that beautiful? Why would you have to torment and walk all over your weaker inferiors if everybody loved you so much? What reason could there possibly be for acting that way?"

"Did she do something terrible to you?"

"Well, let me just say the girl was a pathological liar. She was sick, pure and simple. She made up everything. And while she was making up her stories, she would come to believe them. And then she would change things around her to fit her story. She had such a quick mind, she could always keep a step ahead of you and take care of things that would ordinarily strike you as odd, so it would never cross your mind she was lying. First of all, no one would ever suspect that such a pretty little girl would lie about the most ordinary things. *I* certainly didn't. She told me tons of lies for six months before I had the slightest inkling anything was wrong. She lied about *everything*, and I never suspected. I know it sounds crazy."

"What did she lie about?"

"When I say everything, I mean *everything*." Reiko gave a sarcastic laugh. "When people tell a lie about something, they have to make up a bunch of lies to go with the first one. 'Mythomania' is the word for it. When the usual mythomaniac tells lies, they're usually the innocent kind, and most people notice. But not with that girl. To protect herself, she'd tell hurtful lies without batting an eyelid. She'd use everything she could get her hands on. And she would lie either more or less depending on who she was talking to. To her mother or close friends who would know straight away, she hardly ever lied, or if she had to tell one, she'd be really, really careful to tell lies that wouldn't come out. Or if they did come out,

161

she'd find an excuse or apologize in that clingy voice of hers with tears pouring out of her beautiful eyes. No one could stay mad at her then.

"I still don't know why she chose me. Was I another victim to her, or a source of salvation? I just don't know. Of course, it hardly matters now. Now that everything is over. Now that I'm like this."

A short silence followed.

"She repeated what her mother had told me, that she had been moved when she heard me playing as she passed the house. She had seen me on the street a few times, too, and had begun to worship me. She actually used that word: 'worship'. It made me turn bright red. I mean, to be 'worshipped' by such a beautiful little doll of a girl! I don't think it was an absolute lie, though. I was in my thirties already, of course, and I could never be as beautiful and bright as she was, and I had no special talent, but I must have had something that drew her to me, something that was missing in her, I suppose. That must have been what got her interested in me to begin with. I believe that now, looking back. And I'm not boasting."

"No, I think I know what you mean."

"She had brought some music with her and asked if she could play for me. So I let her. It was a Bach invention. Her performance was . . . interesting. Or should I say strange? It just wasn't ordinary. Of course it wasn't polished. She hadn't been going to a professional school, and what lessons she had taken had been an on-and-off kind of thing; she was very much self-taught. Her sound was untrained. She'd have been rejected immediately at a music-school audition. But she made it work. Although 90 per cent was just terrible, the other 10 per cent was there: she made it sing: it was music. And this was a Bach invention! So I got interested in her. I wanted to know what she was all about.

"Needless to say, the world is full of kids who can play Bach far better than she could. Twenty times better. But most of their performances would have nothing to them. They'd be hollow, empty. This girl's technique was bad, but she had that little bit of something that could draw people – or draw me, at least – into her performance. So I decided it might be worthwhile to teach her. Of course, retraining her at that point to where she could become a pro was out of the question. But I felt it might be possible to make her into the kind of happy pianist I was then – and still am – someone who could enjoy making music for herself. This turned out to be an empty hope, though. She was not the kind of person who quietly goes about doing things for herself. This was a child who would make detailed calculations to use every means at her disposal to impress other people. She knew exactly what she had to do to make people admire and praise her. And she knew exactly what kind of performance it would take to draw me in. She had calculated everything, I'm sure, and put everything she had into practising the most important passages over and over again for my benefit. I can see her doing it.

"Still, even now, after all of this came clear to me, I believe it was a wonderful performance and I would feel the same chills down my spine if I could hear it again. Knowing all I know about her flaws, her cunning and lies, I would still feel it. I'm telling you, there are such things in this world."

Reiko cleared her throat with a dry rasp and broke off.

"So, did you take her as a pupil?" I asked.

"Yeah. One lesson a week. Saturday mornings. Saturday was a day off at her school. She never missed a lesson, she was never late, she was an ideal pupil. She always practised for her lessons. After every lesson, we'd have some cake and chat."

At that point, Reiko looked at her watch as if suddenly remembering something.

"Don't you think we should be getting back to the room? I'm a little worried about Naoko. I'm sure *you* haven't forgotten about her now, have you?"

"Of course not," I laughed. "It's just that I was drawn into your story."

"If you'd like to hear the rest, I'll tell it to you tomorrow. It's a long story – too long for one sitting."

"You're a regular Scheherazade."

"I know," she said, joining her laughter with mine. "You'll never get back to Tokyo."

We retraced our steps through the path in the woods and returned to the flat. The candles had been extinguished and the living room lights were out. The bedroom door was open and the lamp on the night table was on, its pale light spilling into the living room. Naoko sat alone on the sofa in the gloom. She had changed into a loose-fitting blue gown, its collar pulled tight about her neck, her legs folded under her on the sofa. Reiko approached her and rested a hand on her crown.

"Are you all right now?"

"I'm fine. Sorry," answered Naoko in a tiny voice. Then she turned towards me and repeated her apology. "I must have scared you."

"A little," I said with a smile.

"Come here," she said. When I sat down next to her, Naoko, her legs still folded, leaned towards me until her face was nearly touching my ear, as though she were about to share a secret with me. Then she planted a soft kiss by my ear.

"Sorry," she said once more, this time directly into my ear, her voice subdued. Then she moved away from me.

"Sometimes," she said, "I get so confused, I don't know what's happening."

"That happens to me all the time," I said.

Naoko smiled and looked at me.

"If you don't mind," I said, "I'd like to hear more about you. About your life here. What you do every day. The people you meet."

Naoko talked about her daily routine in this place, speaking in short but crystal clear phrases. Wake up at six in the morning. Breakfast in the flat. Clean out the aviary. Then usually farm work. She took care of the vegetables. Before or after lunch, she would have either an hour-long session with her doctor or a group discussion. In the afternoon she could choose from among courses that might interest her, outside work, or sports. She had taken several courses: French, knitting, piano, ancient history.

"Reiko is teaching me piano," she said. "She also teaches guitar. We all take turns as pupils or teachers. Somebody with fluent French teaches French, one person who used to be in social studies teaches history, another good at knitting teaches knitting: that's a pretty impressive school right there. Unfortunately, I don't have anything I can teach anyone."

"Neither do I," I said.

"I put a lot more energy into my studies here than I ever did in university. I work hard and enjoy it – a lot."

"What do you do after supper?"

"Talk with Reiko, read, listen to records, go to other people's flats and play games, stuff like that."

"I do guitar practice and write my autobiography," said Reiko.

"Autobiography?"

"Just kidding," Reiko laughed. "We go to bed around ten. Pretty healthy lifestyle, wouldn't you say? We sleep like babies."

I looked at my watch. It was a few minutes before nine. "I guess you'll be getting sleepy soon."

"That's OK. We can stay up late today," said Naoko. "I haven't seen you in such a long time, I want to talk more. So talk."

"When I was alone before, all of a sudden I started thinking about the old days," I said. "Do you remember when Kizuki and I came to visit you at the hospital? The one on the seashore. I think it was the first year of the sixth-form."

"When I had the chest operation," Naoko said with a smile. "Sure, I remember. You and Kizuki came on a motorbike. You brought me a box of chocolates and they were all melted together. They were so hard to eat! I don't know, it seems like such a long time ago."

"Yeah, really. I think you were writing a poem then, a long one."

"All girls write poems at that age," Naoko tittered. "What reminded you of that all of a sudden?"

"I wonder. The smell of the sea wind, the oleanders: before I knew it, they just popped into my head. Did Kizuki come to see you at the hospital a lot?"

"No way! We had a big fight about that afterwards. He came once, and then he came with you, and that was it for him. He was terrible. And that first time he couldn't sit still and he only stayed about ten minutes. He brought me some oranges and mumbled all this stuff I couldn't understand, and he peeled an orange for me and mumbled more stuff and he was out of there. He said he had a thing about hospitals."

Naoko laughed. "He was always a kid about that kind of stuff. I mean, nobody likes hospitals, right? That's why people visit people in hospitals to make them feel better, and perk up their spirits and stuff. But Kizuki just didn't get it."

"He wasn't so bad when the two of us came to see you, though. He was just his usual self."

"Because you were there," said Naoko. "He was always like that around you. He struggled to keep his weaknesses hidden. I'm sure he was very fond of you. He made a point of letting you see only his best side. He wasn't like that with me. He'd let his guard down. He could be really moody. One minute he'd be chattering away, and the next he'd be depressed. It happened all the time. He was like that from the time he was little. He did keep trying to change himself, to improve himself, though."

Naoko re-crossed her legs on the sofa.

"He tried hard, but it didn't do any good, and that would make him really angry and sad. There was so much about him that was fine and beautiful, but he could never find the confidence he needed. 'I've got to do that, I've got to change this,' he was always thinking, right up to the end. Poor Kizuki!"

"Still," I said, "if it's true that he was always struggling to show me his best side, I'd say he succeeded. His best side was all that I could see."

Naoko smiled. "He'd be thrilled if he could hear you say that. You were his only friend."

"And Kizuki was my only friend," I said. "There was never anybody I could really call a friend, before him or after him."

"That's why I loved being with the two of you. His best side was all that I could see then, too. I could relax and stop worrying when the three of us were together. Those were my favourite times. I don't know how *you* felt about it."

"I used to worry about what *you* were thinking," I said, giving my head a shake.

"The problem was that that kind of thing couldn't go on for ever," said Naoko. "Such perfect little circles are impossible to maintain. Kizuki knew it, and I knew it, and so did you. Am I right?"

I nodded.

"To tell you the truth, though," Naoko went on, "I loved his weak side, too. I loved it as much as I loved his good side. There was absolutely nothing mean or underhand about him. He was weak: that's all. I tried to tell him that, but he wouldn't believe me. He'd always tell me it was because we had been together since we were three. I knew him too well, he'd say: I couldn't tell the difference between his strong points and his flaws, they were all the same to me. He couldn't change my mind about him, though. I went on loving him just the same, and I could never be interested in anyone else."

Naoko looked at me with a sad smile.

"Our boy-girl relationship was really unusual, too. It was as if we were physically joined somewhere. If we happened to be apart, some special gravitational force would pull us back together again. It was the most natural thing in the world when we became boyfriend and girlfriend. It was nothing we had to think about or make any choices about. We started kissing at 12 and petting at 13. I'd go to his room or he'd come to my room and I'd finish him off with my hands. It never occurred to me that we were being precocious. It just happened as a matter of course. If he wanted to play with my breasts or pussy, I didn't mind at all, or if he had cum he wanted to get rid of, I didn't mind helping him with that, either. I'm sure it would have shocked us both if someone had accused us of doing anything wrong. Because we weren't.

We were just doing what we were supposed to do. We had always shown each other every part of our bodies. It was almost as if we owned each other's bodies jointly. For a while, at least, we made sure we didn't go any further than that, though. We were afraid of my getting pregnant, and had almost no idea at that point of how to go about preventing it . . . Anyway, that's how Kizuki and I grew up together, hand in hand, an inseparable pair. We had almost no sense of the oppressiveness of sex or the anguish that comes with the sudden swelling of the ego that ordinary kids experience when they reach puberty. We were totally open about sex, and where our egos were concerned, the way we absorbed and shared each other's, we had no strong awareness of them. Do you see what I mean?"

"I think so," I said.

"We couldn't bear to be apart. So if Kizuki had lived, I'm sure we would have been together, loving each other, and gradually growing unhappy."

"*Un*happy? Why's that?"

With her fingers, Naoko combed her hair back several times. She had taken her hairslide off, which made the hair fall over her face when she dropped her head forward.

"Because we would have had to pay the world back what we owed it," she said, raising her eyes to mine. "The pain of growing up. We didn't pay when we should have, so now the bills are due. Which is why Kizuki did what he did, and why I'm here. We were like kids who grew up naked on a desert island. If we got hungry, we'd just pick a banana; if we got lonely, we'd go to sleep in each other's arms. But that kind of thing doesn't last for ever. We grew up fast and had to enter society. Which is why you were so important to us. You were the link connecting us with the outside. We were struggling

169

through you to fit in with the outside world as best we could. In the end, it didn't work, of course."

I nodded.

"I wouldn't want you to think that we were using you, though. Kizuki really loved you. It just so happened that our connection with you was our first connection with anyone else. And it still is. Kizuki may be dead, but you are still my only link with the outside world. And just as Kizuki loved you, I love you. We never meant to hurt you, but we probably did; we probably ended up making a deep wound in your heart. It never occurred to us that anything like that might happen."

Naoko lowered her head again and fell silent.

"Hey, how about a cup of cocoa?" suggested Reiko.

"Good. I'd really like some," said Naoko.

"I'd like to have some of that brandy I brought, if you don't mind," I said.

"Oh, absolutely," said Reiko. "Could I have a sip?"

"Sure," I said, laughing.

Reiko brought out two glasses and we toasted each other. Then she went into the kitchen to make cocoa.

"Can we talk about something a little more cheerful?" asked Naoko.

I didn't have anything cheerful to talk about. I thought, If only Storm Trooper were still around! That guy could inspire a string of stories. A few of those would have made everybody feel good. The best I could do was talk at length about the filthy habits of the guys in the dormitory. I felt sick just talking about something so gross, but Naoko and Reiko practically fell over laughing, it was all so new to them. Next Reiko did imitations of mental patients. This was a lot of fun, too. Naoko started looking sleepy after eleven o'clock, so Reiko let down the sofa back and handed me a pillow, sheets and blankets.

"If you feel like raping anybody in the middle of the night, don't get the wrong one," she said. "The unwrinkled body in the left bed is Naoko's."

"Liar! Mine's the right bed," said Naoko.

Reiko added, "By the way, I arranged for us to skip some of our afternoon schedule. Why don't the three of us have a little picnic? I know a really nice place close by."

"Good idea," I said.

The women took turns brushing their teeth and withdrew to the bedroom. I poured myself some brandy and stretched out on the sofa bed, going over the day's events from morning to night. It felt like an awfully long day. The room continued to glow white in the moonlight. Aside from the occasional slight creak of a bed, hardly a sound came from the bedroom where Naoko and Reiko lay sleeping. Tiny diagrammatic shapes seemed to float in the darkness when I closed my eyes, and my ears sensed the lingering reverberation of Reiko's guitar, but neither of these lasted for long. Sleep came and carried me into a mass of warm mud. I dreamed of willows. Both sides of a mountain road were lined with willows. An incredible number of willows. A fairly stiff breeze was blowing, but the branches of the willow trees never swayed. Why should that be? I wondered, and then I saw that every branch of every tree had tiny birds clinging to it. Their weight kept the branches from stirring. I grabbed a stick and hit a nearby branch with it, hoping to chase away the birds and allow the branch to sway. But they would not leave. Instead of flying away, they turned into bird-shaped metal chunks that crashed to the ground.

When I opened my eyes, I felt as if I were seeing the continuation of my dream. The moonlight filled the room with the same soft white glow. As if by reflex, I sat up in bed

171

and started searching for the metal birds, which of course were not there. What I saw instead was Naoko at the foot of the bed, sitting still and alone, staring out through the window. She had drawn her knees up and was resting her chin on them, looking like a hungry orphan. I searched for the watch I had left by my pillow, but it was not in the place where I knew it should be. I guessed from the angle of the moonlight that the time must be two or three o'clock in the morning. I felt a violent thirst but I decided to keep still and continue watching Naoko. She was wearing the same blue nightdress I had seen her in earlier, and on one side her hair was held in place by the butterfly hairslide, revealing the beauty of her face in the moonlight. Strange, I thought, she had taken the slide off before going to bed.

Naoko stayed frozen in place, like a small nocturnal animal that has been lured out by the moonlight. The direction of the glow exaggerated the silhouette of her lips. Seeming utterly fragile and vulnerable, the silhouette pulsed almost imperceptibly with the beating of her heart or the motions of her inner heart, as if she were whispering soundless words to the darkness.

I swallowed in hopes of easing my thirst, but in the stillness of the night the sound I made was huge. As if this were a signal to her, Naoko stood and glided towards the head of the bed, gown rustling faintly. She knelt on the floor by my pillow, eyes fixed on mine. I stared back at her, but her eyes told me nothing. Strangely transparent, they seemed like windows to a world beyond, but however long I peered into their depths, there was nothing I could see. Our faces were no more than ten inches apart, but she was light years away from me.

I reached out and tried to touch her, but Naoko drew back, lips trembling faintly. A moment later, she brought her hands

172

up and began slowly to undo the buttons of her gown. There were seven in all. I felt as if it were the continuation of my dream as I watched her slim, lovely fingers opening the buttons one by one from top to bottom. Seven small, white buttons: when she had unfastened them all, Naoko slipped the gown from her shoulders and threw it off completely like an insect shedding its skin. She had been wearing nothing under the gown. All she had on was the butterfly hairslide. Naked now, and still kneeling by the bed, she looked at me. Bathed in the soft light of the moon, Naoko's body had the heartbreaking lustre of newborn flesh. When she moved – and she did so almost imperceptibly – the play of light and shadow on her body shifted subtly. The swelling roundness of her breasts, her tiny nipples, the indentation of her navel, her hipbones and pubic hair, all cast grainy shadows, the shapes of which kept changing like ripples spreading over the calm surface of a lake.

What perfect flesh! I thought. When had Naoko come to possess such a perfect body? What had happened to the body I held in my arms that night last spring?

A sense of imperfection had been what Naoko's body had given me that night as I tenderly undressed her while she cried. Her breasts had seemed hard, the nipples oddly jutting, the hips strangely rigid. She was a beautiful girl, of course, her body marvellous and alluring. It aroused me that night and swept me along with a gigantic force. But still, as I held her and caressed her and kissed her naked flesh, I felt a strange and powerful awareness of the imbalance and awkwardness of the human body. Holding Naoko in my arms, I wanted to explain to her, "I am having sex with you now. I am inside you. But really this is nothing. It doesn't matter. It is nothing but the joining of two bodies. All we are doing is telling each

173

other things that can only be told by the rubbing together of two imperfect lumps of flesh. By doing this, we are sharing our imperfection." But of course I could never have said such a thing with any hope of being understood. I just went on holding her tightly. And as I did so, I was able to feel inside her body some kind of stony foreign matter, something extra that I could never draw close to. And that sensation both filled my heart for Naoko and gave my erection a terrifying intensity.

The body that Naoko revealed before me now, though, was nothing like the one I had held that night. This flesh had been through many changes to be reborn in utter perfection beneath the light of the moon. All signs of girlish plumpness had been stripped away since Kizuki's death to be replaced by the flesh of a mature woman. So perfect was Naoko's physical beauty now that it aroused nothing sexual in me. I could only stare, astounded, at the lovely curve from waist to hips, the rounded richness of the breasts, the gentle movement with each breath of the slim belly and the soft, black pubic shadow beneath.

She exposed her nakedness to me this way for perhaps five minutes until, at last, she wrapped herself in her gown once more and buttoned it from top to bottom. As soon as the final button was in place, she rose and glided towards the bedroom, silently opened the door, and disappeared.

I stayed rooted to the spot for a very long time until it occurred to me to leave the bed. I retrieved my watch from where it had fallen on the floor and turned it towards the light of the moon. It was 3.40. I went to the kitchen and drank a few glasses of water before stretching out in bed again, but sleep never came until the morning sunlight crept into every corner of the room, dissolving all traces of the moon's pale glow.

I was somewhere on the edge of sleep when Reiko came and slapped me on the cheek, shouting, "Morning! Morning!"

While Reiko straightened out my sofa bed, Naoko went to the kitchen and started making breakfast. She smiled at me and said "Good morning".

"Good morning," I replied. I stood by and watched her as she put on water to boil and sliced some bread, humming all the while, but I could sense nothing in her manner to suggest that she had revealed her naked body to me the night before.

"Your eyes are red," she said to me as she poured the coffee. "Are you OK?"

"I woke up in the middle of the night and couldn't get back to sleep."

"I bet we were snoring," said Reiko.

"Not at all," I said.

"That's good," said Naoko.

"He's just being polite," said Reiko, yawning.

At first I thought that Naoko was embarrassed or acting innocent for Reiko, but her behaviour remained unchanged when Reiko momentarily left the room, and her eyes had their usual transparent look.

"How'd you sleep?" I asked Naoko.

"Like a log," she answered with ease. She wore a simple hairpin without any kind of decoration.

I didn't know what to make of this, and I continued to feel that way all through breakfast. Buttering my bread or peeling my egg, I kept glancing across the table at Naoko, in search of a sign.

"Why do you keep looking at me like that?" she asked with a smile.

"I think he's in love with somebody," said Reiko.

"*Are* you in love with somebody?" Naoko asked me.

"Could be," I said, returning her smile. When the two women started joking around at my expense, I gave up trying to think about what had happened in the night and concentrated on my bread and coffee.

After breakfast, Reiko and Naoko said they would be going to feed the birds in the aviary. I volunteered to go along. They changed into jeans and work shirts and white rubber boots. Set in a little park behind the tennis courts, the aviary had everything in it from chickens and pigeons to peacocks and parrots and was surrounded by flowerbeds, shrubberies and benches. Two men in their forties, also apparently sanatorium patients, were raking up leaves that had fallen in the pathways. The women walked over to say good morning to the pair, and Reiko made them laugh with another of her jokes. Cosmos were blooming in the flowerbeds, and the shrubberies were extremely well manicured. Spotting Reiko, the birds started chattering and flying about inside the cage.

The women entered the shed by the cage and came out with a bag of feed and a garden hose. Naoko screwed the hose to a tap and turned on the water. Taking care to prevent any birds from flying out, the two of them slipped into the cage, Naoko hosing down the dirt and Reiko scrubbing the floor of the cage with a deck brush. The spray sparkled in the glare of the morning sun. The peacocks flapped around the cage to avoid getting splashed. A turkey raised its head and glowered at me like a crotchety old man, while a parrot on the perch above screeched its displeasure and beat its wings. Reiko meowed at the parrot, which slunk over to the far corner but soon was calling: "Thank you!" "Crazy!" "Shithead!"

"I wonder who taught him *that* kind of language?" said Naoko with a sigh.

"Not *me*," said Reiko. "I would never do such a thing." She started meowing again, and the parrot shut up.

Laughing, Reiko explained, "This guy once had a run-in with a cat. Now he's scared to death of them."

When they had finished cleaning, the two set down their tools and went around filling each of the feeders. Splashing its way through puddles on the floor, the turkey darted to its feed box and plunged its head in, too obsessed with eating to be bothered by Naoko's smacks on its tail.

"Do you do this every morning?" I asked Naoko.

"Every morning!" she said. "They usually give this job to new women. It's so easy. Like to see the rabbits?"

"Sure," I said. The rabbit hutch was behind the aviary. Some ten rabbits lay inside, asleep in the straw. Naoko swept up their droppings, put feed in their box, and picked up one of the babies, rubbing it against her cheek.

"Isn't it precious?" she gushed. She let me hold it. The warm, little ball of fur cringed in my arms, twitching its nose.

"Don't worry, he won't hurt you," she said to the rabbit, stroking its head with her finger and smiling at me. It was such a radiant smile, without a trace of shadow, that I couldn't help smiling myself. And what about Naoko last night? I wondered. I knew for certain that it had been the real Naoko and not a dream: she had definitely taken her clothes off and shown her naked body to me.

Reiko whistled a lovely rendition of "Proud Mary" as she stuffed a plastic bag with the debris they had gathered and tied the opening. I helped them carry the tools and feed bag to the shed.

"Morning is my favourite time of day," said Naoko. "It's like everything's starting out fresh and new. I begin to get sad around noon time, and I hate it when the sun goes down. I live with those same feelings day after day."

"And while you're living with those feelings, you young-sters get old just like me," said Reiko with a smile. "You're thinking about how it's morning now or night and the next thing you know, you're old."

"But you *like* getting old," said Naoko.

"Not really," said Reiko. "But I sure don't wish I was young again."

"Why not?" I asked.

"Because it's such a pain in the neck!" she said. Then she tossed her broom in and closed the door of the shed, whistling "Proud Mary" all the while.

Back at the flat, the women changed their boots for tennis shoes and said they were going to the farm. Reiko suggested I stayed behind with a book or something because the work would be no fun to watch and they would be doing it as part of a group. "And while you're waiting you can wash the pile of dirty underwear we left by the sink," she added.

"You're kidding," I said, taken aback.

"Of course I am," she laughed. "You're so sweet. Isn't he, Naoko?"

"He really is," said Naoko, laughing with her.

"I'll work on my German," I said with a sigh.

"Yeah, do your homework like a good boy," said Reiko. "We'll be back before lunch."

The two of them went out tittering. I heard the footsteps and voices of a number of people walking by downstairs.

I went into the bathroom and washed my face again, then borrowed a nail clipper and trimmed my nails. For a bath-room that was being shared by two women, its contents were incredibly simple. Aside from some neatly arranged bottles of cleansing cream and lip moisturizer and sun block, there was almost nothing that could be called cosmetics. When I finished trimming my nails, I made myself some coffee and drank it at the kitchen table, German book open. Stripping down to a T-shirt in the sun-filled kitchen, I had set about memorizing all the forms in a grammar chart when I was struck by an odd feeling. It seemed to me that the longest imaginable distance separated irregular German verb forms from this kitchen table.

The two women came back from the farm at 11.30, took turns in the shower, and changed into fresh clothes. The three of us went to the dining hall for lunch, then walked to the front gate. This time the guardhouse had a man on duty. He was sitting at his desk, enjoying a lunch that must have been brought to him from the dining hall. The transistor radio on the shelf was playing a sentimental old pop tune. He waved to us with a friendly "Hi" as we approached, and we hello'ed him back.

Reiko explained to him that we were going to walk outside the grounds and return in three hours.

"Great," he said. "You're lucky with the weather. Just stay away from the valley road, though. It got washed out in that big rain. No problem anywhere else."

Reiko wrote her name and Naoko's in a register along with the date and time.

"Enjoy yourselves," said the guard. "And take care."

"Nice guy," I said.

"He's a little strange up here," said Reiko, touching her head.

He had been right about the weather, though. The sky was a fresh-swept blue, with only a trace of white cloud clinging to the dome of heaven like a thin streak of test paint. We walked beside the low stone wall of Ami Hostel for a time, then moved away to climb a steep, narrow trail in single file. Reiko led the way, with Naoko in the middle and me bringing up the rear. Reiko climbed with the confident stride of one who knew every stretch of every mountain in the area. We concentrated on walking, with hardly a word among us. Naoko wore blue jeans and a white blouse and carried her jacket in one hand. I watched her long, straight hair swaying right and left where it met her shoulders. She would glance back at me now and then, smiling when our eyes met. The trail continued upwards so far that it was almost dizzying, but Reiko's pace never slackened. Naoko hurried to keep up with her, wiping the sweat from her face. Not having indulged in such outdoor activities for some time, I found myself running short of breath.

"Do you do this a lot?" I asked Naoko.

"Maybe once a week," she answered. "Having a tough time?"

"Kind of," I said.

"We're almost there," said Reiko. "This is about two-thirds of the way. Come on, you're a boy, aren't you?"

"Yeah, but I'm out of shape."

"Playing with girls all the time," muttered Naoko, as if to herself.

I wanted to answer her, but I was too winded to speak. Every now and then, red birds with tufts on their heads would flit across our path, brilliant against the blue sky. The fields around us were filled with white and blue and yellow flowers, and bees buzzed everywhere. Moving ahead one step at a time, I thought of nothing but the scene passing before my eyes.

The slope gave out after another ten minutes, and we gained a level plateau. We rested there, wiping the sweat off, catching

180

our breath and drinking from our water bottles. Reiko found a leaf and used it to make a whistle.

The trail entered a gentle downward slope amid tall, waving thickets of plume grass. We walked on for some 15 minutes before passing through a village. There were no signs of humanity here, and the dozen or so houses were all in varying states of decay. Waist-high grass grew among the houses, and dry, white gobs of pigeon droppings clung to holes in the walls. Only the pillars survived in the case of one collapsed building, while others looked ready to be lived in as soon as you opened the storm shutters. These dead, silent houses pressed against either side of the road as we slipped through.

"People lived in this village until seven or eight years ago," Reiko informed me. "This was farmland around here. But they all cleared out. Life was just too hard. They'd be trapped when the snow piled up in the winter. And the soil isn't particularly fertile. They could make a better living in the city."

"What a waste," I said. "Some of the houses look perfectly usable."

"Some hippies tried living here at one point, but they gave up. Couldn't take the winters."

A little beyond the village we came to a big fenced area that seemed to be a pasture. Far away on the other side, I caught sight of a few horses grazing. We followed the fence line, and a big dog came running over to us, tail wagging. It stood up leaning on Reiko, sniffing her face, then jumped playfully on Naoko. I whistled and it came over to me, licking my hand with its long tongue.

Naoko patted the dog's head and explained that the animal belonged to the pasture. "I'll bet he's close to 20," she said. "His teeth are so bad, he can't eat anything hard. He sleeps

181

in front of the shop all day, and he comes running when he hears footsteps."

Reiko took a scrap of cheese from her rucksack. Catching its scent, the dog bounded over to her and chomped down on it.

"We won't be able to see this fellow much longer," said Reiko, patting the dog's head. "In the middle of October they put the horses and cows in trucks and take 'em down to the barn. The only time they let 'em graze is the summer, when they open a little café kind of thing for the tourists. The 'tourists'! Maybe 20 hikers in a day. Hey, how about something to drink?"

"Good idea," I said.

The dog led the way to the café, a small, white house with a front porch and a faded sign in the shape of a coffee cup hanging from the eaves. He led us up the steps and stretched out on the porch, narrowing his eyes. When we took our places around a table on the porch, a girl with a ponytail and wearing a sweatshirt and white jeans came out and greeted Reiko and Naoko like old friends.

"This is a friend of Naoko's," said Reiko, introducing me.

"Hi," she said.

"Hi," I answered.

While the three women traded small talk, I stroked the neck of the dog under the table. It had the hard, stringy neck of an old dog. When I scratched the lumpy spots, the dog closed his eyes and sighed with pleasure.

"What's his name?" I asked the girl.

"Pepé," she said.

"Hey, Pepé," I said to the dog, but he didn't budge.

"He's hard of hearing," said the girl. "You have to speak up or he can't hear."

"Pepé!" I shouted. The dog opened his eyes and snapped to attention with a bark.

"Never mind, Pepé," said the girl. "Sleep more and live longer." Pepé flopped down again at my feet.

Naoko and Reiko ordered cold glasses of milk and I asked for a beer.

"Let's hear the radio," said Reiko. The girl switched on an amplifier and tuned into an FM station. Blood, Sweat and Tears came on with "Spinning Wheel".

Reiko looked pleased. "Now *this* is what we're here for! We don't have radios in our rooms, so if I don't come here once in a while, I don't have any idea what's playing out there."

"Do you sleep in this place?" I asked the girl.

"No way!" she laughed. "I'd die of loneliness if I spent the night here. The pasture guy drives me into town and I come out again in the morning." She pointed at a four-wheel drive truck parked in front of the nearby pasture office.

"You've got a holiday coming up soon, too, right?" asked Reiko.

"Yeah, we'll be shutting up this place soon," said the girl. Reiko offered her a cigarette, and they smoked.

"I'll miss you," said Reiko.

"I'll be back in May, though," said the girl with a laugh.

Cream came on the radio with "White Room". After a commercial, it was Simon and Garfunkel's "Scarborough Fair".

"I *like* that," said Reiko when it was over.

"I saw the film," I said.

"Who's in it?"

"Dustin Hoffman."

"I don't know him," she said with a sad little shake of the head. "The world changes like mad, and I don't know what's happening."

183

She asked the girl for a guitar. "Sure," said the girl, switching off the radio and bringing out an old guitar. The dog raised its head and sniffed the instrument.

"You can't eat this," Reiko said with mock sternness. A grass-scented breeze swept over the porch. The mountains lay spread out before us, the ridge line sharp against the sky.

"It's like a scene from *The Sound of Music*," I said to Reiko as she tuned up.

"What's that?" she asked.

She strummed the guitar in search of the opening chord of "Scarborough Fair". This was apparently her first attempt at the song, but after a few false starts she could play it through without hesitating. She had it down pat the third time and even started adding a few flourishes. "Good ear," she said to me with a wink. "I can usually play just about anything if I hear it three times."

Softly humming the melody, she did a full rendition of "Scarborough Fair". The three of us applauded, and Reiko responded with a decorous bow of the head.

"I used to get more applause for a Mozart concerto," she said.

Her milk was on the house if she would play the Beatles' "Here Comes the Sun", said the girl. Reiko gave her a thumbs up and launched into the song. Hers was not a full voice, and too much smoking had given it a husky edge, but it was lovely, with real presence. I almost felt as if the sun really was coming up again as I sat there listening and drinking beer and looking at the mountains. It was a soft, warm feeling.

Reiko gave back the guitar and asked to hear the radio again. Then she suggested to Naoko and me that we take an hour and walk around the area.

"I want to listen to the radio some more and hang out

with her. If you come back by three, that should be OK."

"Is it all right for us to be alone together so long?"

"Well, actually, it's against the rules, but what the hell. I'm not a chaperone, after all. I could use a break. And you came all the way from Tokyo, I'm sure there's tons of stuff you want to talk about."

Reiko lit another cigarette as she spoke.

"Let's go," said Naoko, standing up.

I started after her. The dog woke up and followed us for a while, but it soon lost interest and went back to its place on the porch. We strolled down a level road that followed the pasture fence. Naoko would take my hand every now and then or slip her arm under mine.

"This is kind of like the old days, isn't it?" she said.

"That wasn't 'the old days'," I laughed. "It was spring of this year! If that was 'the old days', ten years ago was ancient history."

"It feels like ancient history," said Naoko. "But anyway, sorry about last night. I don't know, I was a bundle of nerves. I really shouldn't have done that after you came here all the way from Tokyo."

"Never mind," I said. "Both of us have a lot of feelings we need to get out in the open. So if you want to take those feelings and smash somebody with them, smash me. Then we can understand each other better."

"So if you understand me better, what then?"

"You don't get it, do you?" I said. "It's not a question of 'what then'. Some people get a kick out of reading railway timetables and that's all they do all day. Some people make huge model boats out of matchsticks. So what's wrong if there happens to be one guy in the world who enjoys trying to understand you?"

185

"Kind of like a hobby?" she said, amused.

"Yeah, I guess you could call it a hobby. Most normal people would call it friendship or love or something, but if you want to call it a hobby, that's OK, too."

"Tell me," said Naoko, "you liked Kizuki, too, didn't you?"

"Of course," I said.

"How about Reiko?"

"I like her a lot," I said. "She's really nice."

"How come you always like people like that – people like *us*, I mean? We're all kind of weird and twisted and drowning – me and Kizuki and Reiko. Why can't you like more normal people?"

"Because I don't see you like that," I said after giving it some thought. "I don't see you or Kizuki or Reiko as 'twisted' in any way. The guys *I* think of as twisted are out there running around."

"But we *are* twisted," said Naoko. "*I* can see that."

We walked on in silence. The road left the fence and came out to a circular grassy field ringed with trees like a pond.

"Sometimes I wake up in the middle of the night *so* scared," said Naoko, pressing up against my arm. "I'm scared I'll never get better again. I'll always stay twisted like this and grow old and waste away here. I get so chilled it's like I'm all frozen inside. It's horrible . . . so cold . . . "

I put my arm around her and drew her close.

"I feel like Kizuki is reaching out for me from the darkness, calling to me, 'Hey, Naoko, we can't stay apart.' When I hear him saying that, I don't know what to do."

"What *do* you do?"

"Well . . . don't take this the wrong way, now."

"OK, I won't."

"I ask Reiko to hold me. I wake her up and crawl into her

186

bed and let her hold me tight. And I cry. And she strokes me until the ice melts and I'm warm again. Do you think it's sick?"

"No. I wish *I* could be the one to hold you, though," I said.

"So hold me. Now. Right here."

We sat down on the dry grass of the meadow and put our arms around each other. The tall grass surrounded us, and we could see nothing but the sky and clouds above. I gently lay Naoko down and took her in my arms. She was soft and warm and her hands reached out for me. We kissed with real feeling.

"Tell me something, Toru," Naoko whispered in my ear.

"What's that?" I asked.

"Do you want to sleep with me?"

"Of course I do," I said.

"Can you wait?"

"Of course I can."

"Before we do it again, I want to get myself a little better. I want to make myself into a person more worthy of that hobby of yours. Will you wait for me to do that?"

"Of course I'll wait."

"Are you hard now?"

"You mean the soles of my feet?"

"Silly," Naoko tittered.

"If you're asking whether I have an erection, of course I do."

"Will you do me a favour and stop saying 'Of course'?"

"OK, I'll stop."

"Is it difficult?"

"What?"

"To be all hard like that."

"Difficult?"

"I mean, are you suffering?"

"Well, it depends how you look at it."

"Want me to help you get rid of it?"

"With your hand?"

"Uh-huh. To tell you the truth," said Naoko, "it's been sticking into me ever since we lay down. It hurts."

I pulled my hips away. "Better?"

"Thanks."

"You know?" I said.

"What?"

"I wish you would do it."

"OK," she said with a kind smile. Then she unzipped my trousers and took my stiff penis in her hand.

"It's warm," she said.

She started to move her hand, but I stopped her and unbuttoned her blouse, reaching around to undo her bra strap. I kissed her soft, pink nipples. She closed her eyes and slowly started moving her fingers.

"Hey, you're pretty good at that," I said.

"Be a good boy and shut up," said Naoko.

After I came, I held her in my arms and kissed her again. Naoko did up her bra and blouse, and I zipped up my flies.

"Will that make it easier for you to walk?" she asked.

"I owe it all to you."

"Well, then, Sir, if it suits you, shall we walk a little farther?"

"By all means."

We cut across the meadow, through a stand of trees, and across another meadow. Naoko talked about her dead sister, explaining that although she had hardly said anything about this to anyone, she felt she ought to tell me.

"She was six years older than me, and our personalities were *totally* different, but still we were very close. We never fought, not once. It's true. Of course, with such a big difference in our ages, there was nothing much for us to fight about."

Her sister was one of those girls who are successful at everything – a super-student, a super-athlete, popular, a leader, kind, straightforward, the boys liked her, her teachers loved her, her walls were covered with certificates of merit. There's always one girl like that in any school. "I'm not saying this because she's my sister, but she never let any of this spoil her or make her the least bit stuck-up or a show-off. It's just that, no matter what you gave her to do, she would naturally do it better than anyone else.

"So when I was little, I decided that I was going to be the sweet little girl." Naoko twirled a frond of plume grass as she spoke. "I mean, you know, I grew up hearing everybody talking about how smart she was and how good she was at games and how popular she was. Of course I'm going to assume there's no way I could ever compete with her. My face, at least, was a little prettier than hers, so I guess my parents decided they'd bring me up cute. Right from the start they put me in *that* kind of school. They dressed me in velvet dresses and frilly blouses and patent leather shoes and gave me piano lessons and ballet lessons. This just made my sister even crazier about me – you know: I was her cute little sister. She'd give me these cute little presents and take me everywhere with her and help me with my homework. She even took me along on dates. She was the best big sister anyone could ask for.

"Nobody knew why she killed herself. The same as Kizuki. Exactly the same. She was 17, too, and she never gave the slightest hint she was going to commit suicide. She didn't leave a note, either. Really, it was exactly the same, don't you think?"

"Sounds like it."

"Everybody said she was too smart or she read too many books. And she *did* read a lot. She had tons of books. I read a bunch of them after she died, and it was so sad. They had her comments in the margins and flowers pressed between the pages and letters from boyfriends, and every time I came across something like that I'd cry. I cried a lot."

Naoko fell silent for a few seconds, twirling the plume grass again.

"She was the kind of person who took care of things by herself. She'd never ask anybody for advice or help. It wasn't a matter of pride, I think. She just did what seemed natural to her. My parents were used to this and thought she'd be OK if they left her alone. I would go to my sister for advice and she was always ready to give it, but she never went to anyone else. She did what needed to be done, on her own. She never got angry or moody. This is all true, I mean it, I'm not exaggerating. Most girls, when they have their period or something, will get grumpy and take it out on others, but she never even did that. Instead of getting into a bad mood, she would become very subdued. Maybe once in two or three months this would happen to her: she'd shut herself up in her room and stay in bed, avoid school, hardly eat a thing, turn the lights off, and space out. She wouldn't be in a bad mood, though. When I came home from school, she'd call me into her room and sit me down next to her and ask me about my day. I'd tell her all the little things – like what kinds of games I played with my friends or what the teacher said or my exam results, stuff like that. She'd take in every detail and make comments and suggestions, but as soon as I left – to play with a friend, say, or go to a ballet lesson – she'd space out again. After two days, she'd snap out of it just like that and go to

190

school. This kind of thing went on for, I don't know, maybe four years. My parents were worried at first and I think they went to a doctor for advice, but, I mean, she'd be perfectly fine after two days, so they thought it would work itself out if they left her alone, she was such a bright, steady girl.

"After she died, though, I heard my parents talking about a younger brother of my father's who had died long before. He had also been very bright, but he had stayed shut up in the house for *four years* – from the time he was 17 until he was 21. And then suddenly one day he left the house and jumped in front of a train. My father said, 'Maybe it's in the blood – from my side'."

While Naoko was speaking, her fingers unconsciously teased the tassel of the plume grass, scattering its fibres to the wind. When the shaft was bare, she wound it around her fingers.

"I was the one who found my sister dead," she went on. "In autumn when I was in the first year. November. On a dark, rainy day. My sister was in the sixth-form at the time. I came home from my piano lesson at 6.30 and my mother was making dinner. She told me to tell my sister it was ready. I went upstairs and knocked on her door and yelled 'Dinner's ready', but there was no answer. Her room was completely silent. I thought this was strange, so I knocked again, opened the door and peeped inside. I thought she was probably sleeping. She wasn't in bed, though. She was standing by the window, staring outside, with her neck bent at a kind of angle like this, like she was thinking. The room was dark, the lights were out, and it was hard to see anything. 'What are you doing?' I said to her. 'Dinner is ready.' That's when I noticed that she looked taller than usual. What was going on? I wondered: it was so strange! Did she have high heels on?

191

Was she standing on something? I moved closer and was just about to speak to her again when I saw it: there was a rope above her head. It came straight down from a beam in the ceiling – I mean it was amazingly straight, like somebody had drawn a line in space with a ruler. My sister had a white blouse on – yeah, a simple white blouse like this one – and a grey skirt, and her toes were pointing down like a ballerina's, except there was a space between the tip of her toes and the floor of maybe seven or eight inches. I took in every detail. Her face, too. I looked at her face. I couldn't help it. I thought: I've got to go right downstairs and tell my mother. I've got to scream. But my body ignored me. It moved on its own, separately from my conscious mind. It was trying to lower her from the rope while my mind was telling me to hurry downstairs. Of course, there was no way a little girl could have the strength to do such a thing, and so I just stood there, spacing out, for maybe five or six minutes, a total blank, like something inside me had died. I just stayed that way, with my sister, in that cold, dark place until my mother came up to see what was going on."

Naoko shook her head.

"For three days after that I couldn't talk. I just lay in bed like a dead person, eyes wide open and staring into space. I didn't know what was happening." Naoko pressed against my arm. "I told you in my letter, didn't I? I'm a far more flawed human being than you realize. My sickness is a lot worse than you think: it has far deeper roots. And that's why I want you to go on ahead of me if you can. Don't wait for me. Sleep with other girls if you want to. Don't let thoughts of me hold you back. Just do what you want to do. Otherwise, I might end up taking you with me, and that is the one thing I don't want to do. I don't want to interfere with your life. I don't want to interfere with anybody's life. Like I said before, I want you to come to see me every once in a while, and always remember me. That's all I want."

"It's *not* all *I* want, though," I said.

"You're wasting your life being involved with me."

"I'm not wasting anything."

"But I might never recover. Will you wait for me forever? Can you wait 10 years, 20 years?"

"You're letting yourself be scared by too many things," I said. "The dark, bad dreams, the power of the dead. You have to forget them. I'm sure you'll get well if you do."

"If I can," said Naoko, shaking her head.

"If you can get out of this place, will you live with me?" I asked. "Then I can protect you from the dark and from bad dreams. Then you'd have me instead of Reiko to hold you when things got difficult."

Naoko pressed still more firmly against me.

"That would be wonderful," she said.

We got back to the café a little before three. Reiko was reading a book and listening to Brahms' Second Piano Concerto on the radio. There was something wonderful about Brahms playing at the edge of a grassy meadow without a sign of anyone as far as the eye could see. Reiko was whistling along with the cello passage that begins the third movement.

"Backhaus and Böhm," she said. "I wore this record out once, a long time ago. Literally. I wore the grooves out listening to every note. I sucked the music right out of it."

Naoko and I ordered coffee.

"Do a lot of talking?" asked Reiko.

"Tons," said Naoko.

"Tell me all about his, uh, you know, later."

"We didn't do any of that," said Naoko, reddening.

"Really?" Reiko asked me. "Nothing?"

"Nothing," I said.

"Bo-o-o-ring!" she said with a bored look on her face.

"True," I said, sipping my coffee.

The scene in the dining hall was the same as the day before – the mood, the voices, the faces. Only the menu had changed. The balding man in white, who yesterday had been talking about the secretion of gastric juices under weightless conditions, joined the three of us at our table and talked for a long time about the correlation of brain size to intelligence. As we ate our soybean burgers, we heard all about the volume of Bismarck's brain and Napoleon's. He pushed his plate aside and used a ballpoint pen and notepaper to draw sketches of brains. He would start to draw, declare "No, that's not quite it", and begin a new one. This happened several times. When he had finished, he carefully put the remaining notepaper away in a pocket of his white jacket and slipped the pen into his breast pocket, in which he kept a total of three pens, along with pencils and a ruler. Having finished his meal, he repeated what he had told me the day before, "The winters here are really nice. Make sure you come back when it's winter," and left the dining hall.

"Is he a doctor or a patient?" I asked Reiko.

"Which do you think?"

"I really can't tell. In either case, he doesn't seem all that normal."

"He's a doctor," said Naoko. "Doctor Miyata."

"Yeah," said Reiko, "but I bet he's the craziest one here."

"Mr Omura, the gatekeeper, is pretty crazy, too," answered Naoko.

194

"True," said Reiko, nodding as she stabbed her broccoli. "He does these wild callisthenics every morning, screaming nonsense at the top of his lungs. And before you came, Naoko, there was a girl in the business office, Miss Kinoshita, who tried to kill herself. And last year they sacked a male nurse, Tokushima, who had a terrible drinking problem."

"Sounds like patients and staff should swap places," I said.

"Right on," said Reiko, waving her fork in the air. "You're finally starting to see how things work here."

"I suppose so."

"What makes us most normal," said Reiko, "is knowing that we're not normal."

Back in the room, Naoko and I played cards while Reiko practised Bach on her guitar.

"What time are you leaving tomorrow?" Reiko asked me, taking a break and lighting a cigarette.

"Straight after breakfast," I said. "The bus comes at nine. That way I can get back in time for tomorrow night's work."

"Too bad. It'd be nice if you could stay longer."

"If I stayed around too long, I might end up living here," I said, laughing.

"Maybe so," Reiko said. Then, to Naoko, she said, "Oh, yeah, I've got to go get some grapes at Oka's. I totally forgot."

"Want me to go with you?" asked Naoko.

"How about letting me borrow your young Mr Watanabe here?"

"Fine," said Naoko.

"Good. Let's just the two of us go for another nighttime stroll," said Reiko, taking my hand. "We were almost there yesterday. Let's go all the way tonight."

"Fine," said Naoko, tittering. "Do what you like."

The night air was cool. Reiko wore a pale blue cardigan over her shirt and walked with her hands shoved in her jeans pockets. Looking up at the sky, she sniffed the breeze like a dog. "Smells like rain," she said. I tried sniffing too, but couldn't smell anything. True, there were lots of clouds in the sky obscuring the moon.

"If you stay here long enough, you can pretty much tell the weather by the smell of the air," said Reiko.

We entered the wooded area where the staff houses stood. Reiko told me to wait a minute, walked over to the front door of one house and rang the bell. A woman came to the door – no doubt the lady of the house – and stood there chatting and chuckling with Reiko. Then she ducked inside and came back with a large plastic bag. Reiko thanked her and said goodnight before returning to the spot where I was waiting.

"Look," she said, opening the bag.

It held a huge cluster of grapes.

"Do you like grapes?"

"Love them."

She handed me the top bunch. "It's OK to eat them. They're washed."

We walked along eating grapes and spitting the skins and seeds on the ground. They were fresh and delicious.

"I give their son piano lessons once in a while, and they offer me different stuff. The wine we had was from them. I sometimes ask them to do a little shopping for me in town."

"I'd like to hear the rest of the story you were telling me yesterday," I said.

"Fine," said Reiko. "But if we keep coming home late, Naoko might start getting suspicious."

"I'm willing to risk it."

"OK, then. I want a roof, though. It's a little chilly tonight."

She turned left as we approached the tennis courts. We went down a narrow stairway and came out at a spot where several storehouses stood like a block of houses. Reiko opened the door of the nearest one, stepped in and turned on the lights. "Come in," she said. "There's not much to see, though."

The storehouse contained neat rows of cross-country skis, boots and poles, and on the floor were piled snow removal equipment and bags of rock salt.

"I used to come here all the time for guitar practice – when I wanted to be alone. Nice and cosy, isn't it?"

Reiko sat on the bags of rock salt and invited me to sit next to her. I did as I was told.

"Not much ventilation here, but mind if I smoke?"

"Go ahead," I said.

"This is one habit I can't seem to break," she said with a frown, but she lit up with obvious enjoyment. Not many people enjoy tobacco as much as Reiko did. I ate my grapes, carefully peeling them one at a time and tossing the skins and seeds into a tin that served as a rubbish bin.

"Now, let's see, how far did we get last night?" Reiko asked.

"It was a dark and stormy night, and you were climbing the steep cliff to grab the bird's nest."

"You're amazing, the way you can joke around with such a straight face," said Reiko. "Let's see, I think I had got to the point where I was giving piano lessons to the girl every Saturday morning."

"That's it."

"Assuming you can divide everybody in the world into two groups – those who are good at teaching things to people, and those who are not – I pretty much belong to the first group," said Reiko. "I never thought so when I was young, and I suppose I didn't want to think of myself that way, but once

I reached a certain age and had attained a degree of self-knowledge I realized it was true after all: I'm good at teaching people things. Really good."

"I bet you are."

"I have a lot more patience for others than I have for myself, and I'm much better at bringing out the best in others than in myself. That's just the kind of person I am. I'm the scratchy stuff on the side of the matchbox. But that's fine with me. I don't mind at all. Better to be a first-class matchbox than a second-class match. I got this clear in my own mind, I'd say, after I started teaching this girl. I had taught a few others when I was younger, strictly as a sideline, without realizing this about myself. It was only after I started teaching her that I began to think of myself that way. Hey – I'm *good* at teaching people. That's how well the lessons went.

"As I said yesterday, the girl was nothing special when it came to technique, and there was no question of her becoming a professional musician, so I could take it easy. Plus she was going to the kind of girls' school where anybody with half-decent marks automatically got into university, which meant she didn't have to kill herself studying, and her mother was all for going easy with the lessons, too. So I didn't push her to do anything. I knew the first time I met her that she was the kind of girl you *couldn't* push to do anything, that she was the kind of child who would be all sweetness and say 'Yes, yes,' and *absolutely refuse* to do anything she didn't want to do. So the first thing I did was let her play a piece the way she wanted to – 100 per cent her own way. Then I would play the same piece several different ways for her, and the two of us would discuss which was best or which way she liked most. Then I'd have her play the piece again, and her performance would be ten times better than the first. She would see for herself what worked best and bring those features into her own playing."

Reiko paused for a moment, observing the glowing end of her cigarette. I went on eating my grapes without a word.

"I know I have a pretty good sense for music, but she was better than me. I used to think it was such a waste! I thought, 'If only she had started out with a good teacher and received the proper training, she'd be so much farther along!' But I was wrong. She wasn't the kind of child who could stand proper training. There just happen to be people like that. They're blessed with this marvellous talent, but they can't make the effort to systematize it. They end up squandering it in little bits and pieces. I've seen my share of people like that. At first you think they're amazing. They can sight-read some terrifically difficult piece and do a damn good job playing it all the way through. You see them do it, and you're over-whelmed. You think, 'I could never do that in a million years.' But that's as far as it goes. They can't take it any further. And why not? Because they won't put in the effort. They haven't had the discipline pounded into them. They've been spoiled. They have just enough talent so they've been able to play things well without any effort and they've had people telling them how great they are from an early age, so hard work looks stupid to them. They'll take some piece another kid has to work on for three weeks and polish it off in half the time, so the teacher assumes they've put enough into it and lets them go on to the next thing. And they do *that* in half the time and go on to the *next* piece. They never find out what it means to be hammered by the teacher; they lose out on a crucial element required for character building. It's a tragedy. I myself had tendencies like that, but fortunately I had a very tough teacher, so I kept them in check.

"Anyway, it was a joy to teach her. Like driving down the highway in a high-powered sports car that responds to the slightest touch – responds too quickly, sometimes. The trick to teaching children like that is not to praise them too much. They're so used to praise it doesn't mean anything to them. You've got to dole it out wisely. And you can't force anything on them. You have to let them choose for themselves. And you don't let them rush ahead from one thing to the next: you make them stop and think. But that's about it. If you do those things, you'll get good results."

Reiko dropped her cigarette butt on the floor and stamped it out. Then she took a deep breath as if to calm herself.

"When her lessons ended, we'd have tea and chat. Sometimes I'd show her certain jazz piano styles – like, this is Bud Powell, or this is Thelonious Monk. But mostly she talked. And what a talker she was! She could draw you right in. As I told you yesterday, I think most of what she said was made up, but it was *interesting*. She was a keen observer, a precise user of language, sharp-tongued and funny. She could stir your emotions. Yes, really, that's what she was so good at – stirring people's emotions, *moving* you. And she *knew* she had this power. She tried to use it as skilfully and effectively as possible. She could make you feel whatever she wanted – angry or sad or sympathetic or disappointed or happy. She would manipulate people's emotions for no other reason than to test her own powers. Of course, I only realized this later. At the time, I had no idea what she was doing to me."

Reiko shook her head and ate a few grapes.

"It was a sickness," she said. "The girl was sick. She was like the rotten apple that ruins all the other apples. And no one could cure her. She'll have that sickness until the day she dies. In that sense, she was a sad little creature. I would have pitied her, too, if I hadn't been one of her victims. I would have seen *her* as a victim."

Reiko ate a few more grapes. She seemed to be thinking of how best to go on with her story.

"Well, anyway, I enjoyed teaching her for a good six months. Sometimes I'd find something she said a little surprising or odd. Or she'd be talking and I'd have this rush of horror when I realised the intensity of her hatred for some person was completely irrational, or it would occur to me that she was just far too clever, and I'd wonder what she was really thinking. But, after all, everyone has their flaws, right? And finally, what business was it of mine to question her personality or character? I was just her piano teacher. All I had to care about was whether she practised or not. And besides, the truth of the matter is that I liked her. I liked her a lot.

"Still, I was careful not to tell her anything too personal about myself. I just had this sixth sense that I'd better not talk about such things. She asked me hundreds of questions – she was dying to know more about me – but I only told her the most harmless stuff, like things about my childhood or where I'd gone to school, stuff like that. She said she wanted to know more about me, but I told her there was nothing to tell: I'd had a boring life, I had an ordinary husband, an ordinary child, and a ton of housework. 'But I like you so *much*,' she'd say and look me right in the eye in this clingy sort of way. It sent a thrill through me when she did that – a *nice* thrill. But even so, I never told her more than I had to.

"And then one day – a day in May, I think it was – in the middle of her lesson, she said she felt sick. I saw she was pale and sweating and asked if she wanted to go home, but she said she thought she'd feel better if she could just lie down for a while. So I took her – almost carried her – to the bedroom.

201

We had such a small sofa, the bed was the only place she *could* lie down. She apologized for being a nuisance, but I assured her it was no bother and asked if she wanted anything to drink. She said no, she just wanted me to stay near her, which I said I'd be glad to do.

"A few minutes later she asked me to rub her back. She sounded as though she was really suffering, and she was sweating like mad, so I started to give her a good massage. Then she apologized and asked me if I'd mind taking off her bra, as it was hurting her. So, I don't know, I did it. She was wearing a skin-tight blouse, and I had to unbutton that and reach behind and undo the bra hooks. She had big breasts for a 13-year-old. Twice as big as mine. And she wasn't wearing any starter bra but a real adult model, an expensive one. Of course I'm not paying all that much attention at the time, and like an idiot I just carry on rubbing her back. She keeps apologizing in this pitiful voice as if she's really sorry, and I keep telling her it's OK it's OK."

Reiko tapped the ash from her cigarette to the floor. By then I had stopped eating grapes and was giving all my attention to her story.

"After a while she starts sobbing. 'What's wrong?' I ask her. 'Nothing,' she says. 'It's obviously not nothing,' I say. 'Tell me the truth. What's bothering you?' So she says, 'I just get like this sometimes. I don't know what to do. I'm so lonely and sad, and I can't talk to anybody, and nobody cares about me. And it hurts so much, I just get like this. I can't sleep at night, and I don't feel like eating, and coming here for my lesson is the only thing I have to look forward to.' So I say, 'You can talk to *me*. Tell me why this happens to you.' Things are not going well at home, she says. She can't love her parents, and they don't love her. Her father is seeing another woman and is hardly ever around, and that makes her mother half crazy and she takes it out on the girl; she beats her almost every day and she hates to go home. So now the girl is really wailing, and her eyes are full of tears, those beautiful eyes of hers. The sight is enough to make a god weep. So I tell her, if it's so terrible to go home, she can come to my place any time she likes. When she hears that, the girl throws her arms around me and says, 'Oh, I'm so sorry, but if I didn't have you I wouldn't know what to do. Please don't turn your back on me. If you did that, I'd have nowhere to go.'

"So, I don't know, I hold her head against me and I'm caressing her and saying 'There there,' and she's got her arms around me and she's stroking my back, and soon I'm starting to feel very strange, my whole body is kind of hot. I mean, here's this picture-perfect beautiful girl and I'm on the bed with her, and we're hugging, and her hands are caressing my back in this incredibly sensual way that my own husband couldn't even begin to match, and I feel all the screws coming loose in my body every time she touches me, and before I know it she has my blouse and bra off and she's stroking my breasts. So that's when it finally hits me that she's an absolute dyed-in-the-wool lesbian. This had happened to me once before, at school, one of the sixth-form girls. So then I tell her to stop.

"'Oh, please,' she says, 'just a little more. I'm so lonely, I'm so lonely, please believe me, you're the only one I have, oh please, don't turn your back on me,' and she takes my hand and puts it on her breast – her very nicely shaped breast, and, sure, I'm a woman, but this electric something goes through me when my hand makes contact. I have no idea what to do. I just keep repeating no no no no no, like an idiot. It's as if I'm paralyzed, I can't move. I had managed to push the girl away at school, but now I can't do a thing. My body won't take orders. She's holding my right hand against her with her left hand, and she's kissing and licking my nipples, and her right hand is caressing my back, my side, my bottom. So here I am in the bedroom with the curtains closed and a 13-year-old girl has me practically naked – she's been taking my clothes off somehow all along – and touching me all over and I'm writhing with the pleasure of it. Looking back on it now, it seems incredible. I mean, it's insane, don't you think? But at the time it was as if she had cast a spell on me."

Reiko paused to puff at her cigarette.

"You know, this is the first time I've ever told a man about it," she said, looking at me. "I'm telling it to you because I think I ought to, but I'm finding it really embarrassing."

"I'm sorry," I said, because I didn't know what else to say.

"This went on for a while, and then her right hand started to move down, and she touched me through my panties. By then, I was absolutely soaking wet. I'm ashamed to say it, but I've never been so wet before or since. I had always thought of myself as sort of indifferent to sex, so I was astounded to be getting so worked up. So then she puts these slim, soft fingers of hers inside my panties, and . . . well, you know, I can't bring myself to put it into words. I mean, it was totally different from when a man puts his clumsy hands on you there. It was amazing. Really. Like feathers or down. I thought all the fuses in my head were going to pop. Still, somewhere in my fogged-over brain, the thought occurred to me that I had to put a stop to this. If I let it happen once, I'd never stop, and if I had to carry around a secret like that inside me, my head was going to get completely messed up again. I thought about my daughter, too. What if she saw me like this? She was supposed to be at my parents' house until three on

Saturdays, but what if something happened and she came home unexpectedly? This helped me to gather my strength and raise myself on the bed. 'Stop it now, please stop!' I shouted.

"But she wouldn't stop. Instead, she yanked my panties down and started using her tongue. I had rarely let even my husband do that, I found it so embarrassing, but now I had a 13-year-old girl licking me all over down there. I just gave up. All I could do was cry. And it was absolute paradise.

"'Stop it!' I yelled one more time and slapped her on the side of the face as hard as I could. She finally stopped, raised herself up and looked into my eyes. The two of us were stark naked, on our knees, in bed, staring at each other. She was 13, I was 31, but, I don't know, looking at that body of hers, I felt totally overwhelmed. The image is still so vivid in my mind. I could hardly believe I was looking at the body of a 13-year-old girl, and I still can't believe it. By comparison, what I had for a body was enough to make you cry. Believe me."

There was nothing I could say, and so I said nothing.

"'What's wrong?' she says to me. 'You like it this way, don't you? I knew you would the first time I met you. I know you like it. It's much better than doing it with a man – isn't it? Look how wet you are. I can make you feel even better if you'll let me. It's true. I can make you feel like your body's melting away. You want me to, don't you?' And she was right. She was much better than my husband. And I *did* want her to do it even more! But I couldn't let it happen. 'Let's do this once a week,' she said. 'Just once a week. Nobody will find out. It'll be our little secret'."

"But I got out of bed and put on my dressing-gown and told her to leave and never come back. She just looked at me. Her eyes were absolutely flat. I had never seen them like that before. It was as if they were painted on cardboard. They had no depth. After she stared at me for a while, she gathered up her clothes without a word and, as slowly as she could, as though she were making a show of it, she put on each item, one at a time. Then she went back into the piano room and took a brush from her bag. She brushed her hair and wiped the blood from her lips with a handkerchief, put on her shoes, and left. As she went out, she said, 'You're a lesbian, you know. It's true. You may try to hide it, but you'll be a lesbian until the day you die'."

"Is it true?" I asked.

Reiko curved her lips and thought for a while. "Well, it is and it isn't. I definitely felt better with her than with my husband. That's a fact. I had a time there when I really agonized over the question. Maybe I really was a lesbian and just hadn't noticed until then. But I don't think so any more. Which is not to say I don't have the tendencies. I probably do have them. But I'm not a lesbian in the proper sense of the term. I never feel desire when I look at a woman. Know what I mean?"

I nodded.

"Certain kinds of girls, though, do respond to me, and I can feel it when that happens. Those are the only times it comes out in me. I can hold Naoko in my arms, though, and feel nothing special. We go around in the flat practically naked when the weather's hot, and we take baths together, sometimes even sleep in the same bed, but nothing happens. I don't feel a thing. I can see that she has a beautiful body, but that's all. Actually, Naoko and I played a game once. We made believe we were lesbians. Want to hear about it?"

"Sure. Tell me."

"When I told her the story I just told you – we tell each

other everything, you know – Naoko tried an experiment. The two of us got undressed and she tried caressing me, but it didn't work at all. It just tickled. I thought I was going to die laughing. Just thinking about it makes me itchy. She was so clumsy! I'll bet you're glad to hear *that*."

"Yes I am, to tell the truth."

"Well, anyway, that's about it," said Reiko, scratching near an eyebrow with the tip of her little finger. "After the girl left my house, I found a chair and sat there spacing out for a while, wondering what to do. I could hear the dull beating of my heart from deep inside my body. My arms and legs seemed to weigh a ton, and my mouth felt as though I'd eaten a moth or something, it was so dry. But I dragged myself to the bathroom, knowing my daughter would be back soon. I wanted to clean those places where the girl had touched and licked me. I scrubbed myself with soap, over and over, but I couldn't seem to get rid of the slimy feeling she had left behind. I knew I was probably imagining it, but that didn't help. That night, I asked my husband to make love to me, almost as a way to get rid of the defilement. Of course, I didn't tell him anything – I couldn't. All I said to him was that I wanted him to take it slow, to give it more time than usual. And he did. He concentrated on every little detail, he really took a long, long time, and the way I came that night, oh yes, it was like nothing I had ever experienced before, never once in all our married life. And why do you think that was? Because the touch of that girl's fingers was still there in my body. That's all it was.

"Oh, man, is this embarrassing! Look, I'm sweating! I can't believe I'm saying these things – he 'made love' to me, I 'came'!" Reiko smiled, her lips curved again. "But even this didn't help. Two days went by, three, and her touch was still there. And her last words were echoing and echoing in my head.

"She didn't come to my house the following Saturday. My heart was pounding all day long while I waited, wondering what I would do if she showed up. I couldn't concentrate on anything. She never did come, though. Of course. She was a proud little thing, and she had failed with me in the end. She didn't come the next week, either, nor the week after that, and soon a month went by. I decided that I would be able to forget about what had happened when enough time had passed, but I couldn't forget. When I was alone in the house, I would feel her presence and my nerves would be on edge. I couldn't play the piano, I couldn't think, I couldn't do anything during that first month. And then one day I realized that something was wrong whenever I left the house. The neighbours were looking at me in a strange way. There was a new distance in their eyes. They were as polite as ever with their greetings, but there was something different in their tone of voice and in their behaviour towards me. The woman next door, who used to pay me an occasional visit, seemed to be avoiding me. I tried not to let these things bother me, though. Start noticing things like that, and you've got the first signs of illness.

"Then one day I had a visit from another housewife I was on friendly terms with. We were the same age, and she was the daughter of a friend of my mother's, and her child went to the same kindergarten as mine, so we were fairly close. She just showed up one day and asked me if I knew about a terrible rumour that was going around about me. 'What kind of rumour?' I asked. 'I almost can't say it, it's so awful,' she said. 'Well, you've got this far, you have to tell me the rest.'

"Still she resisted telling me, but I finally got it all out of her. I mean, her whole purpose in coming to see me was to

208

tell me what she had heard, so of course she was going to spit it out eventually. According to her, people were saying that I was a card-carrying lesbian and had been in and out of mental hospitals for it. They said that I had stripped the clothes off my piano pupil and tried to do things to her and when she had resisted I had slapped her so hard her face swelled up. They had turned the story on its head, of course, which was bad enough, but what really shocked me was that people knew I had been hospitalized.

"My friend said she was telling everyone that she had known me for ever and that I was not like that, but the girl's parents believed *her* version and were spreading it around the neighbourhood. In addition, they had investigated my background and found that I had a history of mental problems.

"The way my friend heard it, the girl had come home from her lesson one day – *that* day, of course – with her face all bloated, her lip split and bloody, buttons missing from her blouse, and even her underwear torn. Can you believe it? She had done all this to back up her story, of course, which her mother had to drag out of her. I can just see her doing it – putting blood on her blouse, tearing buttons off, ripping the lace on her bra, making herself cry until her eyes were red, messing up her hair, telling her mother a pack of lies.

"Not that I'm blaming people for believing her. I would have believed her, too, this beautiful doll with a devil's tongue. She comes home crying, she refuses to talk because it's too embarrassing, but then she spills it out. Of *course* people are going to believe her. And to make matters worse, it's true, I *do* have a history of hospitalization for mental problems, I *did* hit her in the face as hard as I could. Who's going to believe *me*? Probably just my husband.

"A few more days went by while I wrestled with the

question of whether to tell him or not, but when I did, he believed me. Of course. I told him everything that had happened that day – the kind of lesbian things she did to me, the way I slapped her in the face. Of course, I didn't tell him what I had felt. I couldn't have told him that. So anyway, he was furious and insisted that he was going to go straight to the girl's family. He said, 'You're a married woman, after all. You're married to *me*. And you're a mother. There's no way you're a lesbian. What a joke!'

"But I wouldn't let him go. All he could do was make things worse. I knew. I knew she was sick. I had seen hundreds of sick people, so I knew. The girl was rotten inside. Peel off a layer of that beautiful skin, and you'd find nothing but rotten flesh. I know it's a terrible thing to say, but it's true. And I knew that ordinary people could never know the truth about her, that there was no way we could win. She was an expert at manipulating the emotions of the adults around her, and we had nothing to prove our case. First of all, who's going to believe that a 13-year-old girl set a homosexual trap for a woman in her thirties? No matter what we said, people would believe what they wanted to believe. The more we struggled, the more vulnerable we'd be.

"There was only one thing for us to do, I said: we had to move. If I stayed in that neighbourhood any longer, the stress would get to me; my mind would snap again. It was happening already. We had to get out of there, go somewhere far away where nobody knew me. My husband wasn't ready to go, though. It hadn't dawned on him yet how critical I was. And the timing was terrible: he loved his work, and he had finally succeeded in getting us settled in our own house (we lived in a little prefab), and our daughter was comfortable in her kindergarten. 'Wait a minute,' he said, 'we can't just up sticks and go. I can't find a job just like that. We'd have to sell the house, and we'd have to find another kindergarten. It'll take two months at least.'

"'I can't wait two months,' I told him. 'This is going to finish me off once and for all. I'm not kidding. Believe me, I know what I'm talking about.' The symptoms were starting already: my ears were ringing, and I was hearing things, and I couldn't sleep. So he suggested that I leave first, go somewhere by myself, and he would follow after he had taken care of what had to be done.

"'No,' I said, 'I don't want to go alone. I'll fall apart if I don't have you. I need you. Please, don't leave me alone.' He held me and pleaded with me to hang on a little longer. Just a month, he said. He would take care of everything – leave his job, sell the house, make arrangements for kindergarten, find a new job. There might be a position he could take in Australia, he said. He just wanted me to wait one month, and everything would be OK. What could I say to that? If I tried to object, it would only isolate me even more."

Reiko sighed and looked at the ceiling light.

"I couldn't hold on for a month, though. One day, it happened again: *snap*! And this time it was really bad. I took sleeping pills and turned on the gas. I woke up in a hospital bed, and it was all over. It took a few months before I had calmed down enough to think, and then I asked my husband for a divorce. I told him it would be the best thing for him and for our daughter. He said he had no intention of divorcing me. 'We can make a new start,' he said. 'We can go somewhere new, just the three of us, and begin all over again.' 'It's too late,' I told him. 'Everything ended when you asked me to wait a month. If you really wanted to start again, you shouldn't have said that to me. Now, no matter where we go, no matter how far away we move, the same thing will happen all over again. And I'll ask you for the same thing, and make you suffer. I don't want to do that any more.'

"And so we divorced. Or I should say I divorced him. He married again two years ago, though. I'm still glad I made him leave me. Really. I knew I'd be like this for the rest of my life, and I didn't want to drag anyone down with me. I didn't want to force anyone to live in constant fear that I might lose my mind at any moment.

"He had been wonderful to me: an ideal husband, faithful, strong and patient, someone I could put my complete trust in. He had done everything he could to heal me, and I had done everything I could to *be* healed, both for his sake and for our daughter's. And I had believed in my recovery. I was happy for six years from the time we were married. He got me 99 per cent of the way there, but the other one per cent went crazy. *Snap!* Everything we had built up came crashing down. In one split second, everything turned into nothing. And that girl was the one who did it."

Reiko collected the cigarette butts she had crushed underfoot and tossed them into the tin can.

"It's a terrible story. We worked so hard, so hard, building our world one brick at a time. And when it fell apart, it happened just like that. Everything was gone before you knew it."

She stood up and thrust her hands in her pockets. "Let's go back. It's late."

The sky was darker, the cloud cover thicker than before, the moon invisible. Now, I realized, like Reiko I could smell the rain. And with it mixed the fresh smell of the grapes in the bag I was holding.

"That's why I can't leave this place," she said. "I'm afraid to get involved with the outside world. I'm afraid to meet new people and feel new feelings."

"I understand," I said. "But I think you can do it. I think you can go outside and make it."

Reiko smiled, but said nothing.

Naoko was on the sofa with a book. She had her legs crossed and pressed her hand against her temple as she read. Her fingers almost seemed to be touching and testing each word that entered her head. Scattered drops of rain were beginning to tap on the roof. The lamplight enveloped her, hovering around her like fine dust. After my long talk with Reiko, Naoko's youthfulness struck me in a new way.

"Sorry we're so late," said Reiko, patting Naoko's head.

"Enjoy yourselves?" asked Naoko, looking up.

"Of course," said Reiko.

"Doing what?" Naoko asked me, " – just the two of you."

"Not at liberty to say, Miss," I answered.

Naoko chuckled and set down her book. Then the three of us ate grapes to the sound of the rain.

"When it's raining like this," said Naoko, "it feels as if we're the only ones in the world. I wish it would just keep raining so the three of us could stay together."

"Oh, sure," said Reiko, "and while the two of you are going at it, I'm supposed to be fanning you or playing background music on my guitar like some dumb geisha? No, thanks!"

"Oh, I'd let you have him once in a while," said Naoko, laughing.

"OK, then, count me in," said Reiko. "Come on, rain, pour down!"

*

213

The rain did pour down, and kept pouring. Thunder shook the place from time to time. When we had finished the grapes, Reiko went back to her cigarettes and pulled out the guitar from under her bed and started to play – first, "Desafinado" and "The Girl from Ipanema", then some Bacharach and a few Lennon and McCartney songs. Reiko and I sipped wine again, and when that was gone we shared the brandy that was left in my flask. A warm, intimate mood took hold as the three of us talked into the night, and I began to wish, with Naoko, that the rain would keep on falling.

"Will you come to see me again?" she asked, looking at me.

"Of course I will," I said.

"And will you write?"

"Every week."

"And will you add a few lines for me?" asked Reiko.

"That I will," I said. "I'd be glad to."

At eleven o'clock, Reiko unfolded the sofa and made a bed for me as she had the night before. We said goodnight and turned out the lights. Unable to sleep, I took *The Magic Mountain* and a torch from my rucksack and read for a while. Just before midnight, the bedroom door edged open and Naoko came and crawled in next to me. Unlike the night before, Naoko was the usual Naoko. Her eyes were in focus, her movements brisk. Bringing her mouth to my ear, she whispered, "I don't know, I can't sleep."

"I can't either," I said. Setting my book down and turning out the torch, I took her in my arms and kissed her. The darkness and the sound of the rain enfolded us.

"How about Reiko?"

"Don't worry, she's sound asleep. And when she sleeps, she *sleeps*." Then Naoko asked, "Will you really come to see me again?"

"Of course I will."

"Even if I can't do anything for you?"

I nodded in the darkness. I could feel the full shape of her breasts against me. I traced the outline of her body through her gown with the flat of my hand. From shoulder to back to hips, I ran my hand over her again and again, driving the line and the softness of her body into my brain. After we had been in this gentle embrace for a while, Naoko touched her lips to my forehead and slipped out of bed. I could see her pale blue gown flash in the darkness like a fish.

"Goodbye," she called in a tiny voice.

Listening to the rain, I dropped into a gentle sleep.

It was still raining the following morning – a fine, almost invisible autumn rain unlike the previous night's downpour. You knew it was raining only because of the ripples on puddles and the sound of dripping from the eaves. I woke to see a milky white mist enclosing the window, but as the sun rose a breeze carried the mist away, and the surrounding woods and hills began to emerge.

As we had done the day before, the three of us ate breakfast then went out to attend to the aviary. Naoko and Reiko wore yellow plastic raincapes with hoods. I put on a jumper and a waterproof windcheater. Outside the air was damp and chilly. The birds, too, were avoiding the rain, huddled together at the back of the cage.

"Gets cold here when it rains, doesn't it?" I said to Reiko.

"Every time it rains it'll be a little colder now, until it turns to snow," she said. "The clouds from the Sea of Japan dump tons of snow when they pass through here."

"What do you do with the birds in the winter?"

"Bring them inside, of course. What are we supposed to

do – dig them out of the snow in spring all frozen? We defrost 'em and bring 'em back to life and yell, OK, everybody, come and get it!"

I poked the wire mesh and the parrot flapped its wings and squawked "Shithead!" "Thank you!" "Crazy!"

"Now, *that* one I'd like to freeze," Naoko said with a melancholy look. "I really think I *will* go crazy if I have to hear that every morning."

After cleaning the aviary, we went back to the flat. While I packed my things, the women put on their farm clothes. We left the building together and parted just beyond the tennis court. They turned right and I continued straight ahead. We called goodbye to each other, and I promised I would come again. Naoko gave a little smile and disappeared around a corner.

On my way to the gate I passed several people, all wearing the same yellow raincapes that Naoko and Reiko wore, all with their hoods up. Colours shone with an exceptional clarity in the rain: the ground was a deep black, the pine branches a brilliant green, and the people wrapped in yellow looking like otherworldly spirits that were only allowed to wander the earth on rainy mornings. They floated over the ground in silence, carrying farm tools, baskets and sacks.

The gatekeeper remembered my name and marked it on the list of visitors as I left. "I see you're here from Tokyo," the old fellow said. "I went there once. Just once. They serve great pork."

"They do?" I asked, uncertain how to answer him.

"I didn't like much of what I ate in Tokyo, but the pork was delicious. I expect they have some special way of rearing 'em, eh?"

I said I didn't know, it was the first I'd heard of it. "When

216

was that, by the way, when you went to Tokyo?"

"Hmm, let's see," he said, cocking his head, "was it the time His Majesty the Crown prince got married? My son was in Tokyo and said I ought to see the place at least once. That must have been 1959."

"Oh, well then, sure, pork must have been good in Tokyo back then," I said.

"How about these days?" he asked.

I wasn't sure, I said, but I hadn't heard anything special about it. This seemed to disappoint him. He gave every sign of wanting to continue our conversation, but I told him I had to catch a bus and started walking in the direction of the road. Patches of fog remained floating on the path where it skirted the stream, but the breeze carried them over to the steep flanks of a nearby mountain. Every now and then as I walked along I would stop, turn, and heave a deep sigh for no particular reason. I felt as though I had arrived on a planet where the gravity was a little different. Yes, of course, I told myself, feeling sad: I was in the outside world now.

Back at the dorm by 4.30, I changed straight away and left for the record shop in Shinjuku to put in my hours. I looked after the shop from six o'clock to 10.30 and sold a few records, but mainly I sat there in a daze, watching an incredible variety of people streaming by outside. There were families and couples and drunks and gangsters and lively-looking girls in short skirts and bearded hippies and bar hostesses and some indefinable types. Whenever I put on hard rock, hippies and runaway kids would gather outside to dance and sniff paint thinner or just sit on the ground doing nothing in particular, and when I put on Tony Bennett, they would disappear.

Next door was a shop where a middle-aged, sleepy-eyed

man sold "adult toys". I couldn't imagine why anyone would want the kind of sex paraphernalia he had there, but he seemed to do a roaring trade. In the alley diagonally across from the record shop I saw a drunken student vomiting. In the game arcade across from us at another angle, the cook from a local restaurant was killing time on his break with a game of bingo that took cash bets. Beneath the eaves of a shop that had closed for the night, a swarthy homeless guy was crouching, motionless. A girl with pale pink lipstick who couldn't have been more than 12 or 13 came in and asked me to play the Rolling Stones' "Jumpin' Jack Flash". When I found the record and put it on for her, she started snapping her fingers to the rhythm and shaking her hips as she danced around the shop. Then she asked me for a cigarette. I gave her one of the manager's, which she smoked gratefully, and when the record ended she left the shop without so much as a "thank you". Every 15 minutes or so I would hear the siren of an ambulance or police car. Three drunk company executives in suits and ties came by, laughing at the top of their voices every time they yelled "Nice arse!" at a pretty, long-haired girl in a phone box.

The more I watched, the more confused I became. What the hell was this all about? I wondered. What could it possibly mean?

The manager came back from dinner and said to me, "Hey, know what, Watanabe? Night before last I made it with the boutique chick." For some time now he had had his eye on the girl who worked at a boutique nearby, and every once in a while he would take a record from the shop as a gift for her.

"Good for you," I said to him, whereupon he told me every last detail of his conquest.

"If you really wanna make a chick, here's what ya gotta do,"

218

he began, very pleased with himself. "First, ya gotta give 'er presents. Then ya gotta get 'er drunk. I mean really drunk. Then ya just gotta do it. It's *easy*. See what I mean?"

Head mixed up as ever, I boarded the commuter train and went back to my dorm. Closing the curtains, I turned off the lights, stretched out in bed, and felt as if Naoko might come crawling in beside me at any moment. With my eyes closed, I could feel the soft swell of her breasts on my chest, hear her whispering to me, and feel the outline of her body in my hands. In the darkness, I returned to that small world of hers. I smelled the meadow grass, heard the rain at night. I thought of her naked, as I had seen her in the moonlight, and pictured her cleaning the aviary and tending to the vegetables with that soft, beautiful body of hers wrapped in the yellow raincape. Clutching my erection, I thought of Naoko until I came. This seemed to clear my brain a little, but it didn't help me sleep. I felt exhausted, desperate for sleep, but it simply refused to cooperate.

I got out of bed and stood at the window, my unfocused eyes wandering out towards the flagpole. Without the national flag attached to it, the pole looked like a gigantic white bone thrusting up into the darkness of night. What was Naoko doing now? I wondered. Of course, she must be sleeping, sleeping deeply, shrouded in the darkness of that curious little world of hers. Let her be spared from anguished dreams, I found myself hoping.

第 7 章

In P.E. class the next morning, Thursday, I swam several lengths of the 50-metre pool. The vigorous exercise cleared my head some more and gave me an appetite. After eating a good-sized lunch at a student restaurant known for its good-sized lunches, I was on my way to the literature department library to do some research when I bumped into Midori Kobayashi. She had someone with her, a petite girl with glasses, but when she spotted me, she approached me alone.

"Where you going?" she asked.

"Lit. library," I said.

"Why don't you forget it and come have lunch with me?"

"I've already eaten."

"So what? Eat again."

We ended up going to a nearby café where she had a plate of curry and I had a cup of coffee. She wore a white, long-sleeved shirt under a yellow woollen vest with a fish knitted into the design, a narrow gold necklace, and a Disney watch. She seemed to enjoy the curry and drank three glasses of water with it.

"Where've you been?" Midori asked. "I don't know how many times I called."

"Was there something you wanted to talk about?"

"Nothing special. I just called."

220

"I see."

"You see what?"

"Nothing. Just 'I see'," I said. "Any fires lately?"

"That was fun, wasn't it? It didn't do much damage, but all that smoke made it feel real. Great stuff." Midori gulped another glass of water, took a breath and studied my face for a while. "Hey, what's wrong with you?" she asked. "You've got this spaced-out face. Your eyes aren't focused."

"I'm OK," I said. "I just came back from a trip and I'm tired."

"You look like you've just seen a ghost."

"I see."

"Hey, do you have lectures this afternoon?"

"German and R.E."

"Can you skip 'em?"

"Not German. I've got a test today."

"When's it over?"

"Two."

"OK. How about going into the city with me after that for some drinks?"

"At two in the afternoon?!"

"For a change, why not? You look so spaced. Come on, come drinking with me and get a little life into you. That's what I want to do – drink with you and get some life into myself. What do you say?"

"OK, let's go," I said with a sigh. "I'll look for you in the Lit. quad at two."

After German we caught a bus to Shinjuku and went to an underground bar called DUG behind the Kinokuniya book-shop. We each started with two vodka and tonics.

"I come here once in a while," she said. "They don't make

221

you feel embarrassed to be drinking in the afternoon."

"Do you drink in the afternoon a lot?"

"Sometimes," she said, rattling the ice in her glass. "Sometimes, when the world gets too hard to live in, I come here for a vodka and tonic."

"Does the world get hard to live in?"

"Sometimes," said Midori. "I've got my own special little problems."

"Like what?"

"Like family, like boyfriends, like irregular periods. Stuff."

"So have another drink."

"I will."

I beckoned to the waiter and ordered two more vodka and tonics.

"Remember how, when you came over that Sunday, you kissed me?" Midori asked. "I've been thinking about it. It was nice. Really nice."

"That's nice."

"'That's nice'," she mimicked. "The way you talk is so weird!"

"It is?"

"Anyway, I was thinking, that time. I was thinking how great it would be if that had been the first time in my life a boy had kissed me. If I could switch around the order of my life, I would absolutely, absolutely make that my first kiss. And then I would live the rest of my life thinking stuff like: Hey, I wonder whatever happened to that boy named Watanabe I gave my first kiss to on the laundry deck, now that he's 58? Wouldn't that be great?"

"Yeah, really," I said, cracking a pistachio nut.

"Hey, what is it with you? Why are you so spaced out? You still haven't answered me."

"I probably still haven't completely adapted to the world," I said after giving it some thought. "I don't know, I feel like this isn't the real world. The people, the scene: they just don't seem real to me."

Midori rested an elbow on the bar and looked at me. "There was something like that in a Jim Morrison song, I'm pretty sure."

"People are strange when you're a stranger."

"Peace," said Midori.

"Peace," I said.

"You really ought to go to Uruguay with me," Midori said, still leaning on the bar. "Girlfriend, family, university – just dump 'em all."

"Not a bad idea," I said, laughing.

"Don't you think it would be wonderful to get rid of everything and everybody and just go somewhere where you don't know a soul? Sometimes I feel like doing that. I really, really want to do it sometimes. Like, suppose you whisked me somewhere far, far away, I'd make lots of babies for you as tough as little bulls. And we'd all live happily ever after, rolling on the floor."

I laughed and drank my third vodka and tonic.

"I guess you don't really want lots of babies as tough as little bulls yet," said Midori.

"I'm intrigued," I said. "I'd like to see what they look like."

"That's OK, you don't have to want them," said Midori, eating a pistachio. "Here I am, drinking in the afternoon, saying whatever pops into my head: 'I wanna dump everything and run off somewhere.' What's the point of going to Uruguay? All they've got there is donkey shit."

"You may be right."

"Donkey shit everywhere. Here a shit, there a shit, the

whole world is donkey shit. Hey, I can't open this. You take it."
Midori handed me a pistachio nut. I struggled with it until
I cracked it open. "But oh, what a *relief* it was last Sunday!
Going up to the laundry deck with you, watching the fire,
drinking beer, singing songs. I don't know *how* long it's been
since I had such a total sense of *relief*. People are always trying
to *force* stuff on me. The minute they see me they start telling
me what to do. At least you don't try to force stuff on me."

"I don't know you well enough to force stuff on you."

"You mean, if you knew me better, you'd force stuff on me
like everyone else?"

"It's possible," I said. "That's how people live in the real
world: forcing stuff on each other."

"You wouldn't do that. I can tell. I'm an expert when it
comes to forcing stuff and having stuff forced on you. You're
not the type. That's why I can relax with you. Do you have
any idea how many people there are in the world who *like*
to force stuff on people and have stuff forced on them? *Tons!*
And then they make a big fuss, like 'I forced her', 'You forced
me!' That's what they like. But *I* don't like it. I just do it
because I have to."

"What kind of stuff do you force on people or they force
on you?"

Midori put an ice-cube in her mouth and sucked on it for
a while.

"Do you want to get to know me better?" she asked.

"Yeah, kind of."

"Hey, look, I just asked you, 'Do you want to get to know
me better?' What sort of answer is that?"

"Yes, Midori, I would like to get to know you better," I said.

"Really?"

"Yes, really."

"Even if you had to turn your eyes away from what you saw?"

"Are you that bad?"

"Well, in a way," Midori said with a frown. "I want another drink."

I called the waiter and ordered a fourth round of drinks. Until they came, Midori cupped her chin in her hand with her elbow on the bar. I kept quiet and listened to Thelonious Monk playing "Honeysuckle Rose". There were five or six other customers in the place, but we were the only ones drinking alcohol. The rich smell of coffee gave the gloomy interior an intimate atmosphere.

"Are you free this Sunday?" Midori asked.

"I think I told you before, I'm always free on Sunday. Until I go to work at six."

"OK, then, *this* Sunday, will you hang out with me?"

"Sure," I said.

"I'll pick you up at your dorm Sunday morning. I'm not sure exactly what time, though. Is that OK?"

"Fine," I said. "No problem."

"Now, let me ask you: do you have any idea what I would like to do right now?"

"I can't imagine."

"Well, first of all, I want to lie down in a big, wide, fluffy bed. I want to get all comfy and drunk and not have any donkey shit anywhere nearby, and I want to have you lying down next to me. And then, little by little, you take off my clothes. *Sooo* tenderly. The way a mother undresses a little child. *Sooo* softly."

"Hmm . . ."

"And I'm just spacing out and feeling really nice until, all of a sudden I realize what's happening and I yell at you 'Stop it, Watanabe!' And then I say 'I really like you, Watanabe, but I'm seeing someone else. I can't do this. I'm very proper about these things, believe it or not, so please stop.' But you don't stop."

"But I *would* stop," I said.

"I know that. Never mind, this is just my fantasy," said Midori. "So then you show it to me. Your thing. Sticking right up. I immediately cover my eyes, of course, but I can't help seeing it for a split second. And I say, 'Stop it! Don't *do* that! I don't want anything so big and hard!'"

"It's not so big. Just ordinary."

"Never mind, this is a fantasy. So then you put on this really sad face, and I feel sorry for you and try to comfort you. There there, poor thing."

"And you're telling me that's what you want to do now?"

"That's it."

"Oh boy."

We left the bar after five rounds of vodka and tonic. When I tried to pay, Midori slapped my hand and paid with a brand-new ¥10,000 note she took from her purse.

"It's OK," she said. "I just got paid, and *I* invited *you*. Of course, if you're a card-carrying fascist and you refuse to let a woman buy you a drink . . ."

"No no, I'm OK."

"And I didn't let you put it in, either."

"Because it's so big and hard," I said.

"Right," said Midori. "Because it's so big and hard."

A little drunk, Midori missed one step, and we almost fell back down the stairs. The layer of clouds that had darkened the sky was gone now, and the late afternoon sun poured its gentle light on the city streets. Midori and I wandered around for a while. She said she wanted to climb a tree, but unfortunately there were no climbable trees in Shinjuku, and the Shinjuku Imperial Gardens were closing.

"Too bad," said Midori. "I love climbing trees."

We continued walking and window-shopping, and soon the street scene seemed more real to me than it had before.

"I'm glad I ran into you," I said. "I think I'm a little more adapted to the world now."

Midori stopped short and peered at me. "It's true," she said. "Your eyes are much more in focus than they were. See? Hanging out with me does you good."

"No doubt about it," I said.

At 5.30 Midori said she had to go home and make dinner. I said I would take a bus back to my dorm, and saw her as far as the station.

"Know what I want to do now?" Midori asked me as she was leaving.

"I have absolutely no idea what you could be thinking," I said.

"I want you and me to be captured by pirates. Then they strip us and press us together face to face all naked and wind these ropes around us."

"Why would they do a thing like that?"

"Perverted pirates," she said.

"*You're* the perverted one," I said.

"So then they lock us in the hold and say, 'In one hour, we're gonna throw you into the sea, so have a good time until then'."

"And . . . ?"

"So we enjoy ourselves for an hour, rolling all over the place and twisting our bodies."

"And that's the main thing you want to do now?"

"That's it."

"Oh boy," I said, shaking my head.

Midori came for me at 9.30 on Sunday morning. I had just woken up and hadn't washed my face. Somebody pounded on my door, yelling "Hey, Watanabe, it's a woman!" I went down to the lobby to find Midori sitting there with her legs crossed wearing an incredibly short denim skirt, yawning. Every student passing by on his way to breakfast slowed down to stare at her long, slim legs. She did have really nice legs.

"Am I too early?" she asked. "I bet you just woke up."

"Can you give me 15 minutes? I'll wash my face and shave."

"I don't mind waiting, but all these guys are staring at my legs."

"What d'you expect, coming into a men's dorm in such a short skirt? Of course they're going to stare."

"Oh, well, it's OK. I'm wearing really cute panties today – all pink and frilly and lacy."

"That just makes it worse," I said with a sigh. I went back to my room and washed and shaved as fast as I could, put on a blue button-down shirt and a grey tweed sports coat, then went back down and ushered Midori out through the dorm gate. I was in a cold sweat.

"Tell me, Watanabe," Midori said, looking up at the dorm buildings, "do all the guys in here wank – rub-a-dub-dub?"

"Probably," I said.

"Do guys think about girls when they do that?"

"I suppose so. I kind of doubt that anyone thinks about the stock market or verb conjugations or the Suez Canal when they wank. Nope, I'm pretty sure just about everybody thinks about girls."

"The Suez Canal?"

"For example."

"So I suppose they think about *particular* girls, right?"

"Shouldn't you be asking your boyfriend about that?" I said. "Why should I have to explain stuff like this to you on a Sunday morning?"

"I was just curious," she said. "Besides, he'd get angry if I asked him about stuff like that. He'd say girls aren't supposed to ask all those questions."

"A perfectly normal point of view, I'd say."

"But I want to know. This is pure curiosity. Do guys think about particular girls when they wank?"

I gave up trying to avoid the question. "Well, *I* do at least. I don't know about anybody else."

"Have you ever thought about *me* while you were doing it? Tell me the truth. I won't be angry."

"No, I haven't, to tell the truth," I answered honestly.

"Why not? Aren't I attractive enough?"

"Oh, you're attractive, all right. You're cute, and sexy outfits look great on you."

"So why don't you think about me?"

"Well, first of all, I think of you as a friend, so I don't want to involve you in my sexual fantasies, and second – "

"You've got somebody else you're supposed to be thinking about."

"That's about the size of it," I said.

"You have good manners even when it comes to something like this," Midori said. "That's what I like about you. Still, couldn't you allow me just one brief appearance? I want to be in one of your sexual fantasies or daydreams or whatever you call them. I'm asking you because we're friends. Who else can I ask for something like that? I can't just walk up to anyone and say, 'When you wank tonight, will you please think of me for a second?' It's *because* I think of you as a friend that I'm asking. And I want you to tell me later what it was like. You know, what you did and stuff."

I let out a sigh.

"You can't put it in, though. Because we're just friends. Right? As long as you don't put it in, you can do anything you like, think anything you want."

"I don't know, I've never done it with so many restrictions before," I said.

"Will you just think about me?"

"All right, I'll think about you."

"You know, Watanabe, I don't want you to get the wrong impression – that I'm a nymphomaniac or frustrated or a tease or anything. I'm just *interested* in that stuff. I want to *know* about it. I grew up surrounded by nothing but girls in a girls' school, you know that. I want to find out what guys are thinking and how their bodies are put together. And not just from pull-out sections in the women's magazines but actual *case studies*."

"Case studies?" I groaned.

"But my boyfriend doesn't like it when I want to know things or try things. He gets angry, calls me a nympho or crazy. He won't even let me give him a blow job. Now, that's one thing I'm dying to study."

"Uh-huh."

"Do *you* hate getting blow jobs?"

"No, not really, I don't hate it."

"Would you say you *like* it?"

"Yeah, I'd say that. But can we talk about this next time? Here it is, a really nice Sunday morning, and I don't want to ruin it talking about wanking and blow jobs. Let's talk about something else. Is your boyfriend at the same university as us?"

"Nope, he goes to another one, of course. We met at school during a club activity. I was in the girls' school, he was in the boys', and you know how they do those things, joint concerts and stuff. We got serious after our exams, though. Hey, Watanabe."

"What?"

"You only have to do it once. Just think about me, OK?"

"OK, I'll give it a try, next time," I said, throwing in the towel.

We took a commuter train to Ochanomizu. When we transferred at Shinjuku I bought a thin sandwich at a stand in the station to make up for the breakfast I hadn't eaten. The coffee I had with it tasted like boiled printer's ink. The Sunday morning trains were filled with couples and families on outings. A group of boys with baseball bats and matching uniforms scampered around inside the carriage. Several of the girls on the train had short skirts on, but none as short as Midori's. Midori would pull on hers every now and then as it rode up. Some of the men stared at her thighs, which made me feel uneasy, but she didn't seem to mind.

"Know what I'd like to do right now?" she whispered when we had been travelling a while.

"No idea," I said. "But please, don't talk about that stuff here. Somebody'll hear you."

"Too bad. This one's kind of wild," Midori said with obvious disappointment.

"Anyway, why are we going to Ochanomizu?"

"Just come along, you'll see."

With all the cram schools around Ochanomizu Station, on

Sunday the area was full of school kids on their way to classes or exam practice. Midori barged through the crowds clutching the strap of her shoulder bag with one hand and my hand with the other.

Without warning, she asked me, "Hey, Watanabe, can you explain the difference between the English present subjunctive and past subjunctive?"

"I think I can," I said.

"Let me ask you, then, what possible use is stuff like that for everyday life?"

"None at all," I said. "It may not serve any concrete purpose, but it *does* give you some kind of training to help you grasp things in general more systematically."

Midori gave that a moment's serious thought. "You're amazing," she said. "That never occurred to me before. I always thought of things like the subjunctive case and differential calculus and chemical symbols as totally useless. A pain in the neck. So I've always ignored them. Now I have to wonder if my whole life has been a mistake."

"You've ignored them?"

"Yeah. Like, for me, they didn't exist. I don't have the slightest idea what 'sine' and 'cosine' mean."

"That's incredible! How did you pass your exams? How did you get into university?"

"Don't be silly," said Midori. "You don't have to know anything to pass entrance exams! All you need is a little intuition – and I have great intuition. 'Choose the correct answer from the following three.' I know immediately which one is right."

"My intuition's not as good as yours, so I have to be systematic to some extent. Like the way a magpie collects bits of glass in a hollow tree."

"Does it serve some purpose?"

"I wonder. It probably makes it easier to do some things."

"What kind of things? Give me an example."

"Metaphysical thought, say. Mastering several languages."

"What good does that do?"

"It depends on the person who does it. It serves a purpose for some, and not for others. But mainly it's training. Whether it serves a purpose or not is another question. Like I said."

"Hmm," said Midori, seemingly impressed. She led me by the hand down the hill. "You know, Watanabe, you're really good at explaining things to people."

"I wonder," I said.

"It's true. I've asked hundreds of people what use the English subjunctive is, and not one of them gave me a good, clear answer like yours. Not even English teachers. They either got confused or angry or laughed it off. Nobody ever gave me a decent answer. If somebody like you had been around when I asked my question, and had given me a proper explanation, even I might have been interested in the subjunctive. Damn!"

"Hmm," I said.

"Have you ever read *Das Kapital*?"

"Yeah. Not the whole thing, of course, but parts, like most people."

"Did you understand it?"

"I understood some bits, not others. You have to acquire the necessary intellectual apparatus to read a book like *Das Kapital*. I think I understand the general idea of Marxism, though."

"Do you think a first-year student who hasn't read books like that can understand *Das Kapital* just by reading it?"

"That's pretty nigh impossible, I'd say."

"You know, when I went to university I joined a folk-music club. I just wanted to sing songs. But the members were a load of frauds. I get goose-bumps just thinking about them. The first thing they tell you when you enter the club is you have to read Marx. 'Read page so-and-so to such-and-such for next time.' Somebody gave a lecture on how folk songs have to be deeply involved with society and the radical movement. So, what the hell, I went home and tried as hard as I could to read it, but I didn't understand a thing. It was worse than the subjunctive. I gave up after three pages. So I went to the next week's meeting like a good little scout and said I had read it, but I couldn't understand it. From that point on they treated me like an idiot. I had no critical awareness of the class struggle, they said, I was a social cripple. I mean, this was serious. And all because I said I couldn't understand a piece of writing. Don't you think they were terrible?"

"Uh-huh," I said.

"And their so-called discussions were terrible, too. Everybody would use big words and pretend they knew what was going on. But I would ask questions whenever I didn't understand something. 'What is this imperialist exploitation stuff you're talking about? Is it connected somehow to the East India Company?' 'Does smashing the educational-industrial complex mean we're not supposed to work for a company after we graduate?' And stuff like that. But nobody was willing to explain anything to me. Far from it – they got *really* angry. Can you believe it?"

"Yeah, I can," I said.

"One guy yelled at me, 'You stupid bitch, how do you live like that with nothing in your brain?' Well, that did it. I wasn't going to put up with that. OK, so I'm not so smart. I'm working class. But it's the working class that keeps the world running, and it's the working classes that get exploited. What kind of revolution is it that just throws out big words that working-class people can't understand? What kind of crap social revolution is that? I mean, *I'd* like to make the world a better place, too. If somebody's really being exploited, we've got to put a stop to it. That's what I believe, and that's why I ask questions. Am I right, or what?"

"You're right."

"So that's when it hit me. These guys are fakes. All they've got on their minds is impressing the new girls with the big words they're so proud of, while sticking their hands up their skirts. And when they graduate, they cut their hair short and march off to work for Mitsubishi or IBM or Fuji Bank. They marry pretty wives who've never read Marx and have kids they give fancy new names to that are enough to make you puke. Smash *what* educational-industrial complex? Don't make me laugh! And the new members were just as bad. They didn't understand a thing either, but they pretended to and they were laughing at me. After the meeting, they told me, 'Don't be silly! So what if you don't understand? Just agree with everything they say.' Hey, Watanabe, I've got stuff that made me even madder than that. Wanna hear it?"

"Sure, why not?"

"Well, one time they called a late-night political meeting, and they told each girl to make 20 rice balls for midnight snacks. I mean, talk about sex discrimination! I decided to keep quiet for a change, though, and showed up like a good girl with my 20 rice balls, complete with umeboshi inside and nori outside. And what do you think I got for my efforts? Afterwards people complained because my rice balls had *only* umeboshi inside, and I hadn't brought anything along to go with them! The other girls stuffed theirs with cod roe and salmon, and they included nice, thick slices of fried egg. I got so furious I couldn't talk! Who the hell do these 'revolution'-mongers think they are making a fuss over rice balls? They should be grateful for umeboshi and nori. Think of the children starving in India!"

I laughed. "So then what happened with your club?"

"I left in June, I was so furious," Midori said. "Most of these student types are total frauds. They're scared to death somebody's gonna find out they don't know something. They all read the same books and they all spout the same slogans, and they love listening to John Coltrane and seeing Pasolini movies. You call that 'revolution?'"

"Hey, don't ask me, I've never actually seen a revolution."

"Well, if that's revolution, you can stick it. They'd probably shoot me for putting umeboshi in my rice balls. They'd shoot you, too, for understanding the subjunctive."

"It could happen."

"Believe me, I know what I'm talking about. I'm working class. Revolution or not, the working class will just keep on scraping a living in the same old shitholes. And what *is* a revolution? It sure as hell isn't just changing the name on city hall. But those guys don't know that – those guys with their big words. Tell me, Watanabe, have you ever seen a taxman?"

"Never."

"Well *I* have. Lots of times. They come barging in and acting big. 'What's *this* ledger for?' 'Hey, you keep pretty sloppy records.' 'You call this a *business* expense?' 'I want to see all your receipts *right now*.' Meanwhile, we're crouching in the corner, and when suppertime comes we have to treat them to sushi deluxe – home delivered. Let me tell you, though, my father never once cheated on his taxes. That's just how he is, a real old-fashioned straight arrow. But tell that to the taxman. All he can do is dig and dig and dig and dig. 'Income's a little low here, don't you think?' Well, of *course* the income's low when you're not making any money! I wanted to scream: 'Go do this where they've got some money!' Do you think the taxman's attitude would change if there was a revolution?"

"Highly doubtful, highly doubtful."

"That does it, then. I'm not going to believe in any damned revolution. Love is all I'm going to believe in."

"Peace," I said.

"Peace," said Midori.

"Hey, where are we going?" I asked.

"The hospital," she said. "My father's there. It's my turn to stay with him all day."

"Your father?! I thought he was in Uruguay!"

"That was a lie," said Midori in a matter-of-fact tone. "He's been screaming about going to Uruguay forever, but he could never do that. He can hardly get himself out of Tokyo."

"How bad is he?" I asked.

"It's just a matter of time," she said.

We walked on in silence.

"I know what I'm talking about. It's the same thing my mother had. A brain tumour. Can you believe it? It's hardly been two years since she died of a brain tumour, and now he's got one."

The University Hospital corridors were noisy and crowded with weekend visitors and patients who had less serious symptoms, and everywhere hung that special hospital smell, a cloud of disinfectant and visitors' bouquets, and urine and mattresses, while nurses surged back and forth with a dry clattering of heels.

Midori's father was in a semi-private room in the bed nearest the door. Stretched out, he looked like some tiny creature with a fatal wound. He lay on his side, limp, the drooping left arm inert, jabbed with an intravenous needle. He was a small, skinny man who gave the impression that he would only get smaller and thinner. A white bandage encircled his head, and his pasty white arms were dotted with the holes left by injections or intravenous drips. His half-open eyes stared at a fixed point in space, bloodshot spheres that twitched in our direction when we entered the room. For some ten seconds they stayed focused on us, then drifted back to that fixed point in space.

You knew when you saw those eyes he was going to die soon. There was no sign of life in his flesh, just the barest trace of what had once been a life. His body was like a dilapidated old house from which all the fixtures and fittings have been removed, awaiting its final demolition. Around the dry lips clumps of whiskers sprouted like weeds. So, I thought, even after so much of a man's life force has been lost, his beard continues to grow.

Midori said hello to a fat man in the bed by the window. He nodded and smiled, apparently unable to talk. He coughed a few times and, after sipping some water from a glass by his pillow, he shifted his weight and rolled on his side, turning to gaze out of the window. Beyond the window could be seen only a pole and some power lines, nothing more, not even a cloud in the sky.

"How are you feeling, Daddy?" said Midori, speaking into her father's ear as if testing a microphone. "How are you today?"

Her father moved his lips. ‹Not good› he said, not so much speaking the words as forming them from dried air at the back of his throat. ‹Head› he said.

"You have a headache?" Midori asked.

‹Yuh› he said, apparently unable to pronounce more than a syllable or two at a time.

"Well, no wonder," she said, "you've just had your head cut open. Of course it hurts. Too bad, but try to be brave. This is my friend, Watanabe."

"Glad to meet you," I said. Midori's father opened his lips halfway, then closed them again.

Midori gestured towards a plastic stool near the foot of the bed and suggested I sit down. I did as I was told. Midori gave her father a drink of water and asked if he'd like a piece of fruit or some jellied fruit dessert. ‹No› he said, and when Midori insisted that he had to eat something, he said ‹I ate›.

A water bottle, a glass, a dish and a small clock stood on a night table near the head of the bed. From a large paper bag under the table, Midori took some fresh pyjamas, underwear, and other things, straightened them out and put them into the locker by the door. There was food for the patient at the bottom of the bag: two grapefruits, fruit jelly and three cucumbers.

"Cucumbers?! What are *these* doing in here?" Midori asked. "I can't imagine what my sister was thinking. I told her on the phone exactly what I wanted her to buy, and I'm sure I never mentioned cucumbers! She was supposed to bring kiwi fruit."

"Maybe she misunderstood you," I suggested.

"Yeah, maybe, but if she had thought about it she would have realized that cucumbers couldn't be right. I mean, what's a patient supposed to do? Sit in bed chewing on raw cucumbers? Hey, Daddy, want a cucumber?"

‹No› said Midori's father.

Midori sat by the head of the bed, telling her father snippets of news from home. The TV picture had gone fuzzy and she had called the repairman; their aunt from Takaido would visit in a few days; the chemist, Mr Miyawaki, had fallen off his bike: stuff like that. Her father responded with grunts.

"Are you sure you don't want anything to eat?"

‹No› her father answered.

"How about you, Watanabe? Some grapefruit?"

"No," I answered.

A few minutes later, Midori took me to the TV room and smoked a cigarette on the sofa. Three patients in pyjamas were also smoking there and watching some kind of political discussion programme.

"Hey," whispered Midori with a twinkle in her eye. "That old guy with the crutches has been looking at my legs ever since we came in. The one with glasses in the blue pyjamas."

"What do you expect, wearing a skirt like that?"

"It's nice, though. I bet they're all bored. It probably does them good. Maybe the excitement helps them get better faster."

"As long as it doesn't have the opposite effect."

Midori stared at the smoke rising from her cigarette.

"You know," she said, "my father's not such a bad guy. I get angry with him sometimes because he says terrible things, but deep down he's honest and he really loved my mother. In his own way, he's lived life with all the intensity he could muster. He's a little weak, maybe, and he has absolutely *no* head for business, and people don't like him very much, but he's a hell of a lot better than the cheats and liars who go round smoothing things over because they're so slick. I'm as bad as he is about not backing down once I've said something, so we fight a lot, but really, he's not a bad guy."

Midori took my hand as if she were picking up something someone had dropped in the street, and placed it on her lap. Half my hand lay on the skirt, the rest touching her thigh. She looked into my eyes for some time.

"Sorry to bring you to a place like this," she said, "but would you mind staying with me a little longer?"

"I'll stay with you all day if you want," I said. "Until five. I like spending time with you, and I've got nothing else to do."

"How do you usually spend your Sundays?"

"Doing my laundry," I said. "And ironing."

"I don't suppose you want to tell me too much about her . . . your girlfriend?"

"No, I guess not. It's complicated, and I, kind of, don't think I could explain it very well."

"That's OK. You don't have to explain anything," said Midori. "But do you mind if I tell you what I imagine is going on?"

"No, go ahead. I suspect anything you'd imagine would have to be interesting."

"I think she's a married woman."

"You do?"

"Yeah, she's thirty-two or -three and she's rich and beautiful and she wears fur coats and Charles Jourdan shoes and silk underwear and she's hungry for sex and she likes to do really yucky things. The two of you meet on weekday afternoons and devour each other's bodies. But her husband's home on Sundays, so she can't see you. Am I right?"

"Very, very interesting."

"She has you tie her up and blindfold her and lick every square inch of her body. Then she makes you put weird things inside her and she gets into these incredible positions like a contortionist and you take pictures of her with a Polaroid camera."

"Sounds like fun."

"She's dying for it all the time, so she does everything she can think of. And she thinks about it every day. She's got nothing but free time, so she's always planning: Hmm, next time Watanabe comes, we'll do this, or we'll do that. You get in bed and she goes crazy, trying all these positions and coming three times in each one. And she says to you, 'Don't I have a sensational body? You can't be satisfied with young girls any more. Young girls won't do *this* for you, will they? Or *this*. Feel good? But don't come yet!'"

"You've watched too many porno movies," I said with a laugh.

"You think so? I was kind of worried about that. But I *love* porn films. Take me to one next time, OK?"

"Fine," I said. "Next time you're free."

"Really? I can hardly wait. Let's go to a real S&M one, with whips and, like, they make the girl pee in front of everyone. That's my favourite."

"We'll do it."

"You know what I like best about porn cinemas?"

"I couldn't begin to guess."

"Whenever a sex scene starts, you can hear this 'Gulp!' sound when everybody swallows all at once," said Midori. "I *love* that 'Gulp!' It's so sweet!"

Back in the hospital room, Midori aimed a stream of talk at her father again, and he would either grunt in response or say nothing. Around eleven the wife of the man in the other bed came to change her husband's pyjamas and peel fruit for him and so on. She had a round face and seemed like a nice person, and she and Midori shared a lot of small talk. A nurse showed up with a new intravenous drip and talked a little while with Midori and the wife before she left. I let my eyes wander around the room and out the window to the power lines. Sparrows would turn up every now and then and perch on them. Midori talked to her father and wiped the sweat from his brow and helped him spit phlegm into a tissue and chatted with the neighbouring patient's wife and the nurse and sent an occasional remark my way and checked the intravenous contraption.

The doctor did his rounds at 11.30, so Midori and I stepped outside to wait in the corridor. When he came out, Midori asked him how her father was doing.

"Well, he's just come out of surgery, and we've got him on painkillers so, well, he's pretty drained," said the doctor. "I'll need another two or three days to evaluate the results of the operation. If it went well, he'll be OK, and if it didn't, we'll have to make some decisions at that point."

"You're not going to open his head up again, are you?"

"I really can't say until the time comes," said the doctor. "Wow, that's some short skirt you're wearing!"

"Nice, huh?"

"What do you do on stairways?" the doctor asked.

"Nothing special. I let it all hang out," said Midori. The nurse chuckled behind the doctor.

"Incredible. You ought to come and let us open *your* head one of these days to see what's going on in there. Do me a favour and use the lifts while you're in the hospital. I can't afford to have any more patients. I'm way too busy as it is."

Soon after the doctor's rounds it was lunchtime. A nurse was circulating from room to room pushing a trolley loaded with meals. Midori's father was given pottage, fruit, boiled, deboned fish, and vegetables that had been ground into some kind of jelly. Midori turned him on his back and raised him up using the handle at the foot of the bed. She fed him the soup with a spoon. After five or six swallows, he turned his face aside and said ‹No more›.

"You've got to eat at least this much," Midori said.

‹Later› he said.

"You're hopeless – if you don't eat properly, you'll never get your strength back," she said. "Don't you have to pee yet?"

‹No› he said.

"Hey, Watanabe, let's go down to the cafeteria."

I agreed to go, but in fact I didn't much feel like eating. The cafeteria was packed with doctors, nurses and visitors. Long lines of chairs and tables filled the huge, windowless underground cavern where every mouth seemed to be eating or talking – about sickness, no doubt, the voices echoing and re-echoing as in a tunnel. Now and then the PA system would break through the reverberation with calls for a doctor or nurse. While I laid claim to a table, Midori bought two set meals and carried them over on an aluminium tray. Croquettes with cream sauce, potato salad, shredded cabbage, boiled vegetables, rice and miso soup: these were lined up in the tray in the same white plastic dishes they used for patients. I ate about half of mine and left the rest. Midori seemed to enjoy her meal to the last mouthful.

"Not hungry?" she asked, sipping hot tea.

"Not really," I said.

"It's the hospital," she said, scanning the cafeteria. "This always happens when people aren't used to the place. The smells, the sounds, the stale air, patients' faces, stress, irritation, disappointment, pain, fatigue – that's what does it. It grabs you in the stomach and kills your appetite. Once you get used to it, though, it's no problem at all. Plus, you can't really take care of a sick person unless you eat properly. It's true. I know what I'm talking about because I've done it with my grandfather, my grandmother, my mother, and now my father. You never know when you're going to have to miss your next meal, so it's important to eat when you can."

"I see what you mean," I said.

"Relatives come to visit and they eat with me here, and they always leave half their food, just like you. And they always say, 'Oh, Midori, it's wonderful you've got such a healthy appetite. I'm too upset to eat.' But get serious, *I'm* the one who's actually here taking care of the patient! They just have to drop by and show a little sympathy. *I'm* the one who wipes up the shit and collects the phlegm and mops the brows. If sympathy was all it took to clean up shit, I'd have 50 times as much sympathy as anybody else! Instead, they see me eating all my food and they give me this look and say, 'Oh Midori, you've got such a healthy appetite.' What do they think I am, a donkey pulling a cart? They're old enough to know how the world really works, so why are they so stupid? It's easy to talk big, but the important thing is whether or not you clean up the shit. I can be hurt, you know. I can get as exhausted as anyone else. I can feel so bad I want to cry, too. I mean, *you* try watching a gang of doctors get together and cut open somebody's head when there's no hope of saving them, and stirring things up in there, and doing it again and again, and every time they do it it makes the person worse and a little bit crazier, and see how *you* like it! And on top of it, you see your savings disappear. I don't know if I can keep going to university for another three-and-a-half years, and there's no way my sister can afford a wedding ceremony at this rate."

"How many days a week do you come here?" I asked.

"Usually four," said Midori. "This place claims to offer total nursing care, and the nurses are great, but there's just too much for them to do. Some member of the family has to be around to take up the slack. My sister's watching the shop, and I've got my studies. Still, she manages to get here three days a week, and I come four. And we sneak in every now and then. Believe me, it's a full schedule!"

"How can you spend time with me if you're so busy?"

"I like spending time with you," said Midori, playing with a plastic cup.

"Get out of here for a couple of hours and go for a walk," I said. "I'll take care of your father for a while."

"Why?"

"You need to get away from the hospital and relax by yourself – not talk to anybody, just clear your mind."

Midori thought about it for a minute and nodded. "Hmm, you may be right. But do you know what to do? How to take care of him?"

"I've been watching. I've pretty much got it. You check the intravenous thing, give him water, wipe the sweat off, and help him spit phlegm. The bedpan's under the bed, and if he gets hungry I feed him the rest of his lunch. Anything I can't work out I'll ask the nurse."

"I think that should do it," said Midori with a smile. "There's just one thing, though. He's starting to get a little funny in the head, so he says weird things once in a while – things that nobody can understand. Don't let it bother you if he does that."

"I'll be fine," I said.

Back in the room, Midori told her father she had some business to take care of and that I would be watching him while she was out. He seemed to have nothing to say to this. It might have meant nothing to him. He just lay there on his back, staring at the ceiling. If he hadn't been blinking every once in a while, he could have passed for dead. His eyes were bloodshot as if he had been drinking, and each time he took

246

a deep breath his nostrils flared a little. Other than that, he didn't move a muscle, and made no effort to reply to Midori. I couldn't begin to grasp what he might be thinking or feeling in the murky depths of his consciousness.

After Midori left, I thought I might try speaking to her father, but I had no idea what to say to him or how to say it, so I just kept quiet. Before long, he closed his eyes and went to sleep. I sat on the stool by the head of the bed and studied the occasional twitching of his nose, hoping all the while that he wouldn't die now. How strange it would be, I thought, if this man were to breathe his last with me by his side. After all, I had just met him for the first time in my life, and the only thing binding us together was Midori, a girl I happened to know from my History of Drama class.

He was not dying, though, just sleeping peacefully. Bringing my ear close to his face, I could hear his faint breathing. I relaxed and chatted to the wife of the man in the next bed. She talked of nothing but Midori, assuming I was her boyfriend.

"She's a really wonderful girl," she said. "She takes great care of her father; she's kind and gentle and sensitive and solid, and on top of all that, she's pretty. You'd better treat her right. Don't ever let her go. You won't find another one like her."

"I'll treat her right," I said without elaborating.

"I have a son and daughter at home. He's 17, she's 21, and neither of them would ever think of coming to the hospital. The minute school finishes, they're off surfing or dating or whatever. They're terrible. They squeeze me for all the pocket money they can get and then they disappear."

At 1.30 she left the hospital to do some shopping. Both men were sound asleep. Gentle afternoon sunlight flooded the room, and I felt as though I might drift off at any moment perching on my stool. Yellow and white chrysanthemums in a vase on the table by the window reminded people it was autumn. In the air floated the sweet smell of boiled fish left over from lunch. The nurses continued to clip-clop up and down the hall, talking to each other in clear, penetrating voices. They would peep into the room now and then and flash me a smile when they saw that both patients were sleeping. I wished I had something to read, but there were no books or magazines or newspapers in the room, just a calendar on the wall.

I thought about Naoko. I thought about her naked, wearing only her hairslide. I thought about the curve of her waist and the dark shadow of her pubic hair. Why had she shown herself to me like that? Had she been sleep-walking? Or was it just a fantasy of mine? As time went by and that little world receded into the distance, I grew increasingly uncertain whether the events of that night had actually happened. If I told myself they were real, I believed they were, and if I told myself they were a fantasy, they seemed like a fantasy. They were too clear and detailed to have been a fantasy, and too whole and beautiful to have been real: Naoko's body and the moonlight.

Midori's father woke suddenly and started coughing, which put a stop to my daydreaming. I helped him spit his phlegm into a tissue, and wiped the sweat from his brow with a towel.

"Would you like some water?" I asked, to which he gave a four-millimetre nod. I held the small glass water bottle so that he could sip a little bit at a time, dry lips trembling, throat twitching. He drank every bit of the lukewarm water in the bottle.

"Would you like some more?" I asked. He seemed to be trying to speak, so I brought my ear closer.

248

‹That's enough› he said in a small, dry voice – a voice even smaller and dryer than before.

"Why don't you eat something? You must be hungry." He answered with a slight nod. As Midori had done, I cranked his bed up and started feeding him alternating spoonfuls of vegetable jelly and boiled fish. It took an incredibly long time to get through half his food, at which point he shook his head a little to signal he had had enough. The movement was almost imperceptible; it apparently hurt him to make larger gestures.

"What about the fruit?" I asked him.

‹No› he said. I wiped the corners of his mouth with a towel and made the bed level again before taking the dishes to the corridor.

"Was that good?" I asked him.

‹Awful› he answered.

"Yeah," I said with a smile. "It looked pretty bad." Midori's father could not seem to decide whether to open his eyes further or close them as he lay there silently, staring at me. I wondered if he knew who I was. He seemed more relaxed when alone with me than when Midori was around. He had probably mistaken me for someone else. Or at least that was how I preferred to think of it.

"Beautiful day out there," I said, perching on the stool and crossing my legs. "It's autumn, Sunday, great weather, and crowded everywhere you go. Relaxing indoors like this is the best thing you can do on such a nice day. It's exhausting in those crowds. And the air is bad. I mostly do laundry on Sundays – wash the stuff in the morning, hang it out on the roof of my dorm, take it in before the sun goes down, do a good job of ironing it. I don't mind ironing at all. There's a special satisfaction in making wrinkled things smooth. And

I'm pretty good at it, too. Of course I was terrible at it at first. I put creases in everything. After a month of practice, though, I knew what I was doing. So Sunday is my day for laundry and ironing. I couldn't do it today, of course. Too bad: wasted a perfect laundry day.

"That's OK, though. I'll wake up early and take care of it tomorrow. Don't worry. I've got nothing else to do on a Sunday.

"After I do my laundry tomorrow morning and hang it out to dry, I'll go to my ten o'clock class. It's the one I'm in with Midori: History of Drama. I'm working on Euripides. Are you familiar with Euripides? He was an ancient Greek – one of the 'Big Three' of Greek tragedy along with Aeschylus and Sophocles. He supposedly died when a dog bit him in Macedonia, but not everybody believes this. Anyway, that's Euripides. I like Sophocles better, but I suppose it's a matter of taste. I really can't say which is better.

"What marks his plays is the way things get so mixed up the characters are trapped. Do you see what I mean? Lots of different people appear, and they all have their own situations and reasons and excuses, and each one is pursuing his or her own idea of justice or happiness. As a result, nobody can do anything. Obviously. I mean, it's basically impossible for *everybody's* justice to prevail or *everybody's* happiness to triumph, so chaos takes over. And then what do you think happens? Simple – a god appears at the end and starts directing the traffic. '*You* go over *there*, and *you* come *here*, and *you* get together with *her*, and *you* just sit still for while.' Like that. He's a kind of fixer, and in the end everything works out perfectly. They call this '*deus ex machina*'. There's almost always a *deus ex machina* in Euripides, and that's where critical opinion divides over him.

"But think about it – what if there were a *deus ex machina* in real life? Everything would be so easy! If you felt stuck or trapped, some god would swing down from up there and solve all your problems. What could be easier than that? Anyway, that's History of Drama. This is more or less the kind of stuff we study at university."

Midori's father said nothing, but he kept his vacant eyes on me the whole time I was talking. Of course, I couldn't tell from those eyes whether he understood anything I was saying.

"Peace," I said.

After all that talk, I felt starved. I had had next to nothing for breakfast and had eaten only half my lunch. Now I was sorry I hadn't eaten more at lunch, but feeling sorry wasn't going to help. I looked in a cabinet for something to eat, but found only a can of nori, some Vicks cough drops and soy sauce. The paper bag was still there with the cucumbers and grapefruit.

"I'm going to eat some cucumbers if you don't mind," I said to Midori's father. He didn't answer. I washed three cucumbers in the sink and dribbled a little soy sauce into a dish. Then I wrapped a cucumber in nori, dipped it in soy sauce and gobbled it down.

"Mmm, great!" I said to Midori's father. "Fresh, simple, smells like life. Really good cucumbers. A far more sensible food than kiwi fruit."

I polished off one cucumber and attacked the next. The sickroom echoed with the sound of me munching cucumbers. Only after I had finished the second whole cucumber was I ready to take a break. I boiled some water on the gas burner in the hall and made tea.

"Would you like something to drink? Water? Juice?" I asked Midori's father.

‹Cucumber› he said.

"Great," I said with a smile. "With nori?"

He gave a little nod. I cranked the bed up again. Then I cut a bite-sized piece of cucumber, wrapped it with a strip of nori, stabbed the combination with a toothpick, dipped it in soy sauce, and delivered it to the patient's waiting mouth. With almost no change of expression, Midori's father crunched down on the piece again and again and finally swallowed it.

"How was that? Good, huh?"

‹Good› he said.

"It's good when food tastes good," I said. "It's kind of like proof you're alive."

He ended up eating the entire cucumber. When he had finished it, he wanted water, so I gave him a drink from the bottle. A few minutes later, he said he needed to pee, so I took the urine jar from under the bed and held it by the tip of his penis. Afterwards I emptied the jar into the toilet and washed it out. Then I went back to the sickroom and finished my tea.

"How are you feeling?" I asked.

‹My . . . head› he said.

"Hurts?"

‹A little› he said with a slight frown.

"Well, no wonder, you've just had an operation. Of course, I've never had one, so I don't know what it's like."

‹Ticket› he said.

"Ticket? What ticket?"

‹Midori› he said. ‹Ticket›.

I had no idea what he was talking about, and just kept quiet. He stayed silent for a time, too. Then he seemed to say ‹Please›. He opened his eyes wide and looked at me hard. I guessed that he was trying to tell me something, but I couldn't begin to imagine what it was.

252

‹Ueno› he said. ‹Midori›.

"Ueno Station?"

He gave a little nod.

I tried to summarize what he was getting at: "Ticket, Midori, please, Ueno Station," but I had no idea what it meant. I assumed his mind was muddled, but compared with before his eyes now had a terrible clarity. He raised the arm that was free of the intravenous contraption and stretched it towards me. This must have been a major effort for him, the way the hand trembled in mid-air. I stood and grasped his frail, wrinkled hand. He returned my grasp with what little strength he could muster and said again ‹Please›.

"Don't worry," I said. "I'll take care of the ticket and Midori, too." He let his hand drop back to the bed and closed his eyes. Then, with a loud rush of breath, he fell asleep. I checked to make sure he was still alive, then went out to boil more water for tea. As I was sipping the hot liquid, I realized that I had developed a kind of liking for this little man on the verge of death.

The wife of the other patient came back a few minutes later and asked if everything was OK. I assured her it was. Her husband, too, was sound asleep, breathing deeply.

Midori came back after three.

"I was in the park, spacing out," she said. "I did what you told me, didn't talk to anybody, just let my head go empty."

"How was it?"

"Thanks, I feel much better. I still have that draggy, tired feeling, but my body feels much lighter than before. I guess I was more tired than I realized."

With her father sound asleep, there was nothing for us to do, so we bought coffee from a vending machine and drank it in the TV room. I reported to Midori on what had happened in her absence – that her father had had a good sleep, then woke up and ate some of what was left of his lunch, then saw me eating a cucumber and asked for one himself, ate the whole thing and peed.

"Watanabe, you're amazing," said Midori. "We're all going crazy trying to get him to eat anything, and you got him to eat a whole cucumber! Incredible!"

"I don't know, I think he just saw me enjoying my own cucumber."

"Or maybe you just have this knack for relaxing people."

"No way," I said with a laugh. "A lot of people will tell you just the opposite about me."

"What do you think about my father?"

"I like him. Not that we had all that much to say to each other. But, I don't know, he seems nice."

"Was he quiet?"

"Very."

"You should have seen him a week ago. He was awful," Midori said, shaking her head. "Kind of lost his marbles and went wild. Threw a glass at me and yelled terrible stuff – 'I hope you die, you stupid bitch!' This sickness can do that to people. They don't know why, but it can make people get really vicious all of a sudden. It was the same with my mother. What do you think she said to me? 'You're not my daughter! I hate your guts!' The whole world turned black for me for a second when she said that. But that kind of thing is one of the features of this particular sickness. Something presses on a part of the brain and makes people say all kinds of nasty things. You *know* it's just part of the sickness, but still, it hurts. What do you expect? Here I am, working my fingers to the bone for them, and they're saying all this terrible stuff to me."

"I know what you mean," I said. Then I remembered the strange fragments that Midori's father had mumbled to me.

"Ticket? Ueno Station?" Midori said. "I wonder what that's all about?"

"And then he said, *Please*, and *Midori*."

"'Please take care of Midori?'"

"Or maybe he wants you to go to Ueno and buy a ticket. The order of the four words is such a mess, who knows what he means? Does Ueno Station mean anything special to you?"

"Hmm, Ueno Station." Midori thought about it for a while. "The only thing I can think of is the two times I ran away, when I was eight and when I was ten. Both times I took a train from Ueno to Fukushima. Bought the tickets with money I took from the till. Somebody at home made me really angry, and I did it to get even. I had an aunt in Fukushima, I kind of liked her, so I went to her house. My father was the one who brought me home. Came all the way to Fukushima to get me – a hundred miles! We ate boxed lunches on the train to Ueno. My father told me all kinds of stuff while we were travelling, just little bits and pieces with long spaces in between. Like about the big earthquake of 1923 or about the war or about the time I was born, stuff he didn't usually talk about. Come to think of it, those were the only times my father and I had something like a good, long talk, just the two of us. Hey, can you believe this? – my father was smack bang in the middle of Tokyo during one of the biggest earthquakes in history and he didn't even notice it!"

"No way!"

"It's true! He was riding through Koishikawa with a cart on the back of his bike, and he didn't feel a thing. When he got home, all the tiles had fallen off the roofs in the neighbourhood, and everyone in the family was hugging pillars and quaking in their boots. He still didn't get it and, the way he tells it, he asked, 'What the hell's going on here?' That's my father's 'fond recollection' of the Great Kanto Earthquake!" Midori laughed. "All his stories of the old days are like that. No drama whatsoever. They're all just a little bit off-centre. I don't know, when he tells those stories, you kind of get the feeling like nothing important has happened in Japan for the past 50 or 60 years. The young officers' uprising of 1936, the Pacific War, they're all kind of 'Oh yeah, now that you mention it, I guess something like that once happened' kind of things. It's so funny!

"So, anyway, on the train, he'd tell me these stories in bits and pieces while we were riding from Fukushima to Ueno. And at the end, he'd always say, 'So that goes to show you, Midori, it's the same wherever you go.' I was young enough to be impressed by stuff like that."

"So is that *your* 'fond recollection' of Ueno Station?" I asked.

"Yeah," said Midori. "Did you ever run away from home, Watanabe?"

"Never."

"Why not?"

"Lack of imagination. It never occurred to me to run away."

"You are *so weird*!" Midori said, cocking her head as though truly impressed.

"I wonder," I said.

"Well, anyway, I think my father was trying to say he wanted you to look after me."

"Really?"

"Really! I understand things like that. Intuitively. So tell me, what was your answer to him?"

"Well, I didn't understand what he was saying, so I just said OK, don't worry, I'd take care of both you and the ticket."

"You promised my father that? You said you'd take care of me?" She looked me straight in the eye with a dead-serious expression on her face.

"Not like *that*," I hastened to correct her. "I really didn't know *what* he was saying, and – "

"Don't worry, I'm just kidding," she said with a smile. "I love that about you."

Midori and I finished our coffee and went back to the room. Her father was still sound asleep. If you leaned close you could hear his steady breathing. As the afternoon deepened, the light outside the hospital window changed to the soft, gentle colour of autumn. A flock of birds rested on the electric wire outside, then flew on. Midori and I sat in a corner of the room, talking quietly the whole time. She read my palm and predicted that I would live to 105, marry three times, and die in a traffic accident. "Not a bad life," I said.

When her father woke just after four o'clock, Midori went to sit by his pillow, wiped the sweat from his brow, gave him water, and asked him about the pain in his head. A nurse came and took his temperature, recorded the number of his urinations, and checked the intravenous equipment. I went to the TV room and watched a little football.

At five I told Midori I would be leaving. To her father I explained, "I have to go to work now. I sell records in Shinjuku from six to 10.30."

He turned his eyes to me and gave a little nod.

"Hey, Watanabe, I don't know how to put this, but I *really* want to thank you for today," Midori said to me when she saw me to reception.

"I didn't do that much," I said. "But if I can be of any help, I'll come next week, too. I'd like to see your father again."

"Really?"

"Well, there's not that much for me to do in the dorm, and if I come here I get to eat cucumbers."

Midori folded her arms and tapped the linoleum with the heel of her shoe.

"I'd like to go drinking with you again," she said, cocking her head slightly.

"How about the porno movies?"

"We'll do that first and *then* go drinking. And we'll talk about all the usual disgusting things."

"*I'm* not the one who talks about disgusting things," I protested. "It's *you*."

"Anyway, we'll talk about things like that and get plastered and go to bed."

"And you know what happens next," I said with a sigh. "I try to do it, and you don't let me. Right?"

She laughed through her nose.

"Anyway," I said, "pick me up again next Sunday morning. We'll come here together."

"With me in a little longer skirt?"

"Definitely," I said.

I didn't go to the hospital that next Sunday, though. Midori's father died on Friday morning.

She called at 6.30 in the morning to tell me that. The buzzer letting me know I had a phone call went off and I ran down to the lobby with a cardigan thrown over my pyjamas. A cold rain was falling silently.

"My father died a few minutes ago," Midori said in a small, quiet voice. I asked her if there was anything I could do. "Thanks," she said. "There's really nothing. We're used to funerals. I just wanted to let you know."

A kind of sigh escaped her lips.

"Don't come to the funeral, OK? I hate stuff like that. I don't want to see you there."

"I get it," I said.

"Will you really take me to a porno movie?"

"Of course I will."

"A really disgusting one."

"I'll research the matter thoroughly."

"Good. I'll call you," she said and hung up.

A week went by without a word from Midori. No calls, no sign of her in the lecture hall. I kept hoping for a message from her whenever I went back to the dorm, but there were never any. One night, I tried to keep my promise by thinking of her when I masturbated, but it didn't work. I tried switching over to Naoko, but not even Naoko's image was any help that time. It seemed so ridiculous I gave up. I took a swig of whisky, brushed my teeth and went to bed.

I wrote a letter to Naoko on Sunday morning. One thing I told her about was Midori's father. *I went to the hospital to visit the father of a girl in one of my lectures and ate some cucumbers in his room. When he heard me crunching on them, he wanted some too, and he ate his with the same crunching sound. Five days later, though, he died. I still have a vivid memory of the tiny crunching he made when he chewed his pieces of cucumber. People leave strange, little memories of themselves behind when they die.* My letter went on:

> I think of you and Reiko and the aviary while I lie in
> bed after waking up in the morning. I think about the
> peacock and pigeons and parrots and turkeys – and
> about the rabbits. I remember the yellow raincapes
> you and Reiko wore with the hoods up that rainy

259

morning. It feels good to think about you when I'm warm in bed. I feel as if you're curled up there beside me, fast asleep. And I think how great it would be if it were true.

I miss you terribly sometimes, but in general I go on living with all the energy I can muster. Just as you take care of the birds and the fields every morning, every morning I wind my own spring. I give it some 36 good twists by the time I've got up, brushed my teeth, shaved, eaten breakfast, changed my clothes, left the dorm, and arrived at the university. I tell myself, "OK, let's make this day another good one." I hadn't noticed before, but they tell me I talk to myself a lot these days. Probably mumbling to myself while I wind my spring.

It's hard not being able to see you, but my life in Tokyo would be a lot worse if it weren't for you. It's because I think of you when I'm in bed in the morning that I can wind my spring and tell myself I have to live another good day. I know I have to give it my best here just as you are doing there.

Today's Sunday, though, a day I don't wind my spring. I've done my laundry, and now I'm in my room, writing to you. Once I've finished this letter and put a stamp on it and dropped it into the postbox, there's nothing for me to do until the sun goes down. I don't study on Sundays, either. I do a good enough job on weekdays studying in the library between lectures, so I don't have anything left to do on Sundays. Sunday afternoons are quiet, peaceful and, for me, lonely. I read books or listen to music. Sometimes I think back on the different routes we used to take in our Sunday walks around Tokyo. I can come up with a pretty clear picture of the clothes you were wearing on any particular walk. I remember all kinds of things on Sunday afternoons.

Say "Hi" from me to Reiko. I really miss her guitar at night.

When I had finished the letter, I walked a couple of blocks to a postbox, then bought an egg sandwich and a Coke at a nearby bakery. I had these for lunch while I sat on a bench and watched some boys playing baseball in a local playground. The deepening of autumn had brought an increased blueness and depth to the sky. I glanced up to find two vapour trails heading off to the west in perfect parallel like tram tracks. A foul ball came rolling my way, and when I threw it back to them the young players doffed their caps with a polite "Thank you, sir". As in most junior baseball, there were lots of walks and stolen bases.

After noon I went back to my room to read but couldn't concentrate. Instead I found myself staring at the ceiling and thinking about Midori. I wondered if her father had really been trying to ask me to look after her when he was gone, but I had no way of telling what had been on his mind. He had probably confused me with somebody else. In any case, he had died on a Friday morning when a cold rain was falling, and now it was impossible to know the truth. I imagined that, in death, he had shrivelled up smaller than ever. And then they had burned him in an oven until he was nothing but ashes. And what had he left behind? A nothing-much bookshop in a nothing-much neighbourhood and two daughters, at least one of whom was more than a little strange. What kind of life was that? I wondered. Lying in that hospital bed with his cut-open head and his muddled brain, what had been on his mind as he looked at me?

Thinking thoughts like this about Midori's father put me into such a miserable mood that I had to bring the laundry down from the roof before it was really dry and set off for Shinjuku to kill time walking the streets. The Sunday crowds gave me some relief. The Kinokuniya bookshop was as jam-packed as a rush-hour train. I bought a copy of Faulkner's *Light in August* and went to the noisiest jazz café I could think of, reading my new book while listening to Ornette Coleman and Bud Powell and drinking hot, thick, foul-tasting coffee. At 5.30 I closed my book, went outside and ate a light supper. How many Sundays – how many hundreds of Sundays like this – lay ahead of me? "Quiet, peaceful, and lonely," I said aloud to myself. On Sundays, I didn't wind my spring.

第 8 章

Halfway through that week I managed to cut my palm open on a piece of broken glass. I hadn't noticed that one of the glass partitions in a record shelf was cracked. I could hardly believe how much blood gushed out of me, turning the floor bright red at my feet. The shop manager found some towels and tied them tightly around the wound. Then he made a phone call to casualty. He was a pretty useless guy most of the time, but he acted with surprising efficiency. The hospital was nearby, fortunately, but by the time I got there the towels were soaked in red, and the blood they couldn't soak up had been dripping on the tarmac. People scurried out of the way for me. They seemed to think I had been injured in a fight. I felt no pain to speak of, but the blood wouldn't stop.

The doctor was cool as he removed the blood-soaked towels, stopped the bleeding with a tourniquet on my wrist, disinfected the wound and sewed it up, telling me to come again the next day. Back at the record shop, the manager told me to go home: he would put me down as having worked my shift. I took a bus to the dorm and went straight to Nagasawa's room. With my nerves on edge over the cut, I wanted to talk to somebody, and I hadn't seen Nagasawa for a long time.

I found him in his room, drinking a can of beer and

watching a Spanish lesson on TV. "What the hell happened to you?" he asked when he saw my bandage. I said I had cut myself but that it was nothing much. He offered me a beer and I said no thanks.

"Just wait. This'll be over in a minute," said Nagasawa, and he went on practising his Spanish pronunciation. I boiled some water and made myself a cup of tea with a tea bag. A Spanish woman recited example sentences: "I have never seen such terrible rain!", "Many bridges were washed away in Barcelona." Nagasawa read the text aloud in Spanish. "What awful sentences!" he said. "This kind of shit is all they ever give you."

When the programme ended, he turned off the TV and took another beer from his small refrigerator.

"Are you sure I'm not in the way?" I asked.

"No way. I was bored out of my mind. Sure you don't want a beer?"

"No, I really don't," I said.

"Oh, yeah, they posted the exam results the other day. I passed!"

"The Foreign Ministry exam?"

"That's it. Officially, it's called the 'Foreign Affairs Public Service Personnel First Class Service Examination'. What a joke!"

"Congratulations!" I said and gave him my left hand to shake.

"Thanks."

"Of course, I'm not surprised you passed."

"No, neither am I," laughed Nagasawa. "But it's nice to have it official."

"Think you'll go abroad once you get in?"

"Nah, first they give you a year of training. Then they send you overseas for a while."

I sipped my tea, and he drank his beer with obvious satisfaction.

"I'll give you this fridge if you'd like it when I get out of here," said Nagasawa. "You'd like to have it, wouldn't you? It's great for beer."

"Yeah, I'd like to have it, but won't you need it? You'll be living in a flat or something."

"Don't be stupid! When I get out of this place, I'm buying myself a big fridge. I'm gonna live the high life! Four years in a shithole like this is long enough. I don't want to have to *look* at anything I used in this place. You name it, I'll give it to you – the TV, the thermos flask, the radio . . ."

"I'll take anything you want to give me," I said. I picked up the Spanish textbook on his desk and stared at it. "You're starting Spanish?"

"Yeah. The more languages you know the better. And I've got a knack for them. I taught myself French and it's practically perfect. Languages are like games. You learn the rules for one, and they all work the same way. Like women."

"Ah, the reflective life!" I said with a sarcastic edge.

"Anyway, let's eat out soon."

"You mean cruising for women?"

"No, a real dinner. You, me and Hatsumi at a good restaurant. To celebrate my new job. My old man's paying, so we'll go somewhere really expensive."

"Shouldn't it just be you and Hatsumi?"

"No, it'd be better with you there. I'd be more comfortable, and so would Hatsumi."

Oh no, it was Kizuki, Naoko and me all over again.

"I'll spend the night at Hatsumi's afterwards, so join us just for the meal."

"OK, if you both really want me to," I said. "But, anyway,

what are you planning to do about Hatsumi? You'll be assigned overseas when you finish your training, and you probably won't come back for years. What's going to happen to her?"

"That's her problem."

"I don't get it," I said.

Feet on his desk, Nagasawa took a swig of beer and yawned.

"Look, I'm not planning to get married. I've made that perfectly clear to Hatsumi. If she wants to marry someone, she should go ahead and do it. I won't stop her. If she wants to wait for me, let her wait. That's what I mean."

"I have to hand it to you," I said.

"You think I'm a shit, don't you?"

"I do."

"Look, the world is an inherently unfair place. I didn't write the rules. It's always been that way. I have never once deceived Hatsumi. She knows I'm a shit and that she can leave me whenever she decides she can't take it. I told her that straight from the start."

Nagasawa finished his beer and lit a cigarette.

"Isn't there anything about life that frightens you?" I asked.

"Hey, I'm not a total idiot," said Nagasawa. "Of *course* life frightens me sometimes. I don't happen to take that as the premise for everything else, though. I'm going to give it 100 per cent and go as far as I can. I'll take what I want and leave what I don't want. That's how I intend to live my life, and if things go bad, I'll stop and reconsider at that point. If you think about it, an unfair society is a society that makes it possible for you to exploit your abilities to the limit."

"Sounds like a pretty self-centred way to live," I said.

"Perhaps, but I'm not just looking up at the sky and waiting

266

for the fruit to drop. In my own way, I'm working hard. I'm working ten times harder than you are."

"That's probably true," I said.

"I look around me sometimes and I get sick to my stomach. Why the hell don't these bastards *do* something? I wonder. They don't do a fucking thing, and then they moan about it."

Amazed at the harshness of his tone, I looked at Nagasawa. "The way I see it, people *are* working hard. They're working their fingers to the bone. Or am I looking at things wrong?"

"That's not hard work. It's just manual labour," Nagasawa said with finality. "The 'hard work' I'm talking about is more self-directed and purposeful."

"You mean, like studying Spanish while everyone else is taking it easy?"

"That's it. I'm going to have Spanish mastered by next spring. I've got English and German and French down pat, and I'm almost there with Italian. You think things like that happen without hard work?"

Nagasawa puffed on his cigarette while I thought about Midori's father. There was one man who had probably never even thought about starting Spanish lessons on TV. He had probably never thought about the difference between hard work and manual labour, either. He was probably too busy to think about such things – busy with work, and busy bringing home a daughter who had run away to Fukushima.

"So, about that dinner of ours," said Nagasawa. "Would this Saturday be OK for you?"

"Fine," I said.

Nagasawa picked a fancy French restaurant in a quiet back-street of Azabu. He gave his name at the door and the two of us were shown to a secluded private room. Some 15 prints hung on the walls of the small chamber. While we waited for Hatsumi to arrive, Nagasawa and I sipped a delicious wine and chatted about the novels of Joseph Conrad. He wore an expensive-looking grey suit. I had on an ordinary blue blazer.

Hatsumi arrived 15 minutes later. She was carefully made up and wore gold earrings, a beautiful deep blue dress, and tasteful red court shoes. When I complimented her on the colour of her dress, she told me it was called midnight blue.

"What an elegant restaurant!" she said.

"My old man always eats here when he comes to Tokyo," said Nagasawa. "I came here with him once. I'm not crazy about these snooty places."

"It doesn't hurt to eat in a place like this once in a while," said Hatsumi. Turning to me, she asked, "Don't you agree?"

"I guess so. As long as I'm not paying."

"My old man usually brings his mistress here," said Nagasawa. "He's got one in Tokyo, you know."

"Really?" asked Hatsumi.

I took a sip of wine, as if I had heard nothing.

Eventually a waiter came and took our orders. After choosing hors d'oeuvres and soup, Nagasawa ordered duck, and Hatsumi and I ordered sea bass. The food arrived at a leisurely pace, which allowed us to enjoy the wine and conversation. Nagasawa spoke first of the Foreign Ministry exam. Most of the examinees were scum who might just as well be thrown into a bottomless pit, he said, though he supposed there were a few decent ones in the bunch. I asked if he thought the ratio of good ones to scum was higher or lower than in society at large.

"It's the same," he said. "Of course." It was the same everywhere, he added: an immutable law.

Nagasawa ordered a second bottle of wine and a double Scotch for himself.

Hatsumi then began talking about a girl she wanted to fix me up with. This was a perpetual topic between us. She was always telling me about some "cute girl in my club", and I was always running away.

"She's *really* nice, though, and *really* cute. I'll bring her along next time. You ought to talk to her. I'm sure you'll like her."

"It's a waste of time, Hatsumi," I said. "I'm too poor to go out with girls from your university. I can't talk to them."

"Don't be silly," she said. "This girl is simple and natural and unaffected."

"Come on, Watanabe," said Nagasawa. "Just meet her. You don't have to screw her."

"I should say *not!*" said Hatsumi. "She's a virgin."

"Like you used to be," said Nagasawa.

"Exactly," said Hatsumi with a bright smile. "Like I used to be. But really," she said to me, "don't give me that stuff about being 'too poor'. It's got nothing to do with it. Sure, there are a few super-stuck-up girls in every year, but the rest of us are just ordinary. We all eat lunch in the school cafeteria for ¥250 – "

"Now wait just a minute, Hatsumi," I said, interrupting her. "In *my* school the cafeteria has three lunches: A, B, and C. The A Lunch is ¥120, the B Lunch is ¥100, and the C Lunch is ¥80. Everybody gives me dirty looks when I eat the A Lunch, and anyone who can't afford the C Lunch eats ramen noodles for ¥60. That's the kind of place I go to. You still think I can talk to girls from yours?"

Hatsumi could barely stop laughing. "That's so *cheap!*" she said. "Maybe *I* should go there for lunch! But really, Toru, you're such a nice guy, I'm sure you'd get along with this girl. She might even like the ¥120 lunch."

"No way," I said with a laugh. "*Nobody* eats that stuff because they like it; they eat it because they can't afford anything else."

"Anyway, don't judge a book by its cover. It's true we go to this hoity-toity establishment, but lots of us there are serious people who think serious thoughts about life. Not *everybody* is looking for a boyfriend with a sports car."

"I know that much," I said.

"Watanabe's got a girl. He's in love," said Nagasawa. "But he won't say a word about her. He's as tight-lipped as they come. A riddle wrapped in an enigma."

"Really?" Hatsumi asked me.

"Really," I said. "But there's no riddle involved here. It's just that it's complicated, and hard to talk about."

"An illicit love? Ooh! You can talk to *me*!"

I took a sip of wine to avoid answering.

"See what I mean?" said Nagasawa, at work on his third whisky. "Tight-lipped. When this guy decides he's not going to talk about something, nobody can drag it out of him."

"What a shame," said Hatsumi as she cut a small slice of terrine and brought it to her lips. "If you'd got on with her, we could have double-dated."

"Yeah, we could've got drunk and done a little swapping," said Nagasawa.

"Enough of that kind of talk," said Hatsumi.

"What do you mean 'that kind of talk'? Watanabe's got his eye on you," said Nagasawa.

"That has nothing to do with what I'm talking about," Hatsumi murmured. "He's not that kind of person. He's sincere and caring. I can tell. That's why I've been trying to fix him up."

270

"Oh, sure, he's sincere. Like the time we swapped women once, way back when. Remember, Watanabe?" Nagasawa said this with a blasé look on his face, then slugged back the rest of his whisky and ordered another.

Hatsumi set her knife and fork down and dabbed at her mouth with her napkin. Then, looking at me, she asked, "Toru, did you really do that?"

I didn't know how to answer her, and so I said nothing.

"Tell her," said Nagasawa. "What the hell." The mood was turning sour. Nagasawa could get nasty when he was drunk, but tonight his nastiness was aimed at Hatsumi, not at me. Knowing that made it all the more difficult for me to go on sitting there.

"I'd like to hear about that," said Hatsumi. "It sounds *very* interesting!"

"We were drunk," I said.

"That's all right, Toru. I'm not blaming you. I just want you to tell me what happened."

"The two of us were drinking in a bar in Shibuya, and we got friendly with this pair of girls. They went to some college, and they were pretty plastered, too. So, anyway, we, uh, went to a hotel and slept with them. Our rooms were right next door to each other. In the middle of the night, Nagasawa knocked on my door and said we should change girls, so I went to his room and he came to mine."

"Didn't the girls mind?"

"No, they were drunk too."

"Anyway, I had a good reason for doing it," said Nagasawa.

"A good reason?"

"Well, the girls were too different. One was really good-looking, but the other one was a dog. It seemed unfair to me. I got the pretty girl, but Watanabe got stuck with the

271

other one. That's why we swapped. Right, Watanabe?"

"Yeah, I s'pose so," I said. But in fact, I had liked the not-pretty one. She was fun to talk to and a nice person. After we had sex, we were enjoying talking to each other in bed when Nagasawa showed up and suggested we change partners. I asked the girl if she minded, and she said it was OK with her if that's what we wanted. She probably thought I wanted to do it with the pretty one.

"Was it fun?" Hatsumi asked me.

"Swapping, you mean?"

"The whole thing."

"Not especially. It's just something you do. Sleeping with girls that way is not all that much fun."

"So why do you do it?"

"Because of me," said Nagasawa.

"I'm asking Toru," Hatsumi shot back at Nagasawa. "Why do you do something like that?"

"Because sometimes I have this tremendous desire to sleep with a girl."

"If you're in love with someone, can't you manage one way or another with her?" Hatsumi asked after a few moments' thought.

"It's complicated."

Hatsumi sighed.

At that point the door opened and the food was carried in. Nagasawa was presented with his roast duck, and Hatsumi and I received our sea bass. The waiters heaped fresh-cooked vegetables on our plates and dribbled sauce on them before withdrawing and leaving the three of us alone again. Nagasawa cut a slice of duck and ate it with gusto, followed by more whisky. I took a forkful of spinach. Hatsumi didn't touch her food.

272

"You know, Toru," she said, "I have no idea what makes your situation so 'complicated', but I do think that the kind of thing you just told me about is not right for you. You're not that kind of person. What do you think?" She placed her hands on the table and looked me in the eye.

"Well," I said, "I've felt that way myself sometimes."

"So why don't you stop?"

"Because sometimes I have a need for human warmth," I answered honestly. "Sometimes, if I can't feel something like the warmth of a woman's skin, I get so lonely I can't stand it."

"Here, let me summarize what I think it's all about," interjected Nagasawa. "Watanabe's got this girl he likes, but for certain complicated reasons, they can't do it. So he tells himself 'Sex is just sex', and he takes care of his need with somebody else. What's wrong with that? It makes perfect sense. He can't just stay locked in his room tossing off all the time, can he?"

"But if you really love her, Toru, shouldn't it be possible for you to control yourself?"

"Maybe so," I said, bringing a piece of sea bass in cream sauce to my mouth.

"You just don't understand a man's sexual needs," said Nagasawa to Hatsumi. "Look at me, for example. I've been with you for three years, and I've slept with plenty of women in that time. But I don't remember a thing about them. I don't know their names, I don't remember their faces. I slept with each of them exactly once. Meet 'em, do it, so long. That's it. What's wrong with that?"

"What I can't stand is that arrogance of yours," said Hatsumi in a soft voice. "Whether you sleep with other women or not is beside the point. I've never really been angry with you for sleeping around, have I?"

"You can't even call what I do sleeping around. It's just a game. Nobody gets hurt," said Nagasawa.

"*I* get hurt," said Hatsumi. "Why am I not enough for you?"

Nagasawa kept silent for a moment and swirled the whisky in his glass. "It's not that you're not enough for me. That's another phase, another question. It's just a hunger I have inside me. If I've hurt you, I'm sorry. But it's not a question of whether or not you're enough for me. I can only live with that hunger. That's the kind of man I am. That's what makes me *me*. There's nothing I can do about it, don't you see?"

At last Hatsumi picked up her silverware and started eating her fish. "At least you shouldn't drag Toru into your 'games'."

"We're a lot alike, though, Watanabe and me," said Nagasawa. "Neither of us is interested, essentially, in anything but ourselves. OK, so I'm arrogant and he's not, but neither of us is able to feel any interest in anything other than what we ourselves think or feel or do. That's why we can think about things in a way that's totally divorced from anybody else. That's what I like about him. The only difference is that he hasn't realized this about himself, and so he hesitates and feels hurt."

"What human being *doesn't* hesitate and feel hurt?" Hatsumi demanded. "Are you trying to say that *you* have never felt those things?"

"Of course I have, but I've disciplined myself to where I can minimize them. Even a rat will choose the least painful route if you shock him enough."

"But rats don't fall in love."

"'Rats don't fall in love'." Nagasawa looked at me. "That's great. We should have background music for this – a full orchestra with two harps and – "

"Don't make fun of me. I'm serious."

"We're eating," said Nagasawa. "And Watanabe's here. It might be more civil for us to confine 'serious' talk to another occasion."

"I can leave," I said.

"No," said Hatsumi. "Please stay. It's better with you here."

"At least have dessert," said Nagasawa.

"I don't mind, really."

The three of us went on eating in silence for a time. I finished my fish. Hatsumi left half of hers. Nagasawa had polished off his duck long before and was now concentrating on his whisky.

"That was excellent sea bass," I offered, but no one took me up on it. I might as well have thrown a rock down a deep well.

The waiters took away our plates and brought lemon sherbet and espresso. Nagasawa barely touched his dessert and coffee, moving directly to a cigarette. Hatsumi ignored her sherbet. "Oh boy," I thought to myself as I finished my sherbet and coffee. Hatsumi stared at her hands on the table. Like everything she wore, her hands looked chic and elegant and expensive. I thought about Naoko and Reiko. What would they be doing now? I wondered. Naoko could be lying on the sofa reading a book, and Reiko might be playing "Norwegian Wood" on her guitar. I felt an intense desire to go back to that little room of theirs. What the hell was I doing in this place?

"Where Watanabe and I are alike is, we don't give a shit if nobody understands us," Nagasawa said. "That's what makes us different from everybody else. They're all worried about whether the people around them understand them. But not me, and not Watanabe. We just don't give a shit. Self and others are separate."

"Is this true?" Hatsumi asked me.

"No," I said. "I'm not that strong. I don't feel it's OK if

275

nobody understands me. I've got people I want to understand and be understood by. But aside from those few, well, I feel it's kind of hopeless. I don't agree with Nagasawa. I *do* care if people understand me."

"That's practically the same thing as what I'm saying," said Nagasawa, picking up his coffee spoon. "It *is* the same! It's the difference between a late breakfast or an early lunch. Same time, same food, different name."

Now Hatsumi spoke to Nagasawa. "Don't you care whether *I* understand you or not?"

"You don't get it, do you? Person A understands Person B because the *time* is right for that to happen, not because Person B *wants to be understood by* Person A."

"So is it a mistake for me to feel that I want to be understood by someone – by *you*, for example?"

"No, it's not a mistake," answered Nagasawa. "Most people would call that love, if you think you want to understand me. My system for living is way different from other people's systems for living."

"So what you're saying is you're not in love with me, is that it?"

"Well, my system and your – "

"To hell with your fucking system!" Hatsumi shouted. That was the first and last time I ever heard her shout.

Nagasawa pushed the button by the table, and the waiter came in with the bill. Nagasawa handed him a credit card.

"Sorry about this, Watanabe," said Nagasawa. "I'm going to see Hatsumi home. You go back to the dorm alone, OK?"

"You don't have to apologize to me. Great meal," I said, but no one said anything in response.

The waiter brought the card, and Nagasawa signed with a ballpoint pen after checking the amount. Then the three of us stood and went outside. Nagasawa started to step into the street to hail a taxi, but Hatsumi stopped him.

"Thanks, but I don't want to spend any more time with you today. You don't have to see me home. Thank you for dinner."

"Whatever," said Nagasawa.

"I want Toru to see me home."

"Whatever," said Nagasawa. "But Watanabe's practically the same as me. He may be a nice guy, but deep down in his heart he's incapable of loving anybody. There's always some part of him somewhere that's wide awake and detached. He just has that hunger that won't go away. Believe me, I know what I'm talking about."

I flagged down a taxi and let Hatsumi in first. "Anyway," I said to Nagasawa, "I'll make sure she gets home."

"Sorry to put you through this," said Nagasawa, but I could see that he was already thinking about something else.

Once inside the cab, I asked Hatsumi, "Where do you want to go? Back to Ebisu?" Her flat was in Ebisu.

She shook her head.

"OK. How about a drink somewhere?"

"Yes," she said with a nod.

"Shibuya," I told the driver.

Folding her arms and closing her eyes, Hatsumi sank back into the corner of the seat. Her small gold earrings caught the light as the taxi swayed. Her midnight-blue dress seemed to have been made to match the darkness of the interior. Every now and then her lightly made-up, beautifully formed lips would quiver slightly as though she had caught herself on the verge of talking to herself. Watching her, I could see why Nagasawa had chosen her as his special companion. There were any number of women more beautiful than Hatsumi, and Nagasawa could have made any of them his. But Hatsumi had some quality that could send a tremor through your heart. It was nothing forceful. The power she exerted was a subtle thing, but it called forth deep resonances. I watched her all the way to Shibuya, and wondered, without ever finding an answer, what this emotional reverberation could be that I was feeling.

It finally hit me some dozen or so years later. I had gone to Santa Fe to interview a painter and was sitting in a local pizza parlour, drinking beer and eating pizza and watching a miraculously beautiful sunset. Everything was soaked in brilliant red – my hand, the plate, the table, the world – as if some special kind of fruit juice had splashed down on everything. In the midst of this overwhelming sunset, the image of Hatsumi flashed into my mind, and in that moment I understood what that tremor of the heart had been. It was a kind of childhood longing that had always remained – and would for ever remain – unfulfilled. I had forgotten the existence of such innocent, almost burnt-in longing: forgotten for years that such feelings had ever existed inside me. What Hatsumi had stirred in me was a part of my very self that had long lain dormant. And when the realization struck me, it aroused such sorrow I almost burst into tears. She had been an absolutely special woman. Someone should have done something – anything – to save her.

But neither Nagasawa nor I could have managed that. As so many of those I knew had done, Hatsumi reached a certain stage in life and decided – almost on the spur of the moment – to end it. Two years after Nagasawa left for Germany, she married, and two years after that she slashed her wrists with a razor blade.

It was Nagasawa, of course, who told me what had

happened. His letter from Bonn said this: "Hatsumi's death has extinguished something. This is unbearably sad and painful, even to me." I ripped his letter to shreds and threw it away. I never wrote to him again.

Hatsumi and I went to a small bar and downed several drinks. Neither of us said much. Like a bored, old married couple, we sat opposite each other, drinking in silence and munching peanuts. When the place began to fill up, we went for a walk. Hatsumi said she would pay the bill, but I insisted on paying because the drinks had been my idea.

There was a deep chill in the night air. Hatsumi wrapped herself in her pale grey cardigan and walked by my side in silence. I had no destination in mind as we ambled through the nighttime streets, my hands shoved deep into my pockets. This was just like walking with Naoko, it occurred to me.

"Do you know somewhere we could play pool around here?" Hatsumi asked me without warning.

"Pool? You play?"

"Yeah, I'm pretty good. How about you?"

"I play a little. Not that I'm very good at it."

"OK, then. Let's go."

We found a pool hall nearby and went in. It was a small place at the far end of an alley. The two of us – Hatsumi in her chic dress and I in my blue blazer and regimental tie – clashed with the scruffy pool hall, but this didn't seem to concern Hatsumi at all as she chose and chalked her cue. She pulled a hairslide from her bag and clipped her hair aside at one temple to keep it from interfering with her game.

We played two games. Hatsumi was as good as she had claimed to be, while my own game was hampered by the thick bandage I still wore on my cut hand. She crushed me.

"You're great," I said in admiration.

"You mean appearances can be deceiving?" she asked as she sized up a shot, smiling.

"Where did you learn to play like that?"

"My grandfather – my father's father – was an old playboy. He had a table in his house. I used to play pool with my brother just for fun, and when I got a little bigger my grandfather taught me the right moves. He was a wonderful guy – stylish, handsome. He's dead now, though. He always used to boast how he once met Deanna Durbin in New York."

She got three in a row, then missed on the fourth try. I managed to squeeze out a point, then missed an easy shot.

"It's the bandage," said Hatsumi to comfort me.

"No, it's because I haven't played for so long," I said. "Two years and five months."

"How can you be so sure of the time?"

"My friend died the night after our last game together," I said.

"So you stopped playing?"

"No, not really," I said after giving it some thought. "I just never had the opportunity to play after that. That's all."

"How did your friend die?"

"Traffic accident."

She made several more shots, aiming with deadly seriousness and adjusting the strength of each shot with precision. Watching her in action – her carefully set hair swept back out of her eyes, golden earrings sparkling, court shoes set firmly on the floor, lovely, slender fingers pressing the green baize as she took her shot – I felt as if her side of the scruffy pool hall had been transformed into part of some elegant social event. I had never spent time with her alone before, and this was a marvellous experience for me, as though I had been drawn up to a higher plane of life. At the end of the third game – in which, of course, she crushed me again – my cut began to throb, and so we stopped playing.

"I'm sorry," she said with what seemed like genuine concern, "I should never have suggested this."

"That's OK," I said. "It's not a bad cut, I enjoyed playing. Really."

As we were leaving the pool hall, the skinny woman owner said to Hatsumi, "You've a good eye, sister." Hatsumi gave her a sweet smile and thanked her as she paid the bill.

"Does it hurt?" she asked when we were outside.

"Not much," I said.

"Do you think it opened?"

"No, it's probably OK."

"I know! You should come to my place. I'll change your bandage for you. I've got disinfectant and everything. Come on, I'm right over there."

I told her it wasn't worth worrying about, that I'd be OK, but she insisted we had to check to see if the cut had opened or not.

"Or is it that you don't like being with me? You want to go back to your room as soon as possible, is that it?" she said with a playful smile.

"No way," I said.

"All right, then. Don't stand on ceremony. It's a short walk."

Hatsumi's flat was a 15-minute walk from Shibuya towards Ebisu. By no means a glamorous building, it was more than decent, with a nice little lobby and a lift. Hatsumi sat me at the kitchen table and went to the bedroom to change. She came out wearing a Princeton hooded sweatshirt and cotton trousers – and no more gold earrings. Setting a first-aid box on the table, she undid my bandage, checked to see that the wound was still sealed, put a little disinfectant on the area and tied a new bandage over the cut. She did all this like an expert. "How come you're so good at so many things?" I asked.

"I used to do volunteer work at a hospital. Kind of like playing nurse. That's how I learned."

When Hatsumi had finished with the bandage, she went and fetched two cans of beer from the fridge. She drank half of hers, and I drank mine plus the half she left. Then she showed me pictures of the other girls in her club. She was right: some of them were cute.

"Any time you decide you want a girlfriend, come to me," she said. "I'll fix you up straight away."

"Yes, Miss."

"All right, Toru, tell me the truth. You think I'm an old matchmaker, don't you?"

"To some extent," I said, telling her the truth, but with a smile. Hatsumi smiled, too. She looked good when she smiled.

"Tell me something else, Toru," she said. "What do you think about Nagasawa and me?"

"What do you mean what do I think? About what?"

"About what I ought to do. From now on."

"It doesn't matter what I think," I said, taking a slug of cold beer.

"That's all right. Tell me exactly what you think."

"Well, if I were you, I'd leave him. I'd find someone with a more normal way of looking at things and live happily ever after. There's no way in hell you can be happy with him. The way he lives, it never crosses his mind to try to make himself happy or to make others happy. Staying with him will only wreck your nervous system. To me, it's already a miracle that you've been with him three years. Of course, I'm very fond of him in my own way. He's fun, and he has lots of great qualities.

He has strengths and abilities that I could never hope to match. But in the end, his ideas about things and the way he lives his life are not normal. Sometimes, when I'm talking to him, I feel as if I'm going around and around in circles. The same process that takes him higher and higher leaves me going around in circles. It makes me feel so empty! Finally, our very systems are totally different. Do you see what I'm saying?"

"I do," Hatsumi said as she brought me another beer from the fridge.

"Plus, after he gets into the Foreign Ministry and does a year of training, he'll be going abroad. What are *you* going to do all that time? Wait for him? He has no intention of marrying anyone."

"I know that, too."

"So I've got nothing else to say."

"I see," said Hatsumi.

I slowly filled my glass with beer.

"You know, when we were playing pool before, something popped into my mind," I said. "I was an only child, but all the time I was growing up I never once felt deprived or wished I had brothers or sisters. I was happy being alone. But all of a sudden, playing pool with you, I had this feeling that I wished I had had an elder sister like you – really chic and a knockout in a midnight-blue dress and gold earrings and great with a pool cue."

Hatsumi flashed me a happy smile. "That's got to be the nicest thing anybody's said to me in the past year," she said. "Really."

"All I want for you," I said, blushing, "is for you to be happy. It's crazy, though. You seem like someone who could be happy with just about anybody, so how did you end up with Nagasawa of all people?"

"Things like that just happen. There's probably not much you can do about them. It's certainly true in my case. Of course, Nagasawa would say it's my responsibility, not his."

"I'm sure he would."

"But anyway, Toru, I'm not the smartest girl in the world. If anything, I'm sort of on the stupid side, and old-fashioned. I couldn't care less about 'systems' and 'responsibility'. All I want is to get married and have a man I love hold me in his arms every night and make babies. That's plenty for me. It's all I want out of life."

"And what Nagasawa wants out of life has nothing to do with that."

"People change, though, don't you think?" Hatsumi asked.

"You mean, like, they go out into society and get a kick up the arse and grow up?"

"Yeah. And if he's away from me for a long time, his feelings for me could change, don't you think?"

"Maybe, if he were an ordinary guy," I said. "But he's different. He's incredibly strong-willed – stronger than you or I can imagine. And he only makes himself stronger with every day that goes by. If something smashes into him, he just works to make himself stronger. He'd eat slugs before he'd back down to anyone. What do you expect to get from a man like that?"

"But there's nothing I *can* do but wait for him," said Hatsumi with her chin in her hand.

"You love him that much?"

"I do," she answered without a moment's hesitation.

"Oh boy," I said with a sigh, drinking down the last of my beer. "It must be a wonderful thing to be so sure that you love somebody."

"I'm a stupid, old-fashioned girl," she said. "Have another beer?"

"No, thanks, I must get going. Thanks for the bandage and beer."

As I was standing in the hallway putting on my shoes, the telephone rang. Hatsumi looked at me, looked at the phone, and looked at me again.

"Good night," I said, stepping outside. As I shut the door, I caught a glimpse of Hatsumi picking up the receiver. It was the last time I ever saw her.

It was 11.30 by the time I got back to the dorm. I went straight to Nagasawa's room and knocked on his door. After the tenth knock it occurred to me that this was Saturday night. Nagasawa always got overnight permission on Saturday nights, supposedly to stay at his relatives' house.

I went back to my room, took off my tie, put my jacket and trousers on a hanger, changed into my pyjamas, and brushed my teeth. Oh no, I thought, tomorrow is Sunday again! Sundays seemed to be rolling around every four days. Another two Sundays and I would be 20 years old. I stretched out in bed and stared at my calendar as dark feelings washed over me.

I sat at my desk to write my Sunday morning letter to Naoko, drinking coffee from a big cup and listening to old Miles Davis albums. A fine rain was falling outside, while my room had the chill of an aquarium. The smell of mothballs lingered in the thick jumper I had just taken out of a storage box. High up on the window-pane clung a huge, fat fly, unmoving. With no wind to stir it, the Rising Sun standard hung limp against the flagpole like the toga of a Roman senator. A skinny, timid-looking brown dog that had wandered into the quadrangle was sniffing every blossom in the flowerbed. I couldn't begin to imagine why any dog would have to go around sniffing flowers on a rainy day.

My letter was a long one, and whenever my cut right palm began to hurt from holding the pen, I would let my eyes wander out to the rainy quadrangle.

I began by telling Naoko how I had given my right hand a nasty cut while working in the record shop, then went on to say that Nagasawa, Hatsumi and I had had a sort of celebration the night before for Nagasawa's having passed his Foreign Ministry exam. I described the restaurant and the food. The meal was great, I said, but the atmosphere got uncomfortable halfway through.

I wondered if I should write about Kizuki in connection with having played pool with Hatsumi and decided to go ahead. I felt it was something I ought to write about.

I still remember the last shot Kizuki took that day – the day he died. It was a difficult cushion shot that I never expected him to get. Luck seemed to be with him, though: the shot was absolutely perfect, and the white and red balls hardly made a sound as they brushed each other on the green baize for the last score of the game. It was such a beautiful shot, I still have a vivid image of it to this day. For nearly two-and-a-half years after that, I never touched a cue.

The night I played pool with Hatsumi, though, the thought of Kizuki never crossed my mind until the first game ended, and this came as a real shock to me. I had always assumed that I'd be reminded of Kizuki whenever I played pool. But not until the first game was over and I bought a Pepsi from a vending machine and started drinking it did I even think of him. It was

286

the Pepsi machine that did it: there had been one in the pool hall we used to play in, and we had often bet drinks on the outcome of our games.

I felt guilty that I hadn't thought of Kizuki straight away, as if I had somehow abandoned him. Back in my room, though, I came to think of it like this: two-and-a-half years have gone by since it happened, and Kizuki is still 17 years old. Not that this means my memory of him has faded. The things that his death gave rise to are still there, bright and clear, inside me, some of them even clearer than when they were new. What I want to say is this: I'm going to turn 20 soon. Part of what Kizuki and I shared when we were 16 and 17 has already vanished, and no amount of crying is going to bring that back. I can't explain it any better than this, but I think that you can probably under-stand what I felt and what I am trying to say. In fact, you are probably the only one in the world who can understand.

I think of you now more than ever. It's raining today. Rainy Sundays are hard for me. When it rains I can't do laundry, which means I can't do ironing. I can't go walking, and I can't lie on the roof. About all I can do is put the record player on auto repeat and listen to *Kind of Blue* over and over while I watch the rain falling in the quadrangle. As I wrote to you earlier, I don't wind my spring on Sundays. That's why this letter is so damn long. I'm stopping now. I'm going to the dining hall for lunch.
Goodbye.

第 9 章

There was no sign of Midori at the next day's lecture, either. What had happened to her? Ten days had gone by since we last talked on the phone. I thought about calling her, but decided against it. She had said that *she* would call *me*.

That Thursday I saw Nagasawa in the dining hall. He sat down next to me with a tray full of food and apologized for having made our "party" so unpleasant.

"Never mind," I said. "I should be thanking you for a great dinner. I have to admit, though, it was a funny way to celebrate your first job."

"You can say that again."

A few minutes went by as we ate in silence.

"I made up with Hatsumi," he said.

"I'm not surprised."

"I was kind of tough on you, too, as I recall it."

"What's with all the apologizing?" I asked. "Are you ill?"

"I may be," he said with a few little nods. "Hatsumi tells me you told her to leave me."

"It only makes sense," I said.

"Yeah, I s'pose so," said Nagasawa.

"She's a great girl," I said, slurping my miso soup.

"I know," he said with a sigh. "A little too great for me."

*

I was sleeping the sleep of death when the buzzer rang to let me know I had a call. It brought me back from the absolute core of sleep in total confusion. I felt as if I had been sleeping with my head soaked in water until my brain swelled up. The clock said 6.15 but I had no idea if that meant a.m. or p.m., and I couldn't remember what day it was. I looked out of the window and realized there was no flag on the pole. It was probably p.m. So, raising that flag served some purpose after all.

"Hey, Watanabe, are you free now?" Midori asked.

"I don't know, what day is it?"

"Friday."

"Morning or evening?"

"Evening, of course! You're so weird! Let's see, it's, uh, 6.18 p.m."

So it *was* p.m. after all! That's right, I had been stretched out on my bed reading a book when I dozed off. Friday. My head started working. I didn't have to go to the record shop on Friday nights. "Yeah, I'm free. Where are you?"

"Ueno Station. Why don't you meet me in Shinjuku? I'll leave now."

We set a time and place and hung up.

When I got to DUG, Midori was sitting at the far end of the counter with a drink. She wore a man's wrinkled, white balmacaan coat, a thin yellow jumper, blue jeans, and two bracelets on one wrist.

"What're you drinking?" I asked.

"Tom Collins."

I ordered a whisky and soda, then realized there was a big suitcase by Midori's feet.

"I went away," she said. "Just got back."

289

"Where'd you go?"

"South to Nara and north to Aomori."

"On the same trip?!"

"Don't be stupid. I may be strange, but I can't go north and south at the same time. I went to Nara with my boyfriend, and then took off to Aomori alone."

I sipped my whisky and soda, then struck a match to light the Marlboro that Midori held between her lips. "You must have had a terrible time, what with the funeral and everything."

"Nah, a funeral's a piece of cake. We've had plenty of practice. You put on a black kimono and sit there like a lady and everybody else takes care of business – an uncle, a neighbour, like that. They bring the sake, order the sushi, say comforting things, cry, carry on, divide up the keepsakes. It's a breeze. A picnic. Compared to nursing someone day after day, it's an absolute picnic. We were drained, my sister and me. We couldn't even cry. We didn't have any tears left. Really. Except, when you do that, they start whispering about you: 'Those girls are as cold as ice.' So then, we're *never* going to cry, that's just how the two of us are. I know we could have faked it, but we would never do anything like that. The bastards! The more they wanted to see us cry, the more determined we were not to give them the satisfaction. My sister and I are totally different types, but when it comes to something like that, we're in absolute sync."

Midori's bracelets jangled on her arm as she waved to the waiter and ordered another Tom Collins and a small bowl of pistachios.

"So then, after the funeral ended and everybody went home, the two of us drank sake till the sun went down. Polished off one of those huge half-gallon bottles, and half of another

one, and the whole time we were dumping on everybody –
this one's an idiot, that one's a shithead, one guy looks like
a mangy dog, another one's a pig, so-and-so's a hypocrite,
that one's a crook. You have no idea how great it felt!"

"I can imagine."

"We got pissed and went to bed – both of us out cold. We
slept for hours, and if the phone rang or something, we just
let it go. Dead to the world. Finally, after we woke up, we
ordered sushi and talked about what to do. We decided to
close the shop for a while and enjoy ourselves. We'd been
killing ourselves for months and we deserved a break. My
sister just wanted to hang around with her boyfriend for a
while, and I decided I'd take mine on a trip for a couple of
days and fuck like crazy." Midori clamped her mouth shut
and rubbed her ears. "Oops, sorry."

"That's OK," I said. "So you went to Nara."

"Yeah, I've always liked that place. The temples, the deer
park."

"And did you fuck like crazy?"

"No, not at all, not even once," she said with a sigh. "The
second we walked into the hotel room and dumped our bags,
my period started. A real gusher."

I couldn't help laughing.

"Hey, it's not funny. I was a week early! I couldn't stop
crying when that happened. I think all the stress threw me
off. My boyfriend got *sooo* angry! He's like that: he gets angry
straight away. It wasn't *my* fault, though. It's not like I *wanted*
to get my period. And, well, mine are kind of on the heavy
side anyway. The first day or two, I don't want to do *anything*.
Make sure you keep away from me then."

"I'd like to, but how can I tell?" I asked.

"OK, I'll wear a hat for a couple of days after my period

starts. A red one. That should work," she said with a laugh. "If you see me on the street and I'm wearing a red hat, don't talk to me, just run away."

"Great. I wish all girls would do that," I said. "So anyway, what did you do in Nara?"

"What else *could* we do? We fed the deer and walked all over the place. It was just awful! We had a big fight and I haven't seen him since we got back. I hung around for a couple of days and decided to take a nice trip all by myself. So I went to Aomori. I stayed with a friend in Hirosaki for the first two nights, and then I started travelling around – Shimokita, Tappi, places like that. They're nice. I once wrote a map brochure for the area. Ever been there?"

"Never."

"So anyway," said Midori, sipping her Tom Collins, then wrenching open a pistachio, "the whole time I was travelling by myself, I was thinking of you. I was thinking how nice it would be if I could have you with me."

"How come?"

"How come?!" Midori looked at me with eyes focused on nothingness. "What do you mean 'How come?'?!"

"Just that. How come you were thinking of me?"

"Maybe because I like you, that's how come! Why else would I be thinking of you? Who would ever think they wanted to be with somebody they didn't like?"

"But you've got a boyfriend," I said. "You don't have to think about me." I took a slow sip of my whisky and soda.

"Meaning I'm not allowed to think about you if I've got a boyfriend?"

"No, that's not it, I just – "

"Now get this straight, Watanabe," said Midori, pointing at me. "I'm warning you, I've got a whole month's worth of

292

misery crammed inside me and getting ready to blow. So watch what you say to me. Any more of that kind of stuff and I'll flood this place with tears. Once I get started, I'm good for the whole night. Are you ready for that? I'm an absolute animal when I start crying, it doesn't matter *where* I am! I'm not joking."

I nodded and kept quiet. I ordered a second whisky and soda and ate a few pistachios. Somewhere behind the sound of a sloshing shaker and clinking glasses and the scrape of an ice maker, Sarah Vaughan sang an old-fashioned love song.

"Things haven't been right between me and my boyfriend ever since the tampon incident."

"Tampon incident?"

"Yeah, I was out drinking with him and a few of his friends about a month ago and I told them the story of a woman in my neighbourhood who blew out a tampon when she sneezed. Funny, right?"

"That *is* funny," I said with a laugh.

"Yeah, all the other guys thought so, too. But he got mad and said I shouldn't be talking about such dirty things. Such a wet blanket!"

"Wow."

"He's a wonderful guy, but he can be really narrow-minded when it comes to stuff like that," said Midori. "Like, he gets mad if I wear anything but white underwear. Don't you think that's narrow-minded?"

"Maybe so," I said, "but it's just a matter of taste." It seemed incredible to me that a guy like that would want a girlfriend like Midori, but I kept this thought to myself.

"So, what have *you* been doing?" she asked.

"Nothing. Same as ever," I said, but then I recalled my attempt to masturbate while thinking of Midori as I had promised to do. I told her about it in a low voice that wouldn't carry to the others around us.

Midori's eyes lit up and she snapped her fingers. "How'd it go? Was it good?"

"Nah, I got embarrassed halfway through and stopped."

"You mean you lost your erection?"

"Pretty much."

"Damn," she said, shooting a look of annoyance at me. "You can't let yourself get embarrassed. Think about something really sexy. It's OK, I'm giving you permission. Hey, I know what! Next time I'll get on the phone with you: 'Oh, oh, that's great . . . Oh, I *feel* it . . . Stop, I'm gonna come . . . Oh, don't *do* that!' I'll say stuff like that to you while you're doing it."

"The dormitory phone is in the lobby by the front door, with people coming in and out all the time," I explained. "The dorm Head would kill me with his bare hands if he saw me wanking in a place like that."

"Oh, too bad."

"Never mind," I said. "I'll try again by myself one of these days."

"Give it your best shot," said Midori.

"I will," I said.

"I wonder if it's me," she said. "Maybe I'm just not sexy. Innately."

"That's not it," I assured her. "It's more a question of attitude."

"You know," she said, "I have this tremendously sensitive back. The soft touch of fingers all over . . . mmmmm."

"I'll keep that in mind."

"Hey, why don't we go now and see a dirty film?" Midori suggested. "A really filthy S&M one."

We went from the bar to an eel shop, and from there to one of Shinjuku's most run-down adult cinemas to see a triple bill. It was the only place we could find in the paper that was showing S&M stuff. Inside, the cinema had some kind of indefinable smell. Our timing was good: the S&M film was just starting as we took our seats. It was the story of a secretary and her schoolgirl sister being kidnapped by a bunch of men and subjected to sadistic tortures. The men made the older one to do all kinds of awful things by threatening to rape the sister, but soon the older sister is transformed into a raging masochist, and the younger one gets really turned on from having to watch all the contortions they put her through. It was such a gloomy, repetitive film, I got bored after a while.

"If I were the younger sister, I wouldn't get worked up so easily," said Midori. "I'd keep watching."

"I'm sure you would," I said.

"And anyway, don't you think her nipples are too dark for a schoolgirl – a virgin?"

"Absolutely."

Midori's eyes were glued to the screen. I was impressed: anyone watching a film with such fierce intensity was getting more than her money's worth. She kept reporting her thoughts to me: "Oh my God, will you look at that!" or "Three guys at once! They're going to tear her apart!" or "I'd like to try that on somebody, Watanabe." I was enjoying Midori a lot more than the film.

When the lights went up during the intermission, I realized there were no other women in the place. One young man sitting near us – probably a student – took one look at Midori and changed his seat to the far side.

"Tell me, Watanabe, do you get hard watching this kind of stuff?"

"Well, yeah, sometimes," I said. "That's why they *make* these films."

"So what you're saying is, every time one of those scenes starts, every man in the cinema has his thing standing to attention? Thirty or forty of them sticking up all at once? It's so weird if you stop and think about it, don't you think?"

"Yeah, I guess so, now you mention it."

The second feature was a fairly normal porn flick, which meant it was even more boring than the first. It had lots of oral sex scenes, and every time they started doing fellatio or cunnilingus or sixty-nine the soundtrack would fill the cinema with loud sucking or slurping sound effects. Listening to them, I felt strangely moved to think that I was living out my life on this bizarre planet of ours.

"Who comes up with these sounds, I wonder," I said to Midori.

"I think they're *great!*" she said.

There was also a sound for a penis moving in and out of a vagina. I had never realized that such sounds even existed. The man was into a lot of heavy breathing, and the woman came up with the usual sort of expressions – "Yes!" or "More!" – as she writhed under him. You could also hear the bed creaking. These scenes just went on and on. Midori seemed to be enjoying them at first, but even she got bored after a while and suggested we leave. We went outside and took a few deep breaths. This was the first time in my life the outside air of Shinjuku felt healthy to me.

"That was fun," said Midori. "Let's try it again sometime."

"They just keep doing the same things," I said.

"Well, what else can they do? We all just keep doing the same things."

She had a point there.

We found another bar and ordered drinks. I had more whisky, and Midori drank three or four cocktails of some indefinable kind. Outside again, Midori said she wanted to climb a tree.

"There aren't any trees around here," I said. "And even if there were, you're too wobbly to do any climbing."

"You're always so damn sensible, you ruin everything. I'm drunk 'cause I wanna be drunk. What's wrong with that? And even if I *am* drunk, I can still climb a tree. Shit, I'm gonna climb all the way to the top of a great, big, tall tree and I'm gonna pee all over everybody!"

"You wouldn't happen to need the toilet by any chance?"

"Yup."

I took Midori to a pay toilet in Shinjuku Station, put a coin in the slot and bundled her inside, then bought an evening paper at a nearby stand and read it while I waited for her to come out. But she didn't come out. I started getting worried after 15 minutes and was ready to go and check on her when she finally emerged looking pale.

"Sorry," she said. "I fell asleep."

"Are you OK?" I asked, putting my coat around her shoulders.

"Not really," she said.

"I'll take you home. You just have to get home, take a nice, long bath and go to bed. You're exhausted."

"I am *not* going home. What's the point? Nobody's there. I don't want to sleep all by myself in a place like that."

"Terrific," I said. "So what are you going to do?"

"Go to some love hotel around here and sleep with your arms around me all night. Like a log. Tomorrow morning we'll have breakfast somewhere and go to lectures together."

"You were planning this all along, weren't you? That's why you called me."

"Of course."

"You should have called your boyfriend, not me. That's the only thing that makes sense. That's what boyfriends are for."

"But I want to be with you."

"You can't be with me," I said. "First of all, I have to be back in the dorm by midnight. Otherwise, I'll break curfew. The one time I did that there was all hell to pay. And secondly, if I go to bed with a girl, I'm going to want to do it with her, and the last thing I want is to lie there struggling to restrain myself. I'm not kidding, I might end up forcing you."

"You mean you'd hit me and tie me up and rape me from behind?"

"Hey, look, I'm serious."

"But I'm so lonely! I want to *be* with someone! I know I'm doing terrible things to you, making demands and not giving you anything in return, saying whatever pops into my head, dragging you out of your room and forcing you to take me everywhere, but you're the only one I can *do* stuff like that to! I've never been able to have my own way with anybody, not once in the 20 years I've been alive. My father, my mother, they never paid the slightest attention to me, and my boyfriend, well, he's just not that kind of guy. He gets angry if I try to have my own way. So we end up fighting. You're the only one I can say these things to. And now I'm really, really, really tired and I want to fall asleep listening to someone tell me how much they like me and how pretty I am and stuff. That's all I want. And when I wake up, I'll be full of energy and I'll never make these kinds of selfish demands again. I swear. I'll be a good girl."

"I hear you, believe me, but there's nothing I can do."

"Oh, please! Otherwise, I'm going to sit down right here

on the ground and cry my head off all night long. And I'll sleep with the first guy that talks to me."

That did it. I called the dorm and asked for Nagasawa. When he got to the phone I asked him if he would make it look as if I had come back for the evening. I was with a girl, I explained.

"Fine," he said. "It's a worthy cause, I'll be glad to help you out. I'll just turn over your name tag to the 'in' side. Don't worry. Take all the time you need. You can come in through my window in the morning."

"Thanks. I owe you one," I said and hung up.

"All set?" Midori asked.

"Pretty much," I said with a sigh.

"Great, let's go to a disco, it's so early."

"Wait a minute, I thought you were tired."

"For something like this, I'm just fine."

"Oh boy."

And she was right. We went to a disco, and her energy came back little by little as we danced. She drank two whisky and cokes, and stayed on the dance floor until her forehead was drenched in sweat.

"This is *so* much *fun!*" she exclaimed when we took a break at a table. "I haven't danced like this in ages. I don't know, when you move your body, it's kind of like your spirit gets liberated."

"Your spirit is *always* liberated, I'd say."

"No way," she said, shaking her head and smiling. "Anyway, now that I'm feeling better, I'm starved! Let's go for a pizza."

I took her to a pizzeria I knew and ordered draught beer and an anchovy pizza. I wasn't very hungry and ate only four of the twelve slices. Midori finished the rest.

"You sure made a fast recovery," I said. "Not too long ago you were pale and wobbly."

"It's because my selfish demands got through to somebody," she answered. "It unclogged me. Wow, this pizza is great!"

"Tell me, though. Is there really nobody at home?"

"It's true. My sister's staying at her friend's place. Now, that girl's got a *real* case of the creeps. She can't sleep alone in the house if I'm not there."

"Let's forget this love hotel crap, then. Going to a place like that just makes you feel cheap. Let's go to your house. You must have enough bedding for me?"

Midori thought about it for a minute, then nodded. "OK, we'll spend the night at mine."

We took the Yamanote Line to Otsuka, and soon we were raising the metal shutter that sealed off the front of the Kobayashi Bookshop. A paper sign on the shutter read TEMPORARILY CLOSED. The smell of old paper filled the dark shop, as if the shutter had not been opened for a long time. Half the shelves were empty, and most of the magazines had been tied in bundles for returns. That hollow, chilly feeling I had experienced on my first visit had only deepened. The place looked like a hulk abandoned on the shore.

"You're not planning to open shop again?" I asked.

"Nah, we're going to sell it," said Midori. "We'll divide the money and live on our own for a while without anybody's 'protection'. My sister's getting married next year, and I've got three more years at university. We ought to make enough to see us through that much at least. I'll keep my part-time job, too. Once the place is sold, I'll live with my sister in a flat for a while."

"You think somebody'll want to buy it?

"Probably. I know somebody who wants to open a wool

shop. She's been asking me recently if I want to sell. Poor Dad, though. He worked *so* hard to get this place, and he was paying off the loan he took out little by little, and in the end he hardly had anything left. It all melted away, like foam on a river."

"He had *you*, though," I said.

"Me?!" Midori said with a laugh. She took a deep breath and let it out. "Let's go upstairs. It's cold down here."

Upstairs, she sat me at the kitchen table and went to warm the bath water. While she busied herself with that, I put a kettle on to boil and made tea. Waiting for the tank to heat up, we sat across from each other at the kitchen table and drank tea. Chin in hand, she took a long, hard look at me. There were no sounds other than the ticking of the clock and the hum of the fridge motor turning on and off as the thermostat kicked in and out. The clock showed that midnight was fast approaching.

"You know, Watanabe, study it hard enough, and you've got a pretty interesting face."

"Think so?" I asked, a bit hurt.

"A nice face goes a long way with me," she said. "And yours . . . well, the more I look at it, the more I get to thinking, 'He'll do'."

"Me, too," I said. "Every once in a while, I think about myself, 'What the hell, I'll do'."

"Hey, I don't mean that in a bad way. I'm not very good at putting my feelings into words. That's why people misunderstand me. All I'm trying to say is I like you. Have I told you that before?"

"You have," I said.

"I mean, I'm not the only one who has trouble working out what men are all about. But I'm getting there, a little at a time."

Midori brought over a box of Marlboro and lit one up. "When you start at zero, you've got a lot to learn."

"I wouldn't be surprised."

"Oh, I almost forgot! You want to burn a stick of incense for my father?"

I followed Midori to the room with the Buddhist altar, lit a stick of incense in front of her father's photo, and brought my hands together.

"Know what I did the other day?" Midori asked. "I got all naked in front of my father's picture. Took off every stitch of clothing and let him have a good, long look. Kind of in a yoga position. Like, 'Here, Daddy, these are my tits, and this is my cunt'."

"Why in the hell would you do something like that?" I asked.

"I don't know, I just wanted to show him. I mean, half of me comes from his sperm, right? Why shouldn't I show him? 'Here's the daughter you made.' I *was* a little drunk at the time. I suppose that had something to do with it."

"I suppose."

"My sister walked in and almost fell over. There I was in front of my father's memorial portrait all naked with my legs spread. I guess you would be kind of surprised."

"I s'pose so."

"I explained why I was doing it and said, 'So take off your clothes too Momo (her name's Momo), and sit down next to me and show him,' but she wouldn't do it. She went away shocked. She has this really conservative streak."

"In other words, she's relatively normal, you mean."

"Tell me, Watanabe, what did you think of my father?"

"I'm not good with people I've just met, but it didn't bother me being alone with him. I felt pretty comfortable.

We talked about all kinds of stuff."

"What kind of stuff?"

"Euripides," I said.

Midori laughed out loud. "You're so *weird*! *Nobody* talks about Euripides with a dying person they've just met!"

"Well, *nobody* sits in front of her father's memorial portrait with her legs spread, either!"

Midori chuckled and gave the altar bell a ring. "Night-night, Daddy. We're going to have some fun now, so don't worry and get some sleep. You're not suffering any more, right? You're dead, OK? I'm sure you're not suffering. If you are, you'd better complain to the gods. Tell 'em it's just too cruel. I hope you meet Mum and the two of you really do it. I saw your willy when I helped you pee. It was pretty impressive! So give it everything you've got. Goodnight."

We took turns in the bath and changed into pyjamas. I borrowed a nearly new pair of her father's. They were a little small but better than nothing. Midori spread out a mattress for me on the floor of the altar room.

"You're not scared sleeping in front of the altar?" she asked.

"Not at all. I haven't done anything bad," I said with a smile.

"But you're going to stay with me and hold me until I fall asleep, right?"

"Right," I said.

Practically falling over the edge of Midori's little bed, I held her in my arms. Nose against my chest, she placed her hands on my hips. My right arm curled around her back while I tried to keep from falling out by hanging on to the bed frame with my left hand. It was not exactly a situation conducive to sexual excitement. My nose was resting on her head and her short-cut hair would tickle every now and then.

"Come on, *say* something to me," Midori said, her face buried in my chest.

"What do you want me to say?"

"Anything. Something to make me feel good."

"You're really cute," I said.

" – Midori," she said. "Say my name."

"You're really cute, Midori," I corrected myself.

"What do you mean *really* cute?"

"So cute the mountains crumble and the oceans dry up."

Midori lifted her face and looked at me. "You have this special way with words."

"I can feel my heart softening when you say that," I said, smiling.

"Say something even nicer."

"I really like you, Midori. A lot."

"How much is a lot?"

"Like a spring bear," I said.

"A spring bear?" Midori looked up again. "What's that all about? A spring bear."

"You're walking through a field all by yourself one day in spring, and this sweet little bear cub with velvet fur and shiny little eyes comes walking along. And he says to you, 'Hi, there, little lady. Want to tumble with me?' So you and the bear cub spend the whole day in each other's arms, tumbling down this clover-covered hill. Nice, huh?"

"Yeah. *Really* nice."

"That's how much I like you."

"That is the best thing I've ever heard," said Midori, cuddling up against my chest. "If you like me *that* much, you'll do anything I tell you to do, right? You won't get angry, right?"

"No, of course not."

"And you'll take care of me always and always."

"Of course I will," I said, stroking her short, soft, boyish hair. "Don't worry, everything is going to be fine."

"But I'm scared," she said.

I held her softly, and soon her shoulders were rising and falling, and I could hear the regular breathing of sleep. I slipped out of her bed and went to the kitchen, where I drank a beer. I wasn't the least bit sleepy, so I thought about reading a book, but I couldn't find anything worth reading nearby. I considered returning to Midori's room to look for one, but I didn't want to wake her by rummaging around while she was sleeping.

I sat there staring into space for a while, sipping my beer, when it occurred to me that I was in a bookshop. I went downstairs, switched on the light and started looking through the paperback shelves. There wasn't much that appealed to me, and most of what did I had read already, but I had to have something to read no matter what. I picked a discoloured copy of Hermann Hesse's *Beneath the Wheel* that must have been hanging around the shop unsold for a long time, and left the money for it by the till. This was my small contribution to reducing the debts of the Kobayashi Bookshop.

I sat at the kitchen table, drinking my beer and reading *Beneath the Wheel*. I had first read the novel the year I entered school. And now, about eight years later, here I was, reading the same book in a girl's kitchen, wearing the undersized pyjamas of her dead father. Funny. If it hadn't been for these strange circumstances, I would probably never have reread *Beneath the Wheel*.

The book did have its dated moments, but as a novel it wasn't bad. I moved through it slowly, enjoying it line by line, in the hushed bookshop in the middle of the night. A dusty bottle of brandy stood on a shelf in the kitchen. I poured a

305

little into a coffee cup and sipped it. It warmed me but did nothing to help me feel sleepy.

I went to check on Midori a little before three, but she was fast asleep. She must have been exhausted. The lights from the block of shops beyond the window cast a soft white glow, like moonlight, over the room. Midori slept with her back to the light. She lay so perfectly still, she might have been frozen stiff. Bending over, I caught the sound of her breathing. She slept just like her father.

The suitcase from her recent travels stood by the bed. Her white coat hung on the back of a chair. Her desktop was neatly arranged, and on the wall over it hung a Snoopy calendar. I nudged the curtain aside and looked down at the deserted shops. Every shop was closed, their metal shutters down, the vending machines hunched in front of the off-licence the only sign of something waiting for the dawn. The moan of long-distance lorry tyres sent a deep shudder through the air every now and then. I went back to the kitchen, poured myself another shot of brandy, and went on reading *Beneath the Wheel*.

By the time I had finished it the sky was growing light. I made myself some instant coffee and used some notepaper and a ballpoint pen I found on the table to write a message to Midori: *I drank some of your brandy. I bought a copy of* Beneath the Wheel. *It's light outside, so I'm going home. Goodbye.* Then, after some hesitation, I wrote: *You look really cute when you're sleeping.* I washed my coffee cup, switched off the kitchen light, went downstairs, quietly lifted the shutter, and stepped outside. I worried that a neighbour might find me suspicious, but there was no one on the street at 5.50-something in the morning. Only the crows were on their usual rooftop perch, glaring down at the street. I glanced up at the pale pink curtains in Midori's window, walked to the tram stop, rode to the end of the line, and walked to my dorm. On the way I found an open café and ate a breakfast of rice and miso soup, pickled vegetables and fried eggs. Circling around to the back of the dorm, I tapped on Nagasawa's ground-floor window. He let me in immediately.

"Coffee?" he asked.

"Nah."

I thanked him, went up to my room, brushed my teeth, took my trousers off, got under the covers, and clamped my eyes shut. Finally, a dreamless sleep closed over me like a heavy lead door.

I wrote to Naoko every week, and she often wrote back. Her letters were never very long. Soon there were references to the cold November mornings and evenings.

> You went back to Tokyo just about the time the autumn weather was deepening, so for a time I couldn't tell whether the hole that opened up inside me was from missing you or from the change of the season. Reiko and I talk about you all the time. She says be sure to say "Hi" to you. She is as nice to me as ever. I don't think I would have been able to stand this place if I didn't have her with me. I cry when I'm lonely. Reiko says it's good I can cry. But feeling lonely really hurts. When I'm lonely at night, people talk to me from the darkness. They talk to me the way trees moan in the wind at night. Kizuki; my sister: they talk to me like that all the time. They're lonely, too, and looking for someone to talk to.
>
> I often reread your letters at night when I'm lonely and in pain. I get confused by a lot of things that come from outside, but your descriptions of the world

around you give me wonderful relief. It's so strange! I wonder why that should be? So I read them over and over, and Reiko reads them, too. Then we talk about the things you tell me. I really liked the part about that girl Midori's father. We look forward to getting your letter every week as one of our few entertainments – yes, in a place like this, letters are our entertainments.

I try my best to set aside a time in the week for writing to you, but once I actually sit down in front of the blank sheet of paper, I begin to feel depressed. I'm really having to push myself to write this letter, too. Reiko's been yelling at me to answer you. Don't get me wrong, though. I have tons of things I want to talk to you about, to tell you about. It's just hard for me to put them into words. Which is why it's so painful for me to write letters.

Speaking of Midori, she sounds like an interesting person. Reading your letter, I got the feeling she might be in love with you. When I told that to Reiko, she said, 'Well, of *course* she is! Even *I* am in love with Watanabe!' We're picking mushrooms and gathering chestnuts and eating them every day. And I do mean *every* day: rice with chestnuts, rice with matsutake mushrooms, but they taste so great, we never get tired of them. Reiko doesn't eat that much, though. For her, it's still one cigarette after another. The birds and the rabbits are doing fine.

Goodbye.

Three days after my twentieth birthday, a package arrived for me from Naoko. Inside I found a wine-coloured crew neck pullover and a letter.

Happy Birthday! I hope you have a happy year being 20. My own year of being 20 looks like it's going to end with me as miserable as ever, but I'd really like it if you could have your share of happiness and mine combined. Really. Reiko and I each knitted half of this jumper. If I had done it all by myself, it would have taken until next Valentine's Day. The good half is Reiko's, and the bad half is mine. Reiko is so good at everything she does, I sometimes hate myself when I'm watching her. I mean, there's not a single thing I'm really good at!

Goodbye.

Be well.

The package had a short note from Reiko, too.

How are you? For you, Naoko may be the pinnacle of happiness, but for me she's just a clumsy girl. Still, we managed to finish this jumper in time for your birthday. Handsome, isn't it? We chose the colour and the style.

Happy Birthday.

第 10 章

Thinking back on the year 1969, all that comes to mind for me is a swamp – a deep, sticky bog that feels as if it's going to suck off my shoe each time I take a step. I walk through the mud, exhausted. In front of me, behind me, I can see nothing but the endless darkness of a swamp.

Time itself slogged along in rhythm with my faltering steps. The people around me had gone on ahead long before, while my time and I hung back, struggling through the mud. The world around me was on the verge of great transformations. Death had already taken John Coltrane who was joined now by so many others. People screamed there'd be revolutionary changes – which always seemed to be just ahead, at the curve in the road. But the "changes" that came were just two-dimensional stage sets, backdrops without substance or meaning. I trudged along through each day in its turn, rarely looking up, eyes locked on the never-ending swamp that lay before me, planting my right foot, raising my left, planting my left foot, raising my right, never sure where I was, never sure I was headed in the right direction, knowing only that I had to keep moving, one step at a time.

I turned 20, autumn gave way to winter, but in my life nothing changed in any significant way. Unexcited, I went to my lectures, worked three nights a week in the record shop, reread *The Great Gatsby* now and then, and when Sunday came I would do my washing and write a long letter to Naoko. Sometimes I would go out with Midori for a meal or to the zoo or to the cinema. The sale of the Kobayashi Bookshop went as planned, and Midori and her sister moved into a two-bedroom flat near Myogadani, a more upmarket neighbourhood. Midori would move out when her sister got married, and rent a flat by herself, she said. Meanwhile, she invited me to their new place for lunch once. It was a sunny, handsome flat, and Midori seemed to enjoy living there far more than she had above the Kobayashi Bookshop.

Every once in a while, Nagasawa would suggest that we go out on one of our excursions, but I always found something else to do instead. I just didn't want the hassle. Not that I didn't like the idea of sleeping with girls: it was just that, when I thought about the whole process I had to go through – drinking in town, looking for the right kind of girls, talking to them, going to a hotel – it was all too much effort. I had to admire Nagasawa all the more for the way he could continue the ritual without ever getting sick and tired of it. Maybe what Hatsumi had said to me had had some effect: I could make myself feel far happier just thinking about Naoko than sleeping with some stupid, anonymous girl. The sensation of Naoko's fingers bringing me to climax in a grassy field remained vivid inside me.

I wrote to her at the beginning of December to ask if it would be all right for me to come and visit her during the winter holidays. An answer came from Reiko saying they would love to have me. She explained that Naoko was having trouble writing and that she was answering for her. I was not to take this to mean that Naoko was feeling especially bad: there was no need for me to worry. These things came in waves.

When the holidays came, I stuffed my things into my rucksack, put on snow boots and set out for Kyoto. The odd doctor had been right: the winter mountains blanketed in snow were incredibly beautiful. As before, I slept two nights in the flat with Naoko and Reiko, and spent three days with them doing much the same kind of things as before. When the sun went down, Reiko would play her guitar and the three of us would sit around talking. Instead of our picnic, we went cross-country skiing. An hour of tramping through the woods on skis left us breathless and sweaty. We also joined the residents and staff shovelling snow when there was time. Doctor Miyata popped over to our table at dinner to explain why people's middle fingers are longer than their index fingers, while with toes it worked the other way. The gatekeeper, Omura, talked to me again about Tokyo pork. Reiko enjoyed the records I brought as gifts from the city. She transcribed a few tunes and worked them out on her guitar.

Naoko was even less talkative than she had been in the autumn. When the three of us were together, she would sit on the sofa, smiling, and hardly say a word. Reiko seemed to be chattering away to make up for her. "But don't worry," Naoko told me. "This is just one of those times. It's a lot more fun for me to listen to you two than to talk myself."

Reiko gave herself some chores that took her out of the flat so that Naoko and I could get in bed. I kissed her neck and shoulders and breasts, and she used her hands to bring me to climax as before. Afterwards, holding her close, I told her how her touch had stayed with me these two months, that I had thought of her and masturbated.

"You haven't slept with anybody else?" Naoko asked.

"Not once," I said.

"All right, then, here's something else for you to remember." She slid down and kissed my penis, then enveloped it in her warm mouth and ran her tongue all over it, her long, straight hair swaying over my belly and groin with each movement of her lips until I came a second time.

"Do you think you can remember that?" she asked.

"Of course I can," I said. "I'll always remember it."

I held her tight and slid my hand inside her panties, touching her still-dry vagina. Naoko shook her head and pulled my hand away. We held each other for a time, saying nothing.

"I'm thinking of getting out of the dorm when term ends and looking for a flat," I said. "I've had it with dorm life. If I keep working part-time I can pretty much cover my expenses. How about coming to Tokyo to live with me, the way I suggested before?"

"Oh, Toru, thank you. I'm so happy that you would ask me to do something like that!"

"It's not that I think there's anything wrong with this place," I said. "It's quiet, the surroundings are perfect, and Reiko is a wonderful person. But it's not a place to stay for a long time. It's too specialized for a long stay. The longer you're here, I'm sure, the harder it is to leave."

Instead of answering, Naoko turned her gaze to the outside. Beyond the window, there was nothing to see but snow. Snow clouds hung low and heavy in the sky, with only the smallest gap between them and the snow-covered earth.

"Take your time, think it over," I said. "Whatever happens, I'm going to move by the end of March. Any time you decide you want to join me, you can come."

Naoko nodded. I wrapped my arms around her as carefully as if I had been holding a work of art delicately fashioned from glass. She put her arms around my neck. I was naked, and she wore only the skimpiest white underwear. Her body was so beautiful, I could have enjoyed looking at it all day.

"Why don't I get wet?" Naoko murmured. "That one time was the only time it ever happened. The day of my twentieth birthday, that April. The night you held me in your arms. What is wrong with me?"

"It's strictly psychological, I'm sure," I said. "Give it time. There's no hurry."

"All of my problems are strictly psychological," said Naoko. "What if I never get better? What if I can never have sex for the rest of my life? Can you keep loving me just the same? Will hands and lips always be enough for you? Or will you solve the sex problem by sleeping with other girls?"

"I'm a born optimist," I said.

Naoko sat up in bed and slipped on a T-shirt. She put a flannel shirt over this, and then climbed into her jeans. I put my clothes on, too.

"Let me think about it," said Naoko. "And you think about it, too."

"I will," I said. "And speaking of lips, what you did with them just now was great."

She reddened slightly and gave a little smile. "Kizuki used to say that, too."

"He and I had pretty much the same tastes and opinions," I said, smiling.

We sat across from each other at the kitchen table, drinking coffee and talking about the old days. She was beginning to talk more about Kizuki. She would hesitate, and choose her words carefully. Every now and then, the snow would fall for a while and stop. The sky never cleared the whole three days I was there. "I think I can get back here in March," I said as I was leaving. I gave her one last, heavily padded hug with my winter coat on, and kissed her on the lips.

"Goodbye," she said.

1970 – a year with a whole new sound to it – came along, and that put an end to my teenage years. Now I could step out into a whole new swamp. Then it was time for exams, and these I passed with relative ease. If you have nothing else to do and spend all your time going to lectures, it takes no special skill to get through end-of-year exams.

Some problems arose in the dorm, though. A few guys active in one of the political factions kept their helmets and iron pipes hidden in their rooms. They had a run-in with some of the baseball-players under the wing of the dorm Head, as a result of which two of them were injured and six expelled. The aftershock of the incident was felt for a long time, spawning minor fights on an almost daily basis. The atmosphere that hung over the dorm was oppressive, and people's nerves were on edge. I myself was on the verge of getting knocked out by one of the baseball-players when Nagasawa intervened and managed to smooth things over. In any case, it was time for me to get out of there.

Once most of my exams were out of the way, I started looking for a flat in earnest. After a week of searching, I came up with the right place way out in the suburbs of Kichijoji. The location was not exactly convenient, but it was a house: an independent house – a real find. Originally a gardener's shack or some other kind of cottage, it stood by itself in the corner of a good-sized plot of land, separated from the main house by a large stretch of neglected garden. The landlord would use the front gate, and I the back, which would make it possible for me to preserve my privacy. It had one good-sized room, a little kitchen and bathroom, and an unimaginably huge closet.

It even had a veranda facing the garden. A nice old couple were renting the house at way below market value on condition that the tenant was prepared to move out the following year if their grandson decided to come to Tokyo. They assured me that I could live as I pleased there; they wouldn't make any demands.

Nagasawa helped me with the move. He managed to borrow a van to transfer my stuff, and, as promised, he gave me his fridge, TV, and oversize thermos flask. He might not need them any more, but for me they were perfect. He himself was scheduled to move out in two days, to a flat in the Mita neighbourhood.

"I guess we won't be seeing each other for a long time," he said as he left me, "so keep well. I'm still sure we'll run across each other in some strange place years from now."

"I'm already looking forward to it," I said.

"And that time we switched girls, the funny-looking one was way better."

"Right on," I said with a laugh. "But anyway, Nagasawa, take care of Hatsumi. Good ones like her are hard to find. And she's a lot more fragile than she looks."

"Yeah, I know," he said, nodding. "That's why I was hoping you would take her when I was through. The two of you would make a great couple."

"Yeah, right!" I said.

"Just kidding," said Nagasawa. "Anyway, be happy. I get the feeling a lot of shit is going to come your way, but you're a stubborn bastard, I'm sure you'll handle it. Mind if I give you one piece of advice?"

"Go ahead."

"Don't feel sorry for yourself," he said. "Only arseholes do that."

316

"I'll keep it in mind," I said. We shook hands and went our separate ways, he to his new world, and I back to my swamp.

Three days after my move, I wrote to Naoko. I described my new house and said how relieved I was to be away from the idiots in the dorm and all their stupid brainstorms. Now I could start my new life with a new frame of mind.

My window looks out on a big garden, which is used as a meeting place by all the neighbourhood cats. I like to stretch out on the veranda and watch them. I'm not sure how many of them get together, but this is one big gang of cats. They sunbathe in groups. I don't think they're too pleased to see me living here, but once when I put out an old chunk of cheese a few of them crept over and nibbled it. They'll probably be friends of mine before too long. There's one striped tom cat in the bunch with half-eaten ears. It's amazing how much he looks like my old dorm Head. I expect him to start raising the flag any day now.

I'm kind of far from university here, but once I start my third year I won't have too many morning lectures, so it shouldn't be too bad. It may even be better with the time to read on the train. Now all I have to do is find some easy work out here that I can do three or four days a week. Then I can get back to my spring-winding life.

I don't want to rush, but April is a good time of year to start new things, and I can't help feeling that the best thing for us would be to begin living together then. You could go back to university, too, if it worked out well. If there's a problem with us actually living

317

together, I could find a flat for you in the neighbourhood. The most important thing is for us to be always near each other. It doesn't *have* to be spring, of course. If you think summer is better, that's fine by me, too. Just let me know what you're thinking, OK?

I'm planning to put some extra time in at work for a while. To cover my moving expenses. I'm going to need a fair amount of money for one thing or another once I start living alone: pots and pans, dishes, stuff like that. I'll be free in March, though, and I definitely want to come to see you. What dates work best for you? I'll plan a trip to Kyoto then. I look forward to seeing you and hearing your answer.

I spent the next few days buying the things I needed in the nearby Kichijoji shopping district and started cooking simple meals for myself at home. I bought some planks at a local timber yard and had them cut to size so I could make a desk for myself. I thought I could study on it and, for the time being, eat my meals there, too. I made some shelves and got in a good selection of spices. A white cat maybe six months old decided she liked me and started eating at my place. I called her Seagull.

Once I had my place sorted out to some extent, I went into town and found a temporary job as a painter's assistant. I filled two solid weeks that way. The pay was good, but the work was murder, and the fumes made my head spin. Every day after work I'd eat at a cheap restaurant, wash it down with beer, go home and play with the cat, then sleep like a dead man. No answer came from Naoko during that time.

I was in the thick of painting when Midori popped into my mind. I hadn't been in touch with her for nearly three weeks,

I realized, and hadn't even told her I had moved. I had mentioned to her that I was thinking of moving, and she had said, "Oh, really?" and that was the last time we had talked.

I went to a phone box and dialled her number. The woman who answered was probably her sister. When I gave her my name, she said "Just a minute", but Midori never came to the phone.

Then the sister, or whoever she was, got back on the line. "Midori says she's too furious to talk to you. You just moved and never said a thing to her, right? Just disappeared and never told her where you were going, right? Well, now you've got her boiling mad. And once she gets mad, she stays that way. Like some kind of animal."

"Look, could you just put her on the phone? I can explain."

"She says she doesn't want to hear any explanations."

"Can I explain to *you*, then? I hate to do this to you, but could you just listen and tell her what I said?"

"Not *me*! Do it yourself. What kind of man are you? It's *your* responsibility, so *you* do it, and do it right."

It was hopeless. I thanked her and hung up. I really couldn't blame Midori for being angry. What with all the moving and fixing up and working for extra cash, I hadn't given her a second thought. Not even Naoko had crossed my mind the whole time. This was nothing new for me. Whenever I get involved in something, I shut out everything else.

But then I began to think how I would have felt if the tables had been turned and Midori had moved somewhere without telling me where or getting in touch with me for three weeks. I would have been hurt – hurt badly, no doubt. No, we weren't lovers, but in a way we had opened ourselves to each other even more deeply than lovers do. The thought caused me a good deal of grief. What a terrible thing it is to wound someone you really care for – and to do it so unconsciously.

As soon as I got home from work, I sat at my new desk and wrote to Midori. I told her how I felt as honestly as I could. I apologized, without explanations or excuses, for having been so careless and insensitive. *I miss you*, I wrote. *I want to see you as soon as possible. I want you to see my new house. Please write to me*, I said, and sent the letter special delivery.

The answer never came.

This was the beginning of one weird spring. I spent the whole holiday waiting for letters. I couldn't take a trip, I couldn't go home to see my parents, I couldn't even take a part-time job because there was no telling when a letter might arrive from Naoko saying she wanted me to come and see her on such-and-such a date. Afternoons I would spend in the nearby shopping district in Kichijoji, watching double bills or reading in a jazz café. I saw no one and talked to almost no one. And once a week I would write to Naoko. I never suggested to her that I was hoping for an answer. I didn't want to pressure her in any way. I would tell her about my painting job, about Seagull, about the peach blossom in the garden, about the nice old lady who sold tofu, about the nasty old lady in the local restaurant, about the meals I was making for myself. But still, she never wrote.

Whenever I was fed up reading or listening to records, I would work a little in the garden. From my landlord I borrowed a rake and broom and pruning shears and spent my time pulling weeds and trimming bushes. It didn't take much to make the garden look good. Once the owner invited me to join him for a cup of tea, so we sat on the veranda of the main house drinking green tea and munching on rice crackers, sharing small talk. After retirement, he had got a job with an insurance company, he said, but he had left that, too, after a couple of years, and now he was taking it easy. The house and land had been in the family for a long time, his children were grown-up and independent, and he could manage a comfortable old age without working. Which is why he and his wife were always travelling together.

"That's nice," I said.

"No it's not," he answered. "Travelling is no fun. I'd much rather be working."

He let the garden grow wild, he said, because there were no decent gardeners in the area and because he had developed allergies that made it impossible for him to do the work himself. Cutting grass made him sneeze.

When we had finished our tea, he showed me a storage shed and told me I could use anything I found inside, more or less by way of thanks for my gardening. "We don't have any use for any of this stuff," he said, "so feel free."

And in fact the place was crammed with all kinds of things – an old wooden bath, a kids' swimming pool, baseball bats. I found an old bike, a handy-sized dining table with two chairs, a mirror, and a guitar. "I'd like to borrow these if you don't mind," I said.

"Feel free," he said again.

I spent a day working on the bike: cleaning the rust off, oiling the bearings, pumping up the tyres, adjusting the gears, and taking it to a bike repair shop to have a new gear cable installed. It looked like a different bike by the time I had finished. I cleaned a thick layer of dust off the table and gave it a new coat of varnish. I replaced the strings of the guitar and glued a section of the body that was coming apart. I took a wire brush to the rust on the tuning pegs and adjusted those. It wasn't much of a guitar, but at least I got it to stay in tune. I hadn't had a guitar in my hands since school, I realized. I sat on the porch and picked my way through The Drifters' "Up on the Roof" as well as I could. I was amazed to find I still remembered most of the chords.

Next I took a few planks of wood and made myself a square letterbox. I painted it red, wrote my name on it, and set it outside my door. Up until 3 April, the only post that found its way to my box was something that had been forwarded from the dorm: a notice from the reunion committee of my school. A class reunion was the last thing I wanted to have anything to do with. That was the class I had been in with Kizuki. I threw it in the bin.

I found a letter in the box on the afternoon of 4 April. It said *Reiko Ishida* on the back. I made a nice, clean cut across the seal with my scissors and went out to the porch to read it. I had a feeling this was not going to be good news, and I was right.

First Reiko apologized for making me wait so long for an answer. Naoko had been struggling to write me a letter, she said, but she could never seem to write one through to the end.

> I offered to send you an answer in her place, but every time I pointed out how wrong it was of her to keep you waiting, she insisted that it was far too personal a matter, that she would write to you herself, which is why I haven't written sooner. I'm sorry, really. I hope you can forgive me.
>
> I know you must have had a difficult month waiting for an answer, but believe me, the month has been just as difficult for Naoko. Please try to understand what she's been going through. Her condition is not good, I have to say in all honesty. She was trying her best to stand on her own two feet, but so far the results have not been good.

322

Looking back, I see now that the first symptom of her problem was her loss of the ability to write letters. That happened around the end of November or beginning of December. Then she started hearing things. Whenever she would try to write a letter, she would hear people talking to her, which made it impossible for her to write. The voices would interfere with her attempts to choose her words. It wasn't all that bad until about the time of your second visit, so I didn't take it too seriously. For all of us here, these kinds of symptoms come in cycles, more or less. In her case, they got quite serious after you left. She is having trouble now just holding an ordinary conversation. She can't find the right words to speak, and that puts her into a terribly confused state – confused and frightened. Meanwhile, the "things" she's hearing are getting worse.

We have a session every day with one of the specialists. Naoko and the doctor and I sit around talking and trying to find the exact part of her that's broken. I came up with the idea that it would be good to add you to one of our sessions if possible, and the doctor was in favour of it, but Naoko was against it. I can tell you exactly what her reason was: "I want my body to be clean of all this when I meet him." That was not the problem, I said to her; the problem was to get her well as quickly as possible, and I pushed as hard as I could, but she wouldn't change her mind.

I think I once explained to you that this is not a specialized hospital. We do have medical specialists here, of course, and they provide effective treatments, but concentrated therapy is another matter. The point of this place is to create an effective environment in which the patient can treat herself or himself, and that does not, properly speaking, include medical treatment. Which means that if Naoko's condition grows any worse, they will probably have to transfer her to some other hospital or medical facility or what have you. Personally, I would find this very painful, but we would have to do it. That isn't to say that she couldn't come back here for treatment on a kind of temporary "leave of absence". Or, better yet, she could even be cured and finish with hospitals completely. In any case, we're doing everything we can, and Naoko is doing everything she can. The best thing you can do meanwhile is hope for her recovery and keep sending her those letters.

It was dated 31 March. After I had read it, I stayed on the porch and let my eyes wander out to the garden, full now with the freshness of spring. An old cherry tree stood there, its blossoms nearing the height of their glory. A soft breeze blew, and the light of day lent its strangely blurred, smoky colours to everything. Seagull wandered over from some-where, and after scratching at the boards of the veranda for a while, she stretched out next to me and fell asleep.

I knew I should be doing some serious thinking, but I had no idea how to go about it. And, to tell the truth, thinking was the last thing I wanted to do. The time would come soon enough when I had no choice in the matter, and when that time came I would take a good, long while to think things over. Not now, though. Not now.

I spent the day staring at the garden, propped against a pillar and stroking Seagull. I felt completely drained. The afternoon deepened, twilight approached, and bluish shadows enveloped the garden. Seagull disappeared, but I went on staring at the cherry blossoms. In the spring gloom, they looked like flesh that had burst through the skin over festering wounds. The garden filled up with the sweet, heavy stench of rotting flesh. And that's when I thought of Naoko's flesh. Naoko's beautiful flesh lay before me in the darkness, countless buds bursting through her skin, green and trembling in an almost imperceptible breeze. Why did such a beautiful body have to be so ill? I wondered. Why didn't they just leave Naoko alone?

I went inside and drew my curtains, but even indoors there was no escape from the smell of spring. It filled everything from the ground up. But the only thing the smell of spring brought to mind for me now was that putrefying stench. Shut in behind my curtains, I felt a violent loathing for spring. I hated what the spring had in store for me; I hated the dull, throbbing ache it aroused inside me. I had never hated anything in my life with such intensity.

I spent three full days after that all but walking on the bottom of the sea. I could hardly hear what people said to me, and they had just as much trouble catching anything I had to say. My whole body felt enveloped in some kind of membrane, cutting off any direct contact between me and the outside world. I couldn't touch "them", and "they" couldn't touch me. I was utterly helpless, and as long as I remained in that state, "they" were unable to reach out to me.

I sat leaning against the wall, staring up at the ceiling. When I felt hungry I would nibble anything within reach, drink some water, and when the sadness of it got to me, I'd knock myself out with whisky. I didn't bathe, I didn't shave. This is how the three days went by.

A letter came from Midori on 6 April. She invited me to meet her on campus and have lunch on the tenth when we had to enrol for lectures. *I put off writing to you as long as I could, which makes us even, so let's make up. I have to admit it, I miss you.* I read the letter again and again, four times all together, and still I couldn't tell what she was trying to say to me. What could it possibly mean? My brain was so fogged over, I couldn't find the connection from one sentence to the next. How would meeting her on enrolment day make us *"even"*? Why did she want to have *"lunch"* with me? I was really losing it. My mind had gone slack, like the soggy roots of a subterranean plant. But somehow I knew I had to snap out of it. And then those words of Nagasawa's came to mind: "Don't feel sorry for yourself. Only arseholes do that."

"OK, Nagasawa. Right on," I heard myself thinking. I let out a sigh and got to my feet.

I did my laundry for the first time in weeks, went to the public bath and shaved, cleaned my place up, shopped for food and cooked myself a decent meal for a change, fed the starving Seagull, drank only beer, and did 30 minutes of exercise. Shaving, I discovered in the mirror that I was becoming emaciated. My eyes were popping. I could hardly recognize myself.

I went out the next morning on a longish bike ride, and after finishing lunch at home, I read Reiko's letter one more time. Then thought seriously about what I ought to do next. The main reason I had taken Reiko's letter so hard was that it had upset my optimistic belief that Naoko was getting better. Naoko herself had told me, "My sickness is a lot worse than you think: it has far deeper roots." And Reiko had warned me there was no telling what might happen. Still, I had seen Naoko twice, and had gained the impression she was on the

326

mend. I had assumed that the only problem was whether she could regain the courage to return to the real world, and that if she managed to, the two of us could join forces and make a go of it.

Reiko's letter smashed the illusory castle that I had built on that fragile hypothesis, leaving only a flattened surface devoid of feeling. I would have to do something to regain my footing. It would probably take a long time for Naoko to recover. And even then, she would no doubt be more debilitated and would have lost even more of her self confidence than ever. I would have to adapt myself to this new situation. As strong as I might become, though, it would not solve all the problems. I knew that much. But there was nothing else I could do: just keep my own spirits up and wait for her to recover.

Hey, there, Kizuki, I thought. Unlike you, I've chosen to live – and to live the best I know how. Sure, it was hard for you. What the hell, it's hard for *me*. Really hard. And all because you killed yourself and left Naoko behind. But that's something I will never do. I will never, ever, turn my back on her. First of all, because I love her, and because I'm stronger than she is. And I'm just going to keep on getting stronger. I'm going to mature. I'm going to be an adult. Because that's what I have to do. I always used to think I'd like to stay 17 or 18 if I could. But not any more. I'm not a teenager any more. I've got a sense of responsibility now. I'm not the same person I was when we used to hang out together. I'm 20 now. And I have to pay the price to go on living.

"Shit, Watanabe, what happened to *you?*" Midori asked. "You're all skin and bones!"

"That bad, huh?"

327

"Too much you-know-what with that married girlfriend of yours, I bet."

I smiled and shook my head. "I haven't slept with a girl since the beginning of October."

"Whew! That can't be true. We're talking six months here!"

"You heard me."

"So how did you lose so much weight?"

"By growing up," I said.

Midori put her hands on my shoulders and looked me in the eye with a twisted scowl that soon turned into a sweet smile. "It's true," she said. "Something's kind of different. You've changed."

"I told you, I grew up. I'm an adult now."

"You're fantastic, the way your brain works," she said as though genuinely impressed. "Let's eat. I'm starving."

We went to a little restaurant behind the literature department. I ordered the lunch special and she did the same.

"Hey, Watanabe, are you mad at me?"

"What for?"

"For not answering you, just to get even. Do you think I shouldn't have done that? I mean, you apologized and everything."

"Yeah, but it was my fault to begin with. That's just how it goes."

"My sister says I shouldn't have done it. That it was too unforgiving, too childish."

"Yeah, but it made you feel better, didn't it, getting even like that?"

"Uh-huh."

"OK, then, that's that."

"You *are* forgiving, aren't you?" Midori said. "But tell me the truth, Watanabe, you haven't had sex for six months?"

"Not once."

"So, that time you put me to bed, you must have really wanted it bad."

"Yeah, I guess I did."

"But you didn't do it, did you?"

"Look, you're the best friend I've got now," I said. "I don't want to lose you."

"You know, if you *had* tried to force yourself on me that time, I wouldn't have been able to resist, I was so exhausted."

"But I was too big and hard," I said.

Midori smiled and touched my wrist. "A little before that, I decided I was going to believe in you. A hundred per cent. That's how I managed to sleep like that with total peace of mind. I knew I'd be all right, I'd be safe with you there. And I *did* sleep like a log, didn't I?"

"You sure did."

"On the other hand, if you were to say to me, 'Hey, Midori, let's do it. Then everything'll be great,' I'd probably do it with you. Now, don't think I'm trying to seduce you or tease you. I'm just telling you what's on my mind, with total honesty."

"I know, I know."

While we ate lunch, we showed each other our enrolment cards and found that we had enrolled for two of the same courses. So I'd be seeing her twice a week at least. With that out of the way, Midori told me about her living arrangements. For a while, neither she nor her sister could get used to living in a flat – because it was too easy, she said. They had always been used to running around like mad every day, taking care of sick people, helping out at the bookshop, and one thing or another.

"We're finally getting used to it, though," she said. "This is the way we should have been living all along – not having to worry about anyone else's needs, just stretching out any way we felt like it. It made us both nervous at first, as if our bodies were floating a few inches off the ground. It didn't seem real, like real life couldn't actually be like that. We were both tense, as though everything was about to be tipped upside down any minute."

"A couple of worriers," I said with a smile.

"Well, it's just that life has been so cruel to us until now," Midori said. "But that's OK. We're going to get back everything it owes us."

"I bet you are," I said, "knowing you. But tell me, what's your sister doing these days?"

"A friend of hers opened this swanky accessory shop a little while ago. My sister helps out there three times a week. Otherwise, she's studying cookery, going on dates with her fiancé, going to the cinema, vegging out, and just enjoying life."

Midori then asked about my new life. I gave her a description of the layout of the house, and the big garden and Seagull the cat, and my landlord.

"Are you enjoying yourself?" she asked.

"Pretty much," I said.

"Could have fooled me," said Midori.

"Yeah, and it's springtime, too," I said.

"And you're wearing that cool pullover your girlfriend knitted for you."

With a sudden shock I glanced down at my wine-coloured jumper. "How did you know?"

"You're as honest as they come," said Midori. "I'm guessing, of course! Anyway, what's wrong with you?"

"I don't know. I'm trying to whip up a little enthusiasm."

"Just remember, life is a box of chocolates."

I shook my head a few times and looked at her. "Maybe I'm not so smart, but sometimes I don't know what on earth you're talking about."

"You know, they've got these chocolate assortments, and you like some but you don't like others? And you eat all the ones you like, and the only ones left are the ones you don't like as much? I always think about that when something painful comes up. 'Now I just have to polish these off, and everything'll be OK.' Life is a box of chocolates."

"I suppose you could call it a philosophy."

"It's true, though. I've learned it from experience."

We were drinking our coffee when two girls came in. Midori seemed to know them from university. The three of them compared enrolment cards and talked about a million different things: "What kind of mark did you get in German?" "So-and-so got hurt in the campus riots." "Great shoes, where did you buy them?" I half-listened, but it felt as though their comments were coming from the other side of the world. I sipped my coffee and watched the scene passing by the shop window. It was a typical university springtime scene as the new year was getting under way: a haze hanging in the sky, the cherry trees blooming, the new students (you could tell at a glance) carrying armloads of new books. I felt myself drifting off a little and thought about Naoko, unable to return to her studies again this year. A small glass full of anemones stood by the window.

When the other two went back to their table, Midori and I left to walk around the neighbourhood. We visited a few second-hand bookshops, bought some books, went to another café for another cup, played some pinball at an arcade, and sat on a park bench, talking – or, rather, Midori talked while

I merely grunted in response. When she said she was thirsty, I ran over to a newsagent's and bought us two Cokes. I came back to find her scribbling away with her ballpoint pen on some ruled paper.

"What's that?" I asked.

"Nothing," she said.

"I have to go," she announced at 3.30. "I'm supposed to meet my sister at the Ginza."

We walked to the subway station and went off in different directions. As she left, Midori stuffed the piece of paper, now folded in four, into my pocket. "Read this when you get home," she said. I read it on the train.

I'm writing this letter to you while you're off buying drinks. This is the first time in my life I've ever written a letter to somebody sitting next to me on a bench, but I feel it's the only way I can get through to you. I mean, you're hardly listening to anything I say. Am I right?

Do you realize you did something terrible to me today? You never even noticed that my hairstyle had changed, did you? I've been working on it forever, trying to grow it out, and finally, at the end of last week, I managed to get it into a style you could actually call girlish, but you never even noticed. It was looking pretty good, so I thought I'd give you a little shock when you saw me for the first time after so long, but it didn't even register with you. Don't you think that's awful? I bet you can't even remember what I was wearing today. Hey, I'm a girl! So what if you've got something on your mind? You can spare me one decent look! All you had to say was "Cute hair", and I would have been able to forgive you for being sunk in a million thoughts, but no!

Which is why I'm going to tell you a lie. It's not true that I have to meet my sister at the Ginza. I was planning to spend the night at your place. I even brought my pyjamas with me. It's true. I've got my pyjamas and a toothbrush in my bag. I'm such an idiot! I mean, you never even invited me over to see your new place. Oh well, what the hell, you obviously want to be alone, so I'll leave you alone. Go ahead and think away to your heart's content!

But don't get me wrong. I'm not totally mad at you. I'm just sad. You were so nice to me when I was having my problems, but now that you're having yours, it seems there's not a thing I can do for you. You're all locked up in that little world of yours, and when I try knocking on the door, you just sort of look up for a second and go right back inside.

So now I see you coming back with our drinks – walking and thinking. I was hoping you'd trip, but you didn't. Now you're sitting next to me drinking your Coke. I was holding out one last hope that you'd notice and say "Hey, your hair's changed!" but no. If you had, I would have torn up this letter and said: "Let's go to your place. I'll make you a nice dinner. And afterwards we can go to bed and cuddle." But you're about as sensitive as a steel plate. Goodbye.

P.S. Please don't talk to me next time we meet.

I rang Midori's flat from the station when I got off the train in Kichijoji, but there was no answer. With nothing better to do, I ambled around the neighbourhood looking for some part-time work I could take after lectures began. I would be free all day Saturday and Sunday and could work after five o'clock on Mondays, Wednesdays and Thursdays; but finding a job that fitted my particular schedule was no easy matter. I gave up and went home. When I went out to buy groceries for dinner, I tried Midori's place again. Her sister told me that Midori hadn't come home yet and that she had no idea when she'd be back. I thanked her and hung up.

After eating, I tried to write to Midori, but I gave up after several false starts and wrote to Naoko instead.

Spring was here, I said, and the new university year was starting. I told her I missed her, that I had been hoping, one way or another, to be able to meet her and talk. *In any case, I wrote, I've decided to make myself strong. As far as I can tell, that's all I can do.*

> There's one other thing. Maybe it's just to do with me, and you may not care about this one way or another, but I'm not sleeping with anybody any more. It's because I don't want to forget the last time you touched me. It meant a lot more to me than you might think. I think about it all of the time.

I put the letter in an envelope, stuck on a stamp, and sat at my desk a long while staring at it. It was a much shorter letter than usual, but I had the feeling that Naoko might understand me better that way. I poured myself an inch-and-a-half of whisky, drank it in two swallows, and went to sleep.

The next day I found a job near Kichijoji Station that I could do on Saturdays and Sundays: waiting on tables at a smallish Italian restaurant. The conditions were pretty poor, but travel and lunch expenses were included. And whenever somebody on the late shift took the day off on a Monday, Wednesday or Thursday (which happened often) I could take their place. This was perfect for me. The manager said they would raise my pay when I had stayed for three months, and they wanted me to start that Saturday. He was a much more decent guy than the idiot who ran the record shop in Shinjuku.

I tried phoning Midori's flat again, and again her sister answered. Midori hadn't come back since yesterday, she said, sounding tired, and now she herself was beginning to worry: did I have any idea where she might have gone? All I knew was that Midori had her pyjamas and a toothbrush in her bag.

I saw Midori at the lecture on Wednesday. She was wearing a deep green pullover and the dark sunglasses she had often worn that summer. She was seated in the last row, talking with a thin girl with glasses I had seen once before. I approached her and said I'd like to talk afterwards. The girl with glasses looked at me first, and then Midori looked at me. Her hairstyle was, in fact, somewhat more feminine than it had been before: more mature.

"I have to meet someone," she said, cocking her head slightly.

"I won't take up much of your time," I said. "Five minutes."

Midori removed her sunglasses and narrowed her eyes. She might just as well have been looking at a crumbling, abandoned house some hundred yards in the distance.

"I don't want to talk to you. Sorry," she said.

The girl with glasses looked at me with eyes that said: She says she doesn't want to talk to you. Sorry.

I sat at the right end of the front row for the lecture (an

overview of the works of Tennessee Williams and their place in American literature), and when it was over, I did a long count to three and turned around. Midori was gone.

April was too lonely a month to spend all alone. In April, everyone around me looked happy. People would throw off their coats and enjoy each other's company in the sunshine – talking, playing catch, holding hands. But I was always by myself. Naoko, Midori, Nagasawa: all of them had gone away from where I stood. Now I had no one to say "Good morning" to or "Have a nice day". I even missed Storm Trooper. I spent the whole month with this hopeless sense of isolation. I tried to speak to Midori a few times, but the answer I got from her was always the same: "I don't want to talk to you now" – and I knew from the tone of her voice that she meant it. She was always with the girl with glasses, or else I saw her with a tall, short-haired guy. He had these incredibly long legs and always wore white basketball shoes.

April ended and May came along, but May was even worse than April. In the deepening spring of May, I had no choice but to recognize the trembling of my heart. It usually happened as the sun was going down. In the pale evening gloom, when the soft fragrance of magnolias hung in the air, my heart would swell without warning, and tremble, and lurch with a stab of pain. I would try clamping my eyes shut and gritting my teeth, and wait for it to pass. And it *would* pass – but slowly, taking its own time, and leaving a dull ache in its path.

At those times I would write to Naoko. In my letters to her, I would describe only things that were touching or pleasant or beautiful: the fragrance of grasses, the caress of a spring breeze, the light of the moon, a film I'd seen, a song I liked, a book that had moved me. I myself would be comforted by letters like this when I would reread what I had written. And I would feel that the world I lived in was a wonderful one. I wrote any number of letters like this, but from Naoko or Reiko I heard nothing.

At the restaurant where I worked I got to know another student my age named Itoh. It took quite a while before this gentle, quiet student from the oil-painting department of an art college would engage me in conversation, but eventually we started going to a nearby bar after work and talking about all kinds of things. He also liked to read and to listen to music, so we'd usually talk about books and records we liked. He was a slim, good-looking guy with much shorter hair and far cleaner clothes than the typical art student. He never had a lot to say, but he had his definite tastes and opinions. He liked French novels, especially those of Georges Bataille and Boris Vian. For music, he preferred Mozart and Ravel. And, like me, he was looking for a friend with whom he could talk about such things.

Itoh once invited me to his flat. It was not quite as hard to get to as mine: a strange, one-floored house behind Inokashira Park. His room was stuffed with painting supplies and canvases. I asked to see his work, but he said he was too embarrassed to show me anything. We drank some Chivas Regal that he had quietly removed from his father's place, grilled some smelts on his charcoal stove, and listened to Robert Casadesus playing a Mozart piano concerto.

Itoh was from Nagasaki. He had a girlfriend he would sleep with whenever he went home, he said, but things weren't going too well with her lately.

"You know what girls are like," he said. "They turn 20 or 21 and all of a sudden they start having these concrete ideas. They get super-realistic. And when that happens, everything

337

that seemed so sweet and loveable about them begins to look ordinary and depressing. Now when I see her, usually after we do it, she starts asking me, 'What are you going to do after you graduate?'"

"Well, what *are* you going to do after you graduate?" I asked him.

Munching on a mouthful of smelt, he shook his head. "What *can* I do? I'm in oil painting! Start worrying about stuff like that, and *nobody's* going to study oil painting! You don't do it to feed yourself. So she's like, 'Why don't you come back to Nagasaki and become an art teacher?' She's planning to be an English teacher."

"You're not so crazy about her any more, are you?"

"That just about sums it up," Itoh admitted. "And who on earth wants to be an art teacher? I'm not gonna spend my whole fuckin' life teaching teenaged monkeys how to draw!"

"That's beside the point," I said. "Don't you think you ought to break up with her? For both your sakes."

"Sure I do. But I don't know how to say it to her. She's planning to spend her life with me. How the hell can I say, 'Hey, we ought to split up. I don't like you any more'?"

We drank our Chivas straight, without ice, and when we ran out of smelts we cut up some cucumbers and celery and dipped them in miso. When my teeth crunched down on my cucumber slices, I thought of Midori's father, which reminded me how flat and tasteless my life had become without Midori and this put me in a foul mood. Without my being aware of it, she had become a huge presence inside me.

"Got a girlfriend?" asked Itoh.

"Yeah," I said, then, after a pause added, "but I can't be with her at the moment."

"But you understand each other's feelings, right?"

"I like to think so. Otherwise, what's the point?" I said with a chuckle.

Itoh talked in hushed tones about the greatness of Mozart. He knew Mozart inside out, the way a country boy knows his mountain trails. His father loved the music and had exposed him to it ever since he was tiny. I didn't know so much about classical music, but listening to this Mozart concerto with Itoh's smart and heartfelt commentary ("There – that part," "How about *that*?"), I felt myself calming down for the first time in ages. We stared at the crescent moon hanging over Inokashira Park and drank our Chivas Regal to the last drop. Fantastic whisky.

Itoh said I could spend the night there, but I told him I had to do something, thanked him for the whisky and left his flat before nine. On the way back to my place I called Midori from a phone box. Much to my surprise she actually answered.

"Sorry," she said, "but I don't want to talk to you right now."

"I know, I know. But I don't want our relationship to end like this. You're one of the very few friends I have, and it hurts not being able to see you. When *am* I going to be able to talk to you? I want you to tell me that much, at least."

"When *I* feel like talking to *you*," she said.

"How are you?" I asked.

"Fine," she said, and hung up.

A letter came from Reiko in the middle of May.

Thanks for writing so often. Naoko enjoys your letters. And so do I. You don't mind if I read them, do you?

Sorry I haven't been able to answer for such a long

339

time. To tell you the truth, I've been feeling a bit exhausted, and there hasn't been much good news to report. Naoko's not doing well. Her mother came from Kobe the other day. The four of us – she and Naoko and the doctor and I – had a good, long talk and we reached the conclusion that Naoko should move to a real hospital for a while for some intensive treatment and then maybe come back here depending on the results. Naoko says she'd like to stay here if possible and make herself well, and I know I am going to miss her and worry about her, but the fact is that it's getting harder and harder to keep her under control here. She's fine most of the time, but sometimes her emotions become extremely unstable, and when that happens we can't take our eyes off her. There's no telling what she would do. When she has those intense episodes of hearing voices, she shuts down completely and burrows inside herself.

Which is why I myself agree that the best thing for Naoko would be for her to receive therapy at a proper institution for a while. I hate to say it, but it's all we can do. As I told you once before, patience is the most important thing. We have to go on unravelling the jumbled threads one at a time, without losing hope. No matter how hopeless her condition may appear to be, we are bound to find that one loose thread sooner or later. If you're in pitch blackness, all you can do is sit tight until your eyes get used to the dark.

Naoko should have moved to that other hospital by the time you receive this. I'm sorry I waited to tell you until the decisions had been made, but it happened very quickly. The new hospital is a really good one, with good doctors. I'll write the address below: please write to Naoko there. They will be keeping me informed of her progress, too, so I will let you know what I hear. I hope it will be good news. I know this is going to be hard for you, but keep your hopes up. And even though Naoko is not here any more, please write to me once in a while.

Goodbye.

I wrote a huge number of letters that spring: one a week to Naoko, several to Reiko, and several more to Midori. I wrote letters in the lecture hall, I wrote letters at my desk at home with Seagull on my lap, I wrote letters at empty tables during my breaks at the Italian restaurant. It was as if I were writing letters to hold together the pieces of my crumbling life.

To Midori I wrote: *April and May were painful, lonely months for me because I couldn't talk to you. I never knew that spring could be so painful and lonely. Better to have three Februaries than a spring like this. I know it's too late to be saying this, but your new hairstyle looks great on you. Really cute. I'm working at an Italian restaurant now, and the cook taught me a great way to make spaghetti. I'd like to make it for you soon.*

I went to the university every day, worked in the restaurant two or three times a week, talked with Itoh about books and music, read a few Boris Vian novels he lent me, wrote letters, played with Seagull, made spaghetti, worked in the garden, masturbated thinking of Naoko, and saw lots of films.

It was almost the middle of June by the time Midori started talking to me. We hadn't said a word to each other for two months. After the end of one lecture, she sat down next to me, propped her chin in her hand, and sat there, saying nothing.

Beyond the window, it was raining – a really rainy-season rain, pouring straight down without any wind, soaking every single thing beneath. Long after the other students had filed out of the classroom, Midori went on sitting next to me without a word. Then she took a Marlboro from the pocket of her jeans jacket, put it between her lips, and handed me her matches. I struck a match and lit her cigarette. Midori pursed her lips and blew a gentle cloud of tobacco in my face.

"Like my hairstyle?" she asked.

"It's great."

"How great?"

"Great enough to knock down all the trees in all the forests of the world."

"You really think so?"

"I really think so."

She kept her eyes on mine for a while, then held her right hand out to me. I took it. She looked even more relieved than I felt. She tapped her ashes onto the floor and rose to her feet.

"Let's eat. I'm starving," she said.

"Where do you want to go?" I asked.

"To the restaurant of the Takashimaya department store in Nihonbashi."

"Why *there* of all places?"

"I like to go there sometimes, that's all."

And so we took the subway to Nihonbashi. The place was practically empty, maybe because it had been raining all morning. The smell of rain filled the big, cavernous department store, and all the employees had that what-do-we-do-now? kind of look. Midori and I went to the basement restaurant and, after a close inspection of the plastic food in the window, both decided to have an old-fashioned cold lunch assortment with rice and pickles and grilled fish and tempura and teriyaki chicken. Inside, it was far from crowded despite it being midday.

"God, how long has it been since I last had lunch in a department-store restaurant?" I wondered aloud, drinking green tea from one of those slick, white cups you only get in a department-store restaurant.

"I like to do stuff like this," said Midori. "I don't know, it makes me feel like I'm doing something special. Probably reminds me of when I was a kid. My parents almost never took me to department stores."

"And I get the sneaking suspicion that's all mine *ever* did. My mother was crazy about them."

"Lucky you!"

"What are you talking about? I don't particularly like going to department stores."

"No, I mean, you were lucky they cared enough about you to take you places."

"Well, I was an only child," I said.

"When I was little I used to dream about going to a department-store restaurant all by myself when I grew up and eating anything I liked. But what an empty dream! What's the fun of cramming your mouth full of rice all alone in a place like this? The food's not all that great, and it's just big and crowded and stuffy and noisy. Still, every once in a while I think about coming here."

"I've been really lonely these past two months," I said.

"Yeah, I know. You told me in your letters," Midori said, her voice flat. "Anyway, let's eat. That's all I can think about now."

We finished all the little fried and grilled and pickled items in the separate compartments of our fancy lacquered half-moon lunch boxes, drank our clear soup from lacquered bowls, and our green tea from those white cups. Midori followed lunch with a cigarette. When she had finished smoking, she stood up without a word and took her umbrella. I also stood up and took mine.

"Where do you want to go now?" I asked.

"The roof, of course. That's the next stop when you've had lunch in a department-store restaurant."

There was no one on the roof in the rain, no clerk in the pet department, and the shutters were closed in the kiosks and the children's rides ticket booth. We opened our umbrellas and wandered among the soaking wet wooden horses and garden chairs and stalls. It seemed incredible to me that there could be anywhere so devoid of people in the middle of Tokyo. Midori said she wanted to look through a telescope, so I put in a coin and held her umbrella over her while she squinted through the eyepiece.

In one corner of the roof there was a covered game area with a row of children's rides. Midori and I sat next to each other on some kind of platform and looked at the rain.

"So talk," Midori said. "You've got something you want to say to me, I know."

"I'm not trying to make excuses," I said, "but I was really depressed that time. My brain was all fogged over. Nothing was registering with me. But one thing became crystal clear to me when I couldn't see you any more. I realized that the only way I had been able to survive until then was having you in my life. When I lost you, the pain and loneliness really got to me."

"Don't you have any idea how painful and lonely it's been for *me* without *you* these past two months?"

This took me completely off guard. "No," I said. "It never occurred to me. I thought you were angry with me and didn't want to see me."

"How can you be such an idiot? Of *course* I wanted to see you! I *told* you how much I like you! When I like somebody I really like them. It doesn't turn on and off for me just like that. Don't you realize at least *that* much about me?"

"Well, sure, but – "

"*That's* why I was so mad at you! I wanted to give you a good kick up the arse. I mean, we hadn't seen each other that whole time, and you were so spaced out thinking about this other girl you didn't even *look* at me! How could I *not* get angry at you? But apart from all that, I had been feeling for a long time that it would be better for me if I kept away from you for a while. To get things clear in my head."

"What kind of things?"

"Our *relationship*, of course. It was getting to the point where I enjoyed being with *you* far more than being with *him*. I mean, don't you think there's something weird about that? And difficult? Of course I still like him. He's a little self-centred and narrow-minded and kind of a fascist, but he's got a lot of good points, and he's the first man I ever felt serious about. But you, well, you're special to me. When I'm with you I feel something is just right. I believe in you. I like you. I don't want to let you go. I was getting more and more confused, so I went to him and asked him what I should do. He told me to stop seeing you. He said if I was going to see you, I should break up with him."

"So what did you do?"

"I broke up with him. Just like that." Midori put a Marlboro in her mouth, shielded it with her hand as she lit up, and inhaled.

"Why?"

"'Why?'!" she screamed. "Are you *crazy*? You know the English subjunctive, you understand trigonometry, you can

345

read Marx, and you don't know the answer to something as simple as *that*? Why do you even have to *ask*? Why do you have to make a girl *say* something like this? I like *you* more than I like *him*, that's all. I wish I had fallen in love with somebody a little more handsome, of course. But I didn't. I fell in love with *you*!"

I tried to speak, but I felt the words catching in my throat.

Midori threw her cigarette into a puddle. "Will you *please* get that look off your face? You're gonna make me cry. Don't worry, I *know* you're in love with somebody else. I'm not expecting anything from you. But the least you can do is give me a hug. These have been two tough months for me."

I put up my umbrella, and we went behind the game area and held each other close. Our bodies strained against each other, and our lips met. The smell of the rain clung to her hair and her jeans jacket. Girls' bodies were so soft and warm! I could feel her breasts pressing against my chest through our clothing. How long had it been since my last physical contact with another human being?

"The day I last saw you, that night I talked to him, and we broke up," Midori said.

"I love you," I said to her. "From the bottom of my heart. I don't ever want to let you go again. But there's nothing I can do. I can't make a move."

"Because of her?"

I nodded.

"Tell me, have you slept with her?"

"Once. A year ago."

"And you haven't seen her since then?"

"I *have* seen her: twice. But we didn't do anything."

"Why not? Doesn't she love you?"

"That's hard to say," I said. "It's really complicated. And

346

mixed up. And it's been going on for such a long time, I don't know what's what any more. And neither does she. All I know is, I have a sort of responsibility in all this as a human being, and I can't just turn my back on it. At least, that's how I feel about it now. Even if she isn't in love with me."

"Let me just tell you this, Watanabe," said Midori, pressing her cheek against my neck. "I'm a real, live girl, with real, live blood gushing through my veins. You're holding me in your arms and I'm telling you that I love you. I'm ready to do anything you tell me to do. I may be a little bit mad, but I'm a good girl, and honest, and I work hard, I'm kind of cute, I have nice boobs, I'm a good cook, and my father left me a trust fund. I mean, I'm a real bargain, don't you think? If you don't take me, I'll end up going somewhere else."

"I need time," I said. "I need time to think and sort things out, and make some decisions. I'm sorry, but that's all I can say at this point."

"Yeah, but you *do* love me from the bottom of your heart, right? And you never want to let me go again, right?"

"I said it and I meant it."

Midori pulled away from me with a smile on her face. "OK, I'll wait! I believe in you," she said. "But when you take me, you take *only* me. And when you hold me in your arms, you think *only* about *me*. Is that clear?"

"I understand exactly."

"I don't care what you do to me, but I don't want you to hurt me. I've had enough hurt already in my life. More than enough. Now I want to be happy."

I drew her close and kissed her on the mouth.

"Drop the damn umbrella and wrap *both* your arms around me – hard!" she said.

"But we'll get soaking wet!"

347

"So what? I want you to stop thinking and hold me tight! I've been waiting two whole months for this!"

I set down the umbrella and held her close in the rain. The dull rush of tyres on the highway enveloped us like a fog. The rain fell without a break, without a sound, soaking her hair and mine, running like tears down our cheeks, down to her denim jacket and my yellow nylon windcheater, spreading in dark stains.

"How about going back under the roof?" I said.

"Come to my place. There's nobody home now. We'll both catch colds like this."

"It's true."

"It's as if we've just swum across a river," Midori said, smiling. "What a great feeling!"

We bought a good-sized towel in the linen department and took turns going into the bathroom to dry our hair. Then we took the subway, with the necessary top-up tickets, to her flat in Myogadani. She let me shower first and then she showered. Lending me a bathrobe to wear while my clothes dried, Midori changed into a polo shirt and skirt. We sat at the kitchen table drinking coffee.

"Tell me about yourself," Midori said.

"What about me?"

"Hmm, I don't know, what do you hate?"

"Chicken and VD and barbers who talk too much."

"What else?"

"Lonely April nights and lacy telephone covers."

"What else?"

I shook my head. "I can't think of anything else."

"My boyfriend – which is to say, my ex-boyfriend – had all kinds of things he hated. Like when I wore too-short skirts, or when I smoked, or how I got drunk too quickly, or said disgusting things, or criticized his friends. So if there's anything about me you don't like, just tell me, and I'll fix it if I can."

"I can't think of anything," I said after giving it some thought. "There's nothing."

"Really?"

"I like everything you wear, and I like what you do and say and how you walk and how you get drunk. Everything."

"You mean I'm really OK just the way I am?"

"I don't know how you could change, so you must be fine the way you are."

"How much do you love me?" Midori asked.

"Enough to melt all the tigers in the world to butter," I said.

"Far out," she said with a hint of satisfaction. "Will you hold me again?"

We got into her bed and held each other, kissing as the sound of the rain filled our ears. Then we talked about everything from the formation of the universe to our preferences in the hardness of boiled eggs.

"I wonder what ants do on rainy days?" Midori asked.

"No idea," I said. "They're hard workers, so they probably spend the day cleaning house or stock-taking."

"If they work so hard, why don't they evolve? They've been the same for ever."

"I don't know," I said. "Maybe their body structure isn't suited to evolving – compared with monkeys, say."

"Hey, Watanabe, there's a lot of stuff you don't know. I thought you knew everything."

"It's a big world out there," I said.

"High mountains, deep oceans," Midori said. She put her hand inside my bathrobe and took hold of my erection. Then, with a gulp, she said, "Hey, Watanabe, joking aside, this isn't gonna work. I could never get this big, hard thing inside me. No way."

"You're kidding," I said with a sigh.

"Yup," she said, giggling. "Don't worry. It'll be just fine. I'm sure it'll fit. Er, mind if I have a look?"

"Feel free."

Midori burrowed under the covers and groped me all over down there, stretching the skin of my penis, weighing my testicles in the palm of her hand. Then she poked her head out and sighed. "I love it!" she said. "No flattery intended! I really love it!"

"Thank you," I said with simple gratitude.

"But really, Watanabe, you don't want to do it with me, do you – until you get all that business straightened out?"

"There's no way I don't want to do it with you," I said. "I'm going crazy I want to do it so bad. But it just wouldn't be right."

"You're so damned stubborn! If I were you, I'd just *do* it – then think about it afterwards."

"You would?"

"Only kidding," Midori said in a tiny voice. "I probably wouldn't do it, either, if I were you. And that's what I love about you. That's what I really really love about you."

"How much do you love me?" I asked, but she didn't answer. Instead, she pressed against me, put her lips on my nipple and began to move the hand that was wrapped around my penis. The first thing that occurred to me was how different it was to the way Naoko moved her hand. Both were gentle and wonderful, but something was different about the way they did it, and so it felt like a totally different experience.

"Hey, Watanabe, I bet you're thinking about that other girl."

"Not true," I lied.

"Really?"

"Really."

"Because I would really hate that."

"I *can't* think about anybody else," I said.

"Want to touch my breasts, or down there?" Midori asked.

"Oh wow, I'd love to, but I'd better not. If we do all those things at once, it'll be too much for me."

Midori nodded and rustled around under the covers, pulling her panties off and holding them against the tip of my penis.

"You can come on these," she said.

"But it'll make a mess of them."

"Stop it, will you? You're gonna make me cry," said Midori, as if on the verge of tears. "All I have to do is wash them. So don't hold back, just let yourself come all you want. If you're worried about my panties, buy me a new pair. Or are they going to keep you from coming because they're mine?"

"No way," I said.

"Go on then, let go."

When I was through, Midori inspected my semen. "Wow, that's a huge amount!"

"Too much?"

"Nah, it's OK, silly. Come all you want," she said with a smile. Then she kissed me.

In the evening, Midori did some shopping in the neighbourhood and made dinner. We ate tempura and rice with green peas at the kitchen table, and washed it all down with beer.

"Eat a lot and make lots of semen," Midori said. "Then I'll be nice and help you get rid of it."

"Thanks very much," I said.

"I know all sorts of ways to do it. I learned from the women's magazines when we had the bookshop. Once they had this special edition all about how to take care of your husband so he won't cheat on you while you're pregnant and can't have sex. There's tons of ways. Wanna try 'em?"

"I can hardly wait," I said.

After saying goodbye to Midori, I bought a newspaper at the station, but when I opened it on the train, I realized I had absolutely no desire to read a paper and in fact couldn't understand what it said. All I could do was glare at the incomprehensible page of print and wonder what was going to happen to me from now on, and how the things around me would be changing. I felt as if the world was pulsating every now and then. I sighed deeply and closed my eyes. As regards what I had done that day, I felt not the slightest regret; I knew for certain that if I had to do it all over again, I would live this day in exactly the same way. I would hold Midori tight on the roof in the rain; I would get soaking wet with her; and I would let her fingers bring me to climax in her bed. I had no doubts about those things. I loved Midori, and I was happy that she had come back to me. The two of us could make it, that was certain. As Midori herself had said, she was a real, live girl with blood in her veins, and she was putting her warm body in my arms. It had been all I could do to suppress the intense desire I had to strip her naked, throw open her body, and sink myself in her warmth. There was no way I could have made myself stop her once she was holding my penis and moving her hand. I wanted her to do it, she wanted to do it, and we were in love. Who could have stopped such a thing? It was true: I loved Midori. And I had probably known as much for a while. I had just been avoiding the conclusion for a very long time.

The problem was that I could never explain these developments to Naoko. It would have been hard enough at any point, but with Naoko in her present condition, there was no way I could tell her I had fallen in love with another girl. And besides, I still loved Naoko. As twisted as that love might be, I did love her. Somewhere inside me there was still preserved a broad, open space, untouched, for Naoko and no one else.

One thing I could do was write a letter to Reiko that confessed everything with total honesty. At home, I sat on the veranda, watching the rain pour down on the garden at night, and assembling phrases in my head. Then I went to my desk and wrote the letter. *It is almost unbearable to me that I now have to write a letter like this to you,* I began. I summarized my relationship with Midori and explained what had happened that day.

I have always loved Naoko, and I still love her. But there is a decisive finality to what exists between Midori and me. It has an irresistible power that is bound to sweep me into the future. What I feel for Naoko is a tremendously quiet and gentle and transparent love, but what I feel for Midori is a wholly different emotion. It stands and walks on its own, living and breathing and throbbing and shaking me to the roots of my being. I don't know what to do. I'm confused. I'm not trying to make excuses for myself, but I do believe that I have lived as sincerely as I know how. I have never lied to anyone, and I have taken care over the years not to hurt other people. And yet I find myself tossed into this labyrinth. How can this be? I can't explain it. I don't know what I should do. Can you tell me, Reiko? You're the only one I can turn to for advice.

I posted the letter that night by special delivery.

Reiko's answer came five days later, dated 17 June.

Let me start with the good news. Naoko has been improving far more rapidly than anyone could have expected. I talked to her once on the phone, and she spoke with real lucidity. She may even be able to come back here before long.

Now, about you.

I think you take everything too seriously. Loving another person is a wonderful thing, and if that love is sincere, no one ends up tossed into a labyrinth. You have to have more faith in yourself.

My advice to you is very simple. First of all, if you are drawn so strongly to this Midori person, it is only natural for you to have fallen in love with her. It might go well, or it might not. But love is like that. When you fall in love, the natural thing to do is give yourself to it. That's what I think. It's just a form of sincerity.

Second, as to whether or not you should have sex with Midori, that is for you to work out. I can't say a thing. Talk it over with Midori and reach your own conclusion, one that makes sense to you.

Third, don't tell any of this to Naoko. If things should develop to the point where you absolutely have to tell her, then you and I will come up with a good plan together. So now, just keep it quiet. Leave it to me.

The fourth thing I have to say is that you have been such a great source of strength for Naoko that even if you no longer have the feelings of a lover towards her, there is still a lot you can do for her. So don't brood over everything in that super-serious way of yours. All of us (by which I mean *all* of us, both normal and not-so-normal) are imperfect human beings living in an imperfect world. We don't live with the mechanical precision of a bank account or by measuring all our lines and angles with rulers and protractors. Am I right?

My own personal feeling is that Midori sounds like a great girl. I understand just reading your letter why you would be drawn to her. And I understand, too, why you would also be drawn to Naoko. There's nothing the least bit sinful about it. Things like that happen all the time in this great big world of ours. It's like taking a boat out on a beautiful lake on a beautiful day and thinking both the sky and the lake are beautiful. So stop eating yourself up. Things will go where they're supposed to go if you just let them take their natural course. Despite your best efforts, people are going to be hurt when it's time for them to be hurt. Life is like that. I know I sound like I'm preaching from a pulpit, but it's about time you learned to live like this. You try too hard to make life fit your way of doing things. If you don't want to spend time in an insane asylum, you have to open up a little more and let yourself go with life's natural flow. I'm just a powerless and imperfect woman, but still there are times when I think to myself how wonderful life can be! Believe me, it's true! So stop what you're doing this minute and get happy. *Work* at making yourself happy!

Needless to say, I do feel sorry that you and Naoko could not see things through to a happy ending. But who can say what's best? That's why you need to grab whatever chance you have of happiness where you find it, and not worry about other people too much. My experience tells me that we get no more than two or three such chances in a lifetime, and if we let them go, we regret it for the rest of our lives.

I'm playing the guitar every day for no one in particular. It seems a bit pointless. I don't like dark, rainy nights, either. I hope I'll have another chance to play my guitar and eat grapes with you and Naoko in the room with me.

Ah, well, until then –

Reiko Ishida

第 11 章

Reiko wrote to me several times after Naoko's death. It wasn't my fault, she said. It was nobody's fault, any more than you could blame someone for the rain. But I never answered her. What could I have said? What good would it have done? Naoko no longer existed in this world; she had become a handful of ashes.

They held a quiet funeral for Naoko in Kobe at the end of August, and when it was over, I went back to Tokyo. I told my landlord I would be away for a while and my boss at the Italian restaurant that I wouldn't be coming in to work. To Midori I wrote a short note: I couldn't say anything just yet, but I hoped she would wait for me a little longer. I spent the next three days in cinemas, and after I had seen every new film in Tokyo, I packed my rucksack, took out all my savings from the bank, went to Shinjuku Station, and got the first express train I could find going out of town.

Where I went on my travels, it's impossible for me to recall. I remember the sights and sounds and smells clearly enough, but the names of the towns are gone, as well as any sense of the order in which I travelled from place to place. I would move from town to town by train or bus or hitching a lift in a lorry, spreading out my sleeping bag in empty car parks or stations or parks or on river banks or the seashore. I once persuaded them to let me sleep in the corner of a local police station, and another time slept alongside a graveyard. I didn't care where I slept, provided I was out of people's way and could stay in my sleeping bag as long as I felt like it. Exhausted from walking, I would crawl into it, gulp down some cheap whisky, and fall fast asleep. In nice towns, people would bring me food and mosquito coils, and in not-so-nice towns, people would call the police and have me chased out of the parks. It made no difference to me one way or another. All I wanted was to put myself to sleep in towns I didn't know.

When I ran low on money, I would work as a labourer for a few days until I had what I needed. There was always work for me to do. I just kept moving from one town to the next, no destination in mind. The world was big and full of weird things and strange people. One time I called Midori because I had to hear her voice.

"Term started a long time ago, you know," she said. "Some courses are even asking for papers already. What are you going to *do*? Do you realize you've been out of touch for three whole weeks now? Where are you? What are you doing?"

"Sorry, but I can't go back to Tokyo yet. Not yet."

"And that's all you're going to tell me?"

"There's really nothing more I can say at this point. Maybe in October . . ."

Midori hung up without a word.

I went on with my travels. Every now and then I'd stay at a dosshouse and have a bath and shave. What I saw in the mirror looked terrible. The sun had dried out my skin, my eyes were sunken, and odd stains and cuts marked my cheekbones. I looked as if I had just crawled out of a cave somewhere, but it was me after all. It was me.

By that time, I was moving down the coast, as far from

Tokyo as I could get – maybe in Tottori or the hidden side of Hyogo. Walking along the seashore was easy. I could always find a comfortable place to sleep in the sand. I'd make a fire from driftwood and roast some dried fish I bought from a local fisherman. Then I'd swallow some whisky and listen to the waves while I thought about Naoko. It was too strange to think that she was dead and no longer part of this world. I couldn't absorb the truth of it. I couldn't believe it. I had heard the nails being driven into the lid of her coffin, but I still couldn't adjust to the fact that she had returned to nothingness.

No, the image of her was still too vivid in my memory. I could still see her enclosing my penis in her mouth, her hair falling across my belly. I could still feel her warmth, her breath against me, and that helpless moment when I could do nothing but come. I could bring all this back as clearly as if it had happened only five minutes ago, and I felt sure that Naoko was still beside me, that I could just reach out and touch her. But no, she wasn't there; her flesh no longer existed in this world.

Nights when it was impossible for me to sleep, images of Naoko would come back to me. There was no way I could stop them. Too many memories of her were crammed inside me, and as soon as one of them found the slightest opening, the rest would force their way out in an endless stream, an unstoppable flood: Naoko in her yellow raincape cleaning the aviary and carrying the feed bag that rainy morning; the caved-in birthday cake and the feel of Naoko's tears soaking through my shirt (yes, it had been raining then, too); Naoko walking beside me in winter wearing her camel-hair coat; Naoko touching the hairslide she always wore; Naoko peering at me with those incredibly clear eyes of hers; Naoko sitting on the sofa, legs drawn up beneath her blue nightdress, chin resting on her knees.

The memories would slam against me like the waves of an incoming tide, sweeping my body along to some strange new place – a place where I lived with the dead. There Naoko lived, and I could speak with her and hold her in my arms. Death in that place was not a decisive element that brought life to an end. There, death was but one of many elements comprising life. There Naoko lived with death inside her. And to me she said, "Don't worry, it's only death. Don't let it bother you."

I felt no sadness in that strange place. Death was death, and Naoko was Naoko. "What's the problem?" she asked me with a bashful smile, "I'm here, aren't I?" Her familiar little gestures soothed my heart like a healing balm. "If this is death," I thought to myself, "then death is not so bad." "It's true," said Naoko, "death is nothing much. It's just death. Things are so easy for me here." Naoko spoke to me in the spaces between the crashing of the dark waves.

Eventually, though, the tide would pull back, and I would be left on the beach alone. Powerless, I could go nowhere; sadness itself would envelop me in deep darkness until the tears came. I felt less that I was crying than that the tears were simply oozing out of me like perspiration.

I had learned one thing from Kizuki's death, and I believed that I had made it a part of myself in the form of a philosophy: "Death exists, not as the opposite but as a part of life."

By living our lives, we nurture death. True as this might be, it was only one of the truths we had to learn. What I learned from Naoko's death was this: no truth can cure the sadness we feel from losing a loved one. No truth, no sincerity, no strength, no kindness, can cure that sorrow. All we can do is see that sadness through to the end and learn something from it, but what we learn will be no help in facing the next sadness that comes to us without warning. Hearing the waves at night, listening to the sound of the wind, day after day I focused on these thoughts of mine. Knapsack on my back, sand in my hair, I moved farther and farther west, surviving on a diet of whisky, bread and water.

One windy evening, as I lay wrapped in my sleeping bag, weeping, by the side of an abandoned hulk, a young fisherman passed by and offered me a cigarette. I accepted it and had my first smoke in over a year. He asked why I was crying, and almost by reflex I told him that my mother had died. I couldn't take the sadness, I said, and so I was on the road. He expressed his deep sympathy and brought a big bottle of sake and two glasses from his house.

The wind tore along the sand beach as we sat there drinking. He told me that he had lost his mother when he was 16. Never healthy, she had worn herself out working from morning to night. I half-listened to him, sipping my sake and grunting in response every now and then. I felt as if I were hearing a story from some far-off world. What the hell was he talking about? I wondered, and all of a sudden I was filled with intense rage: I wanted to strangle him. Who gives a shit about your mother? I've lost Naoko! Her beautiful flesh has vanished from this world! Why the hell are you telling me about your fucking mother?!

But my rage disappeared as quickly as it had flared up. I closed my eyes and went on half-listening to the fisherman's endless talk. Eventually he asked me if I had eaten. No, I said, but in my rucksack I had bread and cheese, a tomato and a piece of chocolate. What had I eaten for lunch? he asked.

Bread and cheese, tomato and chocolate, I answered. "Wait here," he said and ran off. I tried to stop him, but he disappeared into the darkness without looking back.

All I could do was go on drinking my sake. The shore was littered with paper flecks from fireworks that had been exploded on the sand, and waves crashed against the beach with a mad roar. A scrawny dog came up wagging its tail and sniffing around my little campfire for something to eat but eventually gave up and wandered away.

The young fisherman came back half an hour later with two boxes of sushi and a new bottle of sake. I should eat the top box straight away because that had fish in it, he said, but the bottom box had only nori rolls and deep-fried tofu skins so they would last all tomorrow. He filled both our glasses with sake from the new bottle. I thanked him and polished off the whole top box myself, though it had more than enough for two. After we had drunk as much sake as we could manage, he offered to put me up for the night, but when I said I would rather sleep alone on the beach, he left it at that. As he stood to go, he took a folded ¥5,000 note from his pocket and shoved it into the pocket of my shirt. "Here," he said, "get yourself some healthy food. You look awful." I said he had done more than enough for me and that I couldn't accept money on top of everything else, but he refused to take it back. "It's not money," he said, "it's my feelings. Don't think about it too much, just take it." All I could do was thank him and accept it.

When he had gone, I suddenly thought about my old girlfriend, the one I had first slept with in my last year of school. Chills ran through me as I realized how badly I had treated her. I had hardly ever thought about *her* thoughts or feelings or the pain I had caused her. She was such a sweet and gentle thing, but at the time I had taken her sweetness for granted and later hardly gave her a second thought. What was she doing now? I wondered. And had she forgiven me?

A wave of nausea came over me, and I vomited by the old ship. My head hurt from too much sake, and I felt bad about having lied to the fisherman and taken his money. It was time for me to go back to Tokyo, I decided; I couldn't keep this up for ever. I stuffed my sleeping bag into my rucksack, slipped my arms through the straps and walked to the local railway station. I told the man at the ticket-office window that I wanted to get to Tokyo as soon as possible. He checked his timetable and said I could make it as far as Osaka by morning if I transferred from one night train to another, then I could take the bullet train from there. I thanked him and used the ¥5,000 note the fisherman gave me to buy a ticket to Tokyo. Waiting for the train, I bought a newspaper and checked the date: 2 October, 1970. So I had been travelling for a full month. I knew I had to go back to the real world.

The month of travelling neither lifted my spirits nor softened the blow of Naoko's death. I arrived back in Tokyo in pretty much the same state in which I had left. I couldn't even bring myself to phone Midori. What could I say to her? How could I begin? "It's all over now; you and I can be happy together"? No, that was out of the question. However I might phrase it, though, the facts were the same: Naoko was dead, and Midori was still here. Naoko was a mound of white ash, and Midori was a living, breathing human being.

I was overcome with a sense of my own defilement. Though I returned to Tokyo I did nothing for days but shut myself up in my room. My memory remained fixed on the dead rather than the living. The rooms I had set aside in there for Naoko were shuttered, the furniture draped in white, the windowsills dusty. I spent the better part of each day in those rooms. And I thought about Kizuki. "So you finally made Naoko yours," I heard myself telling him. "Oh, well, she was yours to begin with. Now, maybe, she's where she belongs. But in this world, in this imperfect world of the living, I did the best I could for Naoko. I tried to establish a new life for the two of us. But forget it, Kizuki. I'm giving her to you. You're the one she chose, after all. In woods as dark as the depths of her own heart, she hanged herself. Once upon a time, you dragged a part of me into the world of the dead, and now Naoko has dragged another part of me into that world. Sometimes I feel like the caretaker of a museum – a huge, empty museum where no one ever comes, and I'm watching over it for no one but myself."

The fourth day after my return to Tokyo, a letter came from Reiko. Special delivery. It was a simple note: *I haven't been able to get in touch with you for weeks, and I'm worried. Please call me. At 9 a.m. and 9 p.m. I will be waiting by the telephone.*

I called her at nine o'clock that night. Reiko picked up after one ring.

"Are you OK?" she asked.

"More or less," I said.

"Do you mind if I come and visit you the day after tomorrow?"

"Visit me? You mean here in Tokyo?"

"That's exactly what I mean. I want to have a good, long talk with you."

"You're leaving the sanatorium?"

"It's the only way I can come and see you, isn't it? Anyway, it's about time for me to get out of this place. I've been here eight years, after all. If they keep me any longer, I'll start to rot."

I found it difficult to speak. After a short silence, Reiko went on: "I'll be on the 3.20 bullet train the day after tomorrow. Will you meet me at the station? Do you still remember what I look like? Or have you lost interest in me now that Naoko's dead?"

"No way," I said. "See you at Tokyo Station the day after tomorrow at 3.20."

"You won't have any trouble recognizing me. I'm the old lady with the guitar case. There aren't many of those."

And in fact, I had no trouble finding Reiko in the crowd. She wore a man's tweed jacket, white trousers, and red trainers. Her hair was as short as ever, with the usual clumps sticking up. In her right hand she held a brown leather suitcase, and in her left a black guitar case. She gave me a big, wrinkly smile the moment she spotted me, and I found myself grinning back. I took her suitcase and walked beside her to the train for the western suburbs.

"Hey, Watanabe, how long have you been wearing that awful face? Or is that the 'in' look in Tokyo these days?"

"I was travelling for a while, ate junk all the time," I said. "How did you find the bullet train?"

"Awful!" she said. "You can't open the windows. I wanted to buy a box lunch from one of the station buffets."

"They sell them on board, you know."

"Yeah, overpriced plastic sandwiches. A starving horse wouldn't touch that stuff. I always used to enjoy the boxed lunches at Gotenba Station."

"Once upon a time, before the bullet train."

"Well, *I'm* from once upon a time before the bullet train!"

On the train out to Kichijoji, Reiko watched the Musashino

landscape passing the window with all the curiosity of a tourist.

"Has it changed much in eight years?" I asked.

"You don't know what I'm feeling now, do you, Watanabe?"

"No, I don't."

"I'm scared," she said. "So scared, I could go crazy just like that. I don't know what I'm supposed to do, flung out here all by myself." She paused. "But 'Go crazy just like that.' Kind of a cool expression, don't you think?"

I smiled and took her hand. "Don't worry," I said. "You'll be OK. Your own strength got you this far."

"It wasn't my own strength that got me out of that place," Reiko said. "It was Naoko and you. I couldn't stand it there without Naoko, and I had to come to Tokyo to talk to you. That's all. If nothing had happened I probably would have spent the rest of my life there."

I nodded.

"What are you planning to do from now on?" I asked Reiko.

"I'm going to Asahikawa," she said. "Way up in the wilds of Hokkaido! An old college friend of mine runs a music school there, and she's been asking me for two or three years now to help her out. I told her it was too cold for me. I mean, I *finally* get my freedom back and I'm supposed to go to Asahikawa? It's hard to get excited about a place like that – some hole in the ground."

"It's not so awful," I said, laughing. "I've been there. It's not a bad little town. Got its own special atmosphere."

"Are you sure?"

"Absolutely. It's much better than staying in Tokyo."

"Oh, well," she said. "I don't have anywhere else to go, and I've already sent my stuff there. Hey, Watanabe, promise me you'll come and visit me in Asahikawa."

366

"Of course I will. But do you have to leave straight away? Can't you stay in Tokyo for a while?"

"I'd like to hang around here a few days if I can. Can you put me up? I won't get in your way."

"No problem," I said. "I have a big closet I can sleep in, in my sleeping bag."

"I can't do that to you."

"No, really. It's a *huge* closet."

Reiko tapped out a rhythm on the guitar case between her legs. "I'm probably going to have to condition myself a little before I go to Asahikawa. I'm just not used to being in the outside world. There's a lot of stuff I don't get, and I'm nervous. Think you can help me out a little? You're the only one I can ask."

"I'll do anything I can to help you," I said.

"I hope I'm not getting in your way," she said.

"I don't have any *way* for you to get *in*," I said.

She looked at me and turned up the corners of her mouth in a smile but said nothing.

We hardly talked the rest of the way to Kichijoji Station or on the bus back to my place. We traded a few random comments on the changes in Tokyo and Reiko's time at the College of Music and my one trip to Asahikawa, but said nothing about Naoko. Ten months had gone by since I last saw Reiko, but walking by her side I felt strangely calmed and comforted. This was a familiar feeling, I thought, and then it occurred to me it was the way I used to feel when walking the streets of Tokyo with Naoko. And just as Naoko and I had shared the dead Kizuki, Reiko and I shared the dead Naoko. This thought made it impossible for me to go on talking. Reiko continued speaking for a while, but when she realized that I wasn't saying anything, she also fell silent. Neither of us said a word on the bus.

It was one of those early autumn afternoons when the light is sharp and clear, exactly as it had been a year earlier when I visited Naoko in Kyoto. The clouds were white and as narrow as bones, the sky wide open and high. The fragrance of the breeze, the tone of the light, the tiny flowers in the grass, the subtle reverberations that accompanied sounds: all these told me that autumn had come again, increasing the distance between me and the dead with each cycle of the seasons. Kizuki was still 17 and Naoko 21: for ever.

"Oh, what a relief to come to a place like this!" Reiko said, looking all around as we stepped off the bus.

"Because there's nothing here," I said.

As I led her through the back gate through the garden to my cottage, Reiko was impressed by everything she saw.

"This is terrific!" she said. "You *made* these shelves and the desk?"

"Yep," I said, pouring tea.

"You're obviously good with your hands. And you keep the place so clean!"

"Storm Trooper's influence," I said. "He turned me into a cleanliness freak. Not that my landlord's complaining."

"Oh, your landlord! I ought to introduce myself to him. That's his place on the other side of the garden, I suppose."

"Introduce yourself to him? What for?"

"What do you mean 'what for'? Some weird old lady shows up in your place and starts playing the guitar, he's going to wonder what's going on. Better to start out on the right foot. I even brought a box of tea sweets for him."

"Very clever," I said.

"The wisdom that comes with age. I'm going to tell him I'm your aunt on your mother's side, visiting from Kyoto, so don't contradict me. The age difference comes in handy at times like this. Nobody's going to get suspicious."

Reiko took the box of sweets from her bag and went off to pay her respects. I sat on the veranda, drinking another cup of tea and playing with the cat. Twenty minutes went by, and when Reiko finally came back, she pulled a tin of rice crackers from her bag and said it was a present for me.

"What were you talking about for so long?" I asked, munching on a cracker.

"*You*, of course," said Reiko, cradling the cat and rubbing her cheek against it. "He says you're a very proper young man, a serious student."

"Are you sure he was talking about me?"

"There is not the slightest doubt in my mind that he was talking about you," she said with a laugh. Then, noticing my guitar, she picked it up, adjusted the tuning, and played Antonio Carlos Jobim's "Desafinado". It had been months since I last heard Reiko's guitar, and it gave me that old, warm feeling.

"You practising the guitar?" she asked.

"It was kicking around the landlord's storehouse, so I borrowed it and I plunk on it once in a while. That's all."

"I'll give you a lesson later. Absolutely free." Reiko put down the guitar and took off her tweed jacket. Sitting against the veranda post, she smoked a cigarette. She was wearing a madras check short-sleeve shirt.

"Nice shirt, don't you think?" she asked.

"It is," I said. In fact it *was* a good-looking shirt with a handsome pattern.

"It's Naoko's," said Reiko. "I bet you didn't know we were

the same size. Especially when she first came to the sanatorium. She put on a little weight after that, but still we were pretty much the same size: blouses, trousers, shoes, hats. Bras were about the only thing we couldn't share. I've got practically nothing here. So we were always swapping clothes. Actually, it was more like joint ownership."

Now that she mentioned it, I saw that Reiko's build was almost identical to Naoko's. Because of the shape of her face and her thin arms and legs, she had always given me the impression of being smaller and slimmer than Naoko, but in fact she was surprisingly solid.

"The jacket and trousers are hers, too," said Reiko. "It's all hers. Does it bother you to see me wearing her stuff?"

"Not at all," I said. "I'm sure Naoko would be glad to have somebody wearing her clothes – especially you."

"It's strange," Reiko said with a little snap of the fingers. "Naoko didn't leave a will or anything – except where her clothes were concerned. She scribbled one line on a memo pad on her desk. 'Please give all my clothes to Reiko.' She was a funny one, don't you think? Why would she be concerned about her clothes of all things when she's getting ready to die? Who gives a damn about clothes? She must have had tons of other things she wanted to say."

"Maybe not," I said.

Puffing on her cigarette, Reiko seemed lost in thought. Then she said, "You want to hear the whole story, in order, I suppose."

"I do," I said. "Please tell me everything."

"Tests at the hospital in Osaka showed that Naoko's condition was improving for the moment but that she should stay there on a somewhat longer-term basis so that they could continue the intensive therapy for its future benefits. I told you that much in my letter – the one I sent you somewhere around the tenth of August."

"Right. I read that letter."

"Well, on the 24th of August I got a call from Naoko's mother asking if it was OK for Naoko to visit me at the sanatorium. Naoko wanted to pack the things she had left with me and, because she wouldn't be able to see me for a while, she wanted to have a nice long talk with me, and perhaps spend a night in our flat. I said that would be fine. *I* wanted to see *her* really badly and to have a talk with her. So Naoko and her mother arrived the next day, the 25th, in a taxi. The three of us worked together, packing Naoko's things and chatting away. Late in the afternoon, Naoko said it would be OK for her mother to go home, that she'd be fine, so they called a taxi and the mother left. We weren't worried at all because Naoko seemed to be in such good spirits. In fact, until then I had been *very* worried. I had been expecting her to be depressed and worn out and emaciated. I mean, I knew how much the testing and therapy and stuff they do at those hospitals can take it out of you, so I had some real doubts about this visit. But one look at her was all it took to convince me she'd be OK. She looked a lot healthier than I had expected and she was smiling and joking and talking much more normally than when I had seen her last. She had been to the hairdresser's and was showing off her new hairdo. So I thought there would be nothing to worry about even if her mother left us alone. Naoko told me that *this* time she was going to let those hospital doctors cure her once and for all, and I said that that would probably be the best thing to do. So then the two of us went out for a walk, talking all the time, mainly about the future. Naoko told me that what she'd really like was for the two of us to get out of the sanatorium and live together somewhere."

"Live together? You and Naoko?"

"That's right," said Reiko with a little shrug. "So I told her it sounded good to me, but what about Watanabe? And she said, 'Don't worry, I'll get everything straight with him.' That's all. Then she talked about where she and I would live and what we'd do, that kind of thing. After that we went to the aviary and played with the birds."

I took a beer from the fridge and opened it. Reiko lit another cigarette, the cat sound asleep in her lap.

"That girl had everything worked out for herself. I'm sure that's why she was so full of energy and smiling and healthy-looking. It must have been such a load off her mind to feel she knew exactly what she was going to do. So then we finished going through her stuff and throwing what she didn't need into the metal drum in the garden and burning it: the note-book she had used as a diary, and all the letters she had received. Your letters, too. This seemed a bit strange to me, so I asked her why she was burning stuff like that. I mean, she had always been so careful about putting your letters away in a safe place and reading them over and over. She said, 'I'm getting rid of everything from the past so I can be reborn in the future.' I suppose I pretty much took her at her word. It had its own kind of logic to it, sort of. I remember thinking how much I wanted her to get healthy and happy. She was so sweet and lovely that day: I wish you could have seen her!

"When that was over, we went to the dining hall for supper the way we used to. Then we bathed and I opened a bottle of good wine that I had been keeping for a special occasion like this and we drank and I played the guitar. The Beatles, as always, "Norwegian Wood", "Michelle", her favourites. Both of us were feeling pretty good. We turned out the lights, got undressed and lay in our beds. It was one of those steaming hot nights. We had the windows wide open, but there was hardly a breath of wind. It was black as ink outside, the grasshoppers were screaming, and the smell of the summer grass was so thick in the room it was hard to breathe. All of a sudden, Naoko started talking about you – about the night she had sex with you. In incredible detail. How you took her clothes off, how you touched her, how she found herself getting wet, how you went inside her, how wonderful it felt: she told me all of this in vivid detail. So I asked her: why are you telling me this now, all of a sudden? I mean, up to then, she had never spoken openly to me about sex. Of course, we had had some frank sexual talk as a kind of therapy, but she had been too embarrassed to go into details. Now I couldn't stop her. I was shocked.

"So she says, 'I don't know, I just feel like talking about it. I'll stop if you'd rather not hear it.' 'No,' I said, that's OK. 'If there's something you need to talk about, you'd better get it all out. I'll listen to anything you have to say.'

"So she went on with her story: 'When he went inside me, I couldn't believe how much it hurt. It was my first time, after all. I was so wet, he slipped right in, but still, my brain fogged over – it hurt so much. He put it in as far as he could, I thought, but then he lifted my legs and went in even farther. That sent chills all through my body, as if I was soaking in ice water. My arms and legs went numb, and a wave of cold went through me. I didn't know what was happening. I thought I might die right there and then, and I didn't care one way or another. But he realized I was in pain, so he stopped moving, and still deep inside me, he started kissing me all over – my hair, my neck, my breasts – for a long, long time. Little by

373

little, the warmth returned to my body, and then, very slowly, he started to move. Oh, Reiko, it was so wonderful! Now it felt as if my brain was just going to melt away. I wanted to stay like that forever, to stay in his arms for the rest of my life. That's how great it was.'

"So I said to her, 'If it was so great, why didn't you just stay with Watanabe and keep doing it every day?' But she said, 'No, Reiko, I knew it would never happen again. I knew this was something that would come to me once, and leave, and never come back. This would be a once-in-a-lifetime thing. I had never felt anything like it before, and I've never felt anything like it since. I've never felt that I wanted to do it again, and I've never grown wet like that again.'

"Of course, I explained to her that this was something that often happened to young women and that, in most cases, it cures itself with age. And, after all, it *had* worked that one time: there was no need to worry it wouldn't happen again. I myself had had all kinds of trouble when I was first married.

"But she said, 'No, that's not it, Reiko. I'm not worried about that at all. I just don't want anybody going inside me again. I just don't want to be violated like that again – by anybody'."

I drank my beer, and Reiko finished her second cigarette. The cat stretched itself in Reiko's lap, found a new position and went back to sleep. Reiko seemed at a loss how to go on until she had lit her third cigarette.

"After that, Naoko began to sob. I sat on the edge of her bed and stroked her hair. 'Don't worry,' I said, 'everything is going to be all right. A beautiful, young girl like you has *got* to have a man to hold her and make her happy.' Naoko was drenched in sweat and tears. I got a bath towel and dried her face and body. Even her panties were soaked, so I helped her out of them – now wait a minute, don't get any strange ideas, there was nothing funny going on. We always used to bathe together. She was like my little sister."

"I know, I know," I said.

"Well, anyway, Naoko said she wanted me to hold her. I said it was far too hot for holding, but she said it was the last time we'd be seeing each other, so I held her. Just for a while. With a bath towel between us so our sweaty bodies wouldn't stick to each other. And when she calmed down, I dried her off again, got her nightdress on her and put her to bed. She fell sound asleep straight away. Or maybe she was just pretending to sleep. Whatever, she looked so sweet and lovely that night, she had the face of a girl of 13 or 14 who's never had a bit of harm done to her since the day she was born. I saw that look on her face, and I knew I could let myself fall asleep with an easy heart."

When I woke at six in the morning, she was gone. Her nightdress was there, where she had dropped it, but her clothes and trainers and the torch I always keep by my pillow were missing. I knew immediately that something was wrong. I mean, the very fact that she had taken the torch meant she had left in the dark. I checked her desk just in case, and there was the note: *Please give all my clothes to Reiko.* I woke up everybody straight away, and we took different paths to look for her. We searched every inch of the place, from the insides of the dorms to the surrounding woods. It took us five hours to find her. She'd even brought her own rope."

Reiko sighed and patted the cat.

"Want some tea?" I asked.

"Yes, thanks," said Reiko.

I boiled water and brought a pot of tea back to the veranda. Sundown was approaching. The daylight had grown weak, and long shadows of trees stretched to our feet. I sipped my tea and looked at the strangely random garden with its funny mix of yellow globeflowers and pink azaleas and tall, green nandins.

"So then the ambulance came and took Naoko away and the police started questioning me. Not that there was much doubt. There was a kind of suicide note, and it had obviously been a suicide, and they took it for granted that suicide was just one of those things that mental patients *did*. So it was pretty pro forma. As soon as they left, I telegraphed you."

"What a sad little funeral it was," I said. "Her family was obviously upset that I knew Naoko had died. I'm sure they didn't want people to know it was suicide. I probably shouldn't even have been there. Which made me feel even worse. As soon as I got back, I hit the road."

"Hey, Watanabe, let's go for a walk. We can shop for something to make for dinner, maybe. I'm starving."

"Sure. Is there something you want to eat?"

"Sukiyaki," she said. "I haven't had anything like that for years. I used to *dream* about sukiyaki – just stuffing myself with beef and green onions and noodles and roasted tofu and greens."

"Sure, we can have that, but I don't have a sukiyaki pan."

"Just leave it to me. I'll borrow one from your landlord."

She ran off to the main house and came back with a good-sized pan and gas cooker and rubber hose.

"Not bad, eh?"

"Not bad!"

We bought all the ingredients at the little shops in the neighbourhood – beef, eggs, vegetables, tofu. I picked out a fairly decent white wine. I tried to pay, but Reiko insisted on paying for everything.

"Think how the family would laugh at me if they heard I let my nephew pay for the food!" said Reiko. "Besides, I'm carrying a fair amount of cash. So don't worry. I wasn't about to leave the sanatorium broke."

Reiko washed the rice and put it on to boil while I arranged everything for cooking on the veranda. When everything was ready, Reiko took out her guitar and appeared to be testing it with a slow Bach fugue. On the hard parts she would purposely slow down or speed up or make it detached or sentimental, listening with obvious pleasure to the variety of sounds she could draw from the instrument. When she played the guitar, Reiko looked like a 17-year-old girl enjoying the sight of a new dress. Her eyes sparkled, and she pouted with just the hint of a smile. When she had finished the piece, she leaned back against a pillar and looked up at the sky as though deep in thought.

"Do you mind if I talk to you?" I asked.

"Not at all," she said. "I was just thinking how hungry I am."

"Aren't you planning to see your husband or your daughter while you're here? They must be in Tokyo somewhere."

"Close enough. Yokohama. But no, I don't plan to see them. I'm sure I told you before: it's better for them if they don't have anything more to do with me. They've started a new life. And I'd just feel terrible if I saw them. No, the best thing is to keep away."

She crumpled up her empty box of Seven Stars cigarettes and took a new one from her suitcase. She cut the seal and put a cigarette in her mouth, but she didn't light up.

"I'm finished as a human being," she said. "All you're looking at is the lingering memory of what I used to be. The most important part of me, what used to be inside, died

377

years ago, and I'm just functioning by auto-memory."

"But I like you now, Reiko, the way you are, lingering memory or whatever. And what I have to say about it may not make any difference, but I'm really glad that you're wearing Naoko's clothes."

Reiko smiled and lit her cigarette with a lighter. "For such a young man, you know how to make a woman happy."

I felt myself reddening. "I'm just saying what I really think."

"Sure, I know," said Reiko, smiling.

When the rice was done soon after that, I oiled the pan and arranged the ingredients for sukiyaki.

"Tell me this isn't a dream," said Reiko, sniffing the air.

"No, this is 100 per cent realistic sukiyaki," I said. "Empirically speaking, of course."

Instead of talking, we attacked the sukiyaki with our chopsticks, drank lots of beer, and finished up with rice. Seagull turned up, attracted by the smell, so we shared our meat with her. When we had eaten our fill, we sat leaning against the porch pillars looking at the moon.

"Satisfied?" I asked.

"Totally," she groaned. "I've never eaten so much in my life."

"What do you want to do now?"

"Have a smoke and go to a public bath. My hair's a mess. I need to wash it."

"No problem. There's one down the street."

"Tell me, Watanabe, if you don't mind. Have you slept with that girl Midori?"

"You mean have we had sex? Not yet. We decided not to until things get sorted out."

"Well, now they're sorted out, wouldn't you say?"

I shook my head. "Now that Naoko's dead, you mean?"

"No, not that. You made your decision long before Naoko died – that you could never leave Midori. Whether Naoko is alive or dead, it has nothing to do with your decision. You chose Midori. Naoko chose to die. You're all grown up now, so you have to take responsibility for your choices. Otherwise, you ruin everything."

"But I can't forget her," I said. "I told Naoko I would go on waiting for her, but I couldn't do it. I turned my back on her in the end. I'm not saying anyone's to blame: it's a problem for me myself. I do think that things would have worked out the same way even if I hadn't turned my back on her. Naoko was choosing death all along. But that's beside the point. I can't forgive myself. You tell me there's nothing I can do about a natural change in feelings, but my relationship with Naoko was not that simple. If you stop and think about it, she and I were bound together at the border between life and death. It was like that for us from the start."

"If you feel some kind of pain with regard to Naoko's death, I would advise you to keep on feeling that pain for the rest of your life. And if there's something you can learn from it, you should do that, too. But quite aside from that, you should be happy with Midori. Your pain has nothing to do with your relationship with her. If you hurt her any more than you already have, the wound could be too deep to fix. So, hard as it may be, you have to be strong. You have to grow up more, be more of an adult. I left the sanatorium and came all the way up here to Tokyo to tell you that – all the way on that coffin of a train."

"I understand what you're telling me," I said to Reiko, "but I'm still not prepared to follow through on it. I mean, that was *such* a sad little funeral! No one should have to die like that."

Reiko stretched out her hand and stroked my head. "We all have to die like that sometime. I will, and so will you."

We took the five-minute walk along the river bank to the local public baths and came home feeling more refreshed. I opened the bottle of wine and we sat on the veranda drinking it.

"Hey, Watanabe, could you bring out another glass?"

"Sure," I said. "But what for?"

"We're going to have our own funeral for Naoko, just the two of us. One that's not so sad."

When I handed her the glass, Reiko filled it to the brim and set it on the stone lantern in the garden. Then she sat on the veranda, leaning against a pillar, guitar in her arms, and smoked a cigarette.

"And now could you bring out a box of matches? Make it the biggest one you can find."

I brought out an economy-size box of kitchen matches and sat down next to her.

"Now what I want you to do is lay down a match every time I play a song, just set them in a row. I'm going to play every song I can think of."

First she played a soft, lovely rendition of Henry Mancini's "Dear Heart".

"You gave a recording of this to Naoko, didn't you?" she asked.

"I did. For Christmas the year before last. She really liked that song."

"I like it, too," said Reiko. "So sweet and beautiful . . ." and she ran through a few bars of the melody one more time before taking another sip of wine. "I wonder how many songs I can play before I get completely drunk. This'll be a nice funeral, don't you think – not so sad?"

380

Reiko moved on to the Beatles, playing "Norwegian Wood", "Yesterday", "Michelle", and "Something". She sang and played "Here Comes the Sun", then played "The Fool on the Hill". I laid seven matches in a row.

"Seven songs," said Reiko, sipping more wine and smoking another cigarette. "Those guys sure knew something about the sadness of life, and gentleness."

By "those guys" Reiko of course meant John Lennon, Paul McCartney and George Harrison. After a short breather, Reiko crushed her cigarette out and picked up her guitar again. She played "Penny Lane", "Blackbird", "Julia", "When I'm 64", "Nowhere Man", "And I Love Her", and "Hey Jude".

"How many songs is that?"

"Fourteen," I said.

She sighed and asked me, "How about you? Can you play something – maybe one song?"

"No way. I'm terrible."

"So play it terribly."

I brought out my guitar and stumbled my way through "Up on the Roof". Reiko took a rest, smoking and drinking. When I was through, she applauded.

Next she played a guitar transcription of Ravel's "Pavanne for a Dying Queen" and a beautifully clean rendition of Debussy's "Claire de Lune".

"I mastered both of these after Naoko died," said Reiko. "To the end, her taste in music never rose above the sentimental."

She performed a few Bacharach songs next: "Close to You", "Raindrops Keep Falling on my Head", "Walk on By", "Wedding Bell Blues".

"Twenty," I said.

"I'm like a human jukebox!" exclaimed Reiko. "My professors would faint if they could see me now."

She went on sipping and puffing and playing: several bossa novas, Rogers and Hart, Gershwin, Bob Dylan, Ray Charles, Carole King, The Beach Boys, Stevie Wonder, Kyu Sakamoto's "Sukiyaki Song", "Blue Velvet", "Green Fields". Sometimes she would close her eyes and nod or hum to the melody.

When the wine was gone, we turned to whisky. The wine in the glass in the garden I poured over the stone lantern and replaced it with whisky.

"How's our count going?" Reiko asked.

"Forty-eight," I said.

For our forty-ninth song Reiko played "Eleanor Rigby", and the fiftieth was another performance of "Norwegian Wood". After that she rested her hands and drank some whisky. "Maybe that's enough," she said.

"It is," I answered. "Amazing."

Reiko looked me in the eye and said, "Now listen to me, Watanabe. I want you to forget all about that sad little funeral you saw. Just remember this marvellous one of ours."

I nodded.

"Here's one more for good measure," she said, and for her fifty-first piece she played her favourite Bach fugue. When she was through, she said in a voice just above a whisper, "How about doing it with me, Watanabe?"

"Strange," I said. "I was thinking the same thing."

We went inside and drew the curtains. Then, in the darkened room, Reiko and I sought out each other's bodies as if it were the most natural thing in the world for us to do. I removed her blouse and trousers, and then her underwear.

"I've lived a strange life," said Reiko, "but I never thought I'd have my panties removed for me by a man 19 years my junior."

382

"Would you rather take them off yourself?"

"No, go ahead. But don't be too shocked at all my wrinkles."

"I like your wrinkles."

"You're gonna make me cry," she whispered.

I kissed her all over, taking special care to follow the wrinkled places with my tongue. She had the breasts of a little girl. I caressed them and took her nipples in my teeth, then slid a finger inside her warm, moist vagina and began to move it.

"Wrong spot, Watanabe," Reiko whispered in my ear. "That's just a wrinkle."

"I can't believe you're telling jokes at a time like this!"

"Sorry," she said. "I'm scared. I haven't done this for years. I feel like a 17-year-old girl: I just went to visit a guy in his room, and all of a sudden I'm naked."

"To tell you the truth, I feel as if I'm violating a 17-year-old girl."

With my finger in her "wrinkle", I moved my lips up her neck to her ear and took a nipple in my fingers. As her breathing intensified and her throat began to tremble, I parted her long, slim legs and eased myself inside her.

"You're not going to get me pregnant now, are you? You're taking care of that, right?" Reiko murmured in my ear. "I'd be so embarrassed if I got pregnant at this age."

"Don't worry," I said. "Just relax."

When I was all the way in, she trembled and released a sigh. Caressing her back, I moved inside her and then, without warning, I came. It was an intense, unstoppable ejaculation. I clutched at her as my semen pulsed into her warmth again and again.

"I'm sorry," I said. "I couldn't stop myself."

"Don't be silly," Reiko said, giving me a little slap on the rump. "You don't have to worry about that. Do you always have that on your mind when you're doing it with girls?"

"Yeah, pretty much."

"Well, you don't have to think about it with me. Forget it. Just let yourself go as much as you like. Did it feel good?"

"Fantastic. That's why I couldn't control myself."

"This is no time for controlling yourself. This is fine. It was great for me, too."

"You know, Reiko," I said.

"What's that?"

"You ought to take a lover again. You're terrific. It's such a waste."

"Well, I'll think about it," she said. "But I wonder if people take lovers and things in Asahikawa."

Growing hard a few minutes later, I went inside her again. Reiko held her breath and twisted beneath me. I moved slowly and quietly with my arms around her, and we talked. It felt wonderful to talk that way. If I said something funny and made her laugh, the tremors came into me through my penis. We held each other like this for a very long time.

"Oh, this feels marvellous!" Reiko said.

"Moving's not bad either," I said.

"Go ahead. Give it a try."

I lifted her hips and went in as far as I could go, then savoured the sensation of moving in a circular pattern until, having enjoyed it to the full, I let myself come.

Altogether, we joined our bodies four times that night. At the end each time, Reiko would lie in my arms trembling slightly, eyes closed, and release a long sigh.

"I never have to do this again," said Reiko, "for the rest

of my life. Oh, please, Watanabe, tell me it's true. Tell me I can relax now because I've done enough to last a lifetime."

"Nobody can tell you that," I said. "There's no way of knowing."

I tried to convince Reiko that taking a plane would be faster and easier, but she insisted on going to Asahikawa by train.

"I like the ferry to Hokkaido. And I have no desire to fly through the air," she said. I accompanied her to Ueno Station. She carried her guitar and I carried her suitcase. We sat on a platform bench waiting for the train to pull in. Reiko wore the same tweed jacket and white trousers she had on when she arrived in Tokyo.

"Do you really think Asahikawa's not such a bad place?" she asked.

"It's a nice town. I'll visit you there soon."

"Really?"

I nodded. "And I'll write to you."

"I love your letters. Naoko burned all the ones you sent her. And they were such great letters too!"

"Letters are just pieces of paper," I said. "Burn them, and what stays in your heart will stay; keep them, and what vanishes will vanish."

"You know, Watanabe, truth is, I'm scared, going to Asahikawa by myself. So be sure to write to me. Whenever I read your letters, I feel you're right there next to me."

"If that's what you want, I'll write all the time. But don't worry. I know you: you'll do fine wherever you go."

"And another thing. I kind of feel like there's something stuck inside me. Could it be my imagination?"

"Just a lingering memory," I said and smiled. Reiko smiled, too.

385

"Don't forget about me," she said.

"I won't forget you," I said. "Ever."

"We may never meet again, but no matter where I go, I'll always remember you and Naoko."

I saw that she was crying. Before I knew it, I was kissing her. Others on the platform were staring at us, but I didn't care about such things any more. We were alive, she and I. And all we had to think about was continuing to live.

"Be happy," Reiko said to me as she boarded the train. "I've given you all the advice I have to give. There's nothing left for me to say. Just be happy. Take my share and Naoko's and combine them for yourself."

We held hands for a moment, and then we parted.

I phoned Midori.

"I have to talk to you," I said. "I have a million things to talk to you about. A million things we have to talk about. All I want in this world is you. I want to see you and talk. I want the two of us to begin everything from the beginning."

Midori responded with a long, long silence – the silence of all the misty rain in the world falling on all the new-mown lawns of the world. Forehead pressed against the glass, I shut my eyes and waited. At last, Midori's quiet voice broke the silence: "Where are you now?"

Where was I now?

Gripping the receiver, I raised my head and turned to see what lay beyond the phone box. Where was I now? I had no idea. No idea at all. Where was this place? All that flashed into my eyes were the countless shapes of people walking by to nowhere. Again and again I called out for Midori from the dead centre of this place that was no place.

TRANSLATOR'S NOTE

Haruki Murakami was shocked and depressed to find his normal six-figure readership exploding into the millions when he published *Norwegian Wood* in 1987. Fame was one thing, superstardom another, and the craziness of it sent him back to the anonymity of Europe (he had written the book in Greece and Italy). In 1991 he moved to the United States. Not until 1995 was he prepared to resume living in Japan, but strictly on his own terms, without the television appearances and professional pontificating expected of a bestselling Japanese author.

Norwegian Wood is still the one Murakami book that "everyone" in Japan has read, but Murakami's young audience has grown up with him as he has begun wrestling with Japan's dark past (in *The Wind-up Bird Chronicle*) and the 1995 double punch of the Kobe earthquake and, in *Underground*, the sarin gas attack on the Tokyo subway.

Accustomed to his cool, fragmented, American-flavoured narratives on mysterious sheep and disappearing elephants, some of Murakami's early readers were dismayed to find that *Norwegian Wood* seemed to be "just" a love story – and one that bore a suspicious resemblance to the kind of Japanese mainstream autobiographical fiction that Murakami had rejected since his exciting debut in 1979. As Murakami himself tells it, "Many of my readers thought that *Norwegian Wood* was a retreat for me, a betrayal of what my works had stood for until then. For me personally, however, it was just the opposite: it was an adventure, a challenge. I had never written that kind of straight, simple story, and I wanted to test myself. I set *Norwegian Wood* in the late 1960s. I borrowed the details of the protagonist's university environment and daily life from those of my own student days. As a result, many people think it is an autobiographical novel, but in fact it is not autobiographical at all. My own youth was far less dramatic, far more boring than his. If I had simply written the literal truth of my own life, the novel would have been no more than 15 pages long."

The author may joke away its autobiographicality, but the book *feels* like an autobiography; it favours lived experience over mind games and shots at the supernatural, and it does indeed tell us much more straightforwardly than any of his other novels what life was like for the young Haruki Murakami when he first came to Tokyo from Kobe. Back then, in the years 1968–70 that occupy the bulk of the novel, Murakami's experience centred on meeting the love of his life, his wife, Yoko, amid the turbulence of the student movement. The author is right, though: there is a lot of fiction here, and a lot of caricature and humour, and a lot of symbolism that Murakami's regular readers will recognise instantly. It is by no means "just" a love story.

Determined Murakami readers abroad may have succeeded in obtaining copies of Alfred Birnbaum's earlier translation of *Norwegian Wood*, which was produced for distribution in Japan, with grammar notes at the back, to enable students to enjoy their favourite author as they struggled with the mysteries of English. Although the novel has appeared in

French, Italian, Chinese, Korean, Norwegian and Hebrew, the present edition is the first English translation that Murakami has authorized for publication outside Japan.

JAY RUBIN

www.randomhouse.co.uk/vintage